LEAD AND SNOW

TYRANTS OF MARS, BOOK TWO

ALEX P. BERG

1

MARS IS HOME. Mars is love. Mars is death. That's what the locals say, anyway. The death part is self-evident. Step unprotected into the war god's embrace and you'll freeze to death within a matter of minutes. You'll suffocate faster than that, but not before experiencing the unique sensation of the moisture coating your tongue and eyes boiling off even as the cold turns the underlying flesh to stone. But while Mars may be a desolate hellscape, there's a hint of the familiar to it, too. The gentle tug of ten to the forty-ninth atoms, a single order of magnitude making all the difference between it and its blue-green cousin. The whine of a faint breeze playing over rocks or the roar of a violent dust-choked maelstrom, depending on the day. A cool blue sunset, reminiscent of a Michigan afternoon but ever so fleeting, with night always waiting to snatch it away. On Mars, the darkness always waits.

For me, there is no love. But Mars is home now, and it will be my death.

THE WIND HOWLED AROUND ME, cutting through the skin of my Suit, chilling me to the bone despite the best efforts of the built-in resistive heating loops. Somewhere above me stars burned bright in the night sky, a melody of yellow, white, and blue, but I couldn't see them, denied the opportunity by the billions of minuscule fragments of Martian regolith suspended in the air. The microscopic dust worked its way through the Suit's weave, coating my hands with chalky grit that I felt every time I pressed my hand against the grip of my M2145 Remote Sniper Rifle.

I hated it, and it was perfect.

We'd been waiting for such a storm for close to a week. Thanks to the dust-choked wind, the lights of the United Space Corporation settlement of Le Verrier a kilometer and a half away came across as nothing more than a diffuse glow. Even the much closer lights shining upon the outpost's austere spaceport looked fuzzy and indistinct. Thankfully, the dust particles were fine enough that they couldn't interfere much with the infrared spectrum. Even at a distance of four hundred meters, I could still pick out Lauren and Cal's outlines with my visor's IR overlay.

Despite the insulating properties of the Suit, Cal's form showed faintly blue-green against the nearly solid black of the frozen dirt around him. On cue, he spoke from somewhere in the center of my mind. "Charge set on the liquid methane tank."

We communicated wirelessly via Net, the intracranial mesh implant that melded the brain's electrical impulses to those of modern computing, allowing individuals with the appropriate aptitude to do everything from crack into the secure servers of an interplanetary financial services corporation to watch videos of boxer puppies jumping on trampolines, all with the power of the mind. The Net could recreate visual, olfactory, and gustatory sensations that were indiscernible from those generated by the sensory organs that normally produced them, but sound was a little different. The Net couldn't recreate the directional component of spoken communication, making it sound as if all Net conversations took place with someone inside your own skull.

"Roger, Cal," I said. "You're clear to move to the oxygen tank."

I zoomed in on Cal and Lauren using my visor, watching their colorful forms disappear as they passed behind the methane tank only for them to reappear on the other side. I flexed my fingers and squeezed them into a fist, trying to keep the blood circulating. The Suit might be a miracle of modern engineering, but it couldn't stop thermodynamics. I'd seen enough frostbitten fingers and toes to respect Mars's bite.

As I kept an eye on my compatriots, I brought up the Le Verrier spaceport surveillance feed and superimposed it over my vision via Net. The video continued to show the looped clip I'd seamlessly cropped and inserted into the USC servers I'd hacked the week prior. I hadn't been sure which of the two landing pads might've been occupied at the time of our mission given that we were dependent on the weather for cover, so I'd prepared a number of similar clips for whichever occasion presented itself. In an ideal situation, both of the pads would've been occupied, giving us a greater opportunity for sabotage, but since we'd already been waiting a week for the storm to hit, we'd decided to take what we could.

Lauren and Cal's forms stopped next to the oxygen tank. Cal stooped, looped the backpack off his shoulder, and rummaged around in it.

"Everything golden?" asked Lauren.

"It's four AM, I've spent the past two weeks with only the two of you for company, and Mars is doing its best to make sure I'll never procreate," I said. "Hurry it up. I'm freezing my everything off."

"And we're not?" said Cal.

"At least you're moving. Next time we blow something up, I call dibs on whatever job involves the most physical activity."

Net communication might not be able to convey directionality, but it could do just fine with tone. "But Ambrose, you're *soooo* good at working security," said Lauren in a fawning voice. "What would we do if you weren't in charge of covering our asses?"

"Are you suggesting I couldn't plant explosive charges while simultaneously keeping an eye on the security feeds? How little do you think of me?"

"Well, there was that one time you nearly got us captured and exposed the entire resistance because you forgot to silence your tablet before we trespassed on USC property."

I sighed. "That was two and a half years ago. Am I going to hear about that for the rest of my life?"

"You know what they say," said Lauren. "Comedy is tragedy plus time. Given that you almost got us killed, I'd say that one's only going to get funnier."

Cal straightened as he pulled something from the pack. "I'll be happy to act as scout next time. I'm a better shot with the RSR than you are, anyway."

"With your fingers on the grip, maybe," I said. "But I can beat you in remote fire mode any day of the week. I've already got the tripod set up. Sights and wireless cameras aligned. Honestly, I could do this whole operation on my own. No need to watch your asses when I can watch my own ass."

Lauren snorted. "A little vain, are we?"

"On second thought, that came out wrong."

I saw a light activate on the command panel I'd minimized on my Net. "Oxygen tank charge set," said Cal. "Are we clear to move to the booster?"

I looked toward the settlement. "Yeah, we're good to... actually. Wait a second."

The buildings of Le Verrier continued to glow rust red through the storm, but they lacked their previous uniform luminosity. I noticed a section of greater intensity toward the bottom of the diffuse glow.

"What's going on?" asked Lauren.

"Settlement brightness has increased. Which either means someone cranked the juice on the floodlights, or..." I played with the filtering settings on my visor and zoomed toward the settlement.

"Or someone's on their way over," finished Cal.

I caught it by the engine's heat signatures, but I would've seen the headlights in another few seconds. "Shit. It's a Marauder. Heading straight toward us, cruising speed. You guys need to get out of there."

Cal swore. "You've got to be kidding me. After all that grand-standing about covering our asses, you botched security?"

"I didn't botch it," I said. "I'm looking at the surveillance feed right now. We're not on it. Neither have any of the alarms in the military base gone off."

"What about comms?" asked Lauren.

"They're clear. My tracking scripts haven't hit anything regarding Reds, the resistance, sabotage. Nothing." The intensity of the glow from the settlement was increasing, more so than it should've been from the approaching lights of a single transport. "Seriously, you guys need to move. Something's not right."

"What about the booster?" said Cal.

"Forget the booster," I said. "We'll blow the tanks. That'll have to be enough."

"ETA on the Marauder?" asked Lauren.

"Not sure. Let me get LIDAR on it. The intensity of the light is throwing my sensors off. It's like the whole sky is... *oh, shit.*"

I looked up, suddenly realizing why my light sensors were showing increased intensity across my field of view. The sky was brightening and not because we'd misjudged the hour. "Guys, we've got a rocket incoming. Probably a Mark V Slimline. *Take cover!*"

Cal and Lauren's blue-green outlines took off from behind the liquid oxygen tank, racing through the dark of night before disappearing behind a maintenance building.

Cal growled through the Net connection. "Ambrose, USC doesn't land rockets without warning. There are flight plans. Schedules. Launch windows."

"All of which I've been tracking," I said. "This landing wasn't on any of them."

"Are you suggesting this is a clandestine operation?" said Lauren.

"Either that or someone's been feeding me false information without me knowing, and they'd have to be damned good for me not to know. Besides, if USC were trying to trap us, I think they'd send foot soldiers, not a Mark V."

The sky flared as the Mark V's reentry burn intensified. A roar filled the air, turning the howl of the dust storm to a gentle whine. I activated the noise cancellation feature on my helmet, but even that couldn't dull the blast of the rocket's engines to less than a bellow. My visor automatically tinted to account for the piercing light battering its way through the suspended dust. I still averted my gaze.

I felt a ripple dance through my feet, and when I looked up, the rocket had landed, all seventy meters of her. Her engine sputtered, the last bits of methane burning. She was a sleek lady, designed for speed and agility with a seating capacity of only a couple dozen, but given that the settlement had sent a single Marauder, I guessed there were fewer than that aboard. Either that or the vessel was unmanned and the payload was one of equipment rather than people.

"You've got about a minute and a half before that Marauder arrives," I said. "Get out before anyone spots you."

"Negative, Ambrose," said Cal. "I've got two charges left in my pack. I'm not high-tailing it out of here with only a couple busted fuel tanks to show for the past month of planning. Not when there's a shiny new Mark V on a pad a hundred meters out."

"Cal, what are you talking about? The mission was sabotage, not engagement."

"Do you see an elevator coming to the pad?"

Large spaceports had fixed structures with extendable arms next to the pads to allow for crew to embark and disembark, but small ones like Le Verrier's used a robotic, extendable lift that drove itself onto the pad next to the rocket. I'd located it upon arrival from my position on the hill above. It hadn't moved.

"No," I said. "But that doesn't mean it's a cargo mission. They could be waiting for the Marauder's arrival—which should be in roughly a minute."

"Think, Ambrose! A secret mission? At night? With no mention of it through normal channels? Whatever's aboard that is valuable to USC, never mind the Mark V itself. Lauren, cover me. Ambrose, keep me appraised."

Cal's blue-tinged outline emerged from the shadow of the maintenance shed and bounded across the pad toward the newly landed booster. "Damnit, Cal! What are you doing? Abort, man!"

"Are you forgetting who's in charge, Drake? This is the mission. We're executing it."

I glanced at the Marauder. The engine showed up clear as day through the IR overlay. "You're deliberately breaking the rules, Cal. *Never expose the resistance.* Lauren, talk some sense into him!"

She responded on a private Net channel. "He can do this, Ambrose. The storm's raging. It won't take him but a moment."

My heart pounded in my chest. I glanced at Cal's outline, then at the Mark V, then back at the Marauder, just now reaching the spaceport's outbuildings. I did some mental math and didn't like what I saw.

"God damn it..." I trained the M2145 RSR to the edge of the rocket's legs, switched the operation to remote, grabbed my combat rifle, and took off from my perch at a frantic lope.

2

MAY 31, 2179

THE ELEVATOR DINGED as it reached the thirty-second floor, and I stepped out to find Detective Patterson from the Investigative Analysis Unit waiting for the car. He gave me a cordial nod and we exchanged two word greetings before he hurried into the elevator to catch it before it closed. I continued along my route, skirting the edge of the common area as I headed toward my corner desk. The morning sun streamed through the windows, sparkling as it hit the tops of the tall Elysian skyscrapers. The morning meteorological report called for clear skies without a speck of dust. It portended a good day.

I didn't know how right I was, though, until I reached my workspace. There, a familiar face looked up from the desk adjacent to my own. "Morning, Drake."

Bishop Mwenge stood and extended his left hand. It wasn't his dominant one, but his right one happened to be constrained by a sling.

"Partner! Well, this is a surprise." I shook the man's hand. "I guess the doctors finally decided you weren't a threat to society anymore."

"Or to myself, rather." He lifted the sling arm ever so slightly.

"They wanted to keep me on bed rest for another week, but I threatened to go rogue and join an illegal fight club. In the end they released me, but only if I agreed to stick to my desk and keep my arm immobilized until I'm cleared."

I'd last seen Bishop about a week and a half prior. He'd looked hale and hearty by that point, with bright eyes and his skin back to its usual glossy, chocolate complexion. It was a much better state than he'd been in following the gunshots he'd taken during our last mission, the one where we'd apprehended the rookie service members who'd impersonated the dreaded Snow Leopard from days of yore and used the gambit to terrorize all of Elysium.

"Speaking of your arm," I said. "I'm not crazy, right? You got hit in the chest."

"Yeah. Tore my pectoral muscle up good, too," said Bishop. "The sling's there to keep the pec isolated, not the arm itself, so unfortunately I'm going to have to concede any future bench pressing competitions you might have planned for us."

"Considering my burly Earther physique, I don't think you stood much of a chance in any of those to begin with."

That drew a snort and a smile from Mwenge. I reached out and clapped the guy on his good shoulder. "Seriously though, Bishop. It's good to have you back."

He nodded and patted me on the back in return. "It's good to be back, Ambrose. Now. Pleasantries aside, it's time for me to get up to speed. Please tell me I haven't missed anything fun: high speed chases, midnight raids, making life a living hell for suspects in the exam rooms."

I took a seat and Bishop followed my lead. "Well, in that respect, you have nothing to fear. Life here has been exceedingly boring in your absence. Hey! Wipe that smile off your face. It's not *because* of your absence that it's been boring. More because of protocol. I spent a week under administrative leave while the department reviewed the deaths of Detectives Keller and Watters.

After poring through the evidence, they determined I acted in accordance with established procedures and agreed that the use of deadly force was warranted. But as you're well aware, the red tape doesn't stop there. After I returned to duty, I still had to go through psych exams and reintegration protocols. Really, I've only had about a week and a half of actual work without you. As you're aware, the Captain works under the presumption that partnerships work best with two people, so I've been stuck in the office waiting for you to get better."

"Looks like you'll be stuck here a bit longer." Bishop gestured with his sling arm again. "Any new cases I should know about?"

I activated the holodisplay at my desk. "Not yet. The Captain's had me tying up loose ends from the last case. Looking into the backgrounds of Keller, Watters, and Milovich. Building a better case for the DA."

"Everyone involved is dead," said Mwenge. "How tight of a case does he need?"

"You know how it is. Every i needs to be dotted, every t crossed. Every action we took needs to be justified to a review board. And there's always the possibility that Keller, Watters, and Milovich were acting as part of a broader network. The evidence hasn't supported that, but it was worth taking a look." I pulled up my mail and noticed an alert at the top. "Oh. Captain want to see us."

"Really?" Bishop lifted an eyebrow. "She stopped to welcome me back as soon as I arrived. She didn't mention a meeting."

I scanned the message. "Apparently it's me she wants to see. I have a pretty good idea of what it's about." I minimized the holo. "Even if she didn't mention you, I think you should come."

"Think this is about your application?"

I'd told Bishop about my plans when I'd visited him in the hospital. "That's my guess. Come on."

We trotted to the Captain's office. The door was open, and the

Captain sat in her chair within, parsing through layers of holos. I knocked on the frame. "Captain Reyes?"

She looked up and waved us in. "Drake. Mwenge. Close the door behind you."

The Captain tinkered with a couple of the floating displays as we took our seats in front of her broad desk, her dark brown eyes narrowing in thought as she focused on the superimposed data. She didn't keep it there long, though, causing it to disappear with a flick of her fingers.

"I'm pretty sure I only instructed *you* to join me in my office, Detective Drake."

"I thought Detective Mwenge might want to hear what you had to say."

The Captain lifted an eyebrow. She was a diminutive woman, especially by Martian standards, but she had a no-nonsense severity in her gaze that made her presence more imposing than her rounded cheek bones and pony-tail held hair could otherwise provide. "You presume to know why I called on you?"

Bishop shifted in his seat. "I can leave if you'd prefer, ma'am."

Reyes waved him down. "Stay seated, Detective. I'm giving Drake a hard time. His natural instinct to make assumptions based on limited evidence is one of the characteristics that makes him an excellent detective. Unfortunately, it's also one that can be irksome to his direct superiors. It might be something he wants to keep in mind when said superiors change."

My heart skipped a beat. "Are you saying what I think you're saying, Captain?"

She nodded and flashed me a smile. "Your application has been accepted. Your division head at USC Counterterrorism called a half-hour ago with the news. He wanted to personally clear it with me before sending you official notice. I imagine you'll get a message from him later this morning."

I'd expected the news, and yet hearing the words on Reyes' lips, they didn't quite seem real. "I'm glad to hear it."

Bishop reached out and clapped me on the back. "Dang, Drake. It's okay to show a little emotion. This is a big deal. Congratulations!"

I nodded. "I know. I'm not trying to minimize it. I'm excited. But moving to Counterterrorism? It's going to be a big change, to say the least."

"A change that should've happened a half-decade ago, if you ask me," said Reyes. "Don't get me wrong, Drake. I've loved having you in my division, and I'm not entirely sure what the outcome of the Snow Leopard case would've been without you and Mwenge on the job. But even though you may not have realized it, your expertise has been calling you higher for a long time. Do you recall how long I've been trying to get you to take the lieutenant's exam?"

"It's been years, Captain," I said. "And it's not that I never heard the call. I simply thought the contributions I was making at this level were still meaningful. Not to mention I like working with you guys."

"I have no doubt your contributions at the next level will be even more impactful than the ones you've made here, and that's saying a lot," said Reyes. "As much as we enjoy your company, it's past time for you to go. Honestly, I've been itching to split you and Mwenge up for months except I couldn't because your case closure rate is so damn high. Now I can finally make Bishop transfer some of the knowledge he's gained from you onto the next rising star in the department."

"It's the circle of life," said Bishop. "Or at least the circle of detectivehood. Inspectorship? Something like that."

I smiled. "Well, regardless of whether or not the move was too slow in coming, I'm going to miss the two of you. Captain? It's been an honor."

I stuck out a hand but Reyes waved it off. "Put that thing away.

You're not starting until next Monday, and if I know you at all, you won't spend the week lounging on your couch watching holocasts. Besides, there are important matters to discuss before you leave, not least of which is whether you want your farewell cake to be chocolate or vanilla. Keep in mind there *is* a correct answer."

I groaned. "Do we have to have a party?"

"It's not about you," said Mwenge. "Or at least it's not *entirely* about you. It's an opportunity for everyone else to kick back, have a drink and some sugar at work, and lord the experience over the poor saps who have to be on patrol duty at the time."

"Fair enough. I'll accept my inevitable fate with grace. But speaking of important matters, I have a legitimate one I'd like to discuss now that we're all assembled. In private."

Reyes glanced at the closed door. "Go ahead, Detective."

"You've had me bolstering the file on the Snow Leopard matter since I returned. I feel as if we've built an impregnable case against the detective recruits, but we haven't addressed Giancarlo Vincenzio's testimony. We haven't investigated the validity of his claims or our own theories about the Elysium Planitia ice sheet."

As part of their scheme to impersonate the terrorist Snow Leopard of the revolution, junior detectives Keller, Watters, and Milovich had murdered the chief administrative officer of USC's water division and the city comptroller in charge of water services. While they'd faked the existence and involvement of the Snow Leopard and used his image to sow fear among the city's residents, the conspiracy they'd uncovered regarding USC's extraction and distribution of subsurface water appeared to have legs. Internal data from the CAO's private logs suggested as much as thirty million cubic meters of ice was missing from Elysium's underground sheet. That portion of the investigation hadn't been made public following the deaths of the junior detectives, nor had it been shared with the majority of the police department—or with USC, for obvious reasons.

Reyes nodded, her demeanor more severe and her voice more subdued. "As you're well aware, Detective, because of the subject of that investigation, we're going to have to proceed with the utmost care. If USC suspects we're conducting an investigation into any of their departments, they'll move to kill it. Because of that, I'm proceeding as cautiously as I ever have. It's not murder, so I'm out of my element, but it's also why I haven't included you or Detective Mwenge thus far. Suffice it to say I've been vetting individuals from which I can create an investigative team to address the situation. Not just detectives or division heads, either. I'm looking at subject matter experts who will be able to definitively prove whether or not the water theft occurred. But I want to warn you, Detective. Proving the ice is no longer present is a different thing than proving it was removed by human activity. There are natural causes that could be at play. And even if we can prove the theft, that's a far cry from proving USC involvement. As you know from your experience, there's always a fall guy."

"Don't I know it."

A shadow of a smile passed across the Captain's lips. "Don't worry, Drake. We'll get to the bottom of it. Discovering the truth is our job. The justice department will take care of the rest."

I nodded, but inside I felt anything but confidence. When institutions were designed to protect themselves, justice fell to the hands of the people.

"Anything else I can do for you this morning?" Reyes' eyebrows had a look of finality to them.

"Actually, I have a final request if you don't mind," I said. "I know I'm not leaving yet, but given that I suspect you'll be filing my exit paperwork soon... any chance I could keep my police database access after I move to Counterterrorism?"

"Why would you need that, Detective?"

I had an answer prepared, but I didn't need to deliver it. Bishop did it for me.

The man snorted. "Isn't it obvious, Captain? Because Drake's the kind of guy who'll never stop investigating cases until the day he dies, even if he no longer works for us. I sure hope Counterterrorism appreciates you. I know I'll miss having a partner who willingly does the lion's share of the work."

The Captain smirked. "I can't guarantee anything, but there's always a chance some of the exit forms get lost in the shuffle. Not that I need you prying into cold cases because USC isn't keeping you occupied. Let's simply say it wouldn't hurt to have more cooperation between your current department and your future one, Detective Drake."

It wasn't exactly the reason I had in mind, but I agreed with the Captain nonetheless.

3

FEBRUARY 15, 2158

I SKIDDED down the hill overlooking the spaceport, sliding several meters at a time as the Martian regolith gave way underfoot. Dust sprayed with each of my steps before disappearing into the churning winds. Through the infrared overlay, I watched as Cal rapidly closed the gap between himself and the Mark V booster, using the skipping cadence that worked best in Mars's gravity. All I could spot of Lauren was a faint outline of her arm and head as they poked out from behind cover, the rifle in her hands as cold as the surrounding storm. The lights from the approaching Marauder intensified, coalescing into distinct orbs through the swirling dust.

I gritted my teeth as I stumbled to the bottom of the slope, my fingers digging into the grip of my Browning Defensive Automatic Suppressor, better known as a Badass. It was a USC weapon, stolen in a heist that had netted two thousand other identical arms which I'd subsequently reprogramed to respond to the biometrics of our resistance fighters. On a good day, I was accurate with it to two hundred and fifty meters, but in the dark, with winds whipping at over sixty kilometers an hour, I'd be lucky to land a shot to the chest at a quarter of that. I was more accurate with the sniper.

Its muzzle velocity was high enough that the Martian winds and gravity barely affected it, but its rate of fire was too slow to help Cal in the event of a serious firefight, not to mention I'd only once tried to operate the RSR remotely while simultaneously firing a Badass. The results hadn't been encouraging, to say the least. Best case scenario, I could probably use the RSR as a decoy, firing upon the approaching USC troops to force them into cover, assuming they even heard the shot or noticed its trajectory, which wasn't likely given the conditions.

"Cal, there's still time to turn back," I said, darting to the edge of one of the service buildings. "In these conditions, if the enemy's only monitoring the visual spectrum, they won't see you at more than ten meters."

"I'm counting on it, Ambrose."

The Marauder's lights combined with my visor's IR overlay to give me a peek of the action. Cal jumped as he reached the Mark V, shimmying up one of the landing legs with simian deftness. He jammed his foot into one of the landing leg's hinges as he reached the top, bracing himself against the booster's shiny exterior. His pack slid off his shoulder. He pulled one of the remaining charges and slapped it against the metal, a couple meters above the exposed engines.

The Marauder had stopped moving, barely forty paces from the edge of the rocket. The rocket blocked my view of the transport's rear, preventing me from seeing if the back door had deployed. The automated crane used to remove cargo from the payload hadn't budged, but that didn't give me any confidence that the arriving USC folks were intent on taking their time.

I double-checked the position of the RSR before readying my Badass. I peered through the scope, but the darkness and dust gave me a worse view than through my visor. "Come on, Cal," I whispered inside my helmet. *"Come on."*

I spotted a glimmer of motion near the Marauder. I think Cal noticed it, too. His head swiveled, and he paused with both hands pressed against the charge. His arms flew into action. Another green light appeared in the sidebar of my vision, the third of the four charges now active.

"Get out Cal," said Lauren. "The back door on the Marauder is lowering."

"On my way," said Cal. "Cover my retreat."

He spun and pushed off the landing leg to launch himself to the ground—but his body didn't soar through the air. He jerked and fell, swinging gracelessly from his knee joint. He yelped through the Net connection, and his vitals spiked on my squad panel.

Lauren peered around her cover. "*Cal!* Are you hit?"

For the first time, his response sounded strained. Panicked. "My foot's caught in the hinge. Crap!"

"Well, get it out, man!" I said.

Cal pulled himself into a crouch, the backpack swinging from one arm. *"You think I'm not trying?"*

"Cal, they're coming out of the Marauder," said Lauren. "Eight, I think. Some are armed."

Both of Cal's hands shot to his leg. His body shook as he pulled on his trapped foot. *"Shit!"*

Lauren darted out of her cover. "I'm getting him. Ambrose, cover us!"

Her words sucker-punched me. "What? *Are you insane?*"

"He's right," said Cal. "Get into cover! You know the rules!"

Lauren paused on the pad, her voice taught as a violin string. "I'm not leaving you Cal!"

The movement at the Marauder coalesced. My finger grazed the trigger. "They're coming!"

Cal's voice was cold. *"Damnit.* I hate it when you're right, Ambrose." His hand shot to his hip, and I knew he'd drawn his pistol.

"What are you doing?" I said.

"Warming up to my contingency plan. Drake, if they spot me, you know what to do. You said it yourself. Rule number three."

Lauren realized what he meant at the same time I did. Her scream filled my head. "CAL! *NO!*"

Sometimes I wish my training wasn't so well ingrained. I'd taken off across the edge of the pad before Cal even had time to respond.

I think Cal meant to reply on a private channel, but in the agony of the moment I suppose he forgot. "I love you, Lauren."

"*CAL!*"

She tossed her rifle to the ground and took off toward the Mark V at a full sprint, but at that point I already had a fifty meter head start on her. She might've been a native, but I was faster nonetheless. I tackled her halfway to the pad.

A crack of shots split the air as we fell to the ground. My control panel told me it was Cal's pistol that had discharged, but my sensors couldn't attribute the rounds that followed to his gun. His vitals fluctuated wildly, his heart rate spiking but not out of panic this time.

I couldn't see Lauren's face through her visor, but her cries filled my head. "Cal! *Cal!*"

Cal gurgled back a response, his Suit's stress sensors showing he'd absorbed several shots to the abdomen and chest. They hadn't penetrated the shock absorbent weave, but he'd broken several ribs.

"Get out!" he shouted. "Rule number three!"

I grabbed Lauren by the arm and pulled, but she'd turned to stone, her body frozen and lifeless. Floodlights flared to life around the port, and via Net, I noticed a flood of USC comm chatter as the occupants of the Marauder sent frantic messages back to their base.

My teeth ground together, my jaw a vice. "*Lauren...*"

Cal's voice gurgled in my mind. "*Now, Ambrose. They're moving the thirteen mil gun around on the Marauder.*"

"I can't, Cal! We're still within range. Lauren, *we need to move!*"

More floodlights cut through the storm, roving about, searching the darkness of the pad. Lauren hadn't moved, her sobs a constant background. I picked her up, her body limp in my arms, and took off in the direction of the hill.

Cal's voice pounded against my skull with each of my steps. "They're almost on me, Ambrose. I can't be captured. Do it or I will."

I glanced at the three green lights. My throat felt raw. "Mars is home. Mars is love."

"Mars is death."

I sent the signal. A burst of light enveloped me. Blasts filled my ears, followed by the high-pitched whine of hundreds of thousands of liters of liquid oxygen and methane boiling and racing to escape their tanks through jagged holes. Something slammed into me from behind, delivering a wicked slap to my hindquarters. I tumbled to the ground, dropping Lauren, who rolled along the edge of the pad alongside me. Cal's vitals had flatlined in my readout, but Lauren's had spiked, showing pain and a sudden drop in blood pressure.

I stumbled to my feet, casting a quick glance behind me, much as I didn't want to. Of Cal there was no sign, but the satchel charge had blown one of the Mark V's legs clean off and torn a giant gash through the engines. The entire seventy meter structure tipped slowly, falling toward the entrance to the spaceport, just clear of where the Marauder had parked.

Ignoring the pain in my posterior, I scooped Lauren in my arms and raced as fast as I could toward the nearby hill. I scanned her limbs, looking for the shrapnel-induced gash that must've torpedoed her blood pressure. I had a can of polymer spray in my belt that I could use to seal the wound, but in the dust and darkness, I couldn't tell where she'd been hit. Absent those I could save her, but without dust and darkness, we'd already be dead.

The earth shook as the Mark V fell to its death, and another blast tore through the thin air. My toes bit into the regolith as I sprinted up the hill toward the RSR, my legs burning with the exertion, but I knew I couldn't slow.

There were fourteen kilometers between me and safety. Fourteen kilometers with Lauren in my arms, darkness overhead, and angry marines at my back.

Fourteen kilometers. I prayed the storm would hold.

4

JUNE 4, 2179

THE DOOR to my apartment puffed as I opened it. An herbaceous scent greeted me, a mixture of dill, parsley, and mint with a garlicky overtone. I cast a glance into the living room as I slipped off my shoes, but I didn't spot the familiar brown crest peeking from over the top of the couch. "Sophia? You home?"

"In the kitchen!"

I hung up my coat and turned the corner to find her standing in front of the stove, stirring an aromatic mixture in one of my enameled cast iron pots. She wore a loose, flowing blouse that had been knotted at the midsection and a knee-length black skirt that was the polar opposite of loose. Her dark brown hair had been pulled into a simple three strand braid that hung over her shoulder. She looked at me with her smoky eyes and cast me a casual smile. "Hey."

"Hey." I crossed the space between us, wrapping my arm around the small of her back as I pecked her on the lips. "What are you making?"

"It's called *spanakorizo*," she said. "It's Greek pilaf."

"With spinach, I'm guessing, hence the *spana* prefix."

"Like in *spanakopita*, yes. And like *spanakopita*, it's served with feta, but you sprinkle it over the top at the table instead of cooking it with the rice. Care for a taste?" She plucked a dab from the pot and held it out on the end of her spoon.

I leaned forward and took the bite. My eyebrows rose as I chewed. "*Mmm...*"

Sophia cocked me a leery glance. "Is that a 'this is delicious' sort of *mmm* or a 'how do I break it to her' sort?"

I pulled her closer to me. "More of an 'I can't believe she's this smart, attractive, and can still cook' sort."

She smirked and shrugged out of my embrace. "Don't let it go to your head. The market for daughters of notorious crime lords remains laughably depressed. I had to settle for the first suitor with a pulse. Basic supply and demand."

"And she knows economics, to boot." I nodded toward the pot. "Does that have garlic in it? I swear I smell some, but I couldn't taste any."

Sophia tapped the edge of the cooktop. "Greek chicken with lemon and oregano in the oven. There's a good clove or two in there."

"The nose knows."

Sophia stirred the spinach pilaf. "How about you pour me a drink while you tell me about your party."

I slid past her to the liquor cabinet. "I'm not sure how much there is to tell. There was a lot of shaking hands, getting slapped on the back, being told I was moving on to bigger and better things. The Captain presented me with a medal commemorating my service to the department, and Bishop gave me a quarter liter bottle of Callaghan and Sons and one of the bullets the doctors pulled from his chest. Both are still in my jacket pocket, now that I think about it. Bourbon sound good?"

"On the rocks, half and half with ginger ale, pinch of orange juice," said Sophia. "You make it sound like saying goodbye to your friends of the last decade and a half was a chore."

"I've misrepresented it then," I said as I opened the fridge and fetched the mixers. "There were moments I was so overwhelmed I was on the verge of tears. And I did enjoy myself. Reminiscing with Mwenge and Reyes and the others about past cases was cathartic. I did a lot of good in my time in the department, Sophia."

She turned and smiled at me over the pot. "I wish I could've been there to share it with you."

Ice clinked against glass, and bourbon gurgled as I poured it from the bottle. "As do I. It pains me having to hide you."

"You should be used to hiding."

"That doesn't mean I like it." The ginger ale fizzed as it hit the bourbon and juice. "The good news is, we won't have to hide as much anymore. Your father may be a criminal—though he's never been convicted of anything serious—but he's not a terrorist. Our relationship won't carry the same stigma it would've in the police department."

I returned to the stove and slid the drink into Sophia's waiting hand. She took a sip, and her lips curled in appreciation. "Mmm. Somehow this cocktail always tastes better when you make it."

"It's my secret ingredient. Love. That and an extra finger of bourbon."

Sophia smirked as she returned to stirring the pilaf. "In all seriousness, Ambrose, I'm perfectly aware of why you've had to keep our relationship a secret. It doesn't bother me. I don't want to have to sneak around in the shadows, but at the same time I don't need to shout our love from the rooftops. All I ever wanted was for you to open up to me, to be fully and completely honest. And you did."

A small part of me still wondered if I'd made the right choice telling Sophia everything: about my role in the Martian resistance, USC's role in the bombing of Los Angeles, the true identity of the Snow Leopard, and about the case that had set the entire city of Elysium on the edge of rebellion. I'd endangered myself and her both by telling her and in doing so had broken multiple fundamental tenants of the resistance code. I worried, but only because of her safety, not because I didn't trust her. The years I'd spent in service to the Martian counterintelligence taught me many things, chief among them how to evaluate individuals' true intentions. While Sophia's bloodlines might raise red flags, I judged people on their actions. Sophia's had made me trust her as deeply as anyone I'd ever met.

The oven beeped, and Sophia cracked the door to check on the chicken. "Speaking of *honesty*... Are you ready for USC Counterterrorism?"

"I've spent my entire adult life preparing. It's a move I should've made a decade ago, assuming I was the only variable in the equation, but Mars wasn't ready when I was. It's taken this long for sparks of resentment to rekindle the flame. And the move had to be made at the right time. I won't be able to last in Counterterrorism forever, not without betraying everything I stand for or without giving myself away. I'll stay long enough to learn what they know. Their targets, methods, and most importantly their weaknesses. Then I'll move on."

"To what though?"

"The data I gain will point me in the right direction, but ideally to a free Mars, one way or another."

Sophia flicked the stove off and moved the *spanakorizo* to an unused heating element. "Against your determination, USC and Mars alike don't stand a chance, but the world will have to wait, at least for one night. I have other plans for you."

I brought Sophia back into my embrace. "Such as?"

"A nice dinner."

"A delectable one." I pressed her against me. "And?"

Sophia smiled as she took a sip of her bourbon. "A drink or two."

I leaned in, inhaling her scent. "To set the mood perhaps?"

Sophia's glass clinked as it met the counter. She brought her arms around my shoulders, and she raked her fingernails through the short bristles at the base of my skull. "Oh, the mood has already been set."

Our lips met, though I almost wished I'd waited until after the meal to kiss her. After the kiss, nothing else would taste as sweet.

I SAT IN BED, a pillow propped behind my back for support. A light glowed softly on the nightstand, casting my side of the bed in a mellow glow. I didn't really need it on, but it gave the Net files I was reading a more organic look.

Sophia shifted beside me, rolling toward me onto her side. She emitted a soft moan as she pulled herself into the crook of my arm, pressing her naked flesh against my own. She rubbed her hand lazily across my chest before pulling it back to brush the hair out of her face. "What time is it?"

"Your Net not working?"

"It is. I'm not."

I snorted. "It's too late. Don't worry about it."

Her hand slid down my chest to my abdominals. It didn't stop there. "Did I not wear you out? Clearly you ruined me."

I actually wasn't sure how my body would respond to the prospect of another round, but nothing stirred. "Looks like I'm spent, too. I'd be shocked if I wasn't, to be honest."

Sophia's hand fell to my leg. "Good. You would've had to do everything if you weren't."

I brushed her hair around her earlobe with a finger. "Go back to sleep."

She shook her head, nuzzling closer. "If you're awake, I want to be as well. What's on your mind?"

"Work. Same as always."

Sophia pulled the covers up underneath her arm. "You're between jobs, babe."

"You know I can't turn it off. Besides, this isn't work for the department or for Counterterrorism. I finally got a lead on the Wen case."

Sophia looked up at me as she shifted. "Isn't that case closed? You caught the three junior detectives involved. Well... found one, killed the other two."

"Yes. The department considered the case solved after we were able to tie the murder of Chief Administrative Officer Wen to Detective Watters by DNA analysis, but that doesn't mean there aren't loose threads, the most notable of which is who fire-bombed Wen's apartment. If you'll recall, a masked individual we were never able to identify broke into Wen's apartment after she'd been murdered, torched the place, and escaped by detonating a window and parachuting to safety above the city's pressure barrier. It could've been arson Detective Milovich, but the detectives involved in the conspiracy to kill Wen *wanted* her murder publicized, just as they wanted their murder of Comptroller Jackson to be. The person who fire-bombed Wen's apartment seemed to desire the opposite, or at the very least wanted the evidence destroyed. I've always suspected it was someone who wanted to shift control of the situation to their side of the court, at least until they could get a grasp on the intentions behind the murder."

"You're talking about your former counterintelligence friend, Jorge. The one who was killed trying to stop the arson detective from murdering more people at Musk College."

"Yeah. Except it's not him. Dean ran computer models of the suspect based on height, build, and gait taken from security footage and came to the conclusion that the suspect was female. It was a guess, obviously, but I revisited the computer footage after we found Jorge and realized that based on height alone, he couldn't have been the one who visited the apartment. It was someone else."

"Another member of the resistance?"

I shrugged. "Maybe, but it's no one I know who's currently in the game."

Sophia nuzzled further into me. "You said you had a lead?"

"I had to be careful to submit the requests in a manner in which they wouldn't come back to anyone else. I couldn't let the department know I was still investigating this. I didn't think it would take this long but yeah, I finally got a hit."

Sophia's voice sounded distant. I think she was falling asleep again. "What?"

I stroked her hair. "I put a request in with building owners within a ten block radius of Wen's apartment to see if they discovered the jacket or mask that the fire-bomber was wearing in their lost and found. One of them finally got back to me with a yes."

5

FEBRUARY 17, 2158

THE MONITOR BEEPED STEADILY, the blips of Lauren's heart pulsing evenly on the inset screen. She lay before me on a white hospital bed, her eyes closed, hoses trailing from the intubation tube at her mouth. Fluids dripped from a bag through intravenous lines to the injection site on the inside of her elbow. Not long ago the lines had carried liters of synth blood, shelf stable, pre-oxygenated, and tailored to work with all blood types.

It had barely been enough.

I stuffed my fist into my mouth to stifle a yawn. I blinked, my eyes dry and my lids heavy. My Net clock read twenty after five. How long had it been since I'd arrived at the underground base? Sixteen hours? Lauren hadn't stirred since we'd arrived. The doctor who'd performed her surgery said she might not for several days, but I told myself I'd tough it out in the flimsy plastic chair opposite her bed until she did.

The door at my back creaked—Doctor Wu coming to check Lauren's vitals, no doubt. Except instead of Wu's warm baritone, I heard a voice that was an octave higher, softer, and every bit as somber. "How is she?"

A tall, lithe woman with olive skin and dark, shoulder length hair stood in the doorway, fuller in the face than I remembered her but otherwise the same. "Marina?"

I stood and stepped toward her. She took the remaining step and enveloped me in a hug, squeezing me tight with arms like braided steel. We held each other for a moment, feeling the need for contact if not necessarily for each other.

Eventually, she disengaged and stepped back. She squeezed me on the shoulder, giving me a reluctant smile. "It's good to see you, Ambrose."

"You too. It's been, what? A year? I thought you were up north in the Tempe Terra."

"I was until recently, but you haven't answered me. How is she?"

I glanced at Lauren, her chest rising and falling in slow waves. "She's alive. Doctor Wu put her into a medically-induced coma to improve recovery. Says she'll be up and running in a few days—metaphorically speaking. Her leg is going to require a fair bit of rehab."

"What happened, exactly?"

"You want the abridged version, or should we pull up some chairs?"

"I'll take a full written report later," said Marina. "For now hit the highlights."

I tipped my head toward Lauren. "A piece of shrapnel hit her in the back of the knee, slicing the Suit transverse the weave and lodging itself in her popliteal artery. She collapsed. Couldn't put any weight on it. At the time, I thought she couldn't move because..."

"Because you'd lost Cal."

I nodded slowly. "You heard."

"The barest bones version, yes."

I clenched my teeth, still angry with myself, consumed with guilt despite knowing his death hadn't been my fault. "I told him not to go. I pleaded with him to retreat, but when that Mark V descended on us in the middle of the storm... He made a split second decision."

"A decision he only regretted for an instant, but that Lauren will regret for much longer," said Marina.

I took a deep breath and let it out slowly. It felt good. "Yeah. Anyway, we were forced to detonate the charges while we were still within the blast radius. A blunt object hit me in the ass, but it didn't puncture the suit. Just left me with a nice bruise. I knew Lauren hadn't been so lucky, but in the darkness and with the dust swirling, I couldn't locate the wound. I couldn't risk slowing for risk of getting caught, much less activating a light to search her. Once I reached the hidden manhole, rappelled to the tube, and got the pair of us in a pod, I was able to find it. I stripped her Suit, bound the gash as best I could and added heating packs to fight the frostbite, but it wasn't external bleeding that was the problem. When I arrived and we got her into intensive care, Dr. Wu wasn't sure if he'd be able to save her leg."

Marina nodded, her face a passive mask. "What about the USC forces at Le Verrier?"

"I'm monitoring comms. They're still looking for traces of us, but they haven't found anything. The storm was fierce enough to wipe away all traces of our exit."

"And the tunnel you used?"

"I already imploded it, per protocols."

"Good." Marina stared at Lauren as if she wanted to say something, but she simply shook her head and moved her gaze to me instead. "Why don't you come to my quarters, Ambrose? We need to talk."

I hesitated. "What about Lauren?"

"She's not going to wake any time soon. Even if she does, your presence won't comfort her. She'll need time. Alone."

I swallowed back a lump as I thought of Cal. "Right. Let me grab my coat."

———

I CHUCKLED as I stepped foot into Marina's quarters. "You asked for the presidential suite once again, I see."

If anything, her room was adorned even more sparingly than most of the quarters in the underground base, with a lone couch, a few padded chairs, a desk pushed into the far corner, and in place of a coffee table, a circular multicolored rug. A kitchenette roughly the size of a closet stood to the side, a lone toaster taking up the majority of the counter space.

"My arrival was unexpected," said Marina with a smile. "Otherwise they would've taken even more of the furniture out. Can I get you anything? Coffee?"

The suggestion drew from me another yawn. "I probably should. I can't remember the last time I felt the tender caress of a pillow."

As Marina headed to the kitchen, one of the doors on the side of the apartment opened. A guy with short golden hair and a matching curly beard snuck out and closed the door softly behind him.

I smiled and stuck out a hand. "Jorge. How are you, man?"

He batted my arm down and hugged me. "Good, Ambrose. How about you?"

"I've been better, but I've been worse, too. Tired. Though not as tired as you, it seems." I pointed at my under eyes, which even in my sleep-deprived state must've looked fresher than the bags Jorge sported.

"Occupational hazard," he said. "I haven't slept much in the past three months."

"The Tempe Terra's been that bad, huh?"

"Something like that."

The coffee machine gurgled and sputtered as it delivered its contents to an eager mug. It beeped loudly as the last of the hot liquid streamed from the spout. A moment later, I heard a faint mewling.

Marina's face fell as she glanced at Jorge. "Whoops. Sorry."

Jorge sighed a heavy sigh. "It's alright. I'll take care of it."

The mewling intensified into an unmistakable cry. I blinked. "Is that a... baby?"

Marina chewed on her lip as she handed me the coffee, a cup of tea in her hands. I looked from her to Jorge and back. "Wait... *three months?* And you. Your cheeks. I swear they're... Seriously, you had a *baby* and you didn't tell me?"

The crying got louder, and Jorge excused himself, disappearing back inside the bedroom. Marina motioned me toward the sofa. "Don't take it personally, Ambrose. It's protocol, that's all."

"Sure. Rule number one," I said. "Don't share any information that's not mission critical. But seriously, *you guys had a baby?* I didn't even know you were pregnant."

Marina swirled her tea with a finger as she sat. "Ambrose, the last year has been the most challenging, most stressful, and most magical of my life. You think I didn't want to share it with you, with Cal, Lauren, Castleton, everyone? Of course I did! But the rules are in place for a reason. They don't just protect the movement, they protect those of us within it. What if Cal had been captured? Your identity, Lauren's, all of ours could've been in jeopardy. If he'd known about my daughter..."

I smiled. "A little girl, then."

Marina's face tightened in response to her own lapse. "Ambrose, I brought you here to talk about the movement. You asked Jorge about the Tempe Terra. The truth is both of us aren't tired solely because of our newborn. We've spent more sleepless nights putting out fires than we have singing rock-a-bye baby. USC deployments are up. Security is tighter at points of entry. Their surveillance has gotten more sophisticated, and their firewalls harder to crack."

I sighed. "I know. Our success in the Noachis Terra campaign has been limited as well. I can still gain access to most of the USC systems we need, depending on the target, but it's not as easy as it once was, and the opportunities for sabotage have been fewer and farther between. Every time we hit a target, USC learns and adapts. I think that's what pushed Cal to act. We'd waited so long to strike and to walk away empty handed...?"

Marina frowned. "I know, which is why I brought you here. Ambrose, three years ago when we targeted, captured, and recruited you, it was because of your computer skills. You were and still are one of the most natural hackers I've ever seen, but the fight for Mars's independence won't be won in the digital realm."

I blew on my coffee, feeling my jaw tighten. "I'm aware of that, Marina. Cal didn't die from a nasty text message."

Marina's eyes glinted as she peered at me, and I felt bad for lashing out. "The war won't be won by sabotaging fuel tanks and cargo ships either. If it would, USC would've given up and gone home long ago. The fact of the matter is what we're doing isn't working, not in the grand sense. USC's resolve has only increased since the war started. Their grip upon us has tightened, and all of Mars is suffering the consequences."

I sighed. "What do you want me to say, Marina? You're right. And? What do you propose we do about it? We can't fight USC head on. Our resources are stretched to the limit as it is."

Marina sipped on her tea. The cries of her newborn faded, replaced instead by the gentle monotony of Jorge singing "Row, Row, Row your Boat."

"Let me ask you a question, Ambrose," said Marina after a moment. "How many of us are there? Not just Snow Leopards. The entire resistance."

"I'm not sure. Rule number one again."

"If you had to guess."

I shrugged. "In the range of three thousand? Perhaps thirty-five hundred."

"And how many troops does USC have stationed on and around Mars?"

"At least thirty times that many. A hundred thousand or more."

"And the population of Mars?"

"Is this a quiz?"

Marina raised her eyebrows.

"Alright. There's probably sixty million in the cities in the afterlife triangle south of the Utopia Planitia. Probably another ten to twelve million in Olympus. Hard to know how many there are in the cities in the Hellas Basin, but all together, with all the smaller outposts and settlements thrown in... A hundred million? A hundred and ten?"

"So there's at least a thousand Martians for every USC soldier on Mars."

"What are you getting at? You want to incite every farmer and construction worker and stock broker into armed rebellion? Civilizations throughout history have tried that, generally with poor results. Soldiers are exceedingly capable of mowing down unarmed civilians, and they've only become more so as technology has progressed."

Marina sighed. "I'm not suggesting the sons and daughters of Mars grab their pitchforks and storm USC's castles. But for all our progress, for all our cachet, for all the subversive videos we've released to the underground of the Snow Leopard calling for action, the majority of Martians still aren't with us. Not even close. The people of Utopia, Elysium, Isidis, and Olympus may be angry, they may be frustrated, they may be scared, but they haven't yet joined our cause. And before you mention it, battle isn't the only way to aid us. If the majority of Martians wished to evict USC, *really* wished it, the planet would stop in its tracks. Vactrains would cease to run. Water wouldn't flow. Construction would slow to a crawl. Every single action on the part of USC would grind to a halt, trapped in a web of bureaucracy and inactivity, and USC wouldn't have enough men and women at their disposal to push the wheels back into motion. That's how we win this fight, Ambrose. By recruiting those who remain on the sidelines."

I tested my coffee. It had cooled to a few degrees below scalding. "And you came up with a plan to do this while birthing a child in the Tempe Terra?"

"Not so much a plan as an idea. We need the help of someone who's done it before. Someone who knows how to speak to the people, to rally them to our side. Someone charismatic and sympathetic to the cause."

"Being?"

I thought Marina might smile, but she didn't. "Winsor Salt."

I blinked. "The guy who started the rebellion a decade ago? The spy turned activist who was implicated in the Isidis bombings of 2151? Didn't USC try to assassinate him?"

"Twice," said Marina. "He went into hiding after the first attempt. Ambrose, if you could find him, learn from him, bring him into the fold... To say he'd be an asset would be an understatement. He might be the missing piece of the puzzle we need to foment widespread support for the resistance."

I rubbed my fingertips across my forehead. "If you think it'll help. So where can I find him?"

"Did you miss the part where I said he went into hiding?"

"But you have a bead on him, right?"

Marina leaned back in her chair and sipped her tea.

"I see. You realize I'm not a bounty hunter, right? I don't have any experience tracking people."

"You think the rest of us do?"

The coffee's warmth seeped through the mug into my fingers.

"Is this because of Cal? You don't want me leading combat missions anymore?"

Marina met my eyes when I lifted them. "I won't lie. Yes."

A hollow opened inside me, one that a deep breath couldn't fill.

"It's not what you think, Ambrose. Cal's death brought things into perspective. You're too valuable to risk in sabotage missions, and as amazing a digital technician as you are, you'd be wasted sitting behind a desk twelve hours a day. We need to change the narrative of our conflict with USC. Winsor Salt could harbor the knowledge it takes for us to do so, and even if he doesn't... There are other things you could learn from him."

"You're speaking to his background as a spy."

"You're the only former USC operative in our ranks. No one outside the Snow Leopards knows you're one of us. That combination of background and anonymity is powerful."

I took another deep breath, this one soothing the hurt inside. "I want to end the war, Marina, and I want USC gone from Mars. If you think Salt can help us achieve either of those goals, then I'll do everything I can to find him. But can I ask something first?"

"By all means."

"Can I delay leaving until Lauren wakes? I owe it to her to stay."

Marina smiled. "Given all we deal with, I forget how refreshing a simple act of friendship can be. Of course you can."

I nodded and rose. I took a last sip of my coffee before setting the mug down on a sliver of counter in the kitchenette. Marina left her mug beside mine and walked me to the exit, but I didn't make it to the hall.

"Ambrose. Wait." Marina gave me a nod, then cracked the door to her bedroom. I followed her into the darkened room, finding Jorge swaying by the reflected light of a projector showing calming ocean scenes. His voice was little more than a whisper as he sung to the bundle in his arms.

Marina walked lightly, her feet gliding across the carpet without a sound. She placed her hand on Jorge's arm and smiled.

"Ambrose," she whispered. "I'd like for you to meet someone. Fabia Graciana de la Plata."

I couldn't help but smile as I stared at the tiny, angelic face poking from the swaddled cloths in Jorge's arms. The face of Mars's future.

6

JUNE 7, 2179

THE BUILDING DIDN'T LOOK like much from the outside, just a gleaming rectangular prism of silvery-grey metal, same as those next to it. It didn't look particularly impressive from the inside either. A small lobby greeted me as I stepped inside. To my right, a woman in a crisp blue USC uniform sat in front of a bank of holos, while the lone entrance into the building was blocked by a pair of similarly uniformed men who flanked a body scanner.

My instructions told me to approach the woman at the desk. "Morning. Ambrose Drake, reporting for my first day of work."

The woman glanced at me and nodded. "Just a moment, Mr. Drake. Let's see... Yes, I have you right here. Looks like your application is complete. All we need to do is validate your biometrics for security purposes." She stood and motioned me to a station against the wall, one with a retina scanner and a palm reader. "If you could place your chin against the rest and stare into the green light. There we go. Thank you."

A bright light flashed. I straightened as it faded, blinking away the spots.

"Now place your palm upon the reader. Please keep it there until the system beeps."

I did as I was told. The reader was cool to the touch, but it warmed quickly as I pressed my hand against it. It flashed orange, sending an intense heat into my flesh, but it cooled just as quickly. I pulled my hand back, noting the slight pink hue to my skin. Must've been epidermal ablation.

"You use DNA as well as retinal maps?" I said.

"Most of the systems throughout the building are fingerprint scanners. DNA confirmation is mostly for account initialization, though there are areas where you'll need to use ablative scanners for access. Please wait one moment while I print your badge."

A small printer on the woman's desk buzzed and whirred, spitting out a card with my public database photograph on it. The woman in charge of security gave it to me along with a clip. "Here you are, Mr. Drake. You can wear it if you want, but most people don't. It's not as secure as the biometric readers, and our agents avoid publicity whenever possible. My instructions indicate you're heading to the twenty-second floor. Elevators are through the security gate to your right."

I pulled my tablet from my pocket. "Do I need to relinquish this?"

"Not to me you don't, though your division director will probably issue you a secure one at their discretion. Best of luck, Mr. Drake."

"Thanks."

I moved to the security scanners. The two uniformed guards gave me polite nods as I once again scanned my retina and my palm. When those systems flashed green, they waved me forward into the body scanner. It hummed, and a second later, it too flashed green.

"You're good to go, sir," said the guard.

I thanked the man and proceeded to the elevators. Those didn't require identity verification, and they responded without complaint when I pressed the button for the twenty-second floor.

I stepped off the car into an environment I was familiar with from my days in homicide, though there appeared to be more offices and fewer cubicles than I was used to. My new division director had given me detailed instructions prior to arrival, so I headed confidently down the hall, hooked a right, and proceeded to the office at the corner.

I paused at the door and knocked. I could see into the office through the side windows. A smartly-dressed man sat at his desk inside, slender but wide in the shoulders, with close-cropped brown hair that might've appeared lighter in color than it was thanks to a generous sprinkling of grey. He looked up at my knock and waved me in.

I cracked the door and stepped inside. "Director Schmidt?"

The man stood, rounded his desk, and extended a hand. "Drake. Good to see you again." We'd met remotely via interview. "Everything go smoothly downstairs?"

I shook his hand. "I'm in possession of fewer dead skin cells than when I entered, but otherwise yes. It would appear I'm in the system now."

"It's a rite of passage," said Schmidt. "We all go through it. On the bright side, it eliminates the need for spa treatments, and it's the last step before your application is considered complete. There might not be much fanfare associated with it, but getting your hand zapped is what *officially* elevates you to agent status. Congratulations, Agent Drake."

"Thank you, sir. I'm excited to be here."

"As are we to have you," he said. "You come highly recommended. I suspect your experience will be invaluable to our team."

"I'm eager to get started, sir." I waved to the chairs in front of the man's desk. "Should I take a seat? Or is there a training module ready and waiting for me?"

"Actually, orientation and introductions will have to wait. I've been given specific instructions to bring you to the Inspector General upon arrival."

I blinked. The Inspector General was the highest-ranking official in all of Counterterrorism. "Sir?"

"Your guess is as good as mine, Agent. Sometimes I question orders, but the phrasing on this missive made it clear my input wasn't asked for. Come with me."

A pang of fear stabbed into me as we headed back toward the elevators. What could have prompted a sudden meeting with the Inspector General—on my first day of work, before I met with the rest of my team, no less? USC would've performed a thorough background check on me. Could they have found something in my past that gave them pause? I'd been careful at every stage to keep my identity secret, but no ruse was impermeable forever.

My years of experience helped keep my outward appearance calm. The elevators dinged and we stepped inside. Director Schmidt punched the top button on the panel, but the car didn't respond until he placed his palm against the scanner. Apparently, access even to the same floor as the Inspector General required special clearance.

Schmidt had already expressed his ignorance of the reason for the meeting, so I didn't press him. The numbers on the elevator panel cycled in silence. When we reached our floor, we stepped out to be greeted by another pair of guards, these armed. They didn't require biometric authorization for us to pass, though I did notice another palm reader and retina scanner built into the wall. Perhaps the presence of Director Schmidt precluded the need to have my identity verified once again.

We proceeded to a lobby that qualified as fancy by government standards, mostly because it contained potted plants in addition to its lone desk. A severe woman with heavy eyebrows acknowledged our approach with a pointed glance. "Director Schmidt. The Inspector General is expecting you. Go ahead."

"Thank you, Nouria." We proceeded to a closed door, this one without any windows to the sides of the entrance. Schmidt pressed a thumb against the intercom, but he didn't speak. Apparently, our faces were evidence enough as a moment later, a latch clacked. Schmidt cranked on the handle, and we walked into the Inspector Generals's office.

I'd seen a photo of the man in researching my position at Counterterrorism, but he was far more grizzled and weathered in person than his public bio had suggested. If I had to guess, the man was pushing eighty, with a shaved head that sprouted tiny white bristles from the sides. Genetic conditioning could easily activate the hairs that had stopped growing, but I suspected the man had told his doctors not to bother. It would simply be more hair he'd need to shave, slowing down his weekly routine.

Schmidt came to attention a few paces from the man's desk. "Inspector General Riggs. You asked to see Agent Drake."

"I did. Thank you. Dismissed, Director." He gave a curt nod, and Schmidt left the room, closing the door behind him.

I knew my place, so I remained rooted to the floor, quiet as a mouse. Riggs eyed me carefully, the vast expanse of Elysium visible through the floor to ceiling window behind him. "Ambrose Drake."

"Yes, sir."

"You have quite the resume."

"Thank you, sir."

The man waved at one of the chairs in front of his desk. "Have a seat."

I did as I was told, but I didn't offer any opinions.

Riggs spoke after a moment. "You served in the corps. Tell me about that."

I didn't understand the motivation behind the question, but I didn't let that stop me. "I joined the day the separatists nuked Los Angeles, sir. Progressed through an accelerated basic training program before shipping out. Was injured on my first patrol. After recovering, I joined USC Counterintelligence. Did some work in Utopia before shipping out to Cassini. There, I uncovered the existence of a local separatist cell. We attacked, but they were ready for us. I was captured."

"You spent six years in custody."

"Yes, sir."

"That must've been quite a trial."

It was a question I could answer truthfully. "It was."

"You left the military as soon as you were freed."

"Technically, I still had a few months left on my contract, but yes, I left as soon as I was able."

Riggs' expression didn't change. "Why?"

"The war was over, sir, and my experience as a prisoner of war dwarfed my experience in combat. I decided I wanted to serve in a different way."

"Which is why you joined the police department."

"Correct."

Riggs rubbed his chin. "I spent about thirty years in the corps, you know."

"Yes. I read your biography, sir." I also couldn't have imagined a man like Inspector General Riggs in any other profession.

"It helped prepare me for the second half of my career in Counterterrorism, as I suspect your experience will have helped you, even if much of your time enlisted was spent in enemy hands. All of which brings me to my point. Typically, we like to promote from within. There are certain investigative techniques and methods that aren't learned in other professions, not to mention specific training required for our work that isn't needed for most police or military action. But after your name came to my attention, I realized you warranted an exception."

Internally, I relaxed as I realized why I'd been summoned. Externally, I remained unchanged. "I appreciate that, sir."

Riggs continued. "I generally skim the resumes of all the

agents our directors decide to hire, but I paused when I read yours, in part because of your military service during the rebellion and in part because of your police background. Your role in this most recent debacle with the Snow Leopard imitators was particularly impressive, so I had no qualms with Director Schmidt's decision to bring you on. However, the more I thought about it, the more I realized you wouldn't be an ideal fit for Schmidt's team. The fact that you endured isolation in the hands of the Reds for six years speaks to your mental fortitude. The report I received from your Captain about the Snow Leopard case gives proof to your physical abilities and mental quickness, and the fact that you don't have any family to speak of means you're not tied to local cases. You're a field agent if I've ever seen one, Drake."

Thoughts of Sophia swam in my mind. She wasn't family, at least not yet, but bringing her up to the Inspector General wasn't what I'd thought of when I mentioned that our relationship might be better received among my new coworkers. Besides, a field agent position promised a level of operational freedom that far superseded anything I could've achieved in the Elysium office. "Something tells me you want to deploy me right away, sir."

"Your sixth sense is on point, Agent Drake. In fact, a special mission has developed over the past week that appears to be tailor made for your expertise. Have you heard of the Terby outpost?"

"No, sir."

"It's a small military facility located on the edge of the Hellas Planitia, a short overland trip from the Niesten vactrain stop. Most of the station's efforts are spent tracking and analyzing surveillance of the Mukt people at the bottom of the basin, though there are a number of defensive military systems at the outpost that could be called upon should the Mukt decide to break the terms of their armistice. The exact nature of said facilities isn't important, at least not to you or me. What is important is the presence of several diplomats who work at the outpost and make occasional trips into the basin."

The Mukt, or Bimukta depending on whose language you used, were the descendants of Indian and Bangladeshi climate refugees who'd fled their respective countries during the water wars of the late twentieth century. USC had controlled the ports of immigration into the major cities at the time, as they still did, but the refugees had no intention of integrating themselves into the existing city-state system. Instead, they founded their own communities, all of them at the bottom of the Hellas Planitia, a giant impact basin at a depth of roughly seven kilometers below the standard topographic datum of Mars. The location had some advantages. The atmospheric pressure was significantly higher than it was anywhere else on the planet, and thanks to CO_2 sublimation efforts at the poles, it was now possible to walk outside in the Hellas Planitia without a full pressure suit. The temperature was somewhat milder than in many portions of the globe as well, but the biggest reason the Mukt settled there was that USC hadn't challenged them for the territory. USC correctly assumed that the entire basin would disappear beneath kilometers of water once terraforming efforts flooded the planet, so they hadn't been particularly forceful in trying to evict the Mukt. Diplomatic efforts to convince them to leave hadn't been particularly well received, either.

Despite my two and a half decades on Mars, I'd never been to the Hellas Planitia. "I'm sorry, sir, but I'm not particularly well steeped in diplomacy, or on the Mukt."

"I didn't think you were," said Riggs. "You are, however, an expert on homicide, and as it turns out, three of our Terby-based diplomats have died within the last week."

I felt my brow furrow. *"Died?* I'm assuming there's a reason you chose that particular phrasing."

"Well, they weren't shot or stabbed, so it's hard for me to definitively state they were murdered, but the timing of the deaths has become increasingly suspicious. The first of the three died eight days ago from apparent heart failure. Another passed away the evening of the second, and the last just two days ago."

"Have you performed any autopsies on the dead yet?"

"There's no coroner on site," said Riggs. "The station doctor took a look at the first two bodies but didn't find any external signs of foul play. When the third of the diplomats died, we put the station into immediate quarantine and ordered a hazmat team there stat."

"You suspect it could be a chemical weapon?"

"A biological one is the greater fear. And the fact that the three diplomats who were targeted all make regular trips into the Hellas Basin makes it all the more plausible. For now we're treating it as a potential act of bioterror. While the latter may not be your specialty, homicide certainly is. I'll make sure you have immediate access to the full file. I suggest you study it carefully. I want you on the first vactrain toward Terby tomorrow morning."

"Tomorrow morning?" For once I didn't hide my emotions well. I hadn't consulted with Sophia, and I had important tasks still left unfinished in Elysium. I recovered quickly, though. "Sir, I've only started. I haven't completed a single training module."

The Inspector General's face hardened. "Sometimes life doesn't allow us time for preparation, which is why it's a welcome change you arrived already seasoned. You'll do well, Agent. Dismissed."

I nodded and headed for the door, relieved that my identity remained a secret, proud that my experience had gained attention, and worried nonetheless about what the future held.

7

FEBRUARY 23, 2158

JORGE STUCK out his mitt as I stepped off the pod into the omnipresent darkness of the tunnel. "Good luck out there, Ambrose. You need anything, don't hesitate to reach out."

I activated my Suit's helmet light and shook the man's hand. "I will. Now get some sleep for God's sake. You look half dead."

Jorge smiled. "I'll be out before the pod finishes cycling. Take care, buddy."

Jorge depressed a button, and the pod's door swung closed. The compressors whirred to life, returning air pressure to the cabin. The electric motors underneath hummed, and within seconds, the pod had disappeared down the shaft, taking all trace of its floodlights with it.

I turned and headed into the nearby escape shaft. There I found a carabiner hooked onto a bracket at the wall, the cable that was attached to it stretching into the endless darkness overhead. I unhooked it and clamped it to my Suit's harness before activating the release lever. With a jerk, I lifted into the darkness, zipping through the thin air at whip crack speed. At about the hundred meter mark, my speed slowed, but not enough to keep me from soaring and bouncing at the end of the tether when the winch came to a full stop. I reached out and pulled myself to safety by the hand holds at the side of the tunnel, unhooked and secured the carabiner, and headed up the twelve short rungs of the ladder beside me to the manhole above.

I grunted as I pushed on the heavy cover. Dust flooded through the hole as I tossed it to the side. Above me, stars shone bright in the clear night sky, barely twinkling thanks to the thin atmosphere. I pulled myself out of the shaft into the chill air, replaced the cover, and piled rust red dirt back atop it. There wasn't much breeze to speak of, but I could activate the fan in the bottom of my Suit's backpack to spread the regolith behind me to cover my tracks.

With the cover appropriately hidden, I checked my clock and GPS. It was just after three in the morning, and I had about twenty-five kilometers to traverse to get to the closest stop on the transglobal vactrain line.

I turned on the fan and bounded into the night.

I WOKE as the vactrain's deceleration shoved me forward in my seat. I blinked to find the tall skyscrapers of Isidis approaching rapidly through the clear outer shell of the vactube, the afternoon sun glinting off the pillars of alloyed magnesium and the Mylamene pressure layer stretched between buildings at the three story mark.

I'd needed the sleep, yet I was nonetheless surprised I'd achieved the feat. Despite my training, my heart had beaten hard in my chest as I'd slipped out of my pressure suit into civilian clothes in the changing rooms at the Shatskiy Outpost vactrain station. My ticket had been purchased under an assumed name. I knew from poking around USC's servers that vactrain station security didn't regularly process passenger facial scans against records, but I was rattled nonetheless. After all, I hadn't shown my face in public in over three years. As far as USC was concerned, I was a prisoner of war, and while I had no reason to believe anyone was looking for me, the idea of being identified by a passing acquaintance through an act of ill fate moistened my brow.

Once the train had accelerated to full speed, turning the desolate Martian wastes into a passing blur of red rock and swirling dust, I began to breathe easy, in body if not in mind. While I'd traversed Mars dozens of time via the resistance's underground network of ambient pressure tubes, I hadn't ridden an honest-to-goodness vactrain since leaving USC's employ. Though the ride itself was comparable—faster, in fact, due to the vacuum—the vactrain brought with it memories the underground tubes never had. Memories of my first ride from USC's Chicago recruitment office to the training center in Titusville, Florida.

I glanced at the empty seat beside me as the train pulled into the Isidis station and sighed. Time heals all wounds, they say, but Phoebe Zhao's death still hurt.

I grabbed my pack as the train's doors puffed open and fought my way through the crowds to the changing room. Every vactrain station had one, but Isidis's version wasn't any larger than Shatskiy Outpost's despite the size of the settlement. Few people arrived at the Isidis station in Suits and even fewer wore them in the city, so I rented a locker, transferred a few items to my jacket, and stashed my pack inside one. From there I caught a rideshare toward the Pyramid district in the northern part of town, so named not for any architectural efforts on the parts of the city planners but as a nod toward the Egyptians myths after which the plains bordering Isidis were named. I instructed the car to stop a few blocks from my target, choosing to stretch my legs before I made any moves. It was a few minutes shy of five. I figured it made sense to wait until after the post-work rush anyway.

I wandered the streets, trying to enjoy the sights but finding little to draw my eye. I'd never spent any time in Isidis other than passing through on a vactrain ride when I was a grunt in the USC cog, but it didn't look much different than Utopia. The same silver grey alloy glistened at the front of every high rise, crowding out the light of the falling sun. Trees were few and far between, sprouting sporadically from the concrete like weeds from cracks. Rideshares packed the streets and people the sidewalks, empty space a luxury to be heated and pressurized and paid for only by those with money to burn.

Not that I had to fight to claim a slice of sidewalk of my own. A bubble cradled me as I walked, cleared of passersby as much by my broad Earther shoulders as by the cold, quiet look of calculation I wore.

Counting time spent as a marine and a partisan both, I'd felt the loose soils of Mars underfoot for over three and a half years. I'd adapted my gait to the gravity as well as anyone, I'd shed my fatigues for the thick slacks and knee-length dusters that were the local style, and I'd even grown to accept the taste of the highly sought after maché tea, but based on the dubious looks I received as I walked, so reminiscent of the ones I'd received fresh off the USC rockets, none of it had marked me as anything but a wolf in sheep's clothing.

I might've been overreacting. So much time spent underground in the presence of likeminded idealists had stunted my social growth. But in that moment, striding the crowded streets of downtown Isidis, I felt like an outsider. An outcast, unable to return to Earth out of shame and disgust, yet unwelcome in his new home.

Perhaps I always would be.

I STARED at the apartment building in front of me, checking my Net to make sure I had the right address. When pressed, Marina hadn't provided me with much more information than she'd volunteered at our first meeting. In fact, the number of leads she'd given me could be represented by a single binary digit. I hoped it would be enough.

I headed inside and took to the stairs, hopping to the fourth floor before finding apartment four nineteen. A thumb reader to the side of the door contained the chime, so I pressed it and waited in silence. After a moment, the panel lit up and an annoyed voice emerged from the speaker.

"Who is it?"

"Nam Nguyen?" I asked.

"Yes?"

"I'm looking for Winsor Salt."

The voice failed to respond, and after a moment the panel light blinked out. I stood there, considering whether or not I should press the buzzer again, but the latch clacked and the door puffed as the pressure seal to the hallway was broken.

A middle-aged asian man with a wide nose and three distinct creases in his brow opened the door just wide enough to scowl at me. "Who the hell are you?"

8

JUNE 7, 2179

I LEANED into the plush seats of the rideshare and closed the Net files I'd been poring over. I blinked a few times and rubbed my forehead to clear the strain. While the case file regarding the deaths at Terby outpost wasn't as thorough as I would've liked, there was enough background information to process to last me a month: the roles of the different officials and diplomats at the outpost, their backgrounds and family histories, the projects they'd been assigned, their travel histories, who'd they'd met with, who they were in regular contact with. The list went on and on. I'd tried to sift through it to find the relevant information, something I'd become quite good at as a result of two decades of police work, but I didn't know enough about the presumed murders to drill into the diplomats' circles and find who might've had a motive to come after them. I knew I'd find leads eventually, once I got on the scene and did some real investigation.

Of course, I'd never been on the scene of a bioterror attack. The irrational part of me should've been afraid, but despite my inexperience with nerve agents and bioengineered pathogens, I was confident in USC's ability to keep me safe. The core of the organization might be rotten and black, but externally they functioned with a practiced, cold precision. Even during my time in the corps, we'd trained extensively about how to react to all manner of threats, both organic and inorganic. The fact that a military hazmat unit had already been sent to Terby meant there was virtually no chance of me being exposed to whatever killed the diplomats. The others at the outpost who'd been quarantined might not be so lucky, however...

No, it wasn't fear of the mission that bothered me, but rather trepidation over what the assignment and my new position portended. Being named a field agent was a positive development. I wouldn't be forced to report to work at the same time every day. I could travel, including to places USC didn't direct me to assuming I played my cards right, and the freedom granted to me would only increase as I proved myself and advanced to more clandestine cases. But with freedom came certain downsides. One was Sophia. I still hadn't called to tell her about my meeting with the Inspector General or about the fact that I'd be leaving first thing in the morning. The other more pressing downside was that I had an unfinished case anchoring me in Elysium.

The rideshare slowed, and I glanced out the window. My minimap indicated we were approaching my destination. It wasn't much to look at. Just a multistory apartment building with Mg-Al siding like all the rest, except perhaps shabbier than its neighbors. It stood on the edge of the ten block radius I'd set around Shao Wen's apartment, right where Elysium's downtown faded into the dicier neighborhoods to the southeast, which to me made sense. If I was a criminal parachuting from a crime scene toward safety, I'd steer clear of the glass-faced high rises and head for places where people wouldn't look at a strange face twice.

The building's landlord had messaged me Friday about my lost and found request. I'd replied the same day after my farewell party at the station. I hadn't expected an immediate response. I hadn't waited with baited breath over the weekend either, but I was surprised at the radio silence I'd received today. Perhaps I'd overestimated the landlord's commitment to public service. Either way, given my travel plans for the morning, I didn't have time to wait.

I hopped out of the rideshare and entered the building. There wasn't a lobby or an information kiosk, but I'd done my research. I waltzed past the elevators, took the lone hallway to the back of the building, and pressed the buzzer on the intercom beside apartment 1036. A few seconds passed before a disgruntled voice sprouted from the speaker. "Can I help you?"

I decided to play it straight—mostly. "Detective Ambrose Drake, EPD. Open up."

The speaker squawked. *"EPD? What's this about?"*

"Open the door, Mr. Viswanathan."

The speaker went silent. A moment later a latch clacked and the door puffed open. A brown-skinned man with a three day old beard and a stained white shirt underneath his bathrobe stared at me, a mixture of confusion and apprehension in his eyes. "Uh... hi."

I gave the man my best icy stare. "You're the building manager here, aren't you Mr. Viswanathan?"

"That's right. Look, is this about the tenants in fourteen-twelve? Because if so, they're the ones who were the problem. We had every legal right to evict them. I don't know where they get the gall to file a discrimination complaint, but—"

"This isn't about the tenants," I said. "Your landlord, Mrs. Vasquez, sent me. I need to see your lost and found."

Viswanathan blinked. *"Lost and found?"*

"Did she not relay anything to you?"

"No."

I sighed with an exasperation that I didn't have to fake. "Items that are of concern to us were recently reported to us via Mrs. Vasquez. I assumed that if she knew about the presence of the items, you would've been the one to report them to her."

"Oh." Viswanathan blinked again. "Well, yeah. She asked me for a list of the items in the lost and found, but I didn't realize it had anything to do with the police."

I kept a tight grip on my icy stare. "It does. Perhaps you could show me where they're located."

"Right. Sure. Just a sec." Viswanathan disappeared into his apartment and reappeared wearing fuzzy slippers. He closed the door behind him and gestured to an unmarked door next to the emergency exit at the far end of the hall. "Everything's in the maintenance closet." He led the way and opened the door via the thumb reader at the side. The door popped open, the lights inside flashed to life, and Viswanathan shuffled his way inside. "It's kind of tight. Watch your head, and that supply shelf isn't bolted to the wall."

Maintenance closet was right. There was barely room to move through the maze of shelving, stacked boxes, and piles of junk within. A mop and bucket stood behind the furthest shelf, mostly hidden behind jugs of Wipe and Glo and floor wax. I wondered how anyone managed to maneuver it out the door. Based on the dried out cords at the mop's end, perhaps no one ever did.

"Here you go," said Viswanathan, pulling a box from one of the shelves. "Not much here. Clothes, mostly. What are you looking for, exactly?"

"Clothes, mostly, so I guess I'm in luck." I pulled the item at the top of the box and shook it out, a white puffy jacket with fur trim. I'd revisited the security video of the firebomber walking through Wen's building numerous times. The jacket matched hers perfectly, all except for a large tear in one of the sleeves.

I tossed the jacket over my elbow and sifted through the remaining items in the box. "There's no reflective visor."

Viswanathan shrugged. "I don't control what people lose. Is that jacket stolen?"

"Where was the item found?"

"In the elevator shaft, if you can believe it. We had maintenance here on Thursday to check out an issue with the elevator hitching. Turns out it was that jacket. They found it on top of the elevator with one of the sleeves stuck in the safeties."

"Did maintenance find anything else in the shaft? A parachute for instance?"

"A *parachute?* Is that a joke?"

I fingered the tear. "I'll take that as a no. Does this building have roof access?"

"I mean, there's a safety hatch that leads to a roof lock, but no direct access."

"Let me guess. The airlock access hatch is accessible through the elevator shaft, or is connected to it directly through maintenance channels."

Viswanathan scrunched his brow. "Yeah, I think so. Why?"

If he hadn't figured it out yet, I wasn't about to explain it to him. "Do you have a security system in this building?"

Viswanathan's confusion left him in a hurry. "Sort of."

"What does that mean?"

"It's not the most thorough system. Cameras outside the building, inside the front door, in the elevator, and in the stairwell. That's it."

"No door alarms? Elevator movement logs? Nothing on the roof access hatch?"

The manager shook his head.

"I need to see the video. Where's the system?"

"Right here." Viswanathan tapped an unassuming box affixed to the wall. "Keeps about a month of video. I think we back it up in the cloud. Honestly, I've never asked Mrs. Vasquez."

"This has Net access, I hope."

Viswanathan nodded. "Sure. But don't you need written approval or something?"

I was surprised the man had yet to ask for credentials, but people often failed to do so when flustered. Most people had a natural inclination to believe and trust anyone who projected confidence. "I'm trying to figure out who dumped a jacket in your elevator shaft. You *really* want me to get a warrant?"

The man swallowed hard. "Sorry. It's just... Never mind." His eyes flicked as he accessed his own Net. "Alright. Here you go. Should be getting an access request."

"Got it." The system was extremely simple. I quickly pulled up the four feeds from the night of Wen's death and accelerated the footage to a few minutes after the fire bomber escaped her apartment building. From there, I ran through the feeds at sixteen times speed, looking for anything. A few tenants came and went, all of them through the elevator proper with faces fully exposed.

Viswanathan waited patiently for a few moments before glancing at the door. "You know, it's after hours. You could access the video from the hall if you want. Let me lock up."

I held up a finger as a figure passed through one of the feeds. Someone in a hoodie wearing a backpack stuffed to the brim descended the stairwell from the first floor to the ground. They passed across the camera at the ground floor entrance headed toward the back hallway I'd taken to Viswanathan's apartment.

Two things struck me. The first was that the individual hadn't shown their face in either feed. The cameras in the stairwell pointed down, and the camera at the front door pointed toward the elevators. The second was that the individual's backpack was close to bursting. I wasn't the best judge of volume, but I wagered the thing could've held a reflective visor, a folded pressure suit, and a carefully packed parachute. There certainly wasn't any room left for a puffy white jacket.

I crafted the assailant's movements in my mind, seeing them enter through the roof access hatch, hop on the top of the elevator, ride it to the ground floor, exit through the door on the floor above, head down the stairs, into the hallway on the ground floor, and out the emergency exit to the side of the maintenance closet in which I now stood.

"No security cameras in the back alley outside the emergency exit, correct?" I asked.

"No. Sorry."

It was a perfectly planned escape. If the abandoned jacket hadn't gotten caught in the elevator's safeties, no one would've known the fire bomber had been here.

I shared a still of the individual in the hoodie with Viswanathan via Net. "Is this one of your tenants?"

His brow scrunched as he checked it out. "I'm not sure. I can't see their face. Is that who the jacket belongs to?"

I hefted the jacket. "I'm going to hang on to this if you don't mind, Mr. Viswanathan. I appreciate your time. You have a nice night."

9

FEBRUARY 23, 2158

I KEPT my face impassive as I stared at the man in the doorway. "Mr. Nguyen?"

"I'm still waiting for you to tell me who the hell you are."

"The name's Jordan Fletcher. I'm—"

Nguyen snorted. "Sure it is."

It took an exertion of will to keep my eyebrows at bay. "Excuse me?"

"Why are you packing?"

"Packing?"

"Heat." Nguyen nodded at my jacket, roughly at the spot where I'd hidden the pistol I'd taken from the bags I stashed in the Isidis vactrain station lockers.

I knew better than to deny it. I glanced at the console next to the door, the small circular eye of the video camera glistening. "You noticed that from your feed?"

"And from looking at you in person. Among other things."

"Like what?"

Nguyen snorted again. "You're an Earth boy, but not fresh off the rocket. Not USC, though you look like you could be. And you can probably handle yourself in a fight, assuming you weren't surprised or outgunned."

I tried not to look impressed. "How do you know I'm not USC?"

"Please. If you were, you wouldn't have come alone. Even when they're executing raids, those tyrants are never that discreet." He judged me with hard eyes. "So. Are you here to kill me?"

This time I failed to keep the surprise off my face. *"Pardon?"*

"It's a simply question, *Jordan*. I don't know how else to phrase it."

"I'm not here to kill you, Mr. Nguyen."

Nam held my gaze, measuring me without flinching. After a moment, he nodded. "Good." He opened the door to full width, and his shoulders relaxed ever so slightly.

"That's it?" I said. "You're taking me at my word?"

"For now."

I knew I should leave it alone, but I couldn't. "If you thought I was here to kill you, why did you open the door?"

"Would the door have stopped you if you were?"

I didn't answer. I didn't have to.

"So," said Nam. "You're looking for Salt."

I nodded. "You were one of his closest allies through the later part of the twenty-one forties. Whenever he spoke, you weren't far from his side, either in public or in the reactionary videos he distributed online. As I understand, you two were practically inseparable until... the early part of this decade."

"You can say it. When he bombed the lobby of USC's Office of Civilian Operations and tried to do the same to the homes of several of the company's board of governors. I was never implicated in any of that, you understand."

"I'm aware of that."

"What do you want with Winsor?"

"I'm afraid I can't say."

Nam snorted and shook his head. "Of course you can't. Why don't you come in?"

The man left his post at the door and retreated inside. I found it odd that a man who only seconds prior wondered if I'd arrived at his doorstep to gun him down was now inviting me into his home, but he seemed the sort whose eyes could penetrate beneath the skin into the fleshy, nebulous parts underneath. I wondered what else he saw in me.

Nguyen's apartment was neat and austere, the windows clear of fingerprints and not a speck of dust to be found. He waved a hand at an empty seat in the living room as he headed to the adjacent kitchen. "Care for a maché?"

"I'm not a big fan, actually."

Nam chuckled. "I figured."

He fixed himself a mug, slowly and without care for my well-being. I sat and waited patiently, eying the ticking gallery clock that hung from the walls, the only nod to the non-digital age in the entire space. I'd never cared for the aesthetic even for Earth-based clocks, much the less the twenty-four hour Martian variants where an extra thirty-seven and a half minutes had been squeezed haphazardly between the final hour and the first.

Nam came back with an insulated stainless steel thermos in hand. He sat and took a sip of his brew, eying me with curiosity. "You're a quiet one."

"When I need to be."

"And you're sure you don't want to share what it is you're hoping to get from Salt?"

"It's not that I don't want to. More that I can't."

Nam nodded, and I think he understood my motivations. He wouldn't have let me in if he hadn't.

The man took another sip of his tea. "Winsor and I met seventeen years ago. It was at a seminar at Hubble College. A visiting professor was giving a guest lecture about the colonization of Mars, making the argument that USC's efforts, even though they'd resulted in fewer freedoms and rights for Martians, had ultimately been a boon for civilization on the planet as a whole. He likened it to the exploitation of fossil fuels on Earth. Yes, their use ultimately wrecked the planetary ecosystem, causing untold trillions in damages which are still being mitigated today, but without the use of said fuels, humanity would've never developed the technologies needed to replace them with something better. It was a reasonable argument, but there were holes in it. I challenged him on some of his points in the Q and A at the end.

"Afterwards, I found Winsor sitting at the back of the hall. He was older than me, definitely not in graduate school like I was. He hadn't said a word during the lecture, but even after it was over, he stayed in his seat, smoldering, his face like cut feldspar. There was this quiet determination in his eyes, an inner fire not entirely unlike your own, Mr. *Fletcher*. I knew in that moment he was a man who was going to make a difference in Mars's future, and he did. Just not the difference either of us hoped he would."

Nam sat there eying his mug. He sighed. "Anyway. You want to find him, but I'm afraid I can't help you. I haven't seen him in six and a half years. I'm not sure anyone has."

"You were one of his best friends," I said. "You must have a way to contact him."

"Friendship isn't a concept Winsor ever understood," said Nam. "Whatever I saw him as is irrelevant. He considered me an ally, no more no less. And no, I don't have a way to contact him. For all I know the man is dead. I doubt USC would've publicized it if they ever found him."

I didn't move from my chair. "So why invite me in? If you don't have anything to share with me, why not turn me away at the door?"

"Maybe I'm starved for company."

"You don't seem the type who wants any."

Nguyen sniffed. A hint of smile curled his lips. "You're observant, kid. More observant than most who've come looking for Winsor."

I blinked. "There've been others?"

"You think you're the only idealist who's scaled the peak in search of the prophet? Most of them I turn away, but every now and then, there's one who reminds me enough of Winsor to make me think they might be up to the challenge."

"Of finding him?"

"Of saving Mars." Nguyen took a long draught from his tea and set it on the coffee table. "I told you I didn't have a way to contact him. That's true. He's off the grid, as far as I know. But the last time I saw him, shortly before USC's failed attempt on his life, he told me that if I ever needed to find him, I'd be able to do so."

I leaned forward in my seat. "How?"

"He told me, in these exact words, to 'climb the tallest mountain in the solar system, walk through the capitalist monuments to the palace of glass, and have a bite.'"

I frowned. "What's that supposed to mean?"

Nguyen grabbed his thermos and headed for the kitchen. "I have no idea, but then again I've never given it much thought. I've never had reason to seek his company after the direction he took. But you seem like a smart enough young man. I'm sure you'll figure it out."

10

JUNE 7, 2179

I WATCHED the numbers on the elevator panel climb higher as I headed toward Sophia's floor, my chest heavy. I didn't relish the thought of confrontation, but I couldn't keep the truth from her. I didn't want to, either. There was a reason I'd told Sophia about my past. Part of it was because I knew she could be trusted to keep a secret, but I also trusted her to evaluate each situation rationally and thoughtfully.

The door to her apartment opened at the touch of my thumb. Sophia's condo was infinitely nicer than mine, with high ceilings, gleaming magnesite floors, windows that tinted automatically, and air that was lightly perfumed by a circulator. The lights had been turned low, enveloping the space in a mellow glow. Within that protective cocoon, Sophia sat upon the plush cushions of a divan, her feet propped on an ottoman.

She glanced up at my approach. "There you are. I was expecting you home a couple hours ago."

"I had something to attend to that couldn't wait." I tossed the jacket I'd acquired from Viswanathan over the back of the couch across from Sophia's. "Reading anything good?"

Sophia didn't look surprised that I'd read the look on her face.

She did glance at the jacket with curiosity, though. "Trashy romance like usual. Nothing notable or with any redeeming value."

"On the contrary. The mood those romances put you in has a very tangible value. At least to me."

Sophia shot me a devilish smile. "I've noticed you don't mind when I've been reading them. Oh, well. I suppose I've let the cat out of the bag regarding *my* evening plans, but at least I'm disciplined enough to wait. How was your first day at work?"

"Different than expected." I took a seat. "Sophia, I met with the Inspector General first thing this morning."

One of her eyebrows rose. "He's the official in charge of Counterterrorism, isn't he?"

I nodded. "My division director whisked me to his office the moment I arrived. In case you're wondering, that's not standard protocol for new hires. To say I was perplexed and apprehensive would be accurate, but his reasons for wanting to see me had to do with my track record in the department, not any concerns he might've had. Sophia, he told me I was being immediately elevated to field agent status."

Sophia broke out in a wide smile. "Ambrose! That's fantastic."

"It is and it isn't. It is because it's a position I'm better qualified and suited for. It's not because it means I'll be spending vast chunks of time outside the city. In fact, the Inspector General assigned me to a case right away. I'm leaving town first thing in the morning."

Sophia's enthusiasm faded quickly. "Oh. I see."

I sighed. "I'll be honest. One of the reasons the Inspector General cited for his decision was my lack of family. I could've mentioned you, Sophia, but I didn't."

She waved a hand. "I don't expect you to hide me, but I also don't expect you to inject our relationship into every encounter. It wasn't the right time. You made the right choice—assuming, of course, the promotion is something you want."

"I'm not sure I'd call it a promotion," I said. "It's a different position. One that provides me an immense amount of freedom but could also put me in more danger than a traditional office position would. The case to which I've been assigned is a prime example. They're sending me to a remote USC outpost to investigate an incident of potential bioterror against diplomats."

A note of concern washed across Sophia's face. *"Bioterror?"*

"It's uncertain but possible. Three people are dead of mysterious circumstances. You don't have to worry about that, though. The entire base is in quarantine. I won't be at risk."

"For now, anyway."

"I can handle myself. Trust me."

Sophia rose from her couch and crossed over to sit next to me. She placed her hand on my leg. "I do. I always have. But I also know when something is bothering you. It's not a fear of danger. You have respect for dangerous situations, but they don't cripple you. It shouldn't be a fear of what's going to happen to our relationship. Being apart will be difficult, but we'll work through it. What's gnawing at you?"

I sighed. "Sophia, when I decided to join Counterterrorism, I viewed it as a stepping stone toward achieving what I needed. More information on USC, insider knowledge of their operational methods, their targets, their people. Knowledge that would help me figure out a way to undermine USC from within and give me clues as to how to extract Mars from under their thumb. It's something I've wanted since I joined the resistance. But the resistance isn't and never has been a solitary faction. The case with the detectives who impersonated the Snow Leopard is a prime example. They thought they were advancing the cause of a free Mars. This bioterror attack could be another. Then there's me. I believe I'm approaching the cause in a manner that's thoughtful and reasoned. I know that freedom for Mars won't be without hardship. I want to believe my actions will ultimately make life better for tens of millions of people, not worse, but who's to say I'm right? And what gives me the right to act against others who are hoping to achieve the same goal?"

Sophia took my hand in hers. "You're getting ahead of yourself. There's no way for you to know the motivation behind this bioterror attack yet. You're probably just attributing your feelings about the Snow Leopard case forward. But to answer your question, the reason your path is the correct one is that you stop to think about the bigger picture. The fact that you're sitting here now, agonizing over the broader impacts of your decisions says everything. It says you value the people you're fighting for more than the cause. It's the difference between murdering civilians and diplomats to advance your interests and trying to protect them."

"Except I've done that, too."

"*What?*" Sophia's hand tensed against my own.

"You know I've killed people—in battle, in skirmishes, even during the Snow Leopard case. I've made no secret of that, but I've committed murder, too. Only once. To this day I feel it was justified. That one death saved not only my skin but hundreds if not thousands of others. Even then, I acted to protect life. But I also did it for the cause."

Sophia retightened her grip. "Choices in life aren't black and white, Ambrose. It sounds like you made a difficult decision between shades of grey. If faced with the same situation today, would you deal with it any differently?"

I didn't need to think about it. "No. It was the only choice. It was a sacrifice worth making, and it allowed me to keep fighting for what's just and right."

"Then it's a decision I'm happy you made," said Sophia. "But I have one last question before we move on."

"Anything."

Sophia nodded to the side. "What's up with the jacket?"

I laughed, my anxiety disappearing in Sophia's smile. "That's yet another wrinkle added by my change in assignment. Remember how I was investigating the mysterious fire-bomber who got away following Shao Wen's murder?"

"That's her jacket?" Sophia picked it up and turned it over in her hands.

I nodded. "A maintenance crew found it in the elevator shaft of an apartment complex about ten blocks from Wen's apartment. Security cameras didn't catch the intruder's face. So my lone lead on the bomber's identity is in your hands, and now I'm leaving at sunrise."

"Leaving you without anyone to investigate the bomber's identity further."

"Precisely."

Sophia smiled. "And you still haven't realized that the solution to your dilemma is staring you in the face?"

I blinked, taken aback. "I guess not. What solution are you referring to?"

"Me," said Sophia. "I'm literally staring you in the face."

"You... want to take ownership of the case?"

"Don't give me that look," said Sophia. "It's not as if you can hand this off to your friends at the police department, not without risking the capture of someone who may be on the same side as you. Same with your new employers at Counterterrorism. If you still had quality contacts within the resistance I imagine you'd have followed up with them. And it's not as if I'm impotent. I may not have taken after my father, but growing up in a household built upon organized crime you tend to pick up a few things. Besides, fashion is my jam. I doubt you'd have the faintest idea where to ask about the origins of this coat, whereas for me half a dozen already spring to mind."

Apparently, I hadn't kept the emotions off my face, but I tried to push them back. "Everything you've said is a hundred percent accurate, Sophia, but you have to understand, what you're suggesting goes beyond tracking down the history of a coat. I've exposed you simply by telling you about my past and associations. If you decide to do this, you're venturing fully into my world. You'll be committed, both from my perspective and from the perspective of anyone who manages to find out what we're up to, friend or foe."

Sophia cocked an eyebrow at me. "I'm not a delicate flower, Ambrose."

"I know you're not. I wouldn't be with you if you were. I just want you to be fully aware of what you're choosing. You're sure you want to be a part of this?"

Sophia leaned in and kissed me. She cupped my face with her hands as she pulled back. "It's a part of you, and I want to share it. Of course I'm sure."

I smiled. "That's a relief, and in more ways than one. Welcome aboard, cadet."

"More ways than one?"

"Well, it means I don't have to spend the evening desperately investigating the origins of that coat." I stood and pulled Sophia up with me. "Instead, we can focus on the important things. Like supper and that after-dinner activity you alluded to."

Sophia wrapped her arms around me. "Mmm. Yes. But food first. I did mention I was waiting on you for almost two hours."

"Good thing there's an excellent Vietnamese restaurant around the corner. Got a jacket?"

Sophia nodded toward the white puffy one. *"A* jacket, sure."

"Very funny. We'll grab one on the way out."

11

FEBRUARY 24, 2158

I SAT on a bench in the shadow of a tall conifer, awash in the scent of freshly turned mulch and pine needles. An arching lenticular truss stretched the Mylamene pressure layer up and out, over the tips of the trees in Isidis's Horus Park. Joggers raced past in either direction, their longs limbs giving them the grace of gazelles in the low gravity. I envied them. Only a few days removed from my routine, and I already missed the weights and pool of the resistance base. Even when I'd been stuck in the field with Cal and Lauren with nothing more than our weapons and packs at our sides, we'd always found ways to keep active. Now that I was on my own, I'd have to be more diligent. Find ways to maintain my physique despite the obvious roadblocks presented by my mission.

"You still there?" said Jorge via Net.

"Yeah, I'm here," I said, tearing my eyes from the joggers. "I got distracted by the concept of doing something useful with my time."

"Look, I know you're annoyed Nguyen didn't have a better lead for you, but you should be happy he was able to give you any clue to Salt's whereabouts at all. Not to mention the fact that you're no longer on a mission. You're on a quest!"

"Unfortunately for me, I forgot my plus one vorpal blade at the base."

"Can you look down, Ambrose? Are you standing in knee deep mud? How are your legs looking? Wooden? Sticklike?"

"Seriously, Jorge, who leaves a forwarding address in the form of a riddle? What is this, fifteenth century France?"

Jorge sighed. "It could be worse is all I'm saying. Give it to me one more time."

"Nguyen said Salt told him that to find him, he should climb the tallest mountain in the solar system, walk through the capitalist monuments to the palace of glass, and have a bite. Then I'd need to sing the melody of the night elves while the moons of Jupiter—"

"That's enough, wise guy. Honestly, it shouldn't be too hard to suss out what Salt was talking about. The tallest mountain in the solar system is self-explanatory, for starters."

"Not necessarily," I said. "Contrary to popular belief, the tallest mountain orbiting the sun isn't Olympus Mons. It's the Rheasilvia central peak on the asteroid Vesta, which depending on where you establish the datum is anywhere from a couple hundred meters to a kilometer taller than Olympus Mons."

"I'm pretty sure Winsor Salt isn't hiding out on an asteroid, Ambrose."

"Well, I'm pretty sure he's not hiding out in the Olympus Mons caldera, either. In case you didn't know, there's not much up there besides USC's flagship observatory and some communications towers. Even securing overland transport to and from the observatory is a challenge. Besides, there aren't any monuments to capitalism up there or palaces of glass unless you count the observatory's lenses."

"So it's a metaphor," said Jorge.

"For the city of Olympus, obviously," I said. "It would only make sense Salt would leave Isidis and hide out on the other side of the world."

"Perhaps. Olympus is still a USC controlled city."

"Yes, but that fact notwithstanding, it would still be easier for a Caucasian like Salt to blend in there than it would be for him to avoid attracting notice in the Mukt settlements in the Hellas Basin. But even assuming Salt is in Olympus seven years after delivering his cryptic message to Nguyen, the rest of the riddle doesn't give us much to go on."

"It does if you can figure out what the capitalist monuments surrounding the palace of glass are."

"A big if," I said. "From the searches I've done, nothing in Olympus is referred to as a palace of glass, and while there are plenty of monuments scattered about the city, most of them are in commemoration of the city's first settlers or are blatant ego boosts commissioned by USC to make themselves seem like a more integral part of the establishment of Olympus than they actually were."

"So it's another metaphor," said Jorge.

"Yeah, but for what? What's it referring to?"

"I'm no expert on riddles, but even I know words can having meanings beyond the intended," said Jorge. "A palace doesn't have to be a palace. If it's where Salt is hiding, that would make it his abode which is close enough. But the word palace implies to me he's referring to someplace large or grand. As for glass? Well, it's transparent. I'd seek out places that look as if they're made of the material, regardless of whether or not they are."

"I had the same thought," I said. "The vactrain station in Olympus is well known for its domed honeycomb roof. The Goldwater Bank Stadium has a less artistic and more functional dome overhead, but it's another."

"I can think of fewer monuments to capitalism than an interplanetary banking conglomerate."

"Yeah, but I already checked. Goldwater Bank didn't own the naming rights to the stadium in 2151. Back then it was known as Virtucom Stadium."

"Still a gargantuan corporation. Listen, Ambrose, are you sure about Salt being in Olympus?"

"I'm not sure of anything," I said. "For all I know, Nguyen was screwing with me for kicks. But if he told me the truth and Winsor hasn't pulled up stakes and taken off over the last three quarters of a decade, then yeah, I'd assume it's a reasonable guess. Why?"

"Because you're capable of mulling over the meaning of glass and economic monuments from the cab of a vactrain."

I snorted. "No rest for the weary, is there?"

"You'll get no sympathy from me. I have a baby to attend to."

ONCE AGAIN, I slept on the train. I couldn't claim it to be a refreshing experience, but years of military exercises had taught me to sleep anywhere, even when death lurked around the corner. My nerves still tingled as I settled into my seat, the thought of cameras whisking my visage through wireless relays, bouncing it off geostationary satellites into the corneas of hardened USC operatives making me jumpy. But the fear of capture dulled as the cold reality of the world's indifference to me set in.

There were those who looked at me askance, of course, some with ill-hidden malice and others with a smidgen of fear, but as I studied the gazes of others I noticed two things. Of those whose gaze paused over me for more than a fraction of a second, the dominant emotion in their eyes was sadness, or perhaps wistfulness. The kind of look that said they remembered the days when Mars was filled with Martians and not with planet-hopping immigrants from Earth, except those days only existed in the thoughts of the close-minded. I also noticed that I received fewer pointed glances than I'd imagined upon first setting foot in Isidis. Perhaps while drenched in the cold sweat of my first exposure to humanity in years, I'd overestimated the attention people paid me. The fact was most everyone went about their business in a daze, surrounded with a miasma of apathy and surrender. To them, it wasn't a question of whether I was an Earther or not, USC or not. I was just another soul passing by in a blur of anonymity, a person in theory only.

In that, Marina was right. The fire that had filled Mars at the start of the rebellion barely smoldered. Without oxygen, the flames would die.

After my fitful hours dozing while seated, I stepped off the vactrain into the beating heart of the Olympus station. The transglobal line had been built by USC at the turn of the century, but they'd hired local architects from the four major cities of Utopia, Elysium, Isidis, and Olympus to design each station, giving each of them their own unique flair. Despite having shuttled back and forth through the three cities in the Afterlife triangle several times, I'd never made the trek to Olympus, so I'd never had the chance to marvel at the beauty of the station's construction.

The east and westbound train lines passed through the center of a giant dome constructed from hexagonal panels, each of which were tinted a different color and polarized along a distinct vector. The effect was such that if you moved five or six meters in any given direction, the panels above seemed to change color, and every other object within view would shift along the color spectrum, if only slightly. I imagined the same effect would be achieved if you stayed in one spot and waited for the sun to travel across the sky, but I didn't have the time or patience to test the theory. It seemed a silly thing, adding a playful touch of color to a grand structural element, but in a world dominated by monotones, I appreciated it.

I ascended one of the many elevated walkways over the train lines and headed to the central viewing station, populated mostly by tourists who were even more taken with the dome than I was. There I was able to meld into the background, just one more face enjoying the majesty of the station, even if my eye was keener and more focused than any of the others.

A half hour later, I headed toward the rideshare queue, having convinced myself the only way Salt could be lurking within the station was if he'd mortared himself inside the floor. The lunacy of a man making his residence within a building owned and operated by the company who'd tried to kill him aside, there simply wasn't anywhere for him to hole up. As easy as it was to hide in plain sight among the travelers, the only permanent structures within the dome were clusters of built-in seating, panel displays for advertisements and train schedules, and self-service ticket kiosks. Not that Salt had indicated to Nguyen he'd be *living* at the location embedded in his riddle—simply that he could be found there. I could probably check if Salt frequented the station by hacking into the security network and digging through the camera logs, but the station didn't strike me as the right target. It was too obvious, for one thing, and for another, there wasn't any trace of something that could be considered a monument to capitalism within it. Even the buildings surrounding the station were nothing more than a slice of any urban environment, a mixture of city services, businesses, and high-rise residences.

I shared the ride with a pair of scientists who I suspected were in town for a conference on genetic engineering, based on their lengthy discourse on the cell wall strength of a new variant of arctic lichen by the name of M_5 *rhizocarpon geographicum*. The pair exited at the foot of the Wendly Grand Hotel, which was only a few blocks from the downtown convention center and twice as many blocks shy of my destination at the Goldwater Bank Stadium.

There wasn't a game or concert in progress at the moment, so I was forced to admire the bowl from afar. Unlike the vactrain station's dome, the stadium was covered with nothing more than a two-ply Mylamene barrier, same as what protected the cities at street level, but the trusses supporting the thin protective sheets were similarly made of a transparent plastic, giving the stadium-goers underneath the illusion of being bared to the sky. More importantly as I made my rounds, gazing upon the endless ring of concession stands, beverage dispensers, souvenir shops, and ticket counters that surrounded the stands and playing field within, I began to think I might've cracked the mystery of the capitalist monuments. But the same question bothered me as before: Salt couldn't possibly be hiding in the bowels of the stadium, could he, and if he wasn't, how in the world was one supposed to contact him there?

The question nagged at me as I hailed another rideshare to take me to a section of town where the hotels wouldn't break my expense account.

12

JUNE 8, 2179

A FLAT EXPANSE of rusted earth shot across my window while at the horizon the highlands of the Tyrrhena Terra moved at a crawl. A hazy gray blip flicked across the wasteland a few times per second, giving the environment outside the look of ancient stop motion, but it was an artifact of the vactrain passing by the seals that connected each hundred meter section of clear pipe.

I'd filled a portion of the ride with breakfast, but after clearing the remains of my meal, the train still hadn't arrived in Utopia, never mind the subsequent stop in Isidis before we'd start the last leg toward Niesten. Rather than revisit the file the Inspector General had saddled me with, I decided to be proactive. A faint ringing sounded in my head as I waited for the call to go through, my eyes affixed on the distant terrain.

A mirthless voice answered. "Henderson speaking."

The chair back in each of the vactrain seats had a display with a built in camera for video calls. I'd made the call via Net for privacy reasons, but the fact that a video feed didn't accompany the voice in my head suggested Henderson wasn't in a media connected environment. "Captain Henderson. This is Agent Drake from Counterterrorism."

The voice reminded me of countless military superiors I'd encountered over the years. "Agent Drake. The Inspector General messaged to inform us you'd be on your way. Good to hear from you."

"Likewise, Captain. Do you have a few moments to talk?"

"It's as good a moment as any. What do you need?"

The Captain's voice made it sound like the moment wasn't a good one in the absolute sense, rather that all moments were equally bad. "I was hoping for a quick briefing on the state of the quarantine operation."

"There's not much to report, Agent," said Henderson. "The base is isolated. Thankfully, there's been no movement in or out of the outpost since the first reported death except for military patrols that returned back to the base at the end of their shifts. Over the last two days the people within the outpost have been given cursory exams by the doctor on staff, but no one appears to be exhibiting adverse symptoms that would suggest exposure to a toxin or pathogen. As for us, we arrived on site this morning and have been setting up temporary habitation facilities outside the outpost. We expect to have that complete by this afternoon and to start chemical swabs of the deceased's personal spaces and belongings immediately following."

"What about the diplomats?"

"Terby outpost's medical bay doesn't have designated areas for the dead, so they're being stored in an outdoor storage facility adjacent to the base. We're planning on setting up another temporary tent within the storage facility and heating it to allow for examination of the bodies by our staff, but the doctor at the outpost took blood and tissue samples from the bodies before moving them into storage."

"When do you anticipate that to begin?"

"Examination of the dead? Within a day or two. Our chief

pathologist is arriving with a second batch of personnel, and thawing the bodies to above freezing will take some time."

"You mentioned movements in and out of the outpost. Have there been any shipments or deliveries made since the first death? What about outgoing transfers of materials?"

"I don't believe there have been any of those either, Agent, but I'll be sure to double check. Hold on a moment."

The line went silent, and I could imagine the man yelling at subordinates trying to erect and pump up the portable habs in the freezing cold. When Henderson spoke again his voice sounded tired. "My apologies, Agent. Is there anything else I can do for you at the moment?"

"If you could pass along the contact information for the commander in charge at Terby, I'd appreciate it."

"I'll be sure to do that, Agent Drake. Henderson out."

The contact number arrived in my inbox within the minute. I called it and once again waited.

This time, the Net call produced video as well as audio. A middle-aged woman with short dark hair and a hawkish nose sat in front of a desk, faint bags under her eyes. "Commander Minteguia. Can I help you?"

The woman didn't look like she was in any sort of mood for circumlocution. "Commander, this is Agent Ambrose Drake with Counterterrorism. I've been assigned to investigate the deaths that have occurred at your outpost over the past few days."

The woman nodded in the direction of her camera. "Yes. Agent Drake. I was informed you'd be joining us. Are you on your way?"

"I'm on the vactrain out of Elysium as we speak. I should be arriving at the Niesten station by three PM, and I've arranged over-land transport to Terby shortly after that. I understand it's a little over twenty-four hours to the station?"

"If the weather agrees, but there don't appear to be any dust storms incoming," said Minteguia. "Have you coordinated your arrival with the hazmat teams?"

"I just ended a call with Captain Henderson. I get the impression he's working as hard as possible to get medical care and analytical facilities up and running. Know that we're doing everything in our power not only to get to the bottom of this investigation but to ensure that everyone in your base makes it through this ordeal safe and sound."

Minteguia smiled mirthlessly. "I appreciate the sentiment, Agent Drake, but it's a cold comfort at the moment. Peng, Black, and Navarro were not only quality ambassadors. They were valuable members of our community and good friends to boot. Their deaths have us all rocked, especially given the circumstances."

"My apologies for your loss, Commander. Speaking of the diplomats, do you have a moment to talk to me about them?"

"Did Counterterrorism not provide you with a file?"

"They did, ma'am, but I'd prefer to ask you a few questions about them if you don't mind. Information will be key for me to determine what sort of threat we're dealing with."

Minteguia nodded, looking tired. "I'll do my best."

I accessed the file and pulled it up alongside my feed. "The three individuals who've perished so far. Quan Peng, Hollister Black, and Veronica Navarro. I understand they recently visited New Chennai."

"That's correct. They travelled into the basin with regular frequency, primarily to New Chennai but also to some of the other settlements, New Bangalore and Chandrasekhar among them. Most recently they'd been negotiating with the Mukt regarding shared access to criminal databases, but their plates were never lacking. They tackled dozens of issues simultaneously."

"This criminal database business. Is that what they'd been working on prior to returning from New Chennai?"

"That was what their official negotiations had concerned, yes."

Minteguia was saying she wasn't a hundred percent sure of what they'd been up to—or that she knew what their real mission had been and wasn't willing to tell me. "When did they return from this most recent trip?"

"Ten days ago. Peng had only been back for three days before he passed—which in retrospect comes across as suspicious, but the man exhibited no symptoms before his death. As far as we knew, nothing was wrong until he flatlined in the middle of the night."

The Commander had anticipated my next question. "So you were keeping track of the diplomats' biometrics?"

Minteguia shook her head. "We actively monitor our combat personnel, but not our diplomats. We were alerted to Ambassador Peng's death when his Net signal cut out. If we had any reason to suspect an illness on his behalf, we would've monitored him earlier, but again, Peng hadn't reported any feelings of discomfort or unease to the base's medical staff. The same goes for Ambassador Black, though his death prompted even more concern than Peng's. At that point we expanded our biometric monitoring to everyone in the base, including Ambassador Navarro, and she underwent a precautionary physical with our resident physician. Neither one of those measures prevented her death, however."

"The doctor didn't find anything suspicious during her exam?"

"Nothing. She seemed the picture of perfect health for her age, yet she passed away in her sleep two days later."

"What did her biometric scans show?"

"Not much," said Minteguia. "Her last moments were suggestive of sudden heart failure, which was our best guess for what might've happened to Peng and to Black. But the odds of all three passing within such a short period of time is astronomical, and that's before factoring in their physical conditions."

My brow furrowed as I thought. "So you had Ambassador Navarro under supervision during her last moments. You've mentioned she didn't exhibit any symptoms per se, but what about behaviors? Was she acting oddly?"

Minteguia's cheeks sagged. "It's hard to be sure, Agent Drake. She was devastated by the loss of her coworkers and friends. We all were, but more importantly she was frightened beyond belief. She knew as well as the rest of us that something was seriously wrong. The two people who she'd last travelled with were suddenly and inexplicably dead. What do you think she expected to happen to her?"

I nodded somberly. "It must've been excruciating. You have my sympathies, Commander. Speaking of which, how are you and the rest of your charges faring?"

Minteguia shrugged. "Morale is low. Grief for the dead has mostly been replaced by fear for our own safety. Everyone thinks they'll be the next to go. The good news is no one has exhibited any symptoms that would indicate something is amiss. The bad news is that neither did any of the three who already passed." Minteguia shook her head. "To be honest, Agent Drake, I'm at a loss as to how to deal with this. By not knowing what we're up against, it forces us to fight every opponent imaginable, which isn't possible. If I had to guess, I'd say the diplomats were exposed to some sort of toxin, possibly neural in nature, but our medical staff wasn't able to identify any known agents in any of the deceased's blood samples. How are we supposed to protect ourselves when we don't know the dangers we're facing?"

It was a question I didn't have an answer for, and one I hoped I didn't have to confront head on. "I appreciate your time, Commander. I'll be there as soon as I can."

13

FEBRUARY 26, 2158

I'D ALWAYS LIKED LIBRARIES. Preferably the ones with books printed on actual paper, the central libraries for major cities or the ones on college campuses that served the law schools and science departments. There was something about the aroma of processed wood fiber and glue that gave me a sense of nostalgia. I'm not sure why, exactly. The only physical books my parents kept in our home growing up had been ones passed down from generations back, a mix of ancient science fiction novels and self-published genealogy texts about my ancestors, who apparently had emigrated from the entirety of Europe, South America, and good chunks of the Middle East. But I liked the feel of a book in my hands none-theless, even if a digital text was infinitely easier to index and search. A book was a conduit to the past, a link to the time when it was published, with all the good and bad that entailed. While I supposed other artifacts could be links as well—tools, fossils, even rocks—none of their secrets were as easily accessible as those held by words on a page.

To my knowledge, none of the major libraries on Mars had any collections of printed books. After all, trees were in short supply across the planet, and even the wealthiest of trillionaires weren't ostentatious enough to ship collections of historical texts between planets for sport. Certainly, the small branch library in which I found myself didn't have anything in print, but they had several billion works available digitally through partnerships with the major resellers and legacy publishers who made most of their money squatting on copyrights from the previous three centuries.

I hadn't planted myself on a library couch with hopes of reading my way through a gritty crime thriller, though. More to help me commit a crime or two in anonymity.

In addition to their digital collections, libraries still served as hubs where folks who weren't Net enabled or who'd lost their tablets could access a variety of computational services free of charge. Similarly, folks who *were* Net enabled and happened to know what they were doing could hijack the public network and commit all sorts of clandestine activities without a security system on the other end being able to track it to the hijacker in question.

To be fair, I could've hijacked a private network and done the same thing from a coffee shop, gym, or bank lobby, but as I said, I happened to like libraries.

Besides, I'd classify what I was up to as only mildly illegal. For the most part, I was perusing construction diagrams from the Office of Urban Development, which normally required forms to be filled out, questions to be answered, and thumbs to be twiddled while waiting for a response. Pulling them myself was much simpler. Unfortunately, the plans for Goldwater Bank Stadium—originally Zeiss Stadium as a nod to the famous optician—didn't reveal much my own two eyes hadn't. There were hidden elements to the facility to be sure, including locker rooms, service elevators, and janitorial closets, but after careful analysis, I hadn't found any glaring structural element that could've been hijacked by Salt and turned into an abode. Not that I expected the man to be living there. I'd convinced myself that Salt's riddle, unless it pointed to an apartment complex or condominium, had to be instructions for how to contact him, meaning I wasn't looking for a place he could disappear but rather one in which he could hide in plain sight. As such, I'd moved on to the slightly more illegal activity of breaking into the stadium's security servers and accessing their surveillance videos remotely. While I'd jury-rigged the library's outdated systems to process video and search the still frames for faces that matched the photo of Winsor I'd taken from his last public appearance, the computers weren't really designed for the process-intensive task.

And so I waited. As the hours ticked by I considered diving into one of those aforementioned thrillers, but mostly I worked a groove into my chair and thought about Salt's riddle. The palace of glass surrounded by monuments to capitalism—that certainly seemed to describe the stadium, even if the dome itself wasn't glass and the surrounding stands weren't what I'd call palatial. But the idea of walking past an unbroken ring of shops and quick service restaurants rang true to me as the meaning alluded to in Salt's puzzle. What bothered me was the last bit.

Have a bite.

The stadium made it easy to do so. Taking food and beverages to your seat was encouraged and made easier by the vendors who would walk around during games hawking beers, burgers, and empanadas. But why would Salt specifically add those instructions?

Not to mention that the stadium wasn't a public space. As I'd found on my scouting trip, you couldn't walk inside except during a game or event, and seats were assigned to specific tickets. If Salt were present at a game, how would you sit next to him? Did he have season tickets? Two sets, to allow for a clandestine meeting to take place? Or were you to take his seat and wait for him to find you afterwards?

Again, none of the options seemed to have anything to do with the critical element of eating. What if Salt meant something else by that?

I was poking around the edges of a major server rental company's security to see if I might be able to hijack some of their systems for facial recognition when I got a call from Jorge.

"Hey, old man," I said, responding on a private Net channel. "How's parenthood treating you?"

"It's three in the morning where I am, and I decided this was the best time to get some work done. What does that tell you?"

"That you're a liar who'd rather be sleeping but got woken up abruptly and isn't smart enough to crash back into bed?"

"Mock me all you want, but there are uncountable joys that come with being a parent."

"Really? Name one."

Jorge snorted. "Give me a few years."

"So the reason you're calling in the middle of the night is...?"

"I had an idea about the riddle."

"And the truth comes out about you not being able to sleep. What's your thought?"

"It mostly had to do with the phrasing. Palace of glass, as in palace made of glass. But you could also interpret it to mean palace belonging to glass."

"I'm not sure I follow."

"It's a last name, Ambrose. Wallace H. Glass. Apparently he's a commercial architect. Designed a number of nondescript big box warehouse stores, but he counts among his crowning achievements the design of Slopeside Plaza, a mall on the north side of town with about a hundred and fifty stores in it."

"The monuments to capitalism," I said.

"Yup. And even better—it has a foodcourt."

I smiled. "You're a brilliant mind, Jorge."

"And yet I spend most of my waking hours singing nursery rhymes and changing diapers. Go figure."

"Should've had Marina order me to be your nanny. She could've sent you in my stead."

Jorge's voice softened. "I think you're a better fit for the task at hand. Besides, jokes aside, I'm pretty damn happy with where I am right now."

I couldn't say I understood, but I believed him. Tired, frustrated beyond belief, and as happy as could be was the illogical trifecta of parenthood.

I SIPPED on a frozen orange-guava smoothie that I'd purchased from one of Slopeside Plaza's restaurants, a place by the name of Blenders. The drink itself was delicious, but I wish the place had given me the choice of adding my alcohol of choice to the mixture because I was about ready to bash my head into a wall.

I'd been scouting the mall for three days and counting. I'd browsed every store at least twice. Walked up and down every hallway, every escalator. I'd pulled the three dimensional models from the Office of Urban Development and scoured every corner, and I'd spent a collective twenty-four hours in and around the food-court, peering at every face, trying to catch a glimpse of anyone who might resemble the elusive spy turned revolutionary who'd last been seen when I was in high school. None of it had helped.

The most frustrating part of it was that I was sure Jorge and I had ferreted out the meaning of the riddle. Even the name of the shopping center, Slopeside, further confirmed Salt's reference to climbing the tallest mountain, but nothing in the riddle gave me the foggiest idea about how to contact Salt once here other than the nebulous line about taking a bite. Well, guess what? I'd eaten three meals a day of overly-greasy, preprepared food, and none of it had gotten me any closer to the man.

As I'd already concluded when investigating the stadium, Salt couldn't be hiding out in the mall. He'd have to be watching instead, but how? If he frequented the mall with any regularity, I'd have caught him by now, not simply because I was scouting the place on foot but because I'd hacked my way into the mall's security and repeated the same facial recognition trick with the video logs that I had with the stadium's, this time with a more powerful cluster at my back. Those hadn't produced any sign of the man, even after I'd played with the software to account for the changes he might've undergone over the past seven years. That left another possibility—that Salt also had access to the mall's security and was likewise watching the feeds himself. I'd thought if I dug through the system's logs, I might find someone like me piggybacking off the system, but my best efforts had produced diddly-squat, which either meant Salt wasn't using it or he was better at hiding his tracks than I was at unearthing them.

All of which left me with a few possibilities. The first was that Salt wasn't watching. That he'd lied to Nguyen, or that he'd left long ago, perhaps after having been located by one of the other young idealists Nguyen had referred to. After all, the riddle hadn't been that hard to solve once Jorge and I had gotten our teeth into it. But I refused to accept the possibility, mostly because if true it left me with zero means of tracking the man. Also because I wanted to believe that Winsor was smart enough to leave a means of finding him that wouldn't draw the wrong sort of attention.

So he was watching, then, but how could I draw him out? I couldn't hold up a sign with 'Winsor Salt, Contact me!' and my Net's IP address in giant letters. For one thing, USC still wanted the man, dead or alive, and for another, there's no way someone of his ilk would bother giving me the time of day after such a moronic stunt. But there had to be a way to contact him, and if there was, it had to be contained within the riddle. Climb the tallest mountain in the solar system, walk through the capitalist monuments to the palace of glass, and have a bite, Nguyen had said. What was I missing? I'd checked every box, figured out the meaning in each part of the sentence.

I took another sip of my smoothie and sighed. It simply wasn't there. There must've been something else Salt had said to him, something Nguyen hadn't realized was part of the riddle and therefore hadn't given any weight to. Some additional piece I was missing.

I'd pulled up my Net's search tool to find Nguyen's contact info to ask him some follow up questions when it hit me.

Nguyen hadn't missed any part of the riddle. *I* was the one who hadn't realized which part of the message was important.

Nguyen's specific words were, *he told me*. Me, as in Nguyen. If *Nam* wanted to find him, all *he* needed to do was solve the riddle. Winsor would never reveal himself for someone else, only for his most trusted friend.

I did a bit of mental math and decided Jorge should be awake, so I gave him a call.

He was groggy nonetheless when he responded. "What's up?"

"You know the software we use to create the Snow Leopard videos?"

"Yeah," said Jorge. "What about it?"

"I'm going to need remote access to it. I've got an idea."

14

JUNE 9, 2179

I STEPPED out of the airlock into Mars's cold embrace. My pressure suit clung to me like a second skin, the active compression bands hugging me with all their strength. I hadn't worn a Suit in what seemed like ages, but the sensation wasn't one I'd forgotten. Pulling myself into it and sending the electric signal into the bands that slapped the Suit against me felt like saying hello to an old comrade, even if the Suit was more bodyguard then friend.

Behind me, the automated transport rumbled as it begun its slow turn toward Terby outpost's charging station. The lights from the base glowed ominously in the early evening darkness, sending shadows flickering as the strengthening wind picked up loose dust and sent it flying across their faces. Forty meters of thin, frigid death insulated me from the soldiers, but even so I could feel an energy leaking through from the base's warm interior. A mixture of anxiety and fear, for now kept under wraps but on the verge of boiling over. Everyone I'd talked to via Net showed it in their tense jaws and hollow eyes, even if they didn't give proof to it with their voices.

I hoped the best for the lot of them, but I wasn't their savior. I was here to solve the mystery of how the diplomats had died, nothing more. Hazmat would have to take care of the rest.

I turned away from the base and trudged toward the inflated marshmallow which temporarily housed the hazmat crews. Piercing lights from the boom arm of a motorized cart bathed the hab in white, illuminating every crease in the tight-stretched exterior. The fabric billowed in the wind, ripples playing across its surface, all of which gave me pause as I approached the airlock. The Mylamene was of the same strength as that which protected the Elysium roadways and sidewalks, yet for some reason the idea of an entire habitat made of the stuff seemed inherently unsafe. Not that I let the unease slow my entrance. Everyone on Mars lived with a subtle base level of fear that suffused every other emotion. We'd simply learned to ignore it.

The interior door to the airlock puffed and I stepped into a scene of quiet activity. I pulled my helmet off and tucked it under my arm as individuals in navy USC uniforms checked and tinkered with display panels and readouts built into large machines at the side of the hab, air circulators and water purifiers and communications arrays. Several more sat in folding chairs, their eyes flicking back and forth in the recognizable pattern of furious Net activity. At least three quarters of the hab was blocked off behind opaque barriers, probably housing some of the sleeping quarters, bathrooms, and medical facilities.

A young woman with her hair in a tight bun abandoned her work on the oxygenator and approached me. "Agent Drake? I'm Private Minaj. We've been tracking your arrival. Welcome."

"Thanks for accommodating me. Counterterrorism is in your debt." I nodded toward the opaque partitions. "Can I find Captain Henderson behind one of those?"

"Captain Henderson assigned me to be your guide and liaison. If you need any assistance with your investigation, I'll be the one to provide it."

I couldn't blame Henderson for brushing me off. The man was probably under an ocean's worth of pressure from his superiors to solve the problem at Terby. He'd already refused to answer multiple calls I'd made during the day. At least now someone would be forced to help me with my angle of the investigation.

"I appreciate the help, Private. I was briefed this morning on the status of those inside the outpost. Any changes since?"

"No, sir," said Minaj. "We're tracking biometrics, but everyone appears healthy for now, at least physically. We have counselors working with those inside via Net to help alleviate the emotional strain of the situation. As long as no one else succumbs to the mystery ailment, I think we'll be fine."

Meaning that if anyone else passed away in their sleep, the shit would hit the fan. "Remind me again how long they need to stay in containment?"

"Four weeks is the standard protocol. Given those in the base have been isolated since the return of the ambassadors, that means they have eighteen days to go."

"Eighteen days." I rubbed my chin. "What do you think the chances of everyone making it that long are?"

A flicker of uncertainty passed across the private's face, but she kept it professional. "Sir, my expertise doesn't allow me to make an educated guess on that. You'd have to ask our physicians."

"Speaking of, where can I find them?"

"We've set up a tent within one of the unpressurized storage warehouses adjacent to the base. Same place where the bodies are stored."

"Are the doctors there now?"

"We're used to operating on very little sleep, sir. They'll probably be there all night."

"Which means I will, too. I'm assuming you have other work besides escorting me around?"

"A never ending pile, sir."

"Good. Add the location of the warehouse to my minimap, and I'll get out of your hair." I hefted my helmet. "Just make sure to answer if I call. Counterterrorism wants answers as fast as you do."

I WALKED into the storage unit to a scene from a medical thriller. Lights gleamed through the translucent fabric of the inflatable medical tent, filling the warehouse with an eerie, diffuse glow. Figures passed back and forth in front of the lights, obscured by the polymer. A faint howling of wind sounded from outside the structure, adding to my sense of unease.

My fingertips tingled as I passed through the airlock into the tent, but I didn't remove my helmet. The space had been pressurized and heated to make possible the examination of the deceased, but as far as hazmat was concerned, the dead were to be treated as highly contagious. That meant staying in pressure suits with helmets equipped. Even that wasn't a sufficient safety measure to prevent the spread of potential diseases. A chemical disinfectant shower had been set up in the corner of the tent, and I'd been instructed to stand under its cleansing solution for a minute and a half before leaving the tent to go back outside. The low pressure, cold, and extreme carbon dioxide content of Mars's atmosphere might kill us, but there was no guarantee it would kill whatever organisms might've attacked Ambassadors Peng, Black, and Navarro.

Inside the tent, several tables had been set up. Two of them held tightly sealed black cadaver bags, while upon the third lay the body of Veronica Navarro, covered to her clavicle with a white sheet. Two individuals in Suits sat at a panel of instruments arranged at the far side of the tent. One of them was pipetting samples taken from a centrifuge onto glass slides, while the other sat in front of an expensive-looking instrument, playing with settings on a display. Based on the shape of the machine, I guessed it was some sort of combination electron microscope, spectroscope, and interferometer.

Next to the prone body of Ambassador Navarro stood another individual in a Suit, this one wearing a disposable nylon apron with full sleeves and nitrile gloves. They nodded at me as I entered and spoke to me via the Suit's comms. "Agent Drake, I presume?"

"Yes," I said, approaching the exam table. "Are you Doctor Beaufils?"

"I'm Doctor Olafsdottir, the clinical pathologist," she said. "Doctor Beaufils is our toxicologist. She's working the EMSCAT machine. Private Minaj informed us you were on your way."

"I'm like a maharajah arriving on his elephant. Everyone seems to be aware of my presence before I arrive."

The doctor cocked her head. Thanks to the fact that her face-plate had been cleared of all tint, I could make out the look of confusion she gave me. "Pardon?"

"Sorry. I'm used to operating in more anonymity and without a team as large as this at my beck and call. It's disorienting." Not to mention worrisome—not that everyone anticipated my arrival but the motivation behind said notifications. Perhaps Captain Henderson wanted to integrate me into his operation as seamlessly as possible, but there was an alternative explanation that involved a conspiracy to keep me from really knowing what was going on. I wasn't convinced, but it was a possibility I hadn't thrown out.

"So what can I help you with, Agent?" said Doctor Olafsdottir. "Based on the agency you work for, I assume you're classifying the deaths of Mr. Peng, Mr. Black, and Ms. Navarro as acts of terror."

"We're working under that assumption for the time being. At the moment, my goals are the same as yours. I want to know what killed the ambassadors."

Olafsdottir snorted. "Hurry up and wait, Agent. We're working as hard as we can. We finished setting up the tent only a few hours ago, and we're still in the preliminary stages of running blood and tissue samples through our standard tests. Unless we strike gold, we won't know anything for at least twenty-four hours."

"I understand that, Doctor, but you have a lot of experience in analyzing cases similar to these. The entire population of Terby outpost is waiting on a diagnosis with bated breath. Surely you have some intuition about what we're dealing with here."

Olafsdottir picked a tablet up off the exam table and tapped the surface. "I've found intuition can be misleading when dealing with the unknown, Agent Drake. I'm fully aware of the magnitude of the situation. That said, if you forced me to guess, I'd hazard the people quarantined inside Terby don't have much to fear. The lack of symptoms on the parts of the deceased and the timing of their deaths suggests to me they didn't succumb to a viral infection. If that were the case, the medical staff monitoring Ms. Navarro would've noticed something in her final two days. We'd also have noticed symptoms in the Terby population by now, or at least we would if the virus was transmitted through direct contact or airborne means. I suppose the three deceased could've been infected by a vector, but if so we'll be able to determine that in short order through our tests."

"What about bacterial infections? Protozoans? Funguses?"

"Could be, but those should be even easier to identify and they're not generally as fast acting or as deadly as what we've witnessed. They also tend to leave more obvious external signs of infection which we haven't seen in any of the dead. My suspicion is that all three of the deceased were exposed to a toxin, probably neural, either by inhalation or ingestion."

"Wouldn't someone exposed to a neurotoxin show signs of distress prior to their death?"

"Usually, yes," said Olafsdottir, who'd now started scanning some of the samples in a vial holder with the camera on her tablet. "But if we're dealing with something unknown, something specifically engineered for harm? It might have symptoms no one knows to look for. And it might explain the timing of the deaths. People can metabolize toxins at different rates. Some compounds have different absorptions rates for men versus women or for individuals with certain genetic markers. Still, different exposures for the three individuals would be the most likely reason why some took longer to die than others."

The explanation made sense, and it would probably be the best case scenario. Once the toxin was isolated, those of us in Counterterrorism could track it and eliminate it as a threat.

I pointed to Navarro. "Have you inspected the bodies?"

"Externally, yes."

I picked up the edge of the sheet and lifted it, peering at Navarro's arm and some of her torso. "You didn't observe any injuries, pock marks, rashes, or anything of the sort?"

"Only the normal effects of death and exposure to cold."

I let the sheet fall. I could put gloves on and do a more thorough examination, but I wasn't a doctor. "From the lack of incisions, I take it you haven't completed an autopsy."

"Nor do I plan to."

That stopped me in my tracks. "Pardon?"

"I'm a clinical pathologist, not a forensic pathologist. I haven't carved up a cadaver since medical school. I'm not qualified to perform the full post-mortem examination."

"Then who is? Doctor Beaufils?"

"Neither of us, nor is Doctor Nagoya." Olafsdottir gestured toward the individual at the centrifuge. "It's not a specialty we generally require. Toxicology and clinical pathology are. If it turns out someone died of something other than an infectious disease or a toxin, that's a problem to be dealt with by a branch other than hazmat."

"Yes. By my branch, among others. And I *do* care about exactly how the three diplomats died, because even if all three of them died by being shoved out of an airlock, that would qualify as an act of terror given their professions. We're going to need *someone* to perform a thorough necropsy."

Olafsdottir's annoyance with my presence came across clear as the night sky. "Autopsies *will* be performed. When we're done, we'll arrange for a transport to take the bodies to the nearest USC sanctioned facility for examination, but other analyses take precedence at the moment."

"The other analyses you're mentioning are an incomplete portion of a larger whole. We need the autopsies, Doctor."

Olafsdottir turned her back on me as she moved to another exam table. "Take it up with the Captain. I have my orders."

I took a deep breath to calm myself. Blowing up at the doctors trying their damnedest to keep more people from dying sudden, panicked deaths was a noble goal, even if it delayed mine. "I'll be sure to bring the issue to the attention of both of our superiors. In the meantime I'll need every file and report you've put together on the victims."

Doctor Olafsdottir didn't spare me a second glance as she started pipetting. "The Captain can authorize that."

My dismissal couldn't have been any clearer, but lacking a medical degree, there wasn't much more I could do on my own. Frustrated, I headed for the chemical shower.

15

MARCH 4, 2158

I NURSED a cup of coffee at a table at the foodcourt, watching the mall's security feeds via Net. While the caffeine helped keep me awake, it couldn't do much to banish my growing sense of despair.

I hadn't expected anything to happen two days ago when I'd first initiated my experiment, but I'd been sure yesterday would be the day, sure that the modifications I'd made to the mall's security systems would be enough to draw Winsor Salt from his cave.

I'd been wrong. The entire day passed without incident, including the two hour window in which I was sure Salt would arrive. I flicked my eyes away from the security feeds long enough to check the time. I was an hour and half through today's window, and still nothing.

I sighed as I flicked through several dozen camera angles of the mall's common spaces, waves of bag-toting shoppers crashing against each other in a turbulent froth. I didn't want to admit it, but perhaps I'd been wrong. The question was about what? The meaning of the riddle itself? Salt's delivery of the riddle to Nguyen? Or about Salt's whereabouts and the inability of anyone before me to have found him? Maybe I was wrong about the man. Maybe I'd unravelled his clues perfectly, acted precisely as I should've, and he hadn't shown up not because of a mistake on my part but because he no longer cared.

An alert on the side of my vision blinked red, one from the facial recognition software I was running. A nervous tingle infused me as I tapped it open and read the message: *Partial match found. Probability of match 51%.* I switched to the relevant live feed and zoomed in as I wiped away the bright green overlay of the figure in question.

A man in a knee-length trench coat and a wide-brimmed fedora wove his way through the crowds. A shock of white hair tickled the back of his neck, but I couldn't see his face from the current angle. I pulled up the still frame the software had based its probability assessment on. That one provided a partial view of the man's face—bearded, with a strong jaw line and rounded, unattached ear lobes. Like the computer, I couldn't be a hundred percent sure of the man's identity.

He was, however, heading in the right direction.

With the feed confined to a corner of my vision, I rose from my seat and headed across the edge of the foodcourt toward the escalators. I paused at Dumpling King and pretended to peruse the menu, all while I watched the man in question methodically make his way onto the moving steps. He moved slowly, purposefully, taking in everything around him.

I tried to keep my excitement under control.

As he reached the top of the escalator, I split from the dumpling stand and headed back into the center of the food court. To get to his destination, he'd have to skirt the edge of the tables toward the southernmost edge of the court where, hidden amidst a cluster of potted foliage, he'd find his target. I kept an eye on him via the security cameras, making sure not to look his way as he passed through the crowds ordering their lunch. As he neared the plants, I quickened my pace and changed my angle of attack through the tables.

The man in the trench coat wove around the back of one last queue, turned a corner overflowing with dark green elephant ears, and froze.

I timed my approach perfectly. He'd barely stood there for a couple seconds, staring at the empty table in front of him, when I spoke. "Excuse me. Mr. Salt?"

The man turned, and I got my first look at the legend. Winsor Salt had aged appreciably in the seven years since his photo had been captured in a public database. Grayish-white hair framed his face. A thick beard in darker but less uniform shades of gray sprouted from his cheeks, and a deep furrow creased his forehead under the lip of his fedora. He stared at me with ice blue eyes, refusing to blink.

"Who the hell are you?" he said. "What did you do to Nam?"

"I'm afraid Mr. Nguyen couldn't be here."

"Bullshit. He was right here. I saw..." Salt paused. His eyes didn't leave me, but he snorted. *"Oh.* You're good."

"I'm sorry Mr. Salt, but I've been trying to find you for a while. Digitally inserting Mr. Nguyen's likeness into the mall's security feed was the only way to draw you out of hiding."

Salt's body tensed. His shoulders dipped slightly and his knees bent a few degrees, as if he were readying to pounce. "So what's your plan? Are you going to do it here in the mall? What's the story you're going to feed to the media when this shit gets out of hand?"

"Do what in the mall?"

Winsor snorted again, but there wasn't any mirth in his face. "I've been preparing for death every day for the last seven years, kid. You think I'm going to go quietly if you ask nicely?"

"I think you've misjudged me. I'm not here to kill you, Mr. Salt."

"Really? So USC's decided to forgive and forget after all this time? Forgive my incredulity."

"I'm not with USC."

Salt bore into me with icy daggers.

"Not anymore."

"What the hell is that supposed to mean?" said Salt.

I'd kept my eye on the surroundings using the security feed, and while no one had yet approached us, I could feel several gazes heating me from behind. "Perhaps we could discuss this in a more private setting."

Salt surprised me by bursting forth with a cackle of laughter. He smiled, his teeth straight and white. "You're really not here to kill me."

"No."

His face crashed back into a frown. "Then fuck off."

He pushed past me and headed back into the foodcourt.

My disbelief only caused me a moment of hesitation. I plunged after him. "Wait! I've been on your trail for like a week and a half."

Salt didn't slow. "Is that it? A whopping *ten and a half days*? Jesus Christ. I might as well put a blinking sign over my house."

"Sorry. I didn't mean it that way. It was a solid riddle."

"Go away."

"I can't. I need your help."

Salt wilted me a glance. "Do I look like I care? What part of going into hiding is hard for you to understand?" He picked up his pace. For an older guy, he was surprisingly spry.

I could've reached out and grabbed him, but for all my military training and the twenty-five kilo advantage I had on the guy, I still thought it might be a bad idea.

"You *are* Winsor Salt, right? The former spy turned revolution-ary? One of the pivotal voices who started the Martian rebellion?"

"I'm going to be dead or in prison if you don't *shut the hell up and go away.*"

"What the hell happened to you?" I said. "Where's the fire that precipitated the speeches you gave on the steps of the front forty at Hubble College? The passion that led to the establishment of a protest group spanning every major city along the transglobal vactrain line? Where's the rage that led to you trade rhetoric for action and take up a cudgel against the oppressors of your home?"

With lightning quick speed, Winsor twirled, snagged me by the arm, and pulled me into an empty hallway adjacent to a water fountain. "You want to know what the hell happened? I let emotions get the best of me. I took actions that were fueled by passion instead of logic, and those boneheaded moves not only cost me control of the cause I loved but almost resulted in my capture and death. And now that your nosy ass has shown up on my doorstep, I get to deal with the thrill of running for my life all over again."

"Not unless you want it," I said. "USC isn't even looking for you anymore."

"So you admit you're USC?"

"I was. I haven't been for a while. That doesn't mean I don't know how to pry secrets out of their digital fingers."

Winsor loosened his grip on my arm as a group of teens passed us by. His voice lowered to little more than a whisper, having lost none of its fire. "What do you think you're doing here? You got tired of Earth and decided to take a USC joyride to Mars for shits and giggles? Now you fancy yourself a rebel, a revolutionary, because of what? Taking pot shots at dust farmers wasn't the noble cause you'd dreamed it would be? You don't know the first god damned thing about me or about Mars. How dare you question my fire, my passion, my resolve? You presume to stake a claim to *my* time and *my* cause because you were clever enough to find me, but you're too stupid to see that you stick out worse than a tree on a windswept hillside. You're going to get me killed, and worse, you're going to get a whole lot of other people killed, too. People you probably pretend to care about but don't know a damned thing about either."

Though I couldn't help but be impressed with how much

Winsor had deduced about me in a bare minute or two, my cheeks nonetheless warmed in response to the ferocity of his attack. I forced myself to swallow my pride and do my best by Marina's instructions. "If I stick out like a sore thumb, then help me not to. You've managed to stay hidden for the better part of a decade. Even before that, you proved yourself able to fade into the background as Martian anger spilled into the streets."

Winsor let go of my arm. "I'm not helping you."

"We need you, Mr. Salt. I do. The cause does."

"I said, get lost."

He turned and headed toward the elevators. I sighed, feeling angry enough to throw punches but defeated at the same time. Luckily, logic sliced through the bath of adrenaline and other hormones I soaked in and reminded me I'd already won. I'd found Salt. All I needed was to win him over to my side.

I swallowed my pride and plunged into the crowd after the man.

I knew Salt spotted me as soon as I stepped out of the alcove with the water fountain, but he didn't slow until he neared the escalators.

He dawdled enough to allow me to hop on the moving staircase a couple steps after him. He didn't face me. "What do you think you're doing?"

"Isn't it obvious? I'm following you."

"Are you deaf? I'm not helping you."

"You're not helping me *yet*. But you will."

That caused Winsor to turn. "How do you figure that?"

"My very presence endangers you, doesn't it? Sooner or later you'll decide that having someone next to you who sticks out as badly as I do isn't good for your health."

"I'm not *going* to have you next to me," he growled.

"How do you plan to lose me? No offense, old man, but I'm faster than you, and even if you give me the slip, I know how to crack into security systems. I mean, I tracked you here with nothing to go on but a riddle. Now that you're standing in front of me? Come on."

Salt's face darkened to an unnerving shade of purple. He muttered as he turned away from me. "God *damnit.*"

16

JUNE 12, 2179

DOCTOR OLAFSDOTTIR'S latest report swam in my vision. I flicked through to the other physician's reports, but there wasn't anything to glean from them either. I'd pored over them three or four times already, and each came to the same conclusion the previous day's had.

No one had any idea what had led to the diplomats' deaths.

From the doctors' perspectives, the fact that they hadn't identified any pathogens or toxins after performing dozens of fluid and tissue tests was good news, at least it was considering the continued well-being of everyone in Terby outpost. It suggested that whatever killed Ambassadors Peng, Black, and Navarro wasn't contagious. I had to admit that I shared everyone's relief in that regard, but the conclusion didn't bring us any closer to determining how or even whether or not the ambassadors had been murdered. After spending two and a half days in an inflatable tent with little to do other than read reports and initiate Net searches, I was finding the news less satisfying than I'd hoped.

Perhaps I was most frustrated by my inability to investigate the case the way I wanted to. I'd spent almost two decades in police work and better than half that as a detective, but I'd never been so limited in my investigative options as I was now. Thanks to the quarantine, I wasn't able to interact with anyone inside Terby outpost directly. Remote communication was an option, of course. I'd spoken with over a dozen colleagues of the deceased diplomats via Net, but it wasn't the same as being there and gauging their reactions in person. A physical separation emboldened people to lie or at the very least to misrepresent the truth. It limited my ability as an investigator to lean on people emotionally and produce responses they hadn't planned on giving. Not that I was sure anyone at Terby was lying to me about the diplomats' pasts or persuasions, but the situation made it harder for me to tell. I also couldn't enter Peng, Black, or Navarro's quarters to look through their personal belongings, something I found to be a sorely under-rated investigative technique in the digital age. I'd been granted access to remote video surveillance of their rooms, but it wasn't the same as rifling through their clothes and souvenirs.

The physical separation, combined with a lack of medical insight into their deaths, left me with few methods of investigation at my fingertips. Financial searches hadn't turned up any deposits into the diplomats' accounts that suggested illegal activity. Security feeds of their actions were only available from their time in the base, and skimming those had been as exciting as watching an office drama about computer programmers.

Of course, I imagined that intriguing security footage of the ambassadors existed *somewhere*, probably from their time in New Chennai, but USC didn't have access to it. In fact, the diplomats' failure to complete their latest negotiations was part of the reason I didn't have access to government security feeds from the Hellas Basin. Given my computing chops, I could probably access most of the systems I needed with some effort, but I hadn't received authorization to hack a foreign government. Besides, some of the Hellas Basin servers I'd need to peruse weren't connected to the rest of the planet's intraweb. I needed to travel to New Chennai and start physically retracing the diplomats' steps, but the guidance I'd thus far received from headquarters told me to stay put until hazmat had a better grip on the nature of the suspected murders. I'd need to convince the Inspector General to set me free, but I didn't have an arsenal with which to do it yet.

I pulled up a satellite map of the Hellas Planitia and overlaid the ambassadors' most recent travels over it. Their GPS telemetry record had been mapped with a pixel resolution of under two centimeters. I knew precisely where they'd gone and when, or at least I did in two dimensions. As in Elysium and the other USC controlled cities, the settlements within the Hellas Basin had grown vertically as well as horizontally. Fifty story buildings were the norm rather than the exception, and there were a lot of them.

Having never visited the Hellas Planitia, the population density of the cities surprised me. USC estimated New Chennai, New Bangalore, and Chandrasekhar combined contained almost as many people as Isidis, Elysium, and Utopia. Perhaps fifty million people in total. Fifty million individuals USC was willing to bury under a mountain of ice and snow once the comet Swift-Tuttle arrived and was captured in orbit around the planet. Perhaps they'd introduce the water ice into the planet gradually—the scheme Mwenge and I had uncovered in Elysium suggested USC would make the residents of Mars pay dearly for the comet's water resources—but any amount added would soon displace the residents of Hellas. Any moisture added to the atmosphere would preferentially deposit in the Hellas Planitia over time due to the geography of the impact basin. I suspected it wouldn't take long for the effects to completely alter the lives of the Mukt. Enough water ice to cover the planet in a dozen centimeters of snow would be enough to inundate the basin.

To be fair, USC was making efforts to work with the Mukt, hence the diplomats, but the efforts weren't serious and never had been. USC's stated goal for Mars had always been to terraform it.

Liquid water was necessary for that. Judging by the massive financial and technological efforts they'd undertaken to capture Swift-Tuttle, nothing would stop them, but the Mukt would never willingly abandon cities they'd been building for a century. If USC threatened to drop the comet's ice into the atmosphere without the cities having been evacuated, I imagine the Mukt would call USC's bluff. USC wasn't above killing millions to achieve their goals—evidence suggested they'd nuked Los Angeles, after all—but there wasn't any conceivable way they could bury the Hellas Basin under ice from Swift-Tuttle and claim a lack of involvement. Such a move would be political suicide. Honestly though, I wasn't sure if there was *any* way to get the Mukt to move short of a knowledge of certain, inescapable death. If Swift-Tuttle were on a crash course with the basin itself rather than set to get captured in orbit, then perhaps the residents would evacuate, but otherwise? I doubted it.

I got up from my chair and stretched my arms—and brushed my fingertips against the walls. In the two and a half days I'd been stationed outside Terby outpost, Captain Henderson's hazmat team had set up two additional habs, which meant I'd finally been assigned my own private quarters. It wasn't much. Not even ten meters square, barely enough for a chair, a cot, and a small patch of Mylamene-covered dirt over which to stretch and do pushups, but it was a space all to my own. A private space.

Physical privacy was less important to me than the digital kind, however. I didn't have any reason to think someone was spying on my Net calls, but I still wasn't convinced everyone in the hazmat unit and Terby outpost were being a hundred percent honest with me. I'd made some test calls and run a few scripts I'd put together long ago to test my calls' encryption. In between rereading reports, I'd crunched the data and came away pleased.

I bent over and stretched my hamstrings as I made a call. After a few rings, Sophia answered in her sultry voice. "Well. I was expecting to hear from you days ago."

"And I would've loved to have talked to you days ago, but work intervened."

"The investigation?"

"More like making sure I could speak without anyone listening in." I brought myself back to full height and moaned at the stretch in my muscles. "How have you been?"

"Not bad, I suppose. I've been missing you, but I'll grow used to it. Sounds like things haven't been all sunshine and roses for you, though. You're being spied upon?"

I waved my hand even though Sophia couldn't see it. "I'm probably imagining things. Better safe than sorry. Honestly, other than a suspicion that I'm not being told everything, the case has been as dull as any I've investigated. I've made almost no progress since arriving. The doctors don't know what killed the ambassadors, I can't step foot in Terby due to quarantine measures, and I've been cooped inside a portable hab for the better part of seventy-two hours. It's not ideal."

"I'm sorry to hear it," Sophia purred. "But you can take solace in the fact that *one of us* has made progress in our investigation."

I perked. "You tracked the jacket?"

"Slow down, rocket man. The joy in a story is in the telling."

I smiled, picturing Sophia's smirk. "Regale me then. It's not like I have anything better to do."

"Well, my journey didn't start particularly impressively. I took a photo of the jacket in Fashion Finder, and the app quickly identified the item and gave me a list of local and online retailers that carried it. It's a 2167 Lemond Mackenzie Parkina. Actually a pretty nice jacket. Would've been super trendy a decade ago. Not the sort of thing you leave in an elevator shaft, for sure."

"Hold on. *Fashion Finder?* I guess I shouldn't be surprised there's an app for that."

"There's an app for everything, sweetheart. This is why you need me. You would've been begging some intern at your police station for help when all you needed was a search engine and a fremium app. Anyway, the fact that it was a bit of an older jacket made the search for it both easier and trickier. Easier because there aren't many retailers selling that jacket anymore. In fact, I found only one. Care to take a guess?"

"Congo?"

"The online retailer with a market cap greater than most small nations' GDPs. They really do sell everything under the sun. But the search was also tricker because there are many more listings for *used* Lemond Parkinas, including dozens for the 2167 version. Most of the sellers I found are generic resellers or individuals making quick bucks on Hundred Spot. That's a personal resale app."

"Don't patronize me. I've heard of it."

Sophia's laugh rang through my mind. "Sure you have."

"So in summary, our mystery parachute-using firebomber could've purchased her jacket from any number of sites or sellers. That's not anything to be excited about."

"You're not giving me even an ounce of credit, are you? This is where the story gets good."

"Oh. I guess I better sit down then."

"I thought the same thing as you initially. How do we track who sold her the jacket? But then I had a thought. Someone who'd go to the trouble of blowing a pressure window and parachuting to safety from the fifty-fourth story of a building is someone who's willing to go to extreme lengths to hide their identity. Not the sort of person who'd give their personal information to an online retailer who would send a package to their front door. Sales data is still data, after all. I bet Congo knows more about us than USC does."

"Fair point, but there are ways around that. You can deliver a package to someone else's address and lift it without anyone being the wiser."

"Possibly," said Sophia. "Especially if you use the addressee's name and credit information when ordering the package. But I'm not sure anyone would go to that length over a jacket they planned on abandoning at the end of a job. Which brings me to my second point. Why the 2167 Lemond Parkina? It was a trendy garment. Functional for hiding your head under a fur-lined hood, if that's what you're looking for, but plenty of other jackets do that, too. Our mystery suspect wouldn't have gone out of her way to pick out that jacket."

"Implying she didn't. Implying she bought it because that's what was available."

"At a local thrift store," said Sophia. "Exactly."

I smiled. "I like how you think."

"So do I. Anyway, with that information in mind, I went thrift store hopping with the intent of speaking with store managers. I had stills of the suspect from the security feeds you shared with me, but I figured folks might get suspicious if I showed them security footage and asked them if they'd recently sold a jacket matching the one in the images. Instead I fibbed a little. At each store I visited, I told the attendants that my estranged mother had recently passed and that my vulturine siblings had liquidated her estate the moment her heart stopped, selling everything they could through an estate sale and the rest to pawn shops and thrift stores. Included among the items sold was a 2167 Lemond Parkina that happened to be the last birthday gift I'd ever given her before she shut me out. I know. A sappy story that's not particularly believable, but pulling at the heartstrings like that made managers much more willing to dive into their computer archives to see if they'd ever had that jacket on their shelves. Lo and behold, after a dozen stops, I got a hit."

"Go on."

"Wallace's Secondhand on East Tallow Drive. There was an old guy working the store when I arrived, making sure people actually used the checkout kiosk instead of running off with the goods. I gave him my story, and he remembered the coat right away. Didn't even need to check his computers. Not at first anyway. He did eventually check what the date of sale was."

"*Eventually?*"

"We chatted for a while. The man was quite sweet. Charming even. As soon as I realized the jacket had come from his store, I upped my game a few notches, and the man wasn't too old to be disinterested by my flirting. I doubt he thought I was coming onto him, but he was willing to play along with the gambit. Plus there wasn't anyone else in the store at the time."

"Was he able to tell you anything about the buyer?"

"Surprisingly yes. He was on the clock when she bought it. It was a woman, as expected. She was young, maybe in her twenties, or so he thought. He never interacted with her, so he didn't know her name, but he was nice enough to look up her payment method for me, which I'm pretty sure is illegal. Sadly, she used a prepaid credit slip, so that didn't give us a name, either."

"That old dude broke the consumer privacy act for you? You must've been laying it on thick."

I could picture the self-satisfied smile on Sophia's face. "And I didn't even ask him to do it, if you can believe it."

"Well, it's still a lead," I said. "Did the store have cameras?"

"It was kind of a janky place, but I'm pretty sure it did. At least one on the floor and another by the checkout kiosk, so you should be able to get a look at the woman's face if you can crack your way into the system. Unfortunately, I don't know who the security provider is or if the system was local or cloud based. I figured those sorts of questions would tip the old guy off that the story I gave him about my estranged mother wasn't the real reason I was there."

"Clever thinking. But don't worry. I can pull some records. See if the business has a subscription with any of the major security firms. Getting said video from them without raising any suspicions is another story, but at least we have another lead."

"Maybe two," said Sophia. "As it turns out, one of the reasons the old guy at Wallace's remembered her was that she came back a second time."

I blinked. "Not to return the jacket obviously. To buy another?"

"To buy a suit. A black one. And yes, my old admirer broke the consumer privacy act twice. She paid the same way."

"When did she buy it?"

"May seventeenth, I believe. I made a note of it somewhere."

"And what kind of suit was it?"

"A generic, off the rack sort of ensemble. Nothing that would raise eyebrows."

I rubbed a couple fingers against my forehead. "As the resident fashion expert, what do you suppose our suspect could've needed the suit for?"

Sophia snorted. "Anything, really. Black suits are always in style. Off the top of my head, I'd say a job interview, a funeral, a heist, or a stint impersonating a government official. Not a formal ball or party, though. This particular suit wouldn't have gotten the job done."

I sat there, staring in thought at the pressure-stretched walls of my hab. Apparently, I sat a little too long.

"You still there, Ambrose?"

"Yeah. Sorry. Thinking about the suit. Speaking of which, you did an excellent job, Sophia. Not that I had any doubts, but I'm still impressed."

"As you should be. But I'm on my best behavior. I have to prove I'm ready to fry bigger fish."

She was certainly proving she was. Unfortunately for her, I didn't have any other clandestine assignments for her at the moment. We spoke for a little longer, chatting about our days, before eventually saying our heartfelt goodbyes.

I didn't move from my seat after I hung up. I couldn't stop thinking about what Sophia had said. That the suit might've been used for a job interview or a funeral.

I might not have access to whatever security system Wallace's Secondhand used, but thanks to the request I made of Captain Reyes, I still had access to the city of Elysium's public security database. I logged in via Net and pulled up the security feed overlooking Bethlehem Gardens. It was a small, government owned plot, and it was where Jorge de la Plata had been buried.

Burial rituals were different on Mars than where I'd grown up. On Earth, many people still chose to be buried in caskets. On a planet where wood was easy to come by and any organic material returned to the soil naturally made its way into the carbon cycle, that was a viable option. It wasn't on Mars. All the red planet's dead were cremated and the gaseous outflows from the process captured for reuse. Even the ashes themselves couldn't be wasted, so a ritual had developed over the past century to replace traditional burials. The ashes were ceremonially returned to the earth, always in specially maintained gardens where the soil had been carefully nursed to health.

It was in the Bethlehem Garden that I'd taken part in the ceremony to incorporate Jorge's ashes into the soil. It had been a simple affair, with only myself and two of the first responders from the attack on Musk College in attendance. Thanks to his life spent off the grid, Jorge's body had never been identified. As a result I'd been able to attend the burial without suspicion, as a simple act of respect for an individual who'd died protecting others from a violent act of terror. I'd watched stone-faced as the last remains of his earthly essence was tilled into the moist earth, disappearing among the dark soil.

I watched myself take part in the ceremony on the security

feed, and the emotions I hadn't been able to express at the time came rushing back. A tear cascaded down my face at the thought of Jorge's loss, at the thought of all he'd sacrificed in the name of the resistance.

I took a deep breath, wiped away the tear, and fast-forwarded the footage. I'd been at the ceremony. I knew what had occurred. But I didn't know what followed it.

I didn't have to work hard to find what I was looking for. At roughly ten P.M. on the eighteenth, the night of the funeral, an individual in a black suit entered the garden, plucked a single violet orchid from a blooming plant, and placed it over the soil where Jorge's ashes had been mixed in.

I paused the video and zoomed in on the figure. She didn't wear a hood or even glasses. I was thankful for that, because with them I might not have recognized her. I hadn't seen her in over a decade.

It was Fabia Graciana de la Plata. Jorge's daughter.

17

MARCH 4, 2158

I SNORTED as I entered Winsor's apartment. "Is this it?"

The place reminded me of my quarters at the underground Red base near Schiaparelli crater. Of all the subterranean accommodations I'd shared over the past few years, that one by far had been the worst. If anything, Salt's place was even smaller. It was certainly shabbier. Dirty dishes spilled from a kitchenette sink that resembled a shoebox in size and color, the stove was more of a built-in hotplate, and what little counter space existed between the two had been slathered with two decades' worth of atomized grease. The living room was only wide enough to fit a single couch, which I suspected might be a clandestine breeding ground for a weaponized virus based on the green stains seeping through the slip cover from the other side. A doorway at the side of the room suggested the place wasn't a studio, which was probably good given Salt's furry roommate. Even if I hadn't heard it meow as we'd entered, the scent of unattended cat litter coming from the attached bath was unmistakable.

"So I invite you into my home, and the first thing you do is insult me?" said Winsor. "What were you expecting, the Sistine Chapel?"

"First of all, you didn't *invite* me. You cursed and growled as I followed you here. And no, I wasn't expecting a palace, but I thought you'd have, I don't know... a lair?"

Winsor sneered. "With what? Trap doors? A moat filled with sharks with lasers strapped to their heads? Give me a break. I'm a washed up terrorist who watches way too much news, gets angry, and spends an unhealthy amount of time with his cats."

"*Cats?* You have more than one?" I peered into the bathroom, wondering where they were all hiding.

Winsor collapsed on his couch. "Look, kid. You won. You found me, and you managed to weasel your way into my home by threatening to expose me. So congratulations. You're an asshole, but an effective one. Now for the love of all that's holy, who are you and what the hell do you want?"

Winsor lounged across half of the sofa. My only seating choice was to squeeze past him and plant my posterior beside his on the stained slip cover. I stood instead.

"My name is Ambrose Drake, Mr. Salt. You're—"

"Oh, for Christ's sake. The name's Winsor, okay? *WINSOR.*"

"Got it. Winsor."

Salt flicked an impatient hand at me. "Well?"

I took a deep breath. "As I was saying, you were right about me. I joined USC in the spring of 2154, right after the nuclear attack on Los Angeles. I didn't spend much time in their ranks. I was captured at the end of that same year by resistance forces. I was already regretting my decision to enlist at the time, but evidence I discovered while in the hands of the separatists forced me to reconsider every preconceived notion I'd already established about USC and their motives."

"So you know they dropped the bomb themselves, then," said Winsor.

I blinked. "Yes. Honestly, I'm surprised you do. We haven't publicized it at all."

"You think I'm not capable of coming to my own conclusions? I have eyes and a brain, boy."

Winsor's words raked across me like an angry house cat's nails. My cheeks warmed. "I wasn't insinuating anything of the sort. You seem to be extremely observant, but that doesn't mean you deduced everything about me from a glance. There are things you got wrong. The cause? Freeing Mars? I'm not playing it as a hobby. The lies and deceits USC spread and the oppressive systems of governance they've established on Mars aren't a joke to me. The people I'm fighting with, the ones who've sweat blood at my side, they're not jokes to me either. They're not pawns. They're the reason I'm here. Literally, here in your living room. You think I wanted to leave them to track you down while they risk life and limb taking potshots at USC? Please. And that was *before* I met you. Trust me, my friends are the *only* reason I'm here, and if it was anyone other than Marina who'd asked me to do it, I probably would've told them to take a hike."

"Who's Marina?"

"Marina Vieira Coehlo. Head of Martian counterintelligence."

Winsor blew a raspberry. "Never heard of her."

"Maybe not. But you've heard of Jorge de la Plata. He met you years ago in Huygens. He was a member of one of the cells you established there."

Winsor grunted. "I remember Jorge. *Damnit...*" He shot a piercing glance my way and stuck an accusatory finger into the air. "Not that it matters. Just because you managed to source the name of someone I once mentored, however briefly, doesn't mean the rest of your story isn't bullshit."

"I'm not bullshitting you," I said. "Marina sent me here to find you. To bring you back into the fold. To learn from you."

"Oh, yeah? Why in the world would she send a gump like you after me when she could've sent Jorge instead?"

"Probably because he's busy being the father to her child."

Winsor startled. "Jorge's a... Damn. Never mind. Still doesn't explain *you*, though."

"What's that supposed to mean?"

"It means you've got a much lower chance of bringing me into the fold, but you've also got a *hell* of a lot more to learn."

I clenched my fists at my side. "I may be young, but I'm not an idiot. It took me less than two weeks to track you down and pull you out of hiding, in case in you'd forgotten in your old age."

Winsor snorted and crossed his arms. "Yeah? You're good with computers, are you? Know your way around security systems? From the looks of you, you're also good at beating the crap out of people, and you can probably shoot straight, too. *Punch punch, pew pew.* Big freaking deal. None of that is going to help you blend into an enemy environment, learn from them, evaluate them, and create a strategy of attack against them that has more than a snowball's chance on Mercury of working. None of it is going to make you any less likely of failing miserably in a noble but doomed battle against history's largest, most powerful multi-planetary space corporation."

I swallowed my rage. "Fine. You're right. So teach me."

"Teach you what?"

"How to run a successful sabotage campaign against USC. How to infiltrate them. How to dismantle them, either from the outside or from within. How to build support for our cause and convince people to take up arms at our sides."

Winsor snorted. "I can't teach *you*."

"Why not? Because my Earther shoulders stick out? Because I haven't lived through the struggle in the same way you have? Look, I'll admit when Marina told me to seek you out and gain your counsel, I had a similar reaction as you. Why me? But the fact of the matter is as a former USC counterintelligence agent, someone who was raised on Earth and has no track record, I can do things other people in the resistance simply aren't able to."

One of Winsor's eyebrows inched upward. "You worked in USC counterintelligence? That almost makes it worse."

"Makes what worse?"

Winsor sneered at me. "That you don't know the basic rules of the trade. The resistance used to train their pups before letting them off leash."

Only with great restraint did I keep my voice at an even volume. "Rule one. Don't trust anyone. Rule two. Don't offer information unless absolutely necessary. And rule three. Protect the movement at all costs, even if it threatens your personal safety."

"So you know the rules, but you choose to ignore them? Smart."

I couldn't take it anymore. "Listen here, old man—"

"No, *you listen!*" Winsor jumped to his feet. "You've known me for all of forty-five minutes and you've already told me your name, the name of your direct superior, and the name of her child's father. You've told me intricate details about your life, your past, your military service, your home, not to mention details of the other folks I've already mentioned. You've broken every damned rule you just repeated more times than I care to count."

I paused, feeling like I'd been smacked with a switch. "But... you're Winsor Salt. You're—"

"I already told you, *you don't know the first god damned thing about me!* I could've turned myself in to the authorities years ago and traded my knowledge and cooperation for this measly existence." He swept his arm angrily around his apartment.

"Did you?"

"The point is, *you don't know.* And you didn't let your ignorance stop you from being cocky, reckless, and rash. You. A spy. *Please.*" He practically spat the last word before turning and storming into his bedroom.

The rage inside me had washed away in a wave of embarrassment. "Winsor, I—"

"Oh, go away, will you?" The door slammed shut behind him.

"But, Winsor... I need your help."

"Go away!" His voice carried through the door.

I collapsed on the sofa, an emptiness gnawing at my stomach. Part of me, heck, the greater part of me, wanted nothing else than to get up, walk out Salt's front door, and never look back, but I'd always been stubborn, at least in the things I felt conviction about. I believed in the cause, and more importantly, I believed in Marina. She'd told me I could learn from him. If nothing else, the last few minutes had proven that beyond a reasonable doubt.

I sighed as I leaned against the slipcover. And here I'd thought *finding* Salt would be the hard part.

I LAY on Salt's couch, checking the news while one of his cats meowed and rubbed against my leg. His tag said his name was Rowdy, but so far he hadn't lived up to his moniker. He'd first shown his whisker-framed face about two hours after Winsor barricaded himself in his room, popping out from underneath the couch on which I'd been sitting. He'd peeked at me and withdrawn as soon as I moved my eyes in his direction, but he'd only been scouting. After a few more peek and retreat sessions, he'd ventured beyond the safety of the furniture. He'd cocked his head at me, surveying me for several minutes before flopping to the floor to lick himself clean, or as clean as he could get in a place like Winsor's.

Rowdy stayed there a while, completely uninterested in me. I'd largely shared the sentiment, but after another hour passed and the sun set, he'd approached me, stretched on his hind legs to reach the couch, and meowed. I'd long since given up trying to engage Salt through his closed bedroom door and instead convinced myself I wouldn't contract anything incurable from the couch. I wasn't eager to be kicked from my spot, but Rowdy was insistent. I shooed him. He left for the kitchenette, but he didn't stop his insistent calling. It wasn't until I heard Salt's soft snoring coming from underneath the door that I realized Rowdy might be trying to urge me into action.

Sure enough, when I rose and crossed the room to the kitchen, I found a pair of matching plastic bowls on the floor. Both were empty. I filled the cleaner looking one with water and rifled through the cabinets until I found an open bag of dry food to add to the other. Rowdy meowed with gusto throughout the process, and he downed the majority of the food as soon as I set it down. Winsor had said he owned multiple cats, but none of the others had shown themselves, so I didn't refill the bowl beyond what Rowdy needed. It was clearly enough, as Rowdy had followed me back to the couch and refused to leave me alone since.

I nudged him away as he batted at my foot, trying to ignore him as I appraised myself of current events. Not much had changed in the past few weeks, or even months. Riots in the major cities had subsided after USC forces cracked down and arrested thousands of protestors, many of which were still in custody after being hit with falsified or trumped up charges: incitement, vandalism, and resisting arrest, mostly. Most of the attacks that I knew were proceeding apace against USC outposts hadn't been reported upon except in the underground networks distributed by the Snow Leopards, and despite everything, USC's stock price continued its weeks of record highs.

Before I closed my newsfeeds, I pulled up a curated one, one I'd established a couple years ago after a particularly lonely night spent freezing my ass off performing above-ground surveillance of USC transport routes and reminiscing about evenings spent in Phoebe's loving arms. After my capture and Phoebe's demise, I'd tried to put all thoughts of my time in the corps out of my mind, but as Phoebe's death faded into a dull ache, a nagging curiosity about the fate of the rest of my friends grew to replace it.

Eventually, I'd relented and created a script to troll the net for any news regarding my former company, including my former major, Watkins, and the many member of Zeta squad: Johnson, Franks, Sun, Mandel, Halabi, Nakamoto, and yes, even Maarten Stanić.

I'd rather wished I hadn't, not because I'd discovered anything horrible that had befallen any of them, other than an arm injury that had permanently knocked Nakamoto out of active duty. More that the one who'd deserved a miserable fate hadn't received his comeuppance. Despite his growing racism and aggression, Maarten hadn't suffered at all since my departure from USC's ranks. In fact, he'd thrived, having been promoted first to squad leader and later to lieutenant. Given the accolades he continued to receive, I figured it wouldn't be long until he'd be promoted once again, especially given that Watkins had been promoted to lieutenant colonel.

I scanned the most recent set of news regarding Stanić, a few brief headlines about how the campaigns in which he was involved had reduced Red communication volume in the Promethei Terra by thirty-six percent and resulted in the elimination of several terrorist cells. I flicked the windows away angrily, wondering why I'd even checked. Then again, I could ask myself the same with the regular feeds. If the news reported nothing but misery, why did I bother reading?

Rowdy continued to meow and play with my foot, and Salt's snoring hadn't changed its cadence in a half hour. As much as I didn't want to, now seemed as good a time as any to restore my dignity and prove to myself that I did know how to follow the rules by which I'd been trained.

Via Net, I located Salt's local wireless network, opened a control panel, and got to work.

18

JUNE 14, 2179

AS IT TURNS OUT, I didn't need some convoluted excuse to convince the Inspector General that I should leave Terby. He was as anxious to get answers on the case as I was. Given an increasing confidence on the part of the investigating physicians that we weren't dealing with an outbreak of contagion, he was willing to let me follow the diplomats' trail wherever it took me, so long as I understood the dangers involved. While I had to admit the prospect of dying a sudden death in the middle of the night to unknown causes still bothered me, at least I knew I was heading into my hunt as prepared as I could be.

I left the military outpost the same way I came in, via overland transport, but after the day-long trip to the Niesten station, I didn't hop back on a vactrain. Instead, I headed south via open air rail.

Even without the full speed possible in a vacuum, it wasn't a long ride to the edge of the basin. Technically, the Hellas Planitia was visible from the vactrain line going through Niesten for a fair ways west until the line rose into the highlands of the Noachis Terra, but that was like saying the Grand Canyon was visible from Utah. The fact of the matter was you couldn't get a grasp of the magnitude of the thing until you got up close.

As our train approached the basin, it was as if the earth fell out from underneath the horizon. A vast hole stretched as far as the eye could see, and it wasn't until the train pulled onto the crest at the edge of the impact crater that I was able to spot the bottom. From there, the vista wasn't as dramatic. What had initially appeared like a jagged chasm was more of a gentle slope, less than ten degrees not counting for the hiccups and bumps of smaller impact craters within. What made the basin impressive was its sheer size. At a whopping twenty-three hundred kilometers in diameter it was one of the largest confirmed impact craters in the solar system, behind only Mars's Utopia Planitia, whose slope was so gradual as to be unnoticeable in most spots, and Luna's Aitken basin, which no one ever set eyes on thanks to it being smack dab over the moon's southern pole. By contrast, the Hellas Planitia's seven degree slope was positively steep, and it continued downward at a steady pace for over sixty kilometers before reaching its bottom.

I kept my eyes glued to the window as our train pulled over the edge of the crater and started the descent. We sped along at a steady clip—six hundred kilometers an hour, according to the train's help system. It was over an order of magnitude faster than overland transport but a far cry from vactrain speeds, and we'd slow further as we hit the thicker air at the bottom of the crater. Given that the Hellas Planitia contained the thickest atmosphere on Mars, it struck me as odd that the Mukt hadn't installed vactrains like USC had, but constrained as they were by the edges of the crater, even half-speed travel meant you could get from one side of the basin to the other in a few hours. Perhaps they hadn't been able to justify the extra expense in construction and operations.

Eventually, the train's path flattened. From the window I spotted settlements dotting the pock-marked landscape in the distance. Those grew denser until the train reached the outskirts of Chandrasekhar, at which point towering structures sprung from literal thin air, choking the sky and blocking out the sun. Vehicles whirred to and fro, horns honking, as pedestrians clogged the street corners. For all the similarities between the metropolis and the USC controlled cities, there was a world of difference, too. No pressure barrier protected the streets, leaving them open to the ravages of wind and dust, but it didn't seem to bother anyone. They braved the elements all the same, in nothing more than heavy parkas and breathing masks.

I'd packed my Suit in my luggage, but I'd been warned that wearing it would give me away as an outsider far more than my skin color would. Despite having lived on Earth for two decades, the idea of stepping outside without the snug embrace of a pressure suit sent panicked thoughts shooting through my temples, but I couldn't argue with the teeming throngs making their way along the dusty sidewalks. Atmospheric thickening efforts had worked, plain and simple. The morning report gave a pressure of eleven kilopascals in New Chennai, well above the Armstrong limit, and the number continued to climb every year.

The train slowed to a stop at the Chandrasekhar station. People exited and others boarded, and within fifteen minutes we were off and running again, zipping along elevated rails through the outskirts of the city. The wall of skyscrapers ended as sharply as it had begun, leaving us back on ground level and making our way east toward New Chennai. I napped a little on the journey, but within an hour, the deceleration of the train awoke me from my slumber. When we came to a stop, I hopped off and fought the crowds for my bags. Thankfully, stories I'd heard about the prevalence of luggage thieves turned out to be overblown, as the process was as seamless and organized as any I'd experienced on the USC line. With my possessions in hand, I headed toward the station's exit. I'd already picked out a hotel from which to operate out of, and after settling in, I'd be ready to hit the ground running.

I threw on a heavy overcoat and with a deep breath, slipped

into my freestanding breather mask, trying not to look foolish as I did so.

———

I SAT on a bench in a quiet corridor. Footsteps echoed off the polished stone floor as a pair of individuals engaged in quiet conversation approached me. Their voices faded as they entered the open stairwell some twenty paces away. Once again, I checked the time. It was after six. Based on the exodus I'd observed over the past hour, I assumed pretty much everyone in the building had left, but the door across the hall from me remained steadfastly closed. My stomach rumbled in protest, but I ignored it. I could wait.

My persistence paid off. After another couple minutes, the door cracked open, and a well-kept man in a trim ultramarine suit emerged. His shirt was a pristine white, and sparkling links pinched his French cuffs. "My apologies, Mr. Drake," he said as he stepped toward me. "I was on a conference call that wouldn't end."

I wasn't sure I believed him, but the moment called for diplomacy, not antagonism. "Don't pay it any mind, Councilman Jalil. Hopefully it's not too late for a quick meeting."

He nodded deferentially. "By all means. But quick, yes? My family gets to see little enough of me as it is."

"Absolutely. I won't take much of your time."

I followed his hand into his office and took a seat. The place was as well apportioned as the rest of the building, with high ceilings and a broad desk of the best imitation wood. Maybe the reason Mukt politicians hadn't invested in vactrains and pressure barriers was because they were too busy spending on themselves.

Jalil took his seat opposite me. "So Mr. Drake. You mentioned you were with USC Counterterrorism?"

I noted his second use of the standard honorific. Was he slighting me intentionally, or was it the custom not to refer to a man by his position? "That's correct, Councilman. Specifically, I was hoping to talk to you about Ambassadors Quan Peng, Hollister Black, and Veronica Navarro. I understand you met with all three of them recently."

Jalil's brow furrowed. "I did. They visited less than two weeks ago. We discussed a variety of topics, but we made as little progress as we always do. Negotiating with your parent company is like trying to breathe from a stone. Technically, there may be oxygen trapped within, but that doesn't make it possible. That said, I'm struggling to understand why a Counterterrorism agent would be investigating the ambassadors. Are you suggesting they're involved in some manner of plot?"

"Rather that they might've been the subject of one."

Jalil's eyes widened. "They were attacked?"

I didn't want to give away more than I had to, but certain information had to be shared to get the pieces I wanted in return. "All three are dead, Councilman."

The man leaned back in his chair, his face frozen in shock. "Are you serious? What happened? Was there a bombing?"

"USC has kept the incident under wraps to make the investigation easier for us, but I can assure you it wasn't a bombing. Suffice it to say the ambassadors died under suspicious circumstances. We're not entirely sure they were even murdered, much less that their murder was an act of terror. We simply need to do our due diligence and make sure we understand the causes behind the incident."

Jalil's closed his eyes. He spoke gently. *"Life is uncertain. Only death is certain. Do not dwell in the past, do not dream of the future, concentrate the mind on the present moment. Through our actions, we are reborn."* His eyes reopened. "What can I help you with, then?"

"I'm simply trying to retrace the ambassador's steps. Understand their motivations and determine what activities they took part in during their time here."

"Well, I'm not sure I can help you understand their motivations, but I can certainly tell you why the ambassadors were in New Chennai. They were on one of their regular trips to present and sell to us your employer's relocation plans."

"They'd been traveling here every three months, correct?"

Jalil nodded. "As I'm sure you know, USC has been pushing the pace of negotiations, what with that captured comet of theirs approaching, but despite the fact that we've been going back and forth on the subject for over forty years—more like fifty if you count the initial talks—your superiors seem unable to get it through their thick skulls that nothing, and I mean *nothing,* is going to convince us to abandon our homes, our communities, and our investments to rebuild them from scratch under the auspices of a foreign multi-planetary organization that only cares for itself and its shareholders. No offense."

Whatever peace his Buddhist prayers had brought him had quickly left the man. "None taken. My focus is on seeking truth and justice and maintaining order. The machinations of board members and generals is far above me." Some of which was true. Like it or not, I'd had to consider the intentions of those who ran USC for most of my adult life. "I also understand that while they were here, the ambassadors were negotiating mutual access to criminal databases?"

"Yes. That at least was going better then the efforts to coerce us into leaving our homes, though were weren't close to an agreement yet. We'd yet to draft a formal treaty, and anything that we signed would have to be ratified by the other city states in the basin. Not to mention we had numerous issues to iron out, including what sorts of communications should be shared freely with one another. As you can see, that continues to be a problem."

If the man thought a treaty on criminal databases would've

alerted him to the deaths of Peng, Black, and Navarro, he was more naive then he appeared. I wasn't even sure if the ambassadors' families knew they'd passed yet. "The ambassadors travelled here regularly. Surely people must've known about their presence. How were they received locally?"

"With respect. As we would treat anyone coming to us to negotiate."

"I didn't mean you, the city council, specifically. I meant the population at large. Certainly everyone isn't as diplomatic as you, or as willing to continue to negotiate in the face of USC's plan to flood the Hellas Basin."

Jalil leaned back in his chair. "There have been protests, yes, including during the ambassadors' last visit. While some of them have been spirited and have resulted in arrests, they've never led to outright violence. No one ever attacked your people if that's what you're getting at."

"So there were never any attempts made on their lives?"

"Not to my knowledge. I'm assuming our police would be able to answer that question for you with a greater degree of certainty."

"*Would* the police answer that question for me?"

Jalil tried to hold it back, but his face betrayed the faintest hint of a smile. In that moment, I knew he hadn't been on a conference call for an hour and a half. "If instructed to by the proper individual, yes. But that individual would have to have a reason to make the request."

"What do you want from me, Councilman?"

"I'd like for you to convey to your employer that we're a sovereign group of states that deserve more respect than a stubborn step-child, but I doubt you have the clout to make anyone listen. Instead I'll settle for you telling me what actually happened to the ambassadors."

I'd already given away enough, but I was willing to trade. "The fact of the matter is we don't know what killed them. They died suddenly in their sleep with no apparent cause or previous symptoms. We think they may have been poisoned, but we can't completely rule out a bioengineered infection."

That caused Jalil's eyes to widen again. "I see."

"Has anyone in your building recently passed?"

"No one, thankfully."

"I would appreciate you passing it along if anyone did. Now, about that matter with the police?"

Jalil recovered himself quickly. "I'll see what I can do."

"It would be helpful for me to be able to access local hospital records as well. To see if any similar deaths have occurred around the city."

"There are limits to my influence, Mr. Drake."

And to his interest in helping, but that was left unsaid. His use of my honorific again was a pretty clear punctuation mark to our conversation.

I stood and offered my hand. "I appreciate your time, Councilman. I'll be sure to contact you with any further questions."

19

MARCH 5, 2158

I AWOKE with a start to the slam of a door. I shot up from the couch, blinking sleep from my eyes to find Salt standing a meter to my side. He stood there a moment, his jaw slack, before turning to me.

"You cleaned my kitchen?"

I massaged my neck as I yawned. Sleeping on the couch hadn't been the best idea. "The bathroom, too. It was disgusting."

Salt didn't move. "Why?"

"I needed to use it. I don't like to wallow in filth. Also I fed your cat. Rowdy. I think the others have decided I'm a troll and would rather starve than be eaten by me."

Salt frowned. "I thought you would've left by now."

"Thought or *hoped?*"

Salt grunted and headed to the kitchen. He pulled a bowl from a cabinet, filled it with the dregs from a cereal box, and topped it off with soy milk that I'd already determined was past its prime. He returned with it to the couch and gave me a nod. "Move over."

There wasn't another chair in the place, so I did as he asked.

He munched on his Nutribran in silence, pausing after he'd

gotten about a half-dozen spoonfuls into the bowl. "What are you staring at? If you want some, help yourself."

"You killed the box, and I'd rather not anyway. I can smell the milk from here."

"Then stop complaining."

"I wasn't."

He polished off the rest of the bowl, rose, and dumped it into the sink with a clatter. He returned and stuffed his hands in his pockets. Somewhere, Rowdy voiced his disapproval.

"Well?" said Salt.

"Well, what?"

"You've made your point, kid. You're more resilient than I gave you credit for. You can leave now with your head held high. You made a valiant effort."

I stayed on the couch. "I'm not leaving."

"You're hilarious. Come on. Time to go. Wave goodbye to the kitties."

"I'm not leaving."

Salt exploded. "OH, FOR CHRIST'S SAKE! *What in the world is it going to take to get rid of you?"*

I stood and faced him, my shoulders square and my chin held high. "I'm here for your help. I'm not going anywhere until I get it."

"I could call the cops."

"Who partner with USC. We both know you won't."

Salt clenched his teeth. "So let me get this straight. You're going to squat in my apartment and make my life a living hell until I give in and mold you into a master of espionage and the persuasive arts?"

"Living hell? Come on, man. I cleaned your bathroom."

Salt shook his head, murder in his eyes. "Grab your coat. For both our sakes, I hope you're the world's fastest learner."

"SEE THAT YOUNG WOMAN OVER THERE?" Salt pointed into the thick of the Slopeside Plaza's foodcourt to a table near the central fountain.

"The one with the long brown hair and the half-eaten eclair?"

"That's the one. She's your target."

I blinked. "What do you mean, target?"

Salt tapped the side of his head. "Hello? Think, Drake. Your social skills suck, and that means a lot coming from a guy who's spent the last seven years talking to his cats and screaming at feeds. As you might imagine, conversational skills are rather important when you want to convince someone of, well... anything. So I'm starting you off at level one. Somewhere where the stakes are low."

"Okay," I said. "And you want me to... what? Go talk to her?"

"How are you so bad at this? Yes. Go. Talk to her. Tell her about yourself. Brag a little. Try to pick her up."

"You realize there's quite a bit about myself I can't tell her, right?"

"You mean you'll have to lie?" Winsor slapped his hands to his cheeks. *"Oh, no!* That couldn't possibly be a skill you'd have to practice, would it?"

I stood there, staring at the man, brow furrowed.

"Is there a problem, champ?"

"I'm trying to figure out how someone as abrasive as you spearheaded a global movement."

"Yeah, well, seven years of isolation, miserable news, and avoiding attempts on your life will wear on you. Now go on. You're wasting my time."

I shook my head as I ventured into the mass of tables at the center of the foodcourt. I couldn't believe Salt was subjecting me to such a stupid exercise, all in the name of gaining his trust. It certainly didn't have anything to do with improving my skills as a counterintelligence agent, no matter what he said. I mean, did the man think I'd never walked up to to a pretty girl before and engaged her in conversation? Admittedly, I wasn't the smoothest operator in high school or college, and the years in the Snow Leopards' embrace hadn't broadened my dating horizons, but talking to a girl would be easy—wouldn't it?

My pace had slowed as I'd approached her table, but I told myself it was intentional. She stared in the general direction of the fountain with that blank, detached look of Net activity.

I waited a moment beside the table before clearing my throat. "Excuse me?"

The young woman blinked and looked at me for the first time. She had the tall, slender physique of all Martians, but her long hair had been curled to add as much body to her frame as possible. "Yes?"

I waved to the chair. "Mind if I have a seat?"

She glanced to her side. "There are plenty of free tables."

That sounded like a no, but I sat anyway. "Thanks."

She averted her eyes, sighed heavily, and tried to ignore me.

"So, you like eclairs?" I said. "I like them too, at least when they're made right, but good ones are hard to find outside of France. Or so I've heard. I've never actually been to France. I can't imagine you have, either."

The young woman flicked her eyes at me. "No. I haven't."

"Do you like to travel? I never did much myself until I got out of college."

"I like to be left alone while I eat my breakfast."

"Right. Sure. I understand. I'm... Jordan, by the way." Even though I'd prepared the pseudonym for use with Nam Nguyen, it had taken me a fraction of a second to remember to use it instead of my real name. That was sloppy.

"And I'm not interested," said the young woman.

"I think you've got me all wrong. I'm not trying to pick you up. I'm just... new here. Trying to meet new people. Make some friends." I winced at my own lines.

The young lady turned toward the fountain, quite literally giving me the cold shoulder.

"Are you from around here?"

Nothing.

"I just got into town a few days ago. Work. Haven't really had a chance to see the sights yet, other than the vactrain station and Goldwater Bank Stadium. Well, and this mall, but it's not much to look at, is it? Have any recommendations?"

Still nothing.

"I've heard the museum of natural history is pretty good. A Net search also indicated the spaceflight complex downtown was worth visiting, though I have to admit I don't see the point of the planetarium. Not really sure how it could beat a simulated voyage through the cosmos. The curator at the place is well known and all, but I can get VR versions with recorded narration from the greats. Maudlier. DeGrasse Tyson. Heck, there's one I've experienced where researchers used a trace of Issac Newton's DNA recovered from the pages of his first edition copy of *Philosophiæ Naturalis Principia Mathematica* and used the genetic material to synthesize what his voice would've sounded like and used *that* to narrate the virtual tour. That was pretty wild, although it's probably not an accurate representation of what Newton would've sounded like given that the script used for the recording wasn't as eloquent as so many of Newton's original works were."

The young lady across from me groaned loudly, grabbed her eclair, and left, but not before shooting me an annoyed glance that told me exactly what she thought of me.

I sighed.

Salt snuck up from behind me and took the young woman's empty seat. I hadn't even noticed him approaching. He started clapping. Slowly. "Congratulations. That was a masterpiece to behold."

"Oh, shut up."

"No, really. You know how I said I was starting you at level one? Well, there is now a level zero."

"Are you going to mock me endlessly, or are you going to teach me something instead of throwing me to the wolves? Preferably something that would be a useful skill to someone who wants to succeed in my line of work."

"First of all, you're never going to improve in this game if you don't start taking this seriously. You need to work on your socials skills in a big way. Confidence, geniality, the ability to lie success-fully, the ability to keep people's attention when they don't want to provide it. Those are crucial. Being a spy, a mole, winning people over? It's a performance, not a piece of computer code you can hack and reprogram. And secondly, yes, I would love to mock you endlessly. It would give me great joy. But given that I seem to be stuck with you until I manage to beat some sense through your thick skull, I actually have motivation not to draw this out. So swallow your pride, get focused, and let's get to work."

20

JUNE 16, 2179

TRACKING Fabia turned out to be harder than I'd expected. I'd
known I wouldn't be able to find her in any government databases,
at least not under her given name. That didn't bother me at first.
Even though I'd largely been removed from the resistance during
my time in the police department, I'd managed to keep some level
of contact going with other operatives, including Jorge, who'd
informed me about the presence of other agents via dead drops.
He'd never specifically mentioned his daughter, but over time I
collected the names of several aliases I wasn't familiar with. If
Fabia had been working with him, I figured one or more of them
should be hers.

So I tracked those, too. One of the aliases he'd mentioned
belonged to a man who was imprisoned, but not for terrorism,
thankfully. Rather he'd been arrested and sentenced to twelve
years for aggravated assault. The fact that the assault in question
had been of a regional USC official had apparently gone unno-
ticed. Another of the named individuals was dead, having been
found frozen and asphyxiated outside a mining settlement near
Oudemans Crater in the Sinai Planum. Given that the mining
outpost supplied USC farming facilities with elemental phospho-

rus, I had to imagine her death hadn't been a freak accident. I managed to connect three more aliases Jorge had mentioned with individuals who were still alive but had files on record with either Counterterrorism or with one of the police forces of the major cities. That left two aliases with no government records, no criminal records, and no financial ties that I could find.

Given how well Fabia concealed her identity during the firebombing of Shao Wen's apartment, in a job that she couldn't have anticipated having to perform in advance, I knew she wouldn't have left digital trails for government agencies to follow. She was Jorge's daughter, after all. She knew what she was doing. I just hoped her alias was in fact one of the ones Jorge had dropped over time, and that if so, she was still using it. She might be. Falsifying digital information was an easy task for those who knew what they were doing, but creating an entirely new persona to fit said digital information was a different beast entirely.

At least I knew where to focus my searches. I started with hotel registries around Elysium. I didn't expect to get any hits, so I wasn't disappointed when I didn't. Fabia had probably stayed with her father, or maybe with another acquaintance. The financial checks I was able to run didn't turn anything up either, which also didn't surprise me. Fabia had paid for her jacket and suit with prepaid credit, after all, but I did get a hit tracking vactrain tickets.

Someone by the name of Melissa Beyer, which was one of the two aliases I was tracking, had purchased a ticket from Elysium to Olympus two days after Jorge's funeral. The odd part was that she'd purchased a westbound pass instead of the much shorter eastbound one. It wasn't an error that would've sent alarm bells ringing should anyone have been watching. If you needed to make multiple stops, the pass allowed you to get on and off the vactrain, staying overnight in any number of cities on the way to your ultimate destination. It was a slightly more economical option than an unlimited use pass, which only the most train-lagged of businessmen used. In practice, though, it meant I didn't know where Ms. Beyer exited the train.

Once again, I'd taken advantage of the police database access Captain Reyes had allowed me to retain to quickly pull the security feed from the Elysium vactrain station. Sure enough, after some searching, I identified who I believed to be Fabia boarding the vactrain for which Melissa Beyer had purchased a pass, though once again she wore a hood and glasses to mask her face. With some work, I probably could've accessed the feeds from the Olympus station, but I doubted it would be worth my time. Fabia would've gotten off somewhere else. Where exactly would take some work to figure out.

The good news was that I had a willing assistant eager to take on the task. The bad news was that for all her gung-ho attitude, Sophia didn't have much experience with computer security. When we talked, she'd asked me if there was any way for me to hack the security systems of the various municipalities along which Fabia's vactrain had stopped, thus allowing her to scan the footage for signs of her. The problem was that the hacking of said systems was ninety percent of the work. Sophia had offered to try to find Fabia via other methods, namely dropping her alias into the underground network run by her father, but I'd told her to hold off. While I wasn't above having Sophia exploit her father's criminal network to advance the cause, I wasn't about to waste the connection on something I was confident I could do myself. After all, once I got lured into Kosta Demetriou's debt, there would be few ways out. That left Sophia frustrated with the lack of work for her to do to help me, but at least she took it stoically.

Meanwhile, I had plenty of work to do for my real job. I stepped out of my rideshare into the dust-strewn streets of New Chennai, keeping my head low to keep the wind from blowing the hood of my parka off. I skittered across the sidewalk into the waiting open doors of the Sai Paradise Hotel. The doors slammed shut behind me, and a tornado engulfed me, the sound as loud as a rocket booster from a hundred meters away. As quickly as it surrounded me, it died, and the interior doors snapped open to the hotel's interior. I wasn't sure if my ears would ever get used to the overpowered Mukt airlocks that existed at the entrance and exits to all buildings, but at least they worked quickly.

I pulled my breather mask off and clipped it to my belt. My neck felt itchy, and I wondered how much regolith would slough off me during my next shower. Honestly, I had no idea how the pipes didn't clog from all the dust.

I headed toward the front desk where a young woman in a trim pantsuit sat in front of a holo. She smiled broadly as I approached. "Good morning. Checking in?"

"No, thank you. I'm here on behalf of USC Hazmat. I'm going to need a few moments of your time, if that's all right."

She blinked, her brow furrowed. "Pardon me. *Hazmat?*"

"That's right. There were three USC diplomats who recently stayed at your hotel, were there not? Ambassadors Quan Peng, Hollister Black, and Veronica Navarro. Checked in about three weeks ago. Spent a week here, give or take."

"Uh... I'm sorry, sir, but we're unable to share guest information without explicit approval. What do you mean you're with hazmat?"

I sighed. I didn't have to feign the exasperation, though it helped sell my point. "Yes. *USC* Hazmat. I know the ambassadors stayed here. I was being polite by phrasing it in the form of a question. The point is I'm going to need to see the rooms they stayed in. There's a good chance they could've been contaminated."

The poor woman balked. *"Contaminated?"*

Lucky for me the woman wore a name tag. "Look, Krisha. I'm going to send you some identification documents. I'm forwarding them to the Sai Paradise inbox. I'm sure you can access them from there. They'll prove I'm working with USC Hazmat, as I've told you. Now, here's what's going on. The ambassadors I've mentioned? The outpost they returned to is in a state of quarantine. The entire place is shut down in response to a toxin or bioagent the ambassadors came into contact with. In all likelihood, the contact occurred at an industrial site, not a nice clean hotel such as this, and chances are they didn't transfer any of said poison to this lovely establishment. If I could make some quick tests to determine if that occurred, something I'd need your assistance with to make it happen *smoothly* and *quietly,* then I could hopefully be along my way without any further quarantines. If however this process were to become difficult, then things could get complicated. More quarantines could go into effect, which again, would mean a complete *closure* of any establishment affected. Do I make myself clear?"

Krisha's face had become progressively whiter as I'd spoken. She nodded, her eyes wide. "Yes."

I loved the effect simple confidence and the threat of consequences could have. "Excellent. Feel free to look over those documents I sent you, and then perhaps you could show me to the rooms?"

Krisha swallowed hard. "I'm going to see what I can do, sir."

I SLIPPED a chemical swab into a plastic sleeve and sealed the top. I looked around the hotel room, making sure I'd taken samples from all the surfaces on my list: desk, refrigerator, nightstand, bathroom faucet handles, and drain cover. Satisfied that I'd tested everything, I peeled off my gloves and carefully pushed them into yet another plastic bag. I tucked that alongside the samples in my shoulder bag: the samples to be shipped back to Hazmat, the gloves to be incinerated.

I gathered my things and headed into the hallway. Krisha stood there, sweating bullets as she snuck glances up and down the corridor. "Is that is? That was the last room."

I closed the door behind me. "I have everything I need, thanks."

She looked at me expectantly. "And?"

"I told you, I'm going to have to send out for the toxicology screens. I won't know anything for a while. But you said no one in the hotel has come down with anything. Trust me, if whatever infected the diplomats made it here, you would've known. You should be clear. Just be strict with sheet and towel hygiene for the next couple weeks."

Krisha didn't relax. "But what do I tell the guests who were in these rooms?"

"That there was a mechanical failure. Pipes burst, flooding the floor. They'll understand that you had to relocate them, especially if you comp them a night. It'll be fine. Trust me. You can relax."

Krisha's shoulders sagged. "I'll try."

My efforts at soothing Krisha hadn't been altruistic. The fact that I was in Mukt territory meant I needed her help. "Before I leave, I'll need one more thing."

"Absolutely. Anything to make sure the guests are safe."

"I'm going to need to look at your security feeds. To see if there were other areas of the hotel the diplomats visited where they might've deposited traces of the toxin."

Krisha hesitated for a moment, but her fear of people dying from a sudden illness overwhelmed any security concerns she might've had. "Of course. Come with me."

Krisha led me down the elevators to the basement, through the back hallways to a secure door next to the laundry. She touched the intercom and spoke into the speaker. "It's Krisha, Salman. Can you let me in?"

A latch clacked, and the door swung open. A heavyset man in a suit that was nonetheless too big for him sat in front of a wall panel of displays. He wiped his hair out of his face and patted it back into place among the grease trap atop his head. He didn't smile, but he gave my escort a nod. "What do you need, Krisha?"

Despite my advice, the poor front desk attendant hadn't relaxed. "Yes. Well, this is, ah..."

"Agent Drake, with USC Hazmat." It was what I'd told Krisha anyway. "I'm tracking several USC officials who were here a few weeks ago. Chances are they could've spread bio-contaminants during their visits. Nothing to worry about. I'm simply making sure the establishment is as safe as can be."

The man's thick eyebrows had risen at the mention of the word *bio-contaminants*. "Yeah, I saw you on the feeds. Krisha, what's going on?"

"What's going on is we don't want anyone to catch whatever these USC folks did, and we certainly don't want to get shut down or investigated. The agent here needs to know what areas of the hotel the USC diplomats frequented."

Salman shot me a sideways glance. "You want me to pull security video?"

I nodded. "I'm happy to help. I've had experience with this sort of thing. These aren't the first individuals I've tracked. I know the dates they were here and the rooms they stayed in. Together, we can churn through the feeds in an hour, tops."

Salman frowned. "I can't turn over control of our system. Not without approval."

"You wouldn't need to give me control. I'd simply help you process the video."

Salman looked to Krisha. He pressed his lips together, and I could hear the click of his tongue. "I can't, Krisha. I'll get in trouble."

Krisha dropped her voice, despite the fact that it was just us. "Salman, we can't have this turn into a scene. So far Agent Drake has been very accommodating, but if word of this gets out..." Her teeth squeaked as they ground together in fear.

I could see the wheels churning in Salman's head. He leveled his gaze at me and took his time responding. "I can't give you access to our security system, but if you give me a list of names and dates, I'll put together a list of where these folks went in the hotel."

"I'm afraid that won't be good enough. Knowing where they went won't help me if I can't see what they touched and interacted with. I'll need to see the video myself."

Salman glanced at Krisha. She nodded. He sighed, but I could tell he was uneasy. "Fine. I'll collect the relevant clips and make them available to you on a private drop. Might take me a day or two, though."

"For the sake of all of us, make it one," said Krisha.

Salman grunted his displeasure.

"I'll also need to see who might've visited the officials in their rooms."

Salman shot me a piercing glance. "Why?"

The ferocity of the man's glare didn't catch me off guard at this point. "Because person to person contact is the simplest way for the contagion to have spread. I want to make sure I'm not missing anyone who might've been in their immediate presence."

Salman remained outwardly civil, but his eyes betrayed him. "I'll add it to my list."

I smiled, because I'd already gotten most of the information I needed. "Thanks. Your assistance is much appreciated."

21

MARCH 8, 2158

I LOOKED up from my newsfeeds at the sound of the front door. Salt entered the apartment, a couple of bags in hand. Rowdy uncurled from the ball he'd formed beside me on the couch, stretched his back and paws, and hopped off the cushions, heading to Salt at a leisurely pace. Three days and counting and I'd yet to see more than a blurry glimpse of Winsor's second cat, Sticks, who'd probably disowned his friend Rowdy for treason.

I minimized the feeds and stood. "There you are. Thought you'd ditched me."

Winsor snorted as he leaned over and stroked Rowdy. *"Ditch you?* This is *my* place. Much as you annoy me, I'm not going to let you run me out of my own apartment."

"Admittedly, it would be pretty hard to leave *all this* behind." I waved at the luxury around me. "But you can't blame me for being paranoid. After all, you *did* tell me not to trust anyone."

My appeal didn't so much as draw a smirk from Winsor. He grunted. "Speaking of which, you didn't so much as stir when I left this morning. You might want to add another entry to your espionage playbook: sleep light. You never know when someone's going to try to murder you."

"Duly noted. I'll start sleeping with my pistol under one of your throw pillows."

"You know, there *is* another option. You find yourself a safe place to stay. Alone. Seriously, I never invited you to spend the first night, much less *all* of them."

I nodded at the bags, ignoring his suggestion. "You finally go grocery shopping?"

"No. Why would I? Am I supposed to feed you now as well as shelter you? Did the resistance turn communist in my absence?"

I sighed. "Look, you don't have to attack me at every opportunity. All I'm saying is I'm surprised you can live this way. Not counting the cat food, the only edible items in this place that haven't gone bad are crackers and rice."

Rowdy must've understood us, as he slipped out of Salt's grasp and waltzed his way to his bowl. Winsor moved to fill them. "If you want something to eat, go to a restaurant like a normal person." Dry food rattled against the scoop, and water gurgled from the faucet into Rowdy's bowl. "You work on any of those simulations I assigned you?"

I shrugged. "Yeah, and they're as dopey as I expected. Look, I'll admit my interpersonal skills aren't at the level you'd want from a field agent, but the VR sims you gave me are for gamers who are so introverted they literally can't leave the house without suffering a panic attack. You're the only person who knows I'm using them, and it's still embarrassing."

"Well, what did you expect after that disaster at the mall? You've got to crawl before you can walk."

He set the food and water down, and Rowdy thanked him with an adorable mewl. "Are you ever going to tell me what's in the bags?"

Salt took a step toward me and whipped one of them at me. I caught it in mid air, reached inside, and blinked at what I pulled out. "It's a deadbolt."

"All together, yes, but you're more interested in the locking mechanism. It's a key operated pin tumbler lock. They used to be the most common locking system before most people switched to electronic ones."

"Okay. And?"

"And you need to learn to pick it."

"Uh... why?" I said. "You said it yourself. Nobody uses these."

"It's more accurate to say that *few* people use them, but few isn't the same as none."

I stood there, staring at him blankly.

Salt sighed and rubbed his forehead. "Think of it this way. Imagine you were cracking into a security system—hell, let's imagine you were hacking into a security scanner for a digital lock. But instead of the system's source code being in something normal like Kerbal it's in an archaic programing language like, I don't know... Python. What do you do?"

"It wouldn't be in Python," I said. "Nobody's coded anything in Python for a hundred years."

"You're missing the point, kid," said Salt. "Being a useful intelligence agent requires not just intelligence but *knowledge*. A good spy, the sort of person who might actually be able to make a difference in the resistance, is someone who can react to any situation and do so fluidly, at a moment's notice and without hesitation. The point is, if you ran into that situation, you'd fail to break into your target unless you managed to come up with an alternate solution on the fly. Which, knowing you, you'd fail at."

Salt tossed the other bag through the air. I caught it with my free hand and looked inside as the man kept talking.

"Inside that one, you'll find a set of lock picks, a few bump keys, and a snap gun. You need to learn to use all three of them to pick that deadbolt. I'm sure you can find instructions online. You'll want to practice until you can use all three interchangeably, preferably to crack the lock within a matter of seconds. If I were you, I wouldn't stop there. You might want to try your hand at wafer tumbler locks and tubular locks, too. You still encounter those every now and then. And if you need a break, you can get started on the next set of social virtual reality sims that I'm going to forward your way in a few minutes."

I stood there with the two bags in hand. "And what am I supposed to do in the afternoon?"

"Very funny, wise guy. I'm going to get myself a breakfast sandwich." He threw open the front door. "Oh. And while you're at it—learn Python."

I STARED past the edge of the buildings two blocks down the street at the tall evergreens of Melody Park whose branches reached lazily into the empty space over the sidewalk. Though they'd grown to full size, their boughs full of dark green needles and heavy with prickly cones, they seemed lifeless—more like impersonations of conifers than the real thing. It had taken me a while to realize why they seemed asleep.

It was the lack of wind.

Without it, the trees didn't sway. They didn't dance. They didn't rustle and fill the air with the gentle melody after which the park was named. For all their majesty, for all the strength in their limbs and trunk, they might as well have been dead. What good was strength that wasn't put to the test?

Salt snapped his fingers in front of my face. "Hey. Kid. Are you listening?"

I refocused to the world in front of me. Street corners packed with pedestrians. Rideshares that slowed, dumped their passengers to the side, and zipped off again. Streetlights blinking. Motors whirring. The sound of a power washer blasting grit from polished alloy panels.

"Sorry. I spaced out for a moment."

"You're driving me batty, kid. How the hell are we supposed to get anywhere if you don't focus?"

"I was still listening. And could you stop calling me kid? I'm twenty-two years old."

"Really? You'd rather I call you by your name? What was rule number two again?"

I sighed. "Never mind."

Winsor pulled me further into the shadow of the nearest building as a group of boisterous construction workers passed by. "Well, go on. If you were listening, answer the question. How would you tail me from here to my apartment without getting caught?"

I took a deep breath. "First and foremost I'd keep my distance. I'd use natural cover to my advantage, which in this environment consists of other people. Above all else, I'd make sure to keep eyes on you—and specifically keep track of you using the filtering options available to me via Net. If I suspected you'd spotted me, I *wouldn't* stop and hide, change direction, or try to be inconspicuous. I'd maintain the tail for a brief period and move in a different direction to cast doubt on your suspicions. Then I'd loop back and try to locate you again, this time from a greater distance. But the fact of the matter is, I probably couldn't do as good a job tailing you as I could've if I'd prepared for the situation properly."

Winsor nodded. "Go on."

"In an ideal situation, I'd have performed preliminary surveillance on you, possibly from a coffee shop or store somewhere near your apartment or place of business—assuming you were the working kind. From there I'd be able to learn your patterns. How quickly you walk. Whether you're paranoid or if you pay no attention to the world around you. I'd know your routes, the sorts of places you frequent on a regular basis—which for you is the food cart on the corner outside your apartment and the pet store. I'd also have brought proper equipment for the task. Digital zoom-enhanced spectacles, for one thing, but a tablet with a multi-directional camera would be good, too. Most importantly, I'd try to access local security and tap into cameras along your path to keep a better eye on you, in turn enabling me to stay far enough out of sight that you couldn't spot me no matter how hard you tried."

Winsor clapped his hands together. "Hallelujah! It's a miracle. You were actually paying attention. But knowing the theory is a different matter than executing it."

"So let's get to it," I said. "I know how this works by now. We'll run it through. You'll mock me for being terrible, then we'll do it over and over and over again until you admit I'm not the world's worst at it anymore. Then you'll find some other skill for me to hone and so on and so forth."

"Ah. Pattern recognition," said Winsor. "Good. That's another skill you needed to improve upon. But we're not ready to proceed. You haven't learned how to lose a tail."

"I thought I was following you, not the other way around."

"Yes, but if you don't know the types of tricks I'll pull while you're trailing me, how will you know how to counteract them?"

Someone on a scooter zipped into the street in front of us, causing the ride shares to screech to a halt to avoid running into the man. I thought I heard angry yells coming from within the nearest cabin. "Fine. I'm listening. I'll try not to space out this time."

"Are you familiar with intrusion points, channels, and stair-stepping?"

"Say what?"

"I'll take that as a no. They're important components of a well-developed surveillance detection route. If you're following me and I start to suspect you of it, then as an experienced operative I wouldn't keep going about my merry business in the hopes you'd go away. After all, I don't know what your intentions are. For all I know, you want to kidnap and murder me. So once I suspect I'm being tailed, I'm going to enact measures to protect myself.

"The first of those is to vary my route onto a preprepared path. In anticipation of an experienced tail who's done his or her homework and learned my routine, I'll have prepared alternate routes to take in the event I think I'm being followed, specifically routes that contain at least one channel and multiple intrusion points. Channels are long, straight corridors or paths that have multiple entrances and exits but are limited in the middle sections. Think of subway terminals or long stairwells. They're great for two reasons. First, if you suspect you're being tailed, heading into a channel will force your counterpart into the channel behind you where it's easier to identify them. Then when you get to the end, you give yourself multiple exits and a better chance of losing them. That's the whole idea behind intrusion points, which is a fancy way of referring to any place that has secondary exits you've already mapped out. You always want to give yourself multiple opportunities for escape. The last thing you want to do is corner yourself."

"And stair-stepping? Is that a way to get your exercise while you're on the lam?"

"I refers to the act of taking small deviations to the most direct route. Again, it's a method of identifying whether or not someone is tailing you or merely traveling in a similar direction. You can also take timed stops at preset locations, preferably ones with intrusion points."

"So basically, keep your eyes on a swivel, know your environment, and never wall yourself in. If you're following someone, do all that, and also don't let yourself be seen. Seems pretty straightforward."

Winsor snorted. "Trust me, everything I'll teach you *sounds* easy. And it is, for the most part. It's harder when you have to worry about someone murdering you halfway through, though. You ready to get started?"

"Sure," I said. "But it's not a fair test when you know I'll be following you off the bat."

Winsor smiled. "Life's not fair, but don't worry. I'll go easy on you."

He didn't.

22

JUNE 19, 2179

I PUSHED FORWARD along the sidewalk, my parka's hood pulled high and my glove-encased hands thrust deep in my pockets. My breath made a raspy noise in my ears, the sound reflected off the clear plastic surface of my breather mask, but the steady hum of the city threatened to drown it out. Rideshare horns blared at regular intervals, the cars stopped in their tracks by magnesium pipes that had rolled off a flatbed truck that had taken a turn too fast. A crowd surrounded the mess, some gawking, some trying to get the pipes back into place, and others trying to organize the rest to allow the rideshares a lane through which to pass.

I ignored it all as I kept my eyes fixed on a moving point in the distance, instead using my peripheral vision to avoid obstacles that presented themselves. As I bobbed around a mother pushing an encapsulated stroller, I heard a ringing deep in my skull.

I answered it without wasting any of my focus. "Captain Henderson. Thank you for returning my call." I chose my words carefully, though I was sorely tempted to add a stern *finally*.

Henderson's tired bark seeped into my consciousness. "My apologies, Agent Drake. I've been busy, as you might've guessed. I thought I made it clear that if you needed assistance, Private Minaj would be your contact."

I unclenched my teeth. "You did make that clear, sir. As it so happens, I spoke with Private Minaj recently. Yesterday, in fact. While I was pleased to hear from her that no further illnesses or deaths have been observed at Terby, there's other information I require that she doesn't have or doesn't possess the clearance to give to me, hence why I called you." That was a sufficiently diplomatic way to put it. We might represent different agencies, but I wasn't in the mood to put up with Henderson's bullshit.

"What sort of information do you need, Drake?"

"A status report, mostly. Private Minaj said your toxicologist identified traces of something in the victims' bloodstreams. Apparently, the something was classified."

Henderson sighed, which the Net reproduced as an exaggerated breath. "It was synflurane. A fast onset anesthetic. Apparently the chemical had been mostly metabolized and further denatured by the cold temperatures of the body storage otherwise we might've identified it sooner."

"The ambassadors were dosed with an anesthetic? How is that knowledge worthy of being classified?"

"Not the anesthetic part," said Henderson. "More that they were dosed at all. It means someone targeted them, most likely a Mukt operative. It's a big deal."

"I agree. I simply take offense to the fact that I wasn't informed of this seeing as I'm assigned to the Counterterrorism case."

Another sigh. "I'm working on my report, Agent. I was going to send it to you concurrently with the Inspector General and your division director."

I held my tongue. Anger wasn't going to earn me any favors. "How is synflurane usually administered? Intravenously, orally, or by inhalation?"

"The latter," said Henderson. "It's packaged as a gas, usually alongside pure oxygen to increase absorption."

"I'm assuming Peng, Black, and Navarro weren't given anesthetics alone. What else did your medical team uncover?"

"Nothing. No other known pathogens or toxins were uncovered by our screens, which is another reason why the information is classified and why I haven't sent my report. We're stubbing our toes in the dark here, Agent."

My target disappeared behind a corner in the distance, and I increased my foot speed to catch up. "What about the bodies of the deceased? Have they been transported yet?"

"They arrived in our Utopia facility yesterday. They're being held in storage until we can arrange for the autopsies."

If I'd been on a face call, it would've been difficult to hide my displeasure. *"Arrange for them?* Captain, they should've been seen to a week ago."

"We're in a strange position here, Agent Drake. Because we don't know what killed our men and women, we have to treat the situation with every possible precaution. Those precautions magnify when you reach outside your organization to work with subject matter experts."

"Are you saying Hazmat doesn't have coroners on staff?"

"If we had any, we would've brought them to Terby alongside doctors Olafsdottir, Beaufils, and Nagoya. In the event that we require forensic pathology, we hand that over to local jurisdictions."

I wanted to slug the man. "Why didn't you mention this sooner? I could've pulled some strings."

"You have connections within the Utopia mortuary system?"

"Not the Utopian one, no." I turned the corner to catch a glimpse of my mark entering one of the quick-vac systems I'd gotten used to since arriving in New Chennai. "I have to go,

Captain. I'll try to keep you updated on my progress. I'd appreciate the same courtesy."

"Henderson out."

I forced my frustration down as I approached the airlock outside a quick service restaurant by the name of Curry King. The more I talked to Henderson and his staff, the more I thought they weren't intentionally keeping secrets from me. I think they simply didn't trust anyone outside their division. Much as it rankled me, I preferred that to the possibility that Hazmat and the Terby Outpost commanders were part of a complex conspiracy that had caught me in its pincers. The investigative thread I was following was tricky enough to unknot.

I hopped into the lock, clenched my jaw as the tornado of air buffeted me from all sides, and stepped into the establishment a moment later. I pulled down my hood and undid my mask, scanning the sea of tables and booths within. A sign at the front said to seat yourself, so I did.

I slipped into a booth opposite Salman from the Sai Paradise hotel. His head was turned toward the interactive ordering kiosk built into the table. It wasn't until the booth shook from my entry that he looked up. His brows furrowed. "Hey. What are—"

"Evening, Salman," I said. "You remember me, right? Agent Drake from USC Hazmat."

The man looked over his shoulder, then back at me. "What are you doing here? Did you follow me?"

"I needed to talk to you in a more private setting than what your hotel office offered. Sorry for the inconvenience."

Salman squinted at me. "What do you want? I granted you access to the videos you asked for, despite my better judgement and the fact that it took me half a day to compile them. Isn't that enough? What are you going to ask for next, that I wipe my ass with one of your chemical swabs?"

"The videos were great, Salman. I appreciate the work you put into collating them. I just wish you'd sent me all of them."

Salman stiffened. "What are you talking about?"

"The feeds you granted me access to. They're incomplete. They show the diplomats entering and leaving their rooms, traveling among the hotel's common areas. They're helpful, truthfully they are. But there are gaps in the feeds. Especially of the corridor on the eleventh floor."

Salman's face darkened. "I took the time to trim the feeds to give you the relevant video. You'd rather watch over a hundred hours worth of hallway feeds yourself?"

"I wouldn't enjoy it. But access to the original, *uncut* video would answer some of the questions I have."

Salman turned beet red, but there was more than rage in his eyes. His whole body shook as he pointed a finger at me. "How dare you accuse me of having anything to hide. *You.* Some USC tyrant. I tried to help and you throw it in my face. Well, not any more. If you come near me again, I'm reporting it not only to my manager at the Paradise but to the police. Maybe in Olympus or Utopia you can get away with this fascist garbage, but not here. *Shove off,* bubble breather!"

I stood and pulled my mask off my belt clip. "My apologies. I seem to have made a mistake. I appreciate the help you've already given me. You have yourself a nice meal."

I headed for the airlock without another word, certain that Salman sat there, staring daggers at my back. That was one of many differences between me and the man.

I knew how to hide my anger and save it for when it was useful.

23

MARCH 29, 2158

I'D FINISHED FILLING my cup with bright red punch and was trying to decide if I should grab a glazed doughnut or a danish when I felt a gentle touch at my shoulder.

I turned to find Afaafa Mwangi standing behind me, smiling warmly with her hands clasped before her. Behind her, Zachary pulled the chairs from the meeting circle and stacked them in a corner while the others gathered their jackets and headed for the door.

"Afaafa," I said, setting down my empty plate. "Sorry. I never had a chance to eat a proper lunch today. Do you need help putting away the chairs?"

"Oh, no. Don't worry about them, Jordan," said Afaafa. "You help almost every session. Zachary can handle them by himself for once. And by all means, help yourself to as many snacks as you want. My husband would kill me if I brought home another two-dozen calorie bombs. His doctor uncovered a cholesterol issue at his last checkup and he's been making an effort to reform his diet."

"Oh. Well, I'm glad to hear that. The part about him changing his diet, I mean. So... is there anything I can help you with?"

"No, Jordan. I wanted to reach out and thank you for sharing your story today. I know how hard it can be for survivors of trauma to speak publicly, to share their pain with others. I could see you'd been struggling these past two weeks when it came to your turn to share more about what brought you here, and now I understand why. Hearing about your abusive father, about the years you spent in foster care before you set out on your own? I shared your pain. And then to hear about how you found love only to have her torn from your side in such a senseless, tragic forklift accident." Afaafa reached out and touched my arm. "Know that we're all here for you. That your addiction to alcohol isn't about you, but about your past, and that the courage you've shown by sharing your journey will make it easier for the healing to begin."

"Thanks, Afaafa," I said. "I appreciate you listening. And honestly? It felt good to share."

Which was true. It had felt good to stand there and have the rest of the support group enthralled by my tale, nodding, sharing words of wisdom, even shedding a tear or two—especially because it was all hogwash.

"So. We'll see you Monday?" said Afaafa.

"Of course. Have a nice night."

Still undecided, I grabbed a doughnut and a danish. I polished them off quickly, washed them down with the sickly sweet punch, and headed to the door before Zachary or Afaafa could convince me to take home any more of them. Not that I couldn't have eaten more. On the contrary, the combined sugar punch hadn't even taken the edge off the gnawing hole in my stomach, a side effect of pushing through Winsor's workload during what otherwise would've been lunch. Today he'd tested me on my hand eye coordination by having me throw kitchen knives into a target. I'd suggested that unarmed combat, which I happened to be reasonably proficient at, was much likelier to occur between me and an assailant than a knife fight, never mind a knife fight that occurred at just outside ideal slashing range and where I'd have enough knives on hand that I'd be willing to throw any of them, but he soldiered on, adamant that I needed to be ready for any situation. In fact, he suggested that next time we train with ropes, which he claimed could be used to break limbs and pop limbs from sockets in the hands of a trained professional. At the risk of having him cite a squabble from his youth or some Dubai action serial as proof, I'd kept quiet and nodded.

Besides, I wouldn't mind the exercise. Ever since leaving the cold comfort of the Snow Leopard base, I'd been hard pressed to get enough physical activity. Between that and the poor diet I'd suffered at the hands of Salt's barren cupboard, I'd felt myself growing softer than I liked. As a result, I'd forced myself to start waking earlier to go for jogs in the neighborhood around Salt's place. I'd also located a reasonably priced restaurant that served meals containing only egg whites and vegetables.

With my stomach growling, I headed there and picked up a spinach and feta frittata. I ate it on the way home, finishing it in a few bites, though I wouldn't have brought the leftovers home if I'd had any. As I'd learned, Salt had a *thing* about other people's food in his fridge. Based on the state of his apartment, it couldn't have been a germ issue.

Rowdy meowed as I let myself into the apartment, but Winsor didn't exit his bedroom to greet me. I called to him. "You here, Winsor? I killed it at the support group. Everyone lapped my story up. I'm practically ready for a Hollywood audition."

He didn't respond, but a notification popped up on my Net. Unsurprisingly, it was from Winsor.

I opened it. *Got a surprise for you. Meet me at 12960 S. Flint Ave. Above the judo school. Feed Rowdy and Sticks before you leave. And bring me a sandwich. Get moving.*

I sighed as Rowdy sauntered over. He sat at my feet, stared at me, and delivered an indignant yelp.

I snorted. "Yeah. You and me both, buddy."

I FIGURED it had to be a test, so I scouted the place as best I could before going in. The building itself wasn't anything special, though at three stories it was surprisingly short. The dojo occupied the bottom two floors, although I wasn't sure if the business was still in operation. The lights inside had been turned off, and while I hadn't expected much activity after dark, there weren't any signs or displays in the front windows, either. A staircase on the side of the building led to the address in Salt's message, but there was a fire escape in the back accessible both from the dojo and the address in question—an intrusion point, in Winsor's parlance.

I headed up the front stairs, a bag with a vat burger and polenta fries in my left hand. When I got to the top of the steps, I found the doors and windows of my destination had been covered with black paint on the inside. I tested the door, and it swung in without resistance.

I hesitated. "Winsor? You here?"

"There you are." Winsor sat underneath a conical lamp that illuminated him, the desk at which he sat, and little else. "About time. Brought my dinner?"

I walked over. Even in the dim light, I could spot my reflection rippling off the face of mirrors set into place over the desks, of which there were at least a dozen, each of them with a black and chrome chair paired alongside them. They weren't quite dentist's chairs, though they had a similar look and feel.

I lifted the bag. "Should still be warm. Don't tell me the next thing on our agenda is learning how to torture people. Or worse still, how to suffer it in silence."

"*Torture?*" Winsor grabbed the bag and tore into it. "What the hell are you talking about?"

"You know. Pulling teeth and stuff?" I pointed to one of the chairs.

Winsor snorted. "This is a beauty school, not a dentist's office. Give me a break."

"Yeah, that doesn't answer any of the questions I have, and I have a lot of them. The most pressing is why you're sitting in a vacant beauty school with most of the lights off, and what do you plan on doing to me here?"

"First off, that's two questions," said Winsor as he popped a fry in his mouth. "More like three if you consider the part about the lights being off as separate from what I'm doing here. Doesn't matter. The point is, welcome to your new digs." The man spread his arms wide, and in a coup de grâce, he actually smiled.

I looked around again, my eyes having adjusted to the gloom. The chairs were shabbier than I'd judged on first glance. Half of the desks had mannequin heads on them, some adorned with wigs, others with mascara and eyeliner scattered across their surfaces haphazardly. A couple of large glass-faced cabinets stood along the wall, filled with shampoos and conditioners and other cosmetic items.

"You're going to have to explain this to me, Winsor."

Salt huffed as he stood, approaching me with a pointed finger. "Seriously, kid, are you that dense? You've been crashing on my couch for almost a month. *A month!* It's not like I've been accommodating to you, begging for you to stay. I've done everything I could to get you to bounce. I haven't bought food. I haven't cleaned. I even started peeing with the bathroom door open just to gross you out enough to leave, but did you get the hint? No! You just kept right on taking up my couch every night, obstinately trying to get along with me despite my behavior and terrifying Sticks into a near-vegetative state. Hell, I don't know if he's ever going to be the same again. So let me be very clear, since any other approach risks turning you into a permanent fixture of my living room: *I don't want you in my apartment.* This is your place now.

You can thank me later. And pay me. Trust me, I'm not that charitable."

I stood there, transfixed, the confusion probably evident on my face.

"What?" said Winsor. "What is it? Did I hurt your feelings? Because I've been doing that consistently since you showed up in my life. You should be used to it by now. And you can't act like you didn't know I wanted you out. I must've mentioned it a thousand times by now. So what it is? Go on. Spit it out."

I nodded slowly. "Yeah, no, I knew you wanted me gone. I might've left sooner if I thought you wouldn't disappear into thin air the first time I turned my head. But... *you bought a beauty salon?*"

"Oh." Winsor sat back down in his chair and grabbed another fry, waving it in the air. "I admit it's unconventional, but the place has been vacant forever. I've had my eye on it for a while, given its proximity to my apartment. Thought it could make a good spot to squat if circumstances required it. Anyway, it came up at auction, I put in an embarrassingly low bid, and shockingly enough, I won. But as I said, it's not a donation. I'm expecting you or your resistance friends to reimburse me. Well, technically to reimburse the untraceable shell corporation I used to purchase it, but you know what I mean."

"Yeah, but a beauty salon? Aren't there apartments in your building? I mean, does this place even have a shower? A bed? A kitchen?"

"Shower, yes. Other amenities, no. You can put a cot wherever you want. Are you seriously complaining? This place is heaven compared to my living room."

I crossed my arms. "You didn't get this for me, did you?"

Winsor paused, the fry a few centimeters from his mouth. "What's that supposed to mean?"

"You said you've had your eye on this place for a while. You've been planning to buy this since before I arrived, and now that I'm here, you pulled the trigger so that you can teach me about makeup and disguises and using wigs and stuff. I mean, look. All the supplies are still here. There's makeup in these cases, not to mention hair bleach, nail polish remover, other cosmetics. This is part of the training, isn't it?"

"I assure you, my primary motivation was to get you out of my apartment. But yes, there are ancillary benefits as well. Not just the materials we need to teach you the art of disguise, but there's more room here than in my place, which affords us greater opportunities for teaching certain skills without breaking my furniture."

"What? Like judo? Muay Thai?"

"I was thinking about our knife throwing exercise, but sure. Also there's a broken vending machine in the corner. That's another added bonus." Winsor pointed with another fry.

"How is it a bonus if it's broken?"

"Because you should learn to fix it," said Winsor. "Trust me, you can't hack your way through every problem. Sometimes you have to work with the hardware, not the software. I'm adding that to your calendar for tomorrow."

"You know, Winsor, I'm trying to stay open-minded through all the *lessons* you've given me thus far, but I'm struggling to understand how learning the art of vending machine repair is going to help me be a better spy and revolutionary."

The old man unwrapped his burger. "You still don't get it, kid. Espionage is a lot like crime. If you don't want to get caught, you have to be good at everything. Actually, you have to be better than good. You have to be *perfect*." Winsor picked up the bag with the rest of his fries and brushed past me toward the door.

"So that's it?" I said.

"That's it. I'll contact you in the morning." Winsor paused with his hand on the door. "Oh, and one more thing. Try not to let anyone see you come in or out. Likewise, don't have anyone deliver anything here, and leave the black paint over the windows. Better to let people think this place is still abandoned."

The door clattered shut behind him, leaving me in the near darkness of the salon. I was fairly sure I'd see the cantankerous old bastard again, though I wouldn't put it past him to have engineered the purchase as a ruse to get me out of his hair. Hell, I'd have to check the tax records to make sure Winsor really *had* purchased the beauty parlor at all and that I wasn't trespassing.

That wasn't my greatest concern at the moment, however. Finding a business that sold sleeping bags at this hour of the night was.

24

JUNE 20, 2179

I SAT on a lumpy sofa that felt as if its cushions had been stuffed with Martian regolith. Darkness enveloped me, though my eyes had adjusted enough for me to see the outlines of furniture thanks to the light leaking out from the kitchen. A corner display was black and whisper quiet, and not counting the occasional thump from the upstairs unit, the only sound I could make out was the distant hum of the refrigerator.

I shifted in my seat in a vain attempt to keep my butt from falling asleep. As I settled into a new position, I heard a faint beep, followed by the puff of the door. I felt the slightest change in the air around me as the positive pressure from the apartment equalized with that of the corridor outside.

Footsteps sounded, followed by a muted thud and the snap of a latch. I stood and moved silently across the floor, my bare feet making less than a whisper against the cheap laminate. A heavyset figure emerged from around the corner, his disheveled hair half hiding his face, but he didn't look my way. He was focused on hanging his heavy overcoat in the closet in front of him.

Salman coughed once, a raspy sound that made the excess weight on him shake. I closed to within a meter of him as he finished slipping the parka onto a hanger. He extended an arm to hang it upon the bar, but he never made it. I pressed my shock pen hard against the exposed flesh of his neck. The man shuddered and gurgled, his body shaking as the pen delivered the perfect charge into him based on the resistive load of his body. After a second and a half of mind-numbing pain, Salman slumped. I caught him under the arms with ease, keeping him from making any noise against the floor on impact.

With the shock pen still in hand, I dragged the man into the darkened living room and began the laborious process of getting him secured to a chair.

SALMAN STIRRED before cracking his eyes, but he didn't crack them wide. He groaned as the full force of the high lumen bulb I'd positioned directly in front of him shone into his corneas. He squinted and turned his head, but he wasn't able to turn the rest of his body. It was firmly affixed to the chair by a carbon weave tape that was as strong in tension as it was in shear, thus necessitating the need for rolls to be sold with perforations at set intervals. No amount of squirming would break it.

I dimmed the light slightly via my Net control panel. "Evening, Salman."

The man's ears perked at the sound of my voice, and he turned his head in my direction. He squinted more fiercely, perhaps trying to force his eyes to adjust to the decreased intensity of the light through sheer force of will. I stepped forward to make it easier on him, and his eyes snapped open. He pressed back into the seat at his back—mostly with his neck. Very few other parts of him could still move.

"Yes. It's me," I said. "As you can see, I lied. About a lot of things, but especially about the fact that I'd made a mistake and that I appreciated your help."

A flurry of moaning, grunt-like sounds emerged from Salman, but they couldn't coalesce into words thanks to the tape that covered his mouth. He struggled in vain against his bonds. I moved to the light and tilted it toward his midsection.

Salman stopped struggling as he focused on the items I'd illuminated. A trio of wires snaked into his clothes, two into his shirt and another into his pants. From his vantage, Salman couldn't see where any of the three had been affixed, but his eyes followed the wires in the opposite direction to the shock pen into which the wires had been plugged.

"I can see from the look on your face that you've guessed what that particular piece of equipment is."

Salman struggled against the bonds again and emitted another muffled groan.

"I'm not sure I caught that, but I'll get to your concerns in a moment. First of all, I think you deserve a demonstration of this device so you know precisely what you're dealing with."

The moan turned into a high pitched whine, and the panic that had already sprouted in the man's eyes suddenly bloomed.

I didn't give him a chance to think. Using the same Net control app, I sent a quick jolt of electricity into the electrode attached to Salman's chest. He jerked in his chair. His back arched before sagging as the pulse faded from his system.

I swung the light back into Salman's face and turned the brightness back up. "For the record, that electrode is the least uncomfortable of the three. The second is attached to your neck, which I imagine is still sore from where I first immobilized you. The last is in a spot which I guarantee you'd rather never experience an electrical shock. As you've probably also noticed, I can activate and deactivate the electrical charge at will. I can also control the intensity of the shock. If you lie to me, or I think you're lying to me, I can send your body into immediate convulsions. If you try to scream, the shock pen has a built-in decibel meter that automatically activates the electrical charge, and I've set that particular feature to send the shock to the third electrode. Chances are it'll knock you out, but not before it fills your mind with searing pain. And a couple more notes. You may have noticed you don't have wireless Net access. I've blocked it, but I suggest you try not to do anything *at all* with your Net. My light fixture isn't a simple intimidation tool, you see. There's a camera built into the bulb that searches your eyes for random movement associated with Net usage. It, too, is attached to the same trigger on the shock pen, and the system is *surprisingly* accurate. Do I make myself clear?"

Moisture beaded Salman's forehead. His hair stuck to his face like glue. He nodded furiously.

"Good. Let's remove that gag so we can talk."

The moisture on Salman's skin made the tape over his mouth slide off with little resistance. The man breathed quickly, his chest heaving as his eyes flicked around the room. He opened his mouth, but only a faint croak came out. He licked his lips and tried again. This time, he produced a whisper. "Who are you and what do you want?"

"You don't have to be that quiet," I said. "The system is properly tuned. And I suppose I should've gone over the ground rules. First of all, I ask the questions. You answer them. Who I am isn't important. What I want is, however, and I want the truth."

His voice was stronger now, but only a little. "About what?"

"What I've already asked you about, of course. I want to know who visited the diplomats. I want the video you stripped from your feed dump."

A bead of sweat cut loose from Salman's brow and raced down his cheek into his shirt. "I don't have it."

I clicked my tongue. "*Salman.* This interview is too young to be going this poorly."

"*No*. You don't understand." The man's voice rose slightly before he reined himself in. "What I mean is, the video literally doesn't exist. There's a gap. Twenty-five minutes worth. I trimmed the video files so you wouldn't notice the missing piece."

And yet, I'd noticed. "Start at the beginning, Salman. Tell me what's going on."

"I don't know, I promise you. On the night of May twenty-third, I was approached by an individual. I don't know who. It wasn't face to face. They reached out via private message. Offered me money if I would turn the hotel's security system off at half past midnight on the night of the twenty-fifth. It was a *lot* of money. Twenty-five thousand rupals. More than I earn in six months. They said no one would be hurt, and since there's nothing stored at the hotel that's of any real value, I figured what could be the harm? If anyone asked, I could blame the failure on a system update. So I did it. I turned the system off, all except for the fire suppression and pressure systems which are automatic. When I booted the cameras back up, nothing seemed amiss, so I didn't think anything of it, at least not until you showed up."

I paced slowly, the shoes that I'd long since replaced clicking against the floor. "Three people were dosed with a deadly toxin, Salman. Three people died because of your actions. The number could rise."

"*What?* No. I didn't hurt anyone. The person who contacted me told me no one would be harmed, and I believed them. How was I supposed to know it was a lie? *I needed the money*. Have you seen this place?"

Salman was getting defensive. I needed him off-balance. "The individual who contacted you. What did they tell you?"

"Only what I've told you. They asked me to turn off the system and told me how much they would pay. They said no one would be hurt, that nothing would be traced back to me, and demanded an answer. No questions. No negotiations."

"How would they pay?"

"Direct funds transfer. Half in advance, half upon successful execution."

"Both transfers were made?"

"Yes."

"And you didn't have any other communication with whoever contacted you after the initial message?"

Salman shook his head. "I didn't even give them my bank information. The first half of the payment appeared in my account on the twenty-fourth, the second on the twenty-sixth."

"That doesn't give me a lot to go on, Salman." I picked up the shock pen and twisted it between my fingers. It seemed to have the desired effect.

The heavyset security guard started to shake. "I swear to you, I don't know anything else. Check my message history. Check my bank accounts. I'm telling you the truth."

I continued to play with the pen. "Let's assume you are, Salman. Regardless of whether or not I can prove what you've told me, we have ourselves a predicament. We need to talk about what comes next."

Salman froze, his eyes wide. "What comes... *next?*"

I set the pen down. "As you might've guessed, I don't work for USC Hazmat, but I haven't gone out of my way to hide my identity from you. In fact, I've been rather frank about who I am. That puts me in a predicament. You know too much, Salman."

Salman's brows crumpled like asphalt laid over shifting sands. His mouth moved, but only a croak came out.

"As it turns out, you were right about needing the money. This apartment complex of yours *is* a dump. No security at all? That's unsafe for the residents, who, I'll add, are quite shy. Not one of them greeted me on my way in. In fact, no one saw me at all."

"What...? I—"

I took a step into the light. "I don't like loose ends, Salman."

What I was saying hit him. "No. Please, no. I'll do anything you want. Anything. Just don't kill me. I... Oh. *Oh no.*" He squeezed his eyes shut tight, his teeth chattering as he went into a chant. *"O Blessed One, Gautama Buddha, precious treasury of compassion, bestower of supreme inner peace. You, who love all beings without exception—"*

I'd found prayers were usually an indication that a man was sufficiently scared to buy his silence. I leaned in and spoke in Salman's ear. "I was never here."

Salman jerked as another violent electrical charge surged into him, but this one was over in a moment. He slumped in his chair as his consciousness faded. Based on his body mass, he'd be out somewhere between twenty-five and forty minutes, but I didn't waste any time. I checked his pocket, finding the man's tablet. I used his thumb to unlock it, made a copy of his messages, and sent them to my own tablet for study. I also logged into his banking app and copied the details of his account history, including those of the two payments he'd received. Then I removed the digital evidence of my intrusion, logged out, wiped the tablet down, and returned it to Salman's pocket.

Next, I removed a vial and syringe from my travel bag. I measured two ccs of Kenpam, which was the trade name of a fast-acting, high strength benzodiazepine that would induce short term memory loss, essentially blanking Salman's memory of the past few hours. He might be able to recall bits and pieces of my presence, but if he tried to access a Net enhanced version of the memory, he'd encounter the equivalent of a corrupted file.

I injected the drug into Salman's arm, then checked the time. Only seven minutes since the shock, but no time to dally. I got to work on disassembling the light fixture.

25

APRIL 19, 2158

I STEPPED out of the second level doors on the west side of the Olympus Skytree, crossed the busy thoroughfare outside via the elevated walkway, descended the steps to street level, and hoofed it a block south to the Mallorca Cantina. Salt sat at one of the tables under the covered patio, sipping tea from a rust red clay mug.

I gave him a nod as I joined him. "Alright. I went in. I looked around. Now do you want to tell me what the point of my wandering the Skytree was?"

"The point should be obvious," said Winsor as he played with the handle of his glazed mug. "Now, answer me the following. On the ground level, central to the northern-facing doors, what could you see on the floor?"

I blinked. "Excuse me?"

"It would be difficult for me to be more specific without destroying the exercise I've constructed. Answer the question, please."

"It was a piece of architectural artwork. A criss-crossed network of cables laden with colored globes lit from within."

"What color were the globes?"

"A shade of purple. Mauve, maybe."

"How high did the exhibit stretch?"

"To the ceiling."

"Which was how high?"

"In meters? How in the world should I know?"

"In stories, kid."

"I still don't know. Seven? Eight? Beats me."

"Think. Was it seven or eight?"

I rolled my eyes. "I don't know. Give me a sec."

I pulled up my Net's visual log and started to rewind it, but Salt snapped his fingers at me and shook his head. "No. From memory."

"I told you, I don't know. I wasn't paying attention to how many stories tall the lobby was. If you wanted me to count or measure something, you could've asked me."

"I *wanted* you to pay attention," said Winsor with a frosty tongue. "*That* was the whole point. Tell me, now that you're halfway decent at dodging tails. What's the most important tool in the kit of someone who's trying to evade capture?"

"To plan multiple routes of escape and know where and how to access them."

"And how are you supposed to know where those routes are?"

I sighed. "By paying attention to your environment."

Winsor shook his head and frowned with the practiced ease of a disappointed father. "Get back there. This time don't look. *Observe.* And do it well. I'll still be here when you're done."

I didn't argue. Of all the lessons I'd learned from Winsor, the one that carried the most weight was that arguing with him was a lost cause. I worked my way up the street, onto the elevated walkway, and back into the Olympus Skytree.

In fairness, it was a lovely building, and a marvel of modern engineering. Though it was only the third tallest building on Mars, it towered over its Earth rivals despite using less steel, aluminum, and concrete. Though the requirement of making the structure an airtight pressure vessel added thickness to its windows, the much lower gravitational pull of Mars nonetheless allowed the building to feel light and airy, with less of the internal cross section devoted to structural support and more to open spaces, some of which had been filled with neatly manicured gardens, others with artistic pieces like the one in front of the main doors. There was even a massive aquarium filled with all manner of freshwater fish that flaunted the overall cost of the tower.

I took note of it all as I wandered the bottom of the building, which was open from the ground floor to the top of the *ninth* floor. I took note of each shop, each restaurant, each bar. I memorized the locations of the hotels and made mental notes of where the elevators were. I scanned the displays by said elevators to see which floors held apartments, which ones held businesses, and which ones were committed to building services.

I spent over an hour wandering, watching, and committing specifics to memory, but despite my best efforts, I didn't feel confident. I knew Winsor's motivations in sending me back. I knew who he wanted me to be, who he wanted me to become. Despite his training, I felt worlds away from that platonic ideal.

I sighed and headed back to the cantina. Winsor was still there when I arrived, though a server had cleared the table of his empty mug.

"I hope you paid more attention this time," said Winsor, his eyes trained on the rideshares moving in unison along the road.

"I tried. It's nine stories, by the way."

"Answering the last test's questions won't score you any points. Let's try again. What's the first thing you'll see if you enter the Skytree by the southern entrance?"

I oriented myself quickly. "The indoor park. The third level walkways that weave through the trees. Perhaps the stand of information kiosks to the right of the doors."

"What restaurants are closest to the park?"

"The Vietnamese place. Thuc An Ngon. Though there's a smoothie cart that's closer."

"How many trees are there in the park?"

My brows furrowed. "Are you serious?"

"How many trees are in the park?"

I pictured the grove in my mind as seen from the walkways overhead. The paths snaking among them below. The earthy smell of the fertilizer. The repetitive chatter of the self-help kiosk across the way.

I sighed. "I don't know. Between twenty-four and twenty-six."

Winsor snorted. "Twenty-seven, unless you count the dwarf ficus. But not bad."

A waitress came by and asked if she could get me anything. I told her no as politely as I could, but that didn't stop her from giving me a look that clearly said we should vacate her table if we weren't planning on using it anymore.

As she left, I gave Winsor a nod. "How do you do it?"

Winsor peered at me. "Do what?"

"Memorize your environment the first time through. Locate possible sources of conflict, identify them, and prepare yourself to deal with them."

Winsor didn't flinch. "I don't do any of that. Not the first time through."

"But everything you teach me, every skill you hammer into me, you make it seem like it should come instinctually. Seamlessly. Without effort. With the exception of coding, that's never been the case for me. It still isn't."

Winsor eyed me, but not with his usual disdain. For once I think he mulled over his words before spitting them out. "The skills you're learning *should* come to you seamlessly—eventually. But not yet. It's only through repetition that the things you learn become second nature. You think I was born a living legend of the Martian wastes? I was a useless, idealistic kid like you once, but

I've been teetering on a razor's edge for the past twenty years. Live long enough and work hard enough, and you'll become as good as me—or at least not as bad as you are now."

I smiled. "I know you just called me useless, but that's still the nicest speech you've ever given."

Winsor snorted. "Don't get all mushy on me. How's it going with the document modifications?"

If we weren't in public, I imagine Winsor would've called them what they were. Forgeries. But the man was ever careful. "I've got a good grasp of the software, and I can make the digital signatures indistinguishable from the ones on the original versions."

"And the printers?"

Once again, Winsor was adamant I learn the older methods as well. "I'm not quite as proficient in the physical medium, but I'm getting the hang of it."

"I'll drop by the salon later to give you an official review," said Winsor. "In the meantime, how are your studies progressing?"

"The pile never shrinks," I said. "If you don't mind my asking, why did you add several texts on pediatrics?"

Winsor smiled. "Because it's something you'll need to have a passing understanding of, obviously. Now come on. It's time you change into your suit."

A FOUNTAIN GURGLED BESIDE ME, the water flowing over a polished marble slab before falling into a turbulent froth, though a curved lip at the bottom of the bowl kept any unruly droplets from bouncing out and splashing the patrons. Classical music played through speakers hidden in the ceiling. My suit rustled against the suede of the couch as I moved my legs. Across from me, a secretary sat at an expansive desk, pretending to work at a display. She'd greeted me warmly as I'd entered. Though an AI interface could've served the same purpose she did at a drastically reduced cost, this was the sort of place that prided itself on doing things the traditional way. Heck, the suede on the couch might not even have been lab grown.

A man in a suit not quite as rich as my own appeared through a hallway. He saw me and smiled. "Mr. Anderson?"

I stood and shook the man's hand. "That's right. You must be Herman Fallwell."

"Please, Herman will do just fine, Mr. Anderson. Could I get you anything? A glass of water? Coffee? Maché?"

"Water, if you don't mind," I said. "Sparkling."

"Of course. Eleanor?"

The secretary bobbed her head. "Certainly, Mr. Fallwell."

Herman waved me forward. "Please, follow me. She'll bring it to my office."

Herman led me down a hallway with more polished marble and lots of glass. Through the windows in the adjoining conference room, I could see past the edge of the city all the way to the rust red horizon.

"Beautiful views from this high in the Skytree," I said.

"Aren't they?" said Herman. "One of the many perks of working at Silverman Price. Here we are."

Herman ushered me into his office, which also featured a fantastic view. Eleanor brought the sparking water and a pristine glass before closing the door behind her.

"So, Mr. Anderson," said Herman. "I understand you're in the metals business."

"That's a broad assessment," I said. "My family's business is in rhenium and to a lesser degree molybdenum. We have contractual agreements with companies that refine copper-sulfide ores to take ownership of the flue gas residues involved to further refine them into useable metals for alloying."

Herman nodded as if he understood. "That sounds fascinating,

Mr. Anderson. From your messages I take it you're looking to expand into new markets."

"That's correct. We've had favorable surveys from the Aonia Terra suggesting there are untapped deposits there. It's an excellent business opportunity, which is why I came to you."

Herman smiled again. "Well, I assure you, Mr. Anderson, you won't find a more service-oriented lender than Silverman Price. I believe you've already sent me the documents we need to proceed. From what I've seen, it should be a fairly painless process to get you approved for the amount you indicated."

I returned Herman's smile. "That sounds excellent."

Herman pulled the documents up one by one on his holoprojector, which must've cost him an arm and a leg. I walked him through them all in precise detail. I was calm, cool, and collected, a picture of professionalism and self-assure entitlement.

If I wasn't so proud of my performance, I might've been disgusted with myself. The fact that I had no need for the loan and had no intention of following through on the agreement made the distaste more palatable. After all, it was just an exercise.

And I nailed it.

26

JUNE 21, 2179

I SAT in my fortieth story hotel room, gazing upon the darkened streets of New Chennai. The streetlights cast a different glow than the ones in the USC controlled cities, less diffuse thanks to the lack of the pressure barrier but also hazier due to the dust, which seemed to get into everything.

In my days in the USC marine corps, especially those spent in the remote mining colony of Cassini, I'd grown used to operating outside. The Suits we'd worn were designed for functionality, with pressure bands to keep us from exploding and insulation to keep our fingers and toes warm enough to avoid frostbite, but the Suits weren't impermeable. The fine Martian regolith could still get through the Suit's weave, resulting in finely powdered armpits and butt cracks, but it wasn't anywhere near as bad as the dusting I was getting not wearing a Suit at all. Depending on the weather, walking the streets of New Chennai could be like taking a bath in talcum powder.

Part of me wondered why the Mukt put up with it. It's not as if there weren't alternatives to mitigate the dust. The pressure barriers of the USC cities were one option, though admittedly a more technologically advanced and expensive one. For safety reasons, USC buildings had as many airlocks and pressure seals as Mukt ones, but before the advent of Mylamene, other less advanced options had prevailed. All the USC cities had initially been connected via underground tunnels, and the same systems were still used in smaller settlements to this day. It was simple and effective. The only downside was that living in a system of tunnels and pressurized tubes made you feel more like a rat than a human, and *that,* I believed, was the rub.

The Mukt didn't venture into Mars's open arms each day because they had to but because they *wanted* to. The Mukt were climate refugees, having travelled to Mars when the lands available to them had been swallowed by the seas. The move had been a liberation, from which they'd taken their name. *Mukt* literally translated to *free* or *the liberated,* and freedom was not spent in captivity, trapped within a cage of one's own making. It was spent outside, enjoying the fruits of your labors—and the Mukt's labors had indeed helped advance the terraforming of Mars to a point where they could walk freely outdoors without pressure suits. While efforts to sublimate Mars's carbon dioxide rich poles had largely been run by USC, Mukt factories had been pumping fluorides into the atmosphere as fast as they could collect the precursors, helping to warm the planet in addition to thickening the atmosphere.

In that respect, both USC and the Mukt agreed upon something. Both wanted to terraform the planet. Both harbored dreams of walking outdoors under a butterscotch sky, breathing free and with green life sprouting from the soil at their feet. But one group saw the process as taking millennia, and the other planned to start dumping millions of tons of ice and ammonia onto the planet from above within the next two years.

Less, really. Swift-Tuttle was scheduled to arrive in November of 2180. What would happen as the date approached? Councilman Jalil's words rang in my mind, that nothing would convince the Mukt to abandon their homes, but was that true? Fire and brimstone could be convincing, and if both the Mukt and USC shared the goal of terraforming, didn't it make sense to move now? Every year the Mukt waited, the harder and more painful the eventual exodus would become.

I shook my head and turned back to my holo, where I'd been poring over video taken from the hacked servers of vactrain stations along the USC line. So far, I'd had no luck identifying Fabia's exit from the vactrain she'd boarded headed west from Elysium, but I still had a few stations to go. Something told me spotting her wouldn't be easy. She'd taken a bag with her on the train, one that could've contained numerous changes of clothing. So far, I'd been looking for someone trying to hide their identity—upturned hoods, glasses, hats, anything that obscured the face—but what if Fabia had adopted an identity that required no deception or misdirection? What if she'd waltzed out of the train in plain sight, dressed as a businesswoman or a college student or a migrant laborer and I'd simply missed her? I'd have to revisit the feeds, and perhaps run facial recognition scans, too.

I'd asked myself more than once what she was up to, but I didn't have any solid theories. I'm sure she and Jorge must've been working on multiple missions. As difficult as her father's death must've been, the pair of them would've had contingency plans in place for such an event. She might be aching on the inside, but it wouldn't affect her externally. Fabia would be too disciplined for that. But as important as where Fabia had gone was another question, a question that was even harder to answer.

Why was I tracking her? I didn't have any reason to. Mwenge and I had solved the faux Snow Leopard case to the department's satisfaction, and as far as I could tell, no one within the Elysium police department or USC was looking for her. By continuing to track her, wasn't I putting her at greater risk? Shouldn't I let her be? It's not as if I needed to ask her questions to satisfy my curiosity. I knew she and Jorge had been acting to suppress the rogue detectives' murders until such a point as they could be exposed, so that the citizens of Elysium wouldn't rise up and throw themselves into a conflict they weren't ready to win. So what was it? She could probably act as a conduit to the remaining resistance cells, give me an additional channel through which to talk to my fellow revolutionaries, but I was doing well enough on my own, and I was still in a position to endanger the movement should anyone discover me.

Of course, the simplest answer was also the most obvious. I wanted to find her for selfish reasons. I wanted to see her again, and to apologize for the death of her father.

I flicked the holo off, leaned back in my chair, and made a call.

Sophia answered right away. "Hey, handsome. How's the basin treating you?"

"It's cold, dusty, and the pressure is *just* high enough to fool your body into thinking you won't die a horrible, agonizing death should any piece of technology you're wearing malfunction. So it's Mars, but sneakier."

Sophia laughed. "See? This is what I miss most about not having you around. The biting wit and scientific insights."

"Not the toe-curling smiles and physical pleasures I provide?"

"You know there are sex robots for that."

"Hey, now."

Sophia laughed again. "Are you making any progress on your case?"

"Depends on which case you're talking about. I still haven't managed to locate Fabia, or even figure out what city she's in, but I'm making headway with the Terby murders."

"Not *potential* murders anymore?"

"They were dosed at their hotel while they slept with a sedative and with whatever chemical ultimately killed them, unless I'm way off base. They were specifically targeted, no doubt about it."

"So you're saying there's good news and bad news."

"How is any of that good news?"

"Well, the diplomats being murdered in their sleep is obviously bad, but I was focused on the chemical part. I know you'd been worried about dealing with a genetically engineering virus. Or were you just spit-balling?"

"Well, I still don't know for a fact, but seeing as the population of New Chennai hasn't keeled over mid snore, I'm guessing it was chemical, not biological. Either that or the virus is extremely hard to transmit. Either way, I suppose it's a good thing."

Sophia gave a sniff. "Well, I'm ever the optimist. Anything I can do to help you in the investigation?"

I snorted. "You want to provide aid on Counterterrorism cases now, too? You must be really bored."

"I'm not bored. Well... maybe a little. The sex robot isn't much of a conversationalist."

"Sophia..."

"I'm kidding. Come on. I like to stay involved. And as I've said, if I'm going to help you achieve your dream of a free Mars, I'll need to cut my teeth on something. I mean, should I be taking classes? I'm sure my father could introduce me to cybercriminals that could act as tutors."

I thought back to my time with Winsor Salt. "It's going to take more than that I'm afraid. I'm not opposed to teaching you, though. I'll just treat you with more respect than my old mentor did with me. However, I'll leave the Counterterrorism cases to folks on USC's payroll. We have plenty of data analysts that get paid for that sort of thing."

I paused as another ringing filled my head. "Actually. Speak of the devil..."

"A call from HQ?"

"It's like you can read my mind. Talk to you later tonight?"

"You bet."

I switched the connection to the new one. "Director Schmidt. It's rather late for you to be at work, isn't it?"

"I'm not at work, Agent Drake, but I'm still *working*," he said. "You understand, I'm sure."

"All too well, sir. What can I do for you?"

"It's more about what I can do for you, today. Our analysts tracked the source of those mystery payments for you."

I sat up in my chair. When I'd copied the account data from Salman's banking app, the payments from his mystery contact had shown as having come from a third party payment processor instead of from an individual. It wasn't surprising. It kept Salman from being able to identify his contact, but the payment processor couldn't keep the information secret when approached by government agents.

"So who are we dealing with?" I asked. "Someone with a long criminal record?"

"Not a who," said Schmidt. "At least not yet. The payments were initiated by New Chennai Medical Holdings, Limited. They're the corporation that runs the New Chennai Medical Center near Kandilpura Road and Jhansi Avenue."

"A medical center?"

"That's what the records show."

I chewed on the knowledge. "Alright. I'll investigate as soon as I'm able. I appreciate the call, Director."

"All part of the job, Agent Drake. Keep up the good work."

He clicked off, leaving me to mull over my options in my chair. A simple security guard like Salman had been easy enough to intimidate, but I couldn't do the same to a corporation. I'd need to approach them in a different manner.

27

JUNE 16, 2158

THE PAVEMENT DISAPPEARED BENEATH ME, my feet striking a steady rhythm against it. A light sheen of sweat coated my forehead, and my lungs felt raw from the cool air pumping through them. There was a time when I disliked running in the cold, forced outside in the dead of a Michigan winter by a coach who figured a bit of suffering would improve toughness or team bonding or something nebulous that would somehow help us put a ball through a basket with greater frequency.

Those days felt a world a way. They were, in the literal sense.

While I couldn't say I'd enjoyed forced marches in the Martian wastes with only the thin skin of a Suit protecting me, I'd come to enjoy the feel of a frigid morning jog during my months in Olympus. I'd been forced into the exercise due to the prison-like confines of Winsor's apartment, which allowed for nothing more than light calisthenics, and those hadn't provided me with a quality workout even in Earth's gravity. Since I couldn't continue my USC-ingrained swimming regimen in Winsor's bathtub, I'd turned to running, and that in turn meant I'd needed to modify my schedule.

A glint of sunlight trickled over the tops of the trees as I turned a corner and beat a path into Melody Park. In about thirty minutes, the sidewalks would transform into a hive of activity, buzzing with pedestrians and scooters zipping past each other, both of them doing their best not to spill into the street in front of the cabs. For now, the city remained in slumber, shared only by a few shift workers, transients, and other runners desperately trying to get in their kilometers before heading home to shower and rush off to work.

I slowed as I reached a narrow lawn in the middle of the park, nestled amongst the trees on all sides but one—toward that of the rising sun. I could've checked the time, but I knew from the rays yawning above the tips of the pines at the far end of the expanse that I'd made the same time I always did. To be fair, it was the Martian gravity and not my physique keeping me from going any faster. Regardless, I stood there, breathing in the chill air as I enjoyed the sunrise.

Others might have their routines. This one had become mine.

It wasn't just the physical exercise I enjoyed. In addition to a bed and a microwave, I'd installed a squat rack in my salon turned home, so I had other options. Rather, it was the sunrise. Due to Mie scattering that turned the sky blue, dawn and dusk were the only times I could fool myself into thinking I was still on Earth. When I squinted, staring through the trees of the park, the illusion became more convincing. It didn't take a great stretch of the imagination to find myself back in northern Michigan, kayaking around the Pictured Rocks in Munising, hiking the dunes at Sleeping Bear, or taking in a cool November night under the stars.

I couldn't squint too hard though, lest the trees turn to gleaming monoliths in the sun's glare, their boughs to fins, their trunks to orange yellow streams of combusting gasses, taking off from windswept pads in the Florida heat, because then I'd yearn to turn to my side and share a smile with the equally sweaty soul who'd run at my side.

I tore my eyes from the sunset, banishing thoughts of Phoebe from my mind. Not every memory of Earth was a pleasant one.

I turned and worked my way back into a jog as I headed toward the salon. I hadn't gone more than two blocks before a message popped into my vision.

It was from Winsor. *You up?*

Depends, I sent back. *This isn't a booty call, is it?*

Grow up, kid. I'll be at your place in fifteen. We've got a lot of work to do today.

Fifteen minutes was plenty of time for me to get back to the salon, but not a lot of time to shower and eat. I picked up the pace.

I STEPPED out of the back office, which I'd long since converted into my bedroom. "Well? How do I look?"

Winsor shrugged from his chair. "Like a twenty-two year old kid in a tux."

I studied myself in one of the mirrors. Pearl white shirt. Black bow tie. Gleaming cuffs. Freshly shorn hair, short on the sides and a little longer on the top. Two days of stubble, which had thankfully come in evenly around my upper lip and cheeks.

"You're jealous," I said. "You wish you still looked this good."

"I didn't say you don't look good," said Winsor. "I said you look too young. There's a difference. The point of the night isn't to charm the pants off a bunch of college girls, it's to do so to a thirty-eight year old woman."

"To be clear though, I'm not *actually* trying to get anyone to remove their pants, right? I didn't sign up for that."

"Luckily for you, this is just another exercise," said Winsor. "So no. All pants can stay on. But you need to get to work. Makeup always takes longer than you expect, and I'm banking on you screwing up and needing me to fix it."

"Thanks for the vote of confidence." I sat at one of the stations and opened the compact I'd pilfered from one of the cabinets. I dipped the tip of a fine makeup brush into a foundation that was slightly darker than my skin tone and started working it into the corner of my eyes.

"You know," I said as I worked, "you could do this for me. If anything, practice has taught me why professionals don't do their own makeup."

"Actors, maybe. Professionals in our business always do it themselves. No witnesses that way. Besides this is a skill you need to master. I won't always be there to help."

I moved from my right eye to my left. A bag crinkled as Winsor snapped it open, followed by the loud crunch of him biting into a crisp chip.

"Are you going to stare at me the entire time I do this?"

"How else am I supposed to critique you when you foul it up?" said Winsor. "But we could make use of the time. Ready to test your knowledge of the mission parameters?"

I smoothed the foundation with my fingers. "Bring it, old man."

"Tell me about your target."

"Francesca Guccione, associate head of pediatrics at St. Mary's. A meter eighty-five tall, auburn hair, somewhere in the neighborhood of sixty to sixty five kilos, which I will in no way, shape, or form mention or allude to. She grew up in Isidis to Martian parents who were themselves born of immigrants. Attended Florence Nightingale High School and graduated as salutatorian before traveling to Utopia to study microbiology at Turing University of Science and Technology. She graduated in three years and completed her medical degree in four, though she petitioned the department to let her test out of portions of the curriculum so she could complete it a year ahead of schedule. After that, she served her residency at Isidis General before completing an accelerated fellowship here in Olympus at St. Mary's. Her primary area of focus is on pediatric hematology, though she's publishing fewer papers of late following her promotion to associate head of her department. As is befitting her resume, she's single and extremely work oriented, but her colleagues uniformly applaud her sunny disposition and conversational ease, though it's possible she's better at talking to children than adults. Did I miss anything important?"

"Loads," said Winsor. "What about you?"

I picked a flat clean sponge and used it to apply powder to the creases of my eyes while I smiled, baking the crows feet into the foundation. "I'm Christian Anglemoor. Born in Denver, Colorado, but I moved to Elysium with my parents at the age of seven. Even though my parents work in finance, I've always had more altruistic motivations in life. That's what motivated me to study to become a pediatric surgeon, which is what I currently practice at Elysium's Apgar Clinic. Like Francesca, I'm single and overworked, but I love what I do. I happen to be in town because my nephew, Bredeson, is getting married, but I noticed St. Mary's was having their charity gala during my visit and made plans to attend. I'm making a generous donation in addition to the purchase of my ticket, but the amount is something I'm loathe to boast about."

In the mirror, I saw Winsor nodding. "Good. Did you finish the last of the pediatrics texts I assigned you?"

"Not only did I finish it, I reread the first two *after* passing the online study course. I may not be capable of performing surgery on a kid with neuroblastoma, but I can at least take part in a conversation well enough to not make an ass of myself."

"Fair enough. And what about you?"

I applied more foundation and power to my forehead, deepening and darkening the creases. "What do you mean?"

"I mean, what's your state of mind, kid? It's one thing to regurgitate information. It's another to absorb it. To be able to think and react within the guise of who you're supposed to be, not who you really are."

"Winsor, I've spent the last three months lying to alcoholics, to janitors, to government clerks, to kids at clothing stores. Literally anyone and everyone you've pointed me at, all between soldering circuit boards and practicing Krav Maga and learning how to apply age-altering makeup, for Christ's sake. I think I'm ready."

Winsor stood and crossed the floor to stand behind me. He stared at me through the mirror as I continued to apply the makeup. "I hope you are, kid. I hope you are."

28

JUNE 22, 2179

THE NEW CHENNAI MEDICAL CENTER didn't smell like any hospital I'd ever been to. It wasn't a bad smell. Not the smell of burnt flesh or septic infections or unchanged bedpans. Simply a different smell. Instead of the traditional sterile, citrusy scent I associated with medical facilities, the place reminded me more of a candle shop, with overtones of cinnamon and cardamom and some other subtle warm spice. I assumed it was the scent of the cleaner or perhaps an aerosol that was pumped in via the air purification system. Could be that it was an anti-transmission agent, placed in the air to prevent the spread of airborne pathogens. It was a pleasant if unexpected surprise that helped remind me that nearly everything in the Mukt cities was produced and distributed locally. Not only were communications between the Mukt and USC limited, but commerce was as well.

My shoes clacked off the smooth floors as I worked my way across the main corridor on the fifth floor. A collection of signs at an intersection pointed toward gastroenterology to the right, chapel and temple services to the left, and infectious diseases straight ahead. I kept on my path, through a series of open doors to a nurses's station beyond. I found a middle-aged woman in scrubs there, standing in front of a series of overlaid holos. Behind her in a small room I heard the hum of a refrigerator and the gurgle of a coffee maker.

"Excuse me," I said as I stopped on the other side of the station. "Is this the infectious disease ward?"

The nurse glanced at me quickly before returning to her holos. "Yes. Are you looking for a patient?"

"Not a current one," I said. "A former one. Henry Hines Miller. He was released from your facility seven days ago, if my records are correct."

The nurse spared me another quick glance, but only out of pity. "We can't release records of former patients to family. Only to physicians, and even then only if you fill out a HIFA form and it's approved by the attending. Someone from human resources can help you with that. Second floor."

HIFA stood for the Health Information Freedom Act, one of the few universal medical acts followed by both the Mukt and USC. Of course, pretty much every developed nation on Earth abided by it, too. "My apologies. I should've introduced myself. I'm Bryson Dent. I'm a physician, but not practicing. I'm with USC DPC. That's Disease Prevention and Control."

That tore the woman's eyes from her holos. "Disease prevention?"

"Yes. Infectious diseases?" I pointed at the nearest sign for the ward. "Mr. Miller was here visiting his girlfriend's parents. Slipped on a rug and fractured his tibia on the corner of a coffee table. He should've been admitted on the fifteenth. Apparently he was fitted for a cast, given some painkillers, injected with a skeletal regrowth matrix, and sent on his way. Problem is he showed up in Isidis General five days later with neck stiffness, a severe headache, and a dangerously high fever. It didn't take us long to realize we were dealing with viral meningitis."

One of the woman's eyebrows rose. *"Meningitis?"*

"Yes. A nasty enteroviral strain. If his girlfriend hadn't brought him in when she had, he might've died. The girlfriend is currently under observation to make sure she didn't contract it, as well. Which brings me here, of course."

"You think he contracted it here?"

I shrugged apologetically. "I'm not making insinuations. I'm sure your hygiene is impeccable, but the strain we isolated is no joke. If it originated at this facility, you could have a serious outbreak on your hands. Honestly, we may have gotten lucky that Mr. Miller presented so early. The traditional incubation period is closer to a week."

The poor nurse looked at me like I might be infected myself. "We haven't seen any cases."

"Are you sure?" I said. "No high fevers? No nuchal rigidity? Mr. Miller also presented somnolence. What I'm saying is—"

A loud blast cut me off, and I hunched instinctively. A pressurized hiss followed the initial clap, which itself was drowned by the blare of an alarm. I thought I smelled a hint of smoke in the air. I straightened and stared down the hall. *"Jesus Christ.* What was that?"

The nurse burst around the desk and took off down the hall. She flashed me her palm as she called out over her shoulder. "Stay there."

Another nurse burst from the break room and ran after the first. I tried to get her attention. "Is that a pressure alarm? Should I evacuate?"

She paid me as little attention as the first. "Fire. Head to the stairwell."

They sprinted down the hallway, through the double doors, and hooked a left at the nearest intersection, leaving me alone at the nurse's station.

I checked the hall to make sure no one else was nearby, then slipped around the edge of the counter to the holos. I pulled out the keypad and began typing quickly, pulling up the New Chennai Medical Center employee database, which I had access to thanks to the nurse leaving her station unlocked. I selected the database's root directory and mailed it to my tablet's account, then pulled up the patient database and did the same with those.

I didn't have a lot of time. The compressed nitrogen tank I'd sabotaged in an unoccupied supply closet would decompress in a matter of seconds. Once it stopped hissing and the fumes from the smoke bomb I'd hid behind it cleared, the alarm should shut off and the nurses and security staff would disperse, scratching their heads. If I'd set everything up right, no one would suspect anything other than a freak failure of the pressure valve atop the canister.

Thankfully, I didn't need much time. With a few more keystrokes, I set up the transfers for the hospital's chemical supply records, shipping manifests, and anything I could access that had the word 'billing' in the search results, closed the files, and cleared the logs of the transfers. With a little effort, I could've hacked into the hospital's servers remotely, but sometimes the simpler methods were the most effective.

I hopped back to my spot outside the nurses' station and waited for my contact to reappear. She took longer than I anticipated, but about a minute after the fire alarm went silent, she trotted around the corner and headed back toward me.

"Is everything alright?" I think I looked appropriately mortified.

"It's fine. A false alarm. No fire. We'll have occupational safety investigate. Now... where were we?"

"I was trying to ensure you're not at immediate risk of a viral meningitis outbreak."

"Look, I appreciate your concern," said the nurse. "But we've had no signs of such an outbreak, and our doctors are fully aware of the symptoms. If such an outbreak were to occur, we'd be prepared for it."

A notification popped up via Net telling me the database transfers were complete. All that remained was extraction. "I'm sure you're capable. I didn't mean to imply you're not, but this is a serious matter. The strain we isolated is quite aggressive, and logic dictates that Mr. Miller contracted it here. He *was* treated at your facility, wasn't he?"

The nurse sighed. She typed quickly at her keypad. "What was his full name again?"

"Henry Hines Miller."

More keystrokes. "Actually, no. I'm sorry, but I have no record of him in our system."

I blinked. "There has to be some sort of mistake. He told us quite clearly he was treated at the New Chennai Medical Complex."

The nurse's face drooped, and I could tell she'd encountered this problem before. "Sir, this is the New Chennai Medical *Center*. The New Chennai Medical *Complex* is located off Punapur and Seventh."

I pressed my forehead into my hand. "My God. I'm so sorry."

"It's fine, sir. Happens more often than you might think."

I apologized again and headed for the elevators. It wasn't until the doors closed in front of me that I allowed myself to smile.

29

JUNE 16, 2158

I'D ENTERED the rideshare outside the salon as Ambrose Drake, but it was Christian Anglemoor who stepped through the cab's doors onto the plush red carpet outside the Davies Hotel. My patent lab leather shoes glided across the soft fibers underneath, protected from the coarse texture of the sidewalk. A young man who must've been my age but looked fifteen years younger thanks to my makeup smiled and gave me a nod as I approached the entrance.

"Welcome, sir," he said. "You're here for Clinicians for a Cause?"

"I am."

"Excellent, sir. The registration desk is inside to the right. You'll be able to get your badge there and enter your name into the raffle if you choose. The reception is in the main ballroom. Have a wonderful evening."

"Thank you."

I made my way inside the luxury hotel, stopping by the desk to pick up my identification and dinner assignment, whereupon I was once again thanked for my generosity before being informed about the location of the ballroom, the night's speakers, and the band performing at the afterparty in the bar next door. I smiled and nodded and thanked everyone who assisted me, tipping my head with just the right amount of polite deference. From there, I wound my way through groups of chittering doctors and socialites into the ballroom itself, a sprawling space adorned with gleaming chandeliers, thick draperies, and perfectly mundane folding furniture, the latter of which had been adorned with slip covers, immaculate white cloths, and fine china to make it palatable to the attendees.

I waited in line at the bar, ordered a Manhattan, and surveyed the room while I waited. Tables had been grouped in the center of the space, each of them numbered for ease of location, but for the moment people were evenly split between them and the edges. More clustered upon the elevated stage, laughing and clapping each other on the shoulders in response to jokes that drowned in the crescendo of chatter.

"Sir?"

The bartender held my drink toward me, perfectly ruddy in color. I accepted it and thanked the man, taking it with me as I wove through the maze of tables. My registration ticket listed mine as number twenty-four. When I arrived, there was a single person at my table, a young blonde woman in her mid thirties. She smiled. "Hello."

I switched my drink to my left hand and stuck out my right. "Hi. Christian Anglemoor. Pleasure to meet you... Mrs. Riley?"

The woman looked at her badge, same as I had. "Oh, Deirdre is fine. I prefer it, really. How about you—" She cast a quick glance at my tag. "—Dr. Anglemoor?"

"Christian, please. I get enough of Dr. Anglemoor at work." I took a seat, leaving an empty chair between the two of us. "I suppose I'll be dining with you tonight?"

"You will unless someone mixed up the table numbers, I imagine. Are you here on your own?"

"Yes, unfortunately," I said. "I'm actually in town from Elysium on family business and figured this gala would be a pleasant detour. It's hard enough to convince a date to attend a local charity event most of the time, let alone one on the other side of the globe."

"I was going to say, I didn't recognize your name," said Deirdre. "Not that I know everyone at St. Mary's by any stretch, but I've attended enough events with my husband to get a feel for the regulars."

"Yes, I'm a surgeon at the Apgar Clinic. I work in pediatric oncology. Neuroblastoma, primarily, but also some of the rarer cancers. Rhabdomyosarcoma. Ewing sarcoma."

Deirdre pressed a hand against her heart. "I don't know how you do it. My husband is a cardiologist, and it's hard enough when a middle-aged patient passes from a complication. Working with children is another level, and then to be an oncologist?"

I nodded. "It's the most rewarding profession in the world when we succeed, and one of the most gut-wrenching when we don't. But there are always a steady stream of children in need of care. That keeps me going through the bleak periods."

"Well, thank you for what you do," said Deirdre. "Both for your service and your willingness to give back. We're all better for it."

"It's my pleasure." I took a sip of my Manhattan, the rye whiskey warm against my tongue. It wasn't my beverage of choice, but it *was* Anglemoor's.

"I don't suppose you've had a chance to meet the head of the pediatrics department, seeing as you're from out of town?" said Deirdre. "Dr. Hatsune? I'm sure she'd love to thank you for coming."

"I haven't, though I'm familiar with Dr. Hatsune's work. The entire pediatrics department at St. Mary's is top notch. Any idea where I could find her?"

"I thought I caught a glimpse of her on the stage, schmoozing with some of the donors." Deirdre pursed her lips. "Perhaps schmoozing isn't the right word. It's a necessity to keep the hospital operational. I know that."

"It's an evil we all engage in. No need for apologies. If you'll excuse me for a moment..."

I gave Deirdre a smile as I spoke my goodbye, heading in the direction of the groups around the stage. I knew what Dr. Hatsune looked like from my research. I spotted her after a minute of relaxed observation, but gaining her ear wasn't my goal. I simply figured if she was nearby, my target would be, too.

It only took me another minute of circling with my drink to catch a glimpse of her. In the database photos I'd studied, she'd come across as rather plain, but with her hair done up, a touch of blush and eyeliner applied, and coifed in a resplendent green evening dress, I found myself surprisingly attracted to her, despite the fifteen year age difference. She stood among a group of eight, evenly divided between men and woman, most of whom were at least in their fifties, all of them richly dressed. She smiled as one of the group laughed, and her cheeks dimpled slightly.

Given her entourage, I kept my distance, splitting my gaze from the raffle prizes on display only enough to keep tabs on her. I positioned myself toward one end of the stage near a soccer ball signed by the popular striker Rodiño, anticipating the path she'd take when she grew tired of those around her.

It took a few more minutes than I expected but leave she did, along the exact route I'd expected. I turned at the perfect moment, nearly running into her as she approached the steps. It was only with a quick flick of my wrist that I appeared not to spill my drink all over the two of us.

"Oh, my goodness. I'm terribly sorry," I said. "I didn't even see you."

The woman gave me a nervous smile. "Oh, please. It's my fault. I thought I could sneak through. Clearly I couldn't."

I glanced at the woman's badge and let my eyes widen a smidge. "Oh... You're Dr. Guccione, associate head of pediatrics?"

She smiled, more easily this time. "That's correct. You are...?"

I extended a hand. "Dr. Christian Anglemoor. It's an absolute pleasure to meet you."

***

THE THREE SINGERS of The Probiots bowed in unison, arms crossed over each others' backs amid a shower of applause for their encore set. The lead spoke, his voice projected through the bar's many speakers.

"Once again, thank you to Clinicians for a Cause, to the event's organizers, to the Davies Hotel, Moonlight Bar, to Dr. Hiroko Hatsune, and especially, to all of you for making this happen. We can't thank you enough! Stay safe, and have a wonderful night."

Francesca stood beside me, clapping and shaking her head in wonder, a smile stretching her face. "Oh my goodness, they were *fantastic!* I'd heard good things, but I haven't had that much fun in *years.*"

A thin sheen of sweat dampened her hair at the temples and at the base of her neck. I'd felt warm under the collar myself, but I'd taken the odd break or two, mostly to make sure my makeup wasn't being affected. "I don't think I've danced that much in my entire life," I said, rather truthfully.

Francesca leaned close and squeezed my arm, the scent of alcohol lingering on her lips. "Oh, I don't believe that at all. You move *very* well."

"As do you, and in an evening dress no less. But honesty, I've never even taken a dance class. That was all natural ability."

"By all means, leave modesty aside. But it would be fun though, wouldn't it? To learn to waltz or rumba? Ah, but who has the time? It's almost criminal, the burden that comes with this profession. Not that I'm complaining. I love my work, but sometimes... Sometimes I wish there was time for something more." Francesca's smile widened, and her grip on my arm didn't wane.

For the first time all night, I felt a hint of apprehension. "It's a demanding career. Sometimes too much so."

"Can I be honest with you, Christian?"

The people around us were gathering their things. "Of course."

"This is the first time I've stayed until the end of one of these galas. Even at these, I never truly enjoy myself. I always go home as soon as the ceremony is over, either to work or to catch up on sleep."

"Well, for both our sakes, I'm glad you stayed. I had a wonderful evening, and it was a pleasure to get to know you. Can I escort you to the rideshare queue?"

Francesca gave a little nod. She gathered her coat from a nearby stool. As she turned, her foot caught on the edge of her dress. She stumbled, but luckily I was in front of her. I plucked her from the air as she fell, catching her under the arms.

Francesca clutched me around the chest as we both stood, her face a hands breadth from my own. Her body pressed against mine, more than the slight brushes we'd experienced while dancing. "Christian. I'm..."

I think she was going to say she was sorry, but the words died on her lips.

I swallowed hard, reflexively. "It's alright. I caught you."

"You did."

Francesca shifted her weight onto her own feet, averting her eyes as she did so. She smoothed her dress, even though it didn't need smoothing, then took my arm when I offered it. "Wouldn't want any more stumbles."

Francesca nodded in agreement. "No."

We headed for the exit, following the crowd who'd beaten us to it. The rideshare line wouldn't be a joy to navigate.

"So, how long are you in town?" asked Francesca.

"I leave tomorrow, midmorning." I'd already shared with her the details of my nephew's wedding.

"Ah. Where did you say you were staying?"

"The Continental, in the business district."

Francesca nodded. "I'm close to St. Mary's. Maybe fifteen minutes from the vactrain station. Traffic isn't usually bad."

I already knew where she lived, but I feigned mild surprise. "Is that so?"

Francesca kept her eyes trained on me. "I have extra space. You could stay if you wanted. Would give you a little extra time to sleep in the morning."

I met Francesca's gaze, the apprehension in my stomach having grown into full blown anxiety. "I'm used to waking early."

"So am I," said Francesca. "But I could make an exception for once. Especially if something were to keep me up late."

I wet my bottom lip with my tongue. Francesca may have begun as my mark, but I couldn't claim she hadn't grown on me. She had a soft, inviting face and eyes that spoke louder than she did. When she'd pressed against me after stumbling I'd felt a familiar stirring that begged to be listened to. Perhaps my attraction was a byproduct of my extended dry spell—I hadn't been with a girl since an ill-advised fling with a fellow member of the resistance by the name of Sonja—but I couldn't deny it was a throbbing attraction nonetheless. Not to a girl. A woman.

We'd moved outside into the queue, which wasn't as long as I'd feared. "I'm... not sure if I should."

Francesca lowered her voice. "Christian, I know I've had a few drinks, but I'm in control of my faculties. Come home with me."

"Francesca..."

She bit her lip. "Please."

It was then, as I stared into Francesca's eyes, that I understood for the first time what Winsor had told me. Until that moment, the evening had been a delight. I'd *enjoyed* playing the role of Christian Anglemoor, in part because it had involved sipping cocktails, eating a wonderful dinner, and gyrating to music, but also because I'd been able to do it effortlessly. I hadn't fretted, I hadn't been caught off guard, and the only time I'd sweated had been during the dancing. My preparation had paid off. I'd encompassed my character fully, and I was proud of the performance I'd given.

Until now. Because now the decision I was forced into making was one of consequence. Until this moment, I could've skated out of Francesca Guccione's life as easily as I'd entered, nothing more than a passing face in memory. No more. I'd affected her. Or rather Christian Anglemoor had, and all of the exits available to him involved some level of danger and anguish.

All this in regards to an undercover operation that meant nothing, a simple test of my skills. If instead I'd been assigned by the resistance to gain Francesca's trust, to extract confidential information from her, to deceive her and take what I needed without regards to her finances, career, social status, or emotional wellbeing, I'd be committed to doing it. I'd have to bury any feelings of compassion or disgust so deep that no one would suspect they were there. Not Francesca. Not her friends. Not even me.

That was the hard part. Not playing the role, but living with the choices made.

"Francesca, I would *love* to join you." And I meant it. I ached with pent up desire. "But I don't think it's the right choice. I'm sorry."

Francesca looked down, and her voiced dropped several decibels. "I understand."

The next few minutes spent waiting for an available ride stretched into an eternity. When at last an empty cab arrived, I leaned forward to give Francesca a peck on the cheek, but she pulled back, gave me a disappointed nod, and disappeared into the car by herself. I sighed as it sped off, wondering if I'd made the right decision. I could've just as easily disappeared from her life tomorrow mid-morning. Wouldn't that have been a more pleasurable result for the both of us? Or would it have led to more misery in the long run?

I commandeered the next rideshare for myself and settled into the back seats, instructing it to head to the salon. The second-guessing started as soon as the wheels had spun into motion. Maybe I should go back. Maybe I could intercept Francesca's cab. I could contact her via Net. But I knew they were all stupid ideas. The moment had passed, and beyond that, uncontrolled sexual desire and rampant emotions would ensure I'd fail Winsor's ongoing test. Instead I sat there, feeling sorry for myself and fantasizing about what it would've been like to accept Francesca's offer. She'd come across as shy, but that didn't mean she'd behave that way in private. And I had to assume she'd be more experienced than me, which wouldn't be a bad thing. I felt myself stiffen despite my self-imposed predicament, so I forced my eyes out the windows and tried to empty my mind.

The buildings zipped past, greyscale glimmers in the reflected streetlight, one after another in uniform monotony. My rideshare swerved into the outside lane, the engine whirring as it overtook other, slower ones, causing the buildings to turn into a blur. It was almost as if the car fed off my frustration, channeling it into speed, but the car wasn't sentient, even if I could connect to it via Net.

But the rideshare didn't slow. If anything, it seemed to accelerate. I pulled up the cab's metrics, not trusting myself to make accurate judgement calls based on the speed of passing cars and shaded buildings, but the app clearly showed my ride had surged past the speed limit.

And the accelerometer was climbing.

30

JUNE 24, 2179

I PULLED myself from the pool, stood, and wiped my hands through my hair to squeeze some of the moisture onto the tiles. I plucked a towel from a heated rack and dried my face, breathing deeply to slow my heart. I'd sprinted the last hundred meters, but my body hadn't been up to the task, resulting in my finishing two seconds slower than normal. It didn't sound like much, but I should've gone *faster* in the hotel's twenty-five meter pool compared to the fifty meter I was used to. I'd hit weights in the morning, working on deadlifts, lat pulldowns, and overhead presses, leaving me with a sore back, but I didn't think I could blame my performance on that. Nor could I blame my performance on my new diet, which thanks to Mukt culinary leanings had a lot more spice in it than I was used to. Rather, I think it had more to do with *where* I was.

For all the years I'd spent in service to the resistance, life in Elysium had made me sedentary. I'd grown accustomed to my apartment, to my job, and once Sophia had appeared in my life, I'd eagerly become accustomed to her. Honestly, my apartment wasn't anything special. If not for the aforementioned olympic length pool, I would've moved in with Sophia weeks ago, pending her approval. And I did miss Sophia, but at least I was able to see and speak with her via Net most nights. It wasn't the same as holding her in my arms and waking up to the scent of her shampoo on the pillows in the morning, but it was better than nothing. What surprised me was that I missed my job at the department.

It wasn't just Bishop and Captain Reyes who I missed, or the routine that homicide investigation provided. I missed the unshakable belief that I was doing the right thing. Although occasionally a case with thorny moral implications came along, such as the one involving the junior detectives who'd impersonated the Snow Leopard, in most cases it was plainly clear who the bad guy was once the evidence had been gathered. Now, I'd lost that.

In some ways, I yearned for the ignorance of youth. When I was a naive teen, I'd joined USC with an unshakable certainty that I was fighting on the side of right. Then I'd switched sides to the Martian resistance, and again I'd been certain of the moral imperative of the side I'd joined. I'd been wrong both times. I knew that now. When it came to warfare, there was no black or white, only shades of grey. The question was simply which end of the spectrum you were closer to.

Sophia seemed to think my actions were warranted because of my moral core. That it was okay for me to terrorize someone like Salman because I did it in the pursuit of a larger, nobler goal. That it was okay to unleash an explosion in a hospital because I did it in a manner that I was sure wouldn't harm anyone. But Sophia didn't know everything inside of me. I hadn't shared with her the plan I'd started to hatch. The plan that could free Mars but could jeopardize the lives of millions in the process.

I'd thought about sharing it with her, but for as much as I loved her, she wouldn't be able to help me solidify it into something concrete. Something that could actually be implemented, and perhaps, something that might work.

For that, I needed Fabia.

I finished drying myself off, then slipped into my hotel robe and took the elevator back to my room. There, I took a quick shower and changed while a plate of last night's chicken tikka masala warmed in the microwave. I mixed it with a few scoops of rice and sat down at my room's lone table to eat.

As I spooned the steaming hot mixture into my mouth, I brought up the case files I'd been working on for Counterterrorism. Sifting through the hospital's employee and patient databases had been a time-consuming process, in part because I wasn't sure what I was looking for. Despite leading me to the New Chennai Medical Center, my interrogation of Salman hadn't produced much else. The anonymous messages he'd received had come from an encrypted source, one I wouldn't be able to crack without the aid of the local Net service provider, who wasn't beholden to USC or their interests, and the messages themselves hadn't contained any clues to the individual's identity.

That left me with the payment. Unfortunately, the nurse's station from which I'd copied the hotel records didn't have access to all of billing and accounts receivable's files, which meant I didn't know who had initiated the payment to Salman or from which account it had originated. Needless to say, I was upset that after my foray into the medical center I'd still need to hack their computer systems, but rather than plunk down on my couch and brute force my way into the hospital's security with the hotel's firewall breathing down my neck, I'd decided to outsource the work to someone who could do the process with more anonymity, namely the office staff back at Elysium Counterterrorism.

In the meantime, I was still able to winnow the field with the data I'd acquired. For one thing, I'd learned only accounts receivable staff, department heads, and their secretaries could initiate payments to suppliers. That meant I could immediately discount the majority of the hospital's nurses and doctors as the ones who'd contacted and paid Salman, unless of course they'd blackmailed, seduced, or otherwise coerced one of the above into making the payment. It was a possibility I had to consider, because after running background checks on the people with their hands on the hospital's finances, none of them struck me as the kind to be involved in a terrorist plot. Most of them had families, only two of them had any sort of criminal record, both of them for minor offenses, and none of them had any notes in their internal files for harassment, supply mismanagement, or other issues.

That last one was of particular interest to me, mostly because of what the hazmat physicians had discovered. The three dead diplomats had been dosed with synflurane, an anesthetic that hospital records showed was in use in the facility. As all anesthetics were, synflurane was a controlled substance managed by the hospital's anesthesiologists, the quantities of which were closely tracked and recorded—hence why I copied the hospital's chemical supply records. In analyzing them, I'd come across a discrepancy. Specifically, I'd found a disagreement between the quantities of synflurane at the hospital and those shipped to them. Apparently, the hospital had received a shipment of synflurane from a supplier, noticed the quantity was off, and contacted them over the missing canister, which the supplier had subsequently sent. Given that it was the issue's first occurrence, both the hospital and the supplier seemed content believing the shipment had been mishandled on the supplier's side.

So I could be fairly confident someone stole the synflurane, and that the same individual initiated the payment to Salman, but who? Only the hospital's head of anesthesiology had access both to the drug and the payments system, but a thorough background check of the man in no way, shape, or form suggested he was a terrorist. He had degrees from prestigious universities, a long history of peer-reviewed research, had been a featured speaker at numerous conferences, had a large family that he constantly posted about on social media, was an avid racketball player and an obsessive model rocket booster and spacecraft hobbyist. I was amazed the man had time to sleep, never mind orchestrate an attack on visiting diplomats. That left the rest of the billing staff and anesthesiologists. I tried finding connections between the two groups, something that would tie the actions of multiple people together in a single knot, but so far I'd failed.

I sighed and shook my head. Clearly, I was missing something. I spooned the rest of my lunch into my mouth and took the bowl to my room's kitchenette. As I turned on the faucet, a message popped up in my vision. It was from the Counterterrorism finance department.

I opened it and read as I rinsed. The team had good news and bad news. The good was that they'd successfully accessed the hospital's financial records, including all outgoing payments from the last several years. The bad news was that the two payments of twelve thousand five hundred rupals were nowhere to be found. To be sure, they'd been made. The hospital's account balances reflected that. If the hospital accountants hadn't realized it yet, they'd be more than a little alarmed when they did, but of the individual payments there was no record.

The Counterterrorism team confirmed in their message what I already knew—that payments could be wiped. There would be evidence of such an action hidden in the computer logs of the affected system, but so far Counterterrorism hadn't been able to access those. Even if they did, it probably wouldn't matter. If someone went to the trouble of wiping the history of the payment, they could've further obfuscated their presence, setting up a trail of digital breadcrumbs to point at some unsuspecting sap instead of themselves. Clearly, we were dealing with someone who was both cognizant of digital security and capable of handling themselves in the space.

The news should've dispirited me, but instead it gave me an idea. I put the bowl and utensils in the dishwasher and headed back to my table, bringing up the employee database as I walked. As I sat, I initiated a search for any employees who had degrees in computer science and engineering. Surprisingly, or perhaps not given it was a hospital, the search brought up only four results. Three of the individuals worked in the hospital's IT department. The fourth was a medical oncologist—*not* a surgical oncologist, who would be the kind to require synflurane for operations. None of the four had criminal records, and again, none of them fit the profile for a terrorist, though one of the IT professionals might've needed treatment for video game addiction based on his virtual achievement history.

In a fit of inspiration, I tried one more thing. I expanded the search to include employees who had been fired or otherwise had left the hospital in the past twelve months. That brought up another hit. A man by the name of Vikram Nandi who'd completed his bachelor's degree in computer science before dropping out of his masters program. Seven years after that, he'd been hired by the hospital as a physician's assistant—to an anesthesiologist, surprisingly enough. The man had a single criminal arrest which had been overturned, for incitement. That had been during his stint in graduate school. During the seven years leading up to his hire at the hospital, I couldn't find any records about him at all.

It wasn't proof he was the one I was looking for, but my experience in homicide *highly* suggested it.

31

JUNE 16, 2158

I REFRESHED the rideshare data to make sure there wasn't a mistake, but it didn't budge. At this point the evidence was clear. My cab was zipping past others, leaving them in its wake.

For a moment, I sat there, wondering what the hell was going on. It's not as if I could've accidentally ordered the vehicle to step on it, or even paid a premium to have it do so. The rideshares were programmed to obey local traffic laws, and beyond that they were all interconnected, constantly communicating with each other to ensure traffic as a whole moved as smoothly and safely as possible. Overrides existed which allowed emergency services—police, fire, and paramedics—to order individual vehicles to break certain laws, specifically the speed limit. That allowed individuals to arrive at crime scenes or hospitals as quickly as possible, but other rideshares responded to those emergency overrides, pulling to the side automatically to allow for safe passage. At the moment, other rideshares weren't doing any such thing, instead slowing cautiously as they tried to wrap their primitive AI minds around my cab's speed and erratic behavior. Not to mention, the emergency mode wasn't activated in my rideshare's Net window.

I changed my destination, ordering the rideshare to pull to the side and let me off at the nearest corner. It ignored me, so I pushed the emergency stop button beside the door. Again, nothing happened. At that moment I realized I wasn't heading toward the salon.

Whatever romantic longings I'd felt disappeared in a rush. I pulled up the advanced menu on the rideshare app to see what my options were, but they were all useless—online ratings, frequently asked questions, and a prompt to engage in a live chat with a human representative with an approximate wait time of eighteen minutes. Of course, contacting the rideshare company wasn't my only option. I could call the police to see if they could override my cab remotely, but that struck me as a less than ideal scenario. Law enforcement worked hand in hand with USC, and while I might be able to bullshit physicians into thinking I was Dr. Christian Anglemoor, police would run my name and face through official databases.

I did the next best thing and called Winsor. He didn't answer, coming up as unavailable.

I cursed, but I didn't panic. I delved into my system options, opening the rideshare app's source code in a terminal. I skimmed the code as quickly as I could, trying to reverse engineer it on the fly, looking for vulnerabilities where I might be able to inject a quick snippet of code that could give me access to the rideshare's hardware. The car swerved as I poured through it, slamming me against the armrest as it screeched around a corner. I swore again and glanced at the cab's metrics. It was still gaining speed.

Sweat beaded my brow. I could brute force an attack on the app's online controls, but I didn't have the time. I barfed up a couple quick lines of code and snuck them into the login subroutine, but they failed to give me access, instead causing the compiler to freeze.

"*Damnit.*"

I tested the door handles, but they didn't open. The car was in motion. I called Winsor again. Still nothing.

The car swerved around a slow moving rideshare, veering into the lane of opposing traffic. This time, I couldn't suppress the anxiety building inside me.

I squeezed my eyes shut and took a slow, deep breath, forcing it deliberately through my lips. Before I'd joined the Martian resistance, I'd undergone USC training on how to force the body out of a state of panic and into a state of logical thought. I kept forcing deep breaths in and out of my lungs as I gave the problem my undivided attention.

The car was running out of control—except it wasn't. It was breaking speed limits, taking me somewhere other than my stated destination, but it hadn't gone haywire, otherwise it likely would've accelerated at top speed until it slammed into the closest object. So it was acting deliberately, if erratically. I wasn't in control, nor was the car's native AI, which meant either someone had reprogrammed the car to act this way or it was under direct, remote control from a third party.

The reason for the rideshare's behavior intrigued me, but it didn't matter at the moment. What mattered was figuring out how to stop the car. What could I do? The emergency stop button hadn't worked. The software was similarly unresponsive, and although I might be able to crack it, circumstances suggested I didn't have time for that. But there were other ways to stop an out of control cab. Passive safety measures that kicked in regardless of what the software said. If the car lost steering control, for example, the brakes would automatically activate to protect the passenger.

So all I needed to do was disable the steering control. How could I do that? Sever the electrical connection from the onboard computer to the drivetrain, of course. And where was the onboard computer? Damn. I didn't know that.

The rideshare swerved into oncoming traffic again, and I heard a high pitched whistle as we passed within a half meter of each other.

I stumbled to my knees, yanking on the back bench seat, but it didn't budge. Luckily, the front bench did. I jammed my finger behind the seat, looking for the latch that would fold it down, figuring there would be access panels for the onboard computer either from the back seat or front. After some desperate fumbling, I found the latch, flipped the seat, and tore open the panel. A wired connection for a diagnostic system greeted me, but I managed to rip the face plate off, revealing the motherboard and a maze of wiring underneath. But which bundle of wires fed the steering control? During my training with Winsor, I'd learned how to rewire a vending machine, not a car.

My training with Winsor. *Son of a bitch.*

The tires screeched, and again I lost my footing, banging my elbow and bruising my chin as I pitched forward. Screw it. I figured the passive safety features were there for a reason. I indiscriminately started yanking wires, assuming if I removed *all* of the them, I'd get the steering.

The lights overhead flickered, the circulatory fans whined, and then the car lurched, the tires screeching as brake pads dug into tires. I braced myself against the sidewalls, realizing I should've buckled myself in before attacking the circuitry, but I managed to avoid further injury as we skidded to a halt.

The door control still didn't work when I pulled on the lever, so I planted the sole of my expensive tuxedo shoes against the glass and kicked with all my might. Five or six blows later, with ruined shoes and a bruised heel, I clambered from the shattered remains of the rideshare window and took off into the night at a lope.

WINSOR SAT at one of the salon chair when I slipped through the front door. Despite the hour, I wasn't surprised.

"You." I stalked toward him, anger tightening my jaw. "I know you're responsible for the rideshare. Don't try to deny it."

"Why would I deny it?" said Winsor. "I may be abrasive, but I've done my best not to lie to you."

"Are you insane?" The words burst from my mouth, hot and forceful. "What the hell were you trying to prove? That I can't rely on my computer skills when shit hits the fan? Trust me, you've hammered that point over and over and over. *I get it."*

"The point I was trying to prove is that things don't always go the way you want them to," said Winsor, refusing to rise from his chair. "You have to roll with the punches. Be ready for anything."

"Including purposeful sabotage by your own mentor?"

"It could've been worse, kid. Imagine if you'd been in the rideshare with Francesca when that happened."

I lost it, kicking an empty chair to the ground as my rage boiled over. *"God damnit, Winsor!* You're an asshole. I can't believe I've had to put up with this bullshit for the past three and a half months. I've worked my *ass* off. I've read every text you've given me, completed every exercise, picked locks, soldered circuit boards, learned how to read people's facial expressions, how to control my breathing, where to look when I'm crossing a street or buying a coffee, how to stand to best shift my weight in the event of a sudden attack. I even learned how to use a sewing machine and apply makeup, for god's sake. And it's never enough! You always find some way to demean me. Some way to twist the knife and turn my success into defeat. To tell me I've done a shit job, even though you know it's not true. It's why you kept making our tracking sessions harder. Why you kept piling more on my plate, kept asking the impossible. Not because you thought it would make me a better spy, but because it gives you some sort of *sick pleasure."*

"Settle down, kid. It does give me pleasure, but not a sick one."

"Like I'm supposed to believe that given the way you've treated me? Give me a damn break. Yes, I know I barged into your life, upended your sweet existence of ignoring your cats and getting angry watching the news, but don't pretend you haven't loved it. That you haven't relished being back in the game, being useful again, having someone, *anyone* that cared about you, even if only in a small, passing way. I brought you out of your self-imposed miserable existence. You know it, and yet this is how you show it. You're pathetic."

Winsor stood. "Seriously Ambrose, shut up, okay? You did it."

As far as I could remember, it was the first time he'd ever called me by my name. "Did *what?*"

"You gained Francesca's confidence. You made the right choice in terminating the relationship when you did. You kept your cool, escaped the sabotaged rideshare I set up for you, and managed to disappear into the night without a trace, based on the police scanners I've been keeping tabs on. So, yeah. You did it. You passed the final test. You're done. You've learned everything you can from me."

I squinted, unable to comprehend what I was hearing. "Are you screwing with me?"

"I'm fudging a bit. Obviously, there's more I could teach you, but you'd start to run into diminishing returns. I'd say you've absorbed about eighty-five percent and all of the important stuff."

The rage left me, hot air being let out of a balloon. "So what now?"

"Now it's time to move on."

I breathed a sigh of relief. "It's about time. I can finally message Marina to tell her you'll be joining us."

Winsor cocked his head. "I'm not going anywhere. I'm talking about you."

"I'm not leaving without you. I told Marina I'd bring you in. I gave her my word."

"Look, kid, just because you've learned most of what you can from *me* doesn't mean your training is over. It simply means you're ready to move on to the next stage. Remember when I told you you were at level zero? Now you're maybe at a four. Out of ten. There's a world of knowledge out there for you to acquire. Literally."

"As refreshing as it is that you're back to insulting me, I'm not sure I follow."

"Marina sent you to me for two reasons, correct? To learn to be a successful espionage agent and to learn how to recruit others to your cause. You've got a good grasp on the first part, but you haven't done jack squat about the second. And I can't teach how to do that part. I can only tell you what worked for me."

"Which was?"

Winsor approached me, his face intense. "You have to get out there, Ambrose. You have to talk to people. See the world through their eyes, feel it through their fingers. Experience what they're going through. Tell me. Why do you fight for the resistance?"

"Didn't we go over this when we first met? Because USC's chokehold on Mars is an injustice. It's the right thing to do."

Winsor waved me off. "That's the academic answer. The ten thousand kilometer view. Someone somewhere is always fighting against injustice. How does it affect you personally? What's *your* story? What drives *you*? What brought *you* here?"

"You know that as well. I came here as a soldier, but USC bombed my country. They betrayed me and everything I thought they stood for."

"But do you know anyone *else's* story? Why do the people around you fight? More importantly, *why don't more?* Don't tell me it's out of fear or self-preservation. People are always selfish and afraid. It's in our nature, but we're also noble and generous and brave when the circumstances dictate it. Perhaps most importantly, why should they listen to *you* about whether or not they should care?"

I stood there, more unsure of myself than I'd been in some time. For all the days spent hacking USC servers and poring through classified information, for all the nights spent huddled underground, my fingers chilled to the bone as I planned sabotage missions with Cal and Lauren and the others, I'd never stopped to consider what exactly my role in it all was. "I don't know."

Winsor clapped me on the shoulder. "You can't convince someone of something if you don't understand their motivations. If you don't understand their hopes and fears. That's what you're lacking, kid. It's time for you to go meet the people you're fighting for, and for you to come to grips with your own motivations along the way."

"Something tells me you have an idea about how I should do that."

"To an extent, but this isn't an exercise like the ones I've put you through. This will primarily be up to you. You'll need to travel far and wide. Meet people. Talk to them. Listen to them. Blend in with them. When they're ready, they'll speak their own personal truths to you, and in turn you'll spread the word. I can't help with any of that, but I can provide suggestions for where you might start. Places for you to visit. Professions for you to engage in. I have one lined up already, but I'll have to work on others to keep you moving. To keep you learning from new social groups. Ideally, you'll never stay in one spot for more than a couple months."

I blinked, still not totally sure of the direction into which the conversation had swerved. "What about you?"

"This isn't my fight. It hasn't been in nearly a decade. Besides, I haven't exactly aged gracefully. You know what I've turned into. The movement's passed me by. For better or worse, Mars's future is in the hands of you and your compatriots now. Try not to let everyone down."

Winsor headed toward the exit.

"We could still use you," I called. "Not as the face of the revolution, but you'd still have a place."

The old man paused at the door, but he didn't look back. "Get some sleep, kid. Take the day off tomorrow. You should head out the morning after."

I SHOULD'VE TAKEN Salt's advice, but I couldn't sleep. I was too distraught over how I'd ended the night with Francesca, too wired from my escape from the rideshare, and too confused over my confrontation with Winsor.

There were questions I'd wanted to ask him. How had he controlled the rideshare? Had he doctored the onboard AI, or was he controlling the car remotely? With enough time, I could discover the answers, either by hacking the rideshare company's mainframes or by sifting through Salt's personal data, but I wasn't sure how much it mattered. Either way, he'd risked my life, put me within centimeters of a deadly collision as part of an exercise that, quite frankly, he hadn't fully prepared me for and wasn't particularity well thought out to begin with.

I wasn't a stranger to dangerous simulations. I'd taken part in several during my USC marine corps training, but there'd always been a purpose. The risks had been understood from the beginning. Salt had claimed the *lack* of preparation was crucial to the exercise, but he'd nonetheless risked my life to determine my readiness.

Which made his fatherly pride over my success all the more confusing.

I sat in one of the salon chairs, thinking about what he'd told me. About needing to learn more about myself and the people I'd chosen to fight for. About the fact that he didn't want to be a part of the revolution anymore, instead preferring to linger in quiet solitude. About the fact that he'd been willing to kill me, despite the fact that he'd grown to care about me. And I thought about the rules of the resistance.

Rule number three. Protect the movement at all costs, even if it threatens your personal safety. Salt had taken it one step further. Even though he didn't see himself as part of the resistance anymore, he'd risked the well-being of someone he viewed as the movement's future leadership to ensure the movement's larger continued viability.

It may not have been the lesson he'd intended to teach, but I learned it nonetheless.

I checked the time. Past three, but I wasn't tired. Instead, I got up, unlocked the cabinet with the bleach and the nail polish, and got to work.

32

A THICK CLOUD of dust whipped past the rideshare's window, obscuring everything more than a half-meter from the aluminum and glass shell, but the car didn't swerve, nor did the tires screech. Not for the first time, I wondered at the bravado and stupidity of humans who'd driven vehicles in similar weather back in the days when machines weren't capable of the same, trusting their eyes instead of electromagnetic signals that wouldn't be blocked by free-floating suspensions of fine particles. Perhaps they'd felt that taking their lives in their own hands still beat the prospect of walking in such a storm. Based upon how few of the Mukt walked the streets of New Chennai at the moment, perhaps the sentiment still stood.

With the wind howling, sweeping across the smooth, aerodynamic lines of the cab, I made a call.

Sophia answered after the third ring, her voice the same combination of sultry and playful that I so sorely missed. "Look who the cat dragged in."

"More like who the cat dragged *out*. Or who I dragged out. Myself. Whatever. I'm not good with mixed metaphors. The point is I'd rather be indoors."

"You, too, huh? The local atmospheric forecast called for

sustained sixty kilometer an hour winds, with gusts of up to a hundred and ten. Same there?"

I peered into the swirling dust. "Worse, I'd say. I'm wondering if I can effectively conduct a stake out from the confines of this rideshare."

Sophia snorted. "And here I thought you were actually in the thick of it, with the winds plunging down the neckline of your poorly secured parka."

"If only. I'm not even wearing a shirt. Just slippers, underwear, and a breathing mask. I've got to prove my masculinity."

Sophia made a moan of pleasure. "Well, the breathing mask and shoes part is a little weird, but I do like the thought of you without a shirt. I could go along with it."

I sighed, thinking I shouldn't have led her along that path. Now both our minds were occupied with desires we wouldn't be able to address. "Are you out and about as well?"

"No. At home," said Sophia. "Getting some work done."

"What sort of work?"

"Funny you should ask. I was doing a bit of investigating on your behalf." I could picture the flick of her eyebrow and the sly smile she'd give me.

"I didn't ask you to investigate anything for me."

"I'm an independent woman, Ambrose. I don't need your approval to go out, or sign a new lease, or dive into an investigation."

"You signed a new lease?"

"Bad choice of examples. But you're missing the point, which is that once I sunk my teeth into chasing Fabia's coat, I got a taste for it that's been hard to shake. I've been searching for her ever since, despite the fact that you told me you'd do it yourself."

I took a slow breath to make sure I didn't respond in a way I'd regret. "I hope you've been discreet."

"Of course I have. Is that your worry? That I involved someone else?"

"Mostly, yes. Privacy is security."

"So you're not mad that I didn't tell you about it?"

"I'd rather you would've told me, sure. I don't think there's any reason for us to be dishonest to each other about anything. But I trust you. I wouldn't have shared everything about my past and Fabia and my cases if I didn't."

Sophia sighed. "I know. I didn't mean to keep it from you, but in my defense it didn't start as a full blown investigation. I just kept thinking about how to find her and it morphed into a project over time."

"I'm not mad, Sophia, but I might be if you don't tell me what you found."

"Right. I'll cut to the chase. I'm pretty sure Fabia is in Utopia."

I blinked. "Okay. I never spotted her on the Utopia vactrain security feeds, but I'll bite. How do you figure it?"

"Because there was a break in at a water purification facility there two nights ago."

I sat up in my seat. "There was?"

"That's right. Police didn't find any evidence of wrongdoing, or at least none that they released to the public. I'm basing my guess on a gut instinct that Fabia would've kept investigating the ice theft business you uncovered during your Snow Leopard case. Chances are she and her father stumbled upon it at a similar juncture as you did."

I nodded. "It's not a bad assumption. She'd be as keen to know if USC is robbing the people of Mars as I am. More so, because she'd be the sort to tailor that knowledge into a campaign to recruit people to her side. How'd you find out about it?"

"Police reports."

"*Police reports?*"

"They're public record. You of all people should know that."

"That's not what I meant. I'm surprised you're trolling those. You really got sucked in, didn't you?"

I pictured Sophia rolling her eyes. "What can I say? My romance novels weren't cutting it."

"Do you have any evidence it might've been Fabia?"

"Not yet. I've looked through all the reports. Given how Fabia works, none of the other recent incidents around Utopia strike me as something she would've dipped her toes in. And given that I still haven't been taught the basics of hacking and espionage..."

"Sorry about that. I've had a lot of my plate." A call sounded in my mind. "Speaking of which, looks like I've got more incoming. I've got another call I have to take."

Sophia snorted. "I'd say I have perfect timing, but you're the one who always calls me when you're supposed to be working."

"Problem is I'm always working. I'll talk to you later. And Sophia? Good work. I'm impressed—as always."

"Thanks, love. Till next time."

I hung up and switched over just in time to catch the incoming call. "Trinh. How are you doing today?"

Trinh Pham was a coroner for the Elysium Police Department and one of the best I'd ever worked with. She wasn't the most amiable of colleagues at times, but I was nonetheless surprised with the tone she took with me. *"Detective Drake.* I thought I'd be free of you once you left homicide. You're a real piece of work, you know that?"

"It's Agent Drake now, and I'm sorry I didn't pick up sooner. I was on another call."

"You think I'm upset because you kept me waiting for twenty seconds? What about the fact that I got shepherded onto a train to Utopia, stuffed into a decontamination suit, and told not to come out until I figured out what killed three people in quarantined caskets?"

After the bureaucratic red tape I'd faced battling Captain

Henderson's inability to get coroners assigned to the dead diplomats, I'd called an audible. Literally. I'd called the Inspector General and told him we needed to get the bodies analyzed as soon as possible, preferably by someone who knew what they were doing. I might've dropped a name.

"I apologize for the treatment you've received," I said. "Sounds like Hazmat hasn't provided you with the resources, rest, and respect you deserve. But I figured you'd be eager to figure out what killed those poor individuals. We're facing a medical mystery here, Trinh."

"Buttering someone up works better if you do it *before* you screw them over."

"Fair enough. I should've given you a heads up that we'd need your expertise, but I knew that as much as the trip might've interfered with your schedule, this would be the kind of case to pique your curiosity. And I also know you wouldn't be calling me without results to share."

"Correct on both counts, much as I hate to admit it," said Pham. "But, yes, after four days of intensive work, I've completed my examinations. I have to agree with the assessment the Hazmat physicians came to. The three victims didn't die of an infectious disease, poison, drug, or chemical overdose."

My brow furrowed. "You're kidding. So what killed them?"

"The official answer is cardiac arrest. The unofficial answer is I have no clue. Something weird."

"Trinh, you're not inspiring a lot of confidence at the moment."

"That's because I've never encountered the precise conditions that seem to have led to the ambassadors' deaths."

I felt a ray of hope. "So you *do* know what killed them?"

"Not exactly. The term cardiac arrest, otherwise known as sudden cardiac death, is a catch-all for any mechanism that causes a sudden loss of blood flow stemming from the heart's inability to pump. It can be caused by any number of factors, the most common of which is coronary artery disease, which is the buildup of fatty tissues leading to high-grade stenosis or narrowing of the major cardiac arteries, but there are other possible causes as well. Structural heart diseases such as cardiomyopathy or myocarditis, arrhythmias, or even non-cardiac causes such as those stemming from trauma. Aortic rupture or intracranial hemorrhage, for example. Overdoses can also cause them."

"Given that all three diplomats presumably died from the same mechanism, I would have to assume that last one would be the obvious culprit."

"That would make sense, and in the course of completing my autopsies, I found something the USC doctors hadn't. Injection sites on all three of the deceased. Between the toes. Easy to miss, and very sneaky on behalf of the individual who injected them."

"So it was an overdose."

"Perhaps. The problem with that line of thought is that the toxicology reports didn't find anything other than the traces of synflurane you already know about. I even reran the tox screens myself and got the same results. It's as if the individuals were injected with... I don't know. Saline?"

"So what caused the cardiac arrest?"

"That's the interesting part. I'm not sure. I started out exploring the pericardial cavity. I checked the anatomy of the great arteries and opened the pulmonary artery in situ to identify any emboli—which I found, but none that should've caused an arrest. Then I transected the arteries three centimeters above the aortic and pulmonary valves and—"

"Trinh. I'm not a doctor. You don't need to give me the full blow by blow. I'm assuming the point you're getting at is that you're confident they died of cardiac arrest, perhaps drug-induced, but you're not exactly sure what caused it."

I detected a hint of annoyance when she responded. "Essentially, yes. But I did find *something*."

"What sort of something?"

"It'll be easier to explain with a visual aid. I'm sending you an image."

A message popped up in my inbox. I didn't open it right away. "Is this going to be some gross picture of a dissected heart?"

"A dissected brain, actually. Technically, a close up of the basilar artery."

"And that is?"

"The artery that supplies blood to the brain stem, obviously."

Obviously. I steeled myself and opened the message. It wasn't as gross as I'd feared, just a magnified cross-section of an artery surrounded by waxy grey matter. "Walk me through what I'm staring at."

"You see that dark streak along the interior edge of the artery?"

I saw it. "What is that? Plaque?"

"If you mean atheromatous plaque, no. That's usually yellow in color. That, Agent Drake, is graphite."

"Graphite?"

"That's right. I found trace deposits along the arteries of all three victims, and not just in the basilar artery. I also found it in the superior, anterior, and posterior cerebral arteries."

"Which means what, exactly?"

"Hell if I know, Drake," said Pham. "I've never seen it before in my life."

33

JUNE 20, 2158

I CAUGHT the vactrain line going east, taking it through the high altitude plains, Daedalia, Syrai, Sinai, Solis, and back down through Thaumasia, before eventually hopping off at the transfer station near Hale crater. While the overwhelming majority of passenger traffic followed the main line, primarily along the section connecting Isidis, Utopia, and Elysium in the afterlife triangle, freight traffic wasn't so limited by geography. It travelled wherever rails existed, and it had been the driving reason to establish the north-south line connecting the settlements south of Hale Crater in the Argyre Planitia with the ones to the north in the Margaritifer Terra.

While there were undoubtedly opportunities to be had in mining and manufacturing in the Argyre settlements, I took a train headed north. It shot along its evacuated line, weaving ever lower through the pock-marked plains and into the chaos—literally. The motley jumble of mesas, buttes, and hills, divided by ancient flood plains and alluvial fans, had been referred to since the twentieth century as chaos terrain. But in chaos there was beauty. The jagged peaks and crevices, rust-red, deep, and raw despite hundreds of millions of years of weathering, reminded me of the majesty of the

Grand Canyon but on a grander scale. Instead of one canyon there were dozens, each of them at least as spectacular as Earth's greatest river worn trench, and my route along the rails didn't take me anywhere close to the two hundred kilometer wide Valles Marineris further west.

I couldn't tear my eyes from the windows as we zipped along, marveling at the sterile devastation, but it wasn't long before the first of the settlements appeared amongst the valleys. Nestled among the boulders and jagged rock walls, the long, squat buildings and drilling rigs seemed out of place, but no one had brought the equipment and built the vactrain line to Margaritifer out of charity. A wealth of riches slumbered underground. Not gold and gemstones, but ice, left behind hundreds of millions of years ago after the floods and glaciers had long vanished from the surface.

Subsurface ice wasn't a rarity. It existed all over Mars, but most communities delivered as much as they could process to their citizens and used the rest to humidify the air. Whatever industry needed, they had to pay a hefty premium for. Better instead to extract it themselves, hence the grow farms of the Margaritifer Terra.

I exited the train at an outpost by the name of Aureum, but my journey wasn't over. A painfully-slow overland transport owned by the Beornson AG corporation crawled through the jagged terrain, carrying me in its belly before spitting me out at a cluster of warehouses and wells known only as 52A. Reginaldo met me once I'd stepped through the airlocks and changed out of my Suit, a young man with dark hair and a scraggly beard who treated me with equal amounts of respect and indifference. He gave my hand a shake and tipped his head for me to follow him.

Winsor hadn't told me who Reginaldo was or even if the man had any connection to the resistance, only that he'd be my contact upon arrival and would show me the ropes. He'd nodded as I told him my story, that of an out of luck immigrant looking for any work

I could get after my previous employer shuttered his doors in the wake of dwindling sales. It was a common enough story in the current climate, but Reginaldo nonetheless seemed sympathetic to my tale. Perhaps he'd been in a similar situation once upon a time.

There wasn't enough time the first day to do anything more than assign me a bunk and a corporate account, but we started early the next morning in the command center attached to the almond grove. He walked me through the software that controlled the irrigation and fertilizer schedules, showed me the atmospheric modulator, and explained how to manually control the system in the event that the tree shakers and nut sweepers ran into a problem their AI couldn't handle, such as a downed limb. I nodded through it all, pretending like I was following along when in fact I could've rewritten the entire system from scratch to run more efficiently. Reginaldo seemed pleased with my tech knowledge, but I could tell from the look on his face that he didn't have a lot of faith in my ability to do the manual labor.

After all, not every crop was as automated as the almonds. In the apple orchards, Reginaldo instructed me on the use of the fruit vacuum, which I'd never before seen much less used, but given that I was a competent driver and adept with smaller, handheld vacuums, I picked it up in a hurry. From there, he walked me through picking raspberries, strawberries, asparagus, and other produce that Beornson AG hadn't yet developed a quality mechanical picker for, but I think I surprised him there, too. I worked quickly and efficiently, remembering how to keep the berries and shoots from bruising as I'd been taught in the underground vertical farms of the resistance working under the steady hand of Castleton Fox.

Through it all, Reginaldo nodded and smiled his approval, no doubt happy his friend of a friend hadn't sent a worthless meat bag his way begging for work. He'd given me his stamp of approval at the end of the day and sent me on my way, whereupon I'd returned to my bunk and slept as much as I could, still train-lagged from my journey. I rose bright and early the next day though, picking fruit, emptying the leaf hampers from the sorters into the compost bins, and checking the harvest volumes in real time via Net.

The work was mindless and taxing, but I didn't totally mind it. There was a closeness with nature associated with farming that was hard to achieve any other way on Mars. Nonetheless, when the clock struck six I happily stumbled toward the company cafeteria for my evening meal. Reginaldo was there, once again smiling and nodding his approval, likely more at the fact that I'd met the harvesting quotas rather than anything he'd observed. I gave him a wave as I took a seat at an empty table, but he motioned me over, directing me to a chair next to him and a group of his friends.

I met a half-dozen of them that meal. Wilson, Esmeralda, Nganye, Florence, Taylor, and a heavyset, perpetually happy fellow who went by the name Bowser. I learned some of their backstories that night. Esmeralda had grown up poor as a Martian dust farmer, with only a single Suit to her family of nine's name. Taylor had left Isidis after a rocky end to a marriage, having bought a one-way ticket out of town that ultimately left her high and dry in Hale. And Bowser? He didn't tell me much about his life, but he cracked about two dozen jokes, a quarter of which were acceptable for polite company.

I shared my story, too, but I didn't go into detail. Instead, I did what Winsor had asked of me. I listened. I engaged in conversation, but not with specific motivations in mind. Mostly I learned. I learned the stories of the people around me. I learned what made them happy (their friends and lovers), what made them angry (low wages, corporate indifference, government interference), what made them sad (death, the news, diets in Bowser's case), and what made them frustrated (all of the above). I took all that knowledge in. I incorporated it into my world view, used it to grow, to gain empathy for my fellow man and a better understanding of the world around me. As I did so, my feelings about

Mars, USC, and the resistance shifted from the academic to the personal.

When Winsor's message arrived two months later, instructing me to head to a remote weather outpost at the southern tip of the subsidiary vactrain line serving the Terra Sirenum, it caught me off guard. I didn't want to leave, but more importantly, I couldn't. I hadn't spread the message yet, even if I'd sowed seeds of doubt into the minds of Reginaldo and his friends.

I did the next best thing. I left them a message, hinting at who I really was, why I'd been there, and urging them to keep vigilant. To be there when their homeland needed them. And I disappeared into the night.

34

JUNE 25, 2179

AS IT TURNED OUT, I wasn't able to conduct a stakeout from the confines of my rideshare, which was a disappointment on multiple levels. Not only did it mean I had to brave the cold Martians winds, albeit briefly, but I'd also miss the inevitable look of horror from someone in Counterterrorism billing when they confronted me with the rideshare tab.

Luckily, my stakeout didn't involve a lot of time spent outdoors. I'd travelled to the apartment of Vikram Nandi, the address taken from the rolls of the New Chennai Medical Center employee database, but it wasn't long after I'd set up a hidden microcam in the hall outside his place that someone came out of his apartment. Four someones, in fact. A family, the patriarch of which was decidedly not Vikram. I double checked the public records database, and unsurprisingly, Vikram *wasn't* listed as the occupant of 1505 Hebatpur Drive, Apartment 12C. In fact, the address he had on file was that of a dorm room at Raman College, which I suspected hadn't been updated in over a decade. Of course, the public records database was based on tax records, and something told me Vikram was as adept at avoiding capture by the tax man as he was at avoiding capture by everyone else. Upon doing a reverse search on the address at Hebatpur Drive, I found a much newer listing for Apartment 12C. That of the Saha family, who'd moved in six months prior.

Still, the fact that they'd moved in so recently gave me hope Vikram hadn't lied about his address on his hospital employment application. If he'd lived in the apartment at all, even only for a few months, I could use that to find him. Tracking him wouldn't be easy, though. The profile of Vikram I'd compiled suggested he was a loner. I doubted he would've spoken to his neighbors except for the occasional greeting in the hallway, much less left a forwarding address. Though he might've left something in his apartment to suggest where he'd run off to, I doubted it. In every interaction of his that I'd studied, with Salman, the hotel security systems, and the hospital, Vikram had shown an abundance of caution. He'd be disciplined enough to erase his tracks before leaving.

Still, the fact that he'd presumably dosed USC diplomats with a mysterious, deadly toxin suggested he was still in town. I needed to find him, so I used another public records database to look up the owner of the Hebatpur Drive apartment complex. Although I'd intended to contact the landlord to ask them to put me in touch with the building manager, a quick glance at the facility's online listing told me they were one and the same. Said manager also lived quite close to the complex, as would be expected of someone who'd have to put out fires at the drop of a tenant's hat.

I took a rideshare to the new complex and headed to the seventh floor. The landlord's building was nicer than the one in which her tenants lived but still about six steps shy of luxurious. Perhaps the landlord was a leaser rather than an owner, and the rents from the tenants barely covered the payments to the builder. That or the landlord was abnormally stingy. It wouldn't surprise me. Wealthy people had their fair share of eccentricities.

I pressed the buzzer on the intercom outside the landlord's

apartment and waited. I had to push it a second time before anyone responded. "Yes? Who is it?"

The voice sounded tired and apathetic. I wasn't sure if that would make my job easier or more difficult. "Excuse me. Divya Anagal? The name is Ambrose Drake. I'm with ESG Collection Services. I was wondering if I could have a moment of your time?"

"*Collections?*" The disgust was palpable.

"Yes, ma'am. I'm trying to collect on a past due debt on the part of one of your tenants. I was wondering if you might be able to help me locate them."

"Oh. Just a moment."

The intercom went silent. About fifteen seconds later the door cracked open. The woman who stood in its wake was on the receding end of middle age, with a few deep creases in her forehead and streaks of grey through her otherwise jet black hair. She wore pink slippers with a matching pink micro fleece robe that hung to just below her knees, and she reeked of strawberry scented vapor stimulants.

She nodded at me without smiling. "So. Who owes you? Because if it's someone who's behind on rent, I'll be collecting first."

"No fear of that," I said. "Unless I'm mistaken, I'm looking for a former tenant of yours. Vikram Nandi?"

"Oh. *Nandi.* Good luck getting your money out of him."

"What's that supposed to mean? Was he a problem?"

"You could say that." The woman nodded at me. "Want to come in?"

My nose wrinkled in disgust at the idea. "Sure. I'd love to."

I stepped into her den, breathing shallowly to mitigate the wave of fake-strawberry scented revulsion. I told myself I simply had to weather the storm for a minute or two. The body has a way of processing out pervasive background stimuli once it adjusts.

Divya waved me toward a couch that overlooked the scenic

dust-filled alleyway next to her complex. "Have a seat. You want a drink?"

She headed into the adjacent kitchen without waiting for my response. Good lord, was the woman hitting on me? "No thank you, Ms. Anagal. Now, about Mr. Nandi?"

Divya plucked a lowball glass off a low-hanging shelf, snagged a bottle of what appeared to be cognac from the counter, and begun pouring the deep amber liquid into the glass. "I knew he'd be a problem from the start. Had that look to him, you know? Untrustworthy. Never should've rented to him."

Her musings sounded like the bitter ramblings of someone who'd been snookered rather than actual foresight. "Did he fail to pay you?"

Divya plugged the bottle and slid it back into place, swirling her glass as she brought it into the living room. At least she hadn't poured a second. "No. He always paid me, though he'd wait until the bill was past due. There's a grace period built into the contract, and he'd wait until the last day to send me the money, every month without fail. But that's not why he was a bad tenant. It was the mess he left behind when he moved out. Why haven't you had a seat yet?" She collapsed into the cushions and patted the spot next to her.

I stood at the edge of the couch. The honest answer wouldn't have gone over well, so I bit the bullet and sat. "I take it the man didn't get his security deposit back?"

"Are you kidding? The place *reeked*. I had to have a professional crew steam clean it before I could rent it to the next family."

The irony of her statement was lost on her. "Was he a cat owner?"

"It wasn't pets. That I can handle. This was a whole other level of funk. I don't even know how to describe it. A chemical smell. Pungent and sour at the same time. Goodness knows what he was up to in there. I hope he wasn't making drugs."

I wish I knew what he'd been up to as well. "Did he leave any equipment behind?"

"No. Place was cleaned out when he left. Only the smell remained. Why? Hoping you could impound his belongings and sell them off?"

I forced a smile. "I had to ask. I suppose you would've already done the same if he'd left anything."

Divya swallowed half her brandy in a single gulp. "I know a guy who buys in bulk. It would've been gone by ten A.M. the morning after his lease expired."

I figured I'd played along for long enough. "Do you have any idea where he moved? My employer would love to collect on his debt."

Divya tipped back her glass. The second half of her brandy disappeared with as little fanfare as the first. "Wish I could say, but he didn't tell me a thing. Sorry. Sure you don't want a drink?"

I held up a hand. "I appreciate the offer, but I'll pass. What about his rent? How did he pay for the apartment?"

"Direct deposit, same as everyone else."

"Do you know what financial institution he used?"

Divya lifted an eyebrow. "Why? You think you can squeeze his bank to get them to release to you whatever he owes? You haven't been in collections long, have you?"

"I don't expect them to comply with a polite request to hand over his rupals, but it would give my employer another legal avenue to pursue. If nothing else, it would provide me another institution that might have his current address on file."

"And you're going to shake him down if you find him?"

I smiled. This time I didn't have to force it. "If I do find him, I'd be happy to share his forwarding address with you. I have to imagine his security deposit didn't cover the full cost of that steam cleaning."

Divya snorted. "It didn't. Give me a moment while I check my bank records."

I nodded, the fake strawberry stimulant smell finally fading. "By all means. Take your time."

35

JULY 1, 2159

THE BUILDING at 1800 Marsden Avenue appeared complete, so long as you didn't look up. Its gleaming side panels had been fitted into place and sealed, creating the airtight barrier necessary for any building in Isidis to pass code, but if one's eyes were to drift skyward, you'd notice that above the line where the pressure layer melded into the side of the panels, nothing but bones existed. Shiny I-beams, bolted together with high shear superalloy nuts, reaching toward the heavens, glistening in the morning sun.

I walked through the front doors and headed across the vast swath of unfinished, dusty floor toward the elevators in back, the cars encased in the same pressure-sealed panels as the ones on the building exterior. Heavy vacuum pumps hummed next to the gleaming columns, constantly pulling and pushing gas back into the shafts as workers took the cars through the airlock above the third floor to the upper levels. I passed under a bundle of wires hanging from the ceiling and made my way into the only semi-finished space in the entire building—the changing room.

Yerzhan Marlenov sat in front of his locker flicking at his tablet, his Suit on the bench beside him. I'm not sure he noticed me enter.

"Morning, Yer," I said as I popped open my locker.

He glanced up. "Morning, Jordan."

I pulled my own Suit and worked my way into it. Yer mostly ignored me, his forehead a mess of furrows as he stared at his tablet. He sighed heavily.

"You doing alright there?" I asked.

He flicked his tablet off. "It's nothing."

I shrugged into the Suit's arms, pulling on the fabric to set it in place. "Doesn't sound like nothing."

"Well. Maybe it's not." Yer picked up his Suit, but he didn't don it.

I gave him a moment. Over the past two and a half months, I'd come to learn Yer didn't appreciate intrusions into his personal life. If he wanted to elaborate, he'd do so on his own terms.

I finished getting my Suit into place while Yer sat there, his eyes drilling a hole into the floor. I pulled my helmet and bag with my welding gun, feed unit, wire, and a small tank of compressed shielding gas from my locker. Luckily, the electrical crews had already brought power to the floors we were working on.

"So... I'll see you up there?"

Yer didn't look at me. "You watch the news?"

"Ah. Now I understand." I left my helmet and tool bag where they were and sat next to Yer. "To be honest, sometimes it's better *not* to watch it."

Yer rolled his eyes. "Trust me, I know. Maybe if we lived in the wastes it would be easier to avoid, but here? I don't have to check my tablet, I can just look out a window to see what's wrong. Three hundred protestors. That's how many were arrested at the rally outside USC's corporate offices. Over a dozen injured with an unknown number dead, which probably means a dozen dead and at least five times as many injured. You know how the media is. They're probably controlled by the government, too."

I didn't want to get into *that* particular conversation. "I think the reports are accurate enough. They're bad either way."

"And if only that were it," said Yer. "Seems like every day I get a message from some long lost cousin or friend of a friend looking for a place to stay or a lead on a job or a handout. Tell you what, not a day goes by I'm not grateful for this job. Not only that I have it, but that I make a decent wage—thanks in part to you."

"I barely did anything. You had the will to unionize before I showed up, you just needed a shove in the right direction. It could've worked out poorly. Thankfully it didn't. We got some of what we wanted. Enough to keep us going for the time being."

The locker room intercom crackled and spat, squawking in a harsh voice. "Marlenov. Fletcher. Get your asses up to the eighty-first. You think those girders are going to weld themselves?"

Yer grunted as he cast a sour glance toward the camera. "Didn't get *everything* we wanted, that's for damn sure. Freaking Thompson. *I hate Earthers...*"

"Dude."

Yer grunted. "Right. Sorry. You know I think of you as an honorary Martian. Though to be fair, if you were foreman, I'd probably hate you, too. Never met a foreman I didn't despise."

"*Honorary Martian?* That's probably the nicest insult you've ever called me."

Yer put up his fists, and I danced back. We both chuckled, getting a kick out of our routine.

Thompson's voice came back over the PA. "I'm waiting."

Yer swore and threw on his Suit. We fastened our helmets and breathing packs into place, snagged our tool bags, and headed toward the elevator.

Yer's voice crackled in my ear as we waited for the car to recompress. My Net indicated it was on a private channel. "Seriously, though, Jordan, I appreciated your voice during the negotiations. You've got a way with words. People listen to you, man."

The elevator puffed. The doors opened, and Yer and I stepped inside. When the doors closed, the pumps restarted, humming and vibrating the entire car. It was just the two of us, surrounded by rapidly thinning air and the hiss that went along with it. I thought about Yer's creased face, staring at his tablet. The fact that he'd chosen to speak to me about what was on his mind. I suspected it was time.

"Would *you* listen to me if I told you something?"

"Of course. What's going on?"

I double checked the privacy settings on our Suits. "The protestors. The ones who were arrested. Do you think they were doing the right thing?"

"Right for themselves, or right for everyone else?"

The whine of the pumps died as the last of the air left the elevator. "Obviously, it's not in their best interests to get arrested, Yer. I'm talking about the cause they're fighting for. The rights and concessions they want."

"Jordan, I dislike USC as much as the next guy, but... I don't know. I guess I don't see the point. Yelling, raging, throwing stones. It makes you a target. Better to keep your head down and work harder. Focus on your own life, your own family."

"But in a vacuum—a metaphorical one, not this one. What then? Whose side would you be on?"

"There's no vacuum needed. I'm on the side of the protestors. USC can take a one way booster to the dark side of Pluto for all I care, but there's nothing I can do to get them on it."

The car lurched into motion. "What if there was?"

A long pause filled my helmet. Eventually Yer spoke. "What do you mean?"

"You say people listen to me, Yer, but you're the union rep. You've got the ear of the other workers."

"They're not going to lead a march because I ask them to. Besides, I told you it's pointless. There's nothing we can do against a behemoth like USC."

"I'm not suggesting you lead a march, Yer. There are other ways to resist."

More silence as the service elevator rose, the display showing the approximate floor.

"Resist how?" asked Yer.

"USC is the most powerful corporation in the history of mankind, but that doesn't mean they're invincible. They're only as strong as the pillars that support them. We don't work for them, but when they need construction, they come to *us*. We have a choice of whether or not to say yes."

"We don't have the luxury of turning down projects, Jordan, not in this economy."

I wanted to say that he had it all wrong, that those with skills could dictate their employers, not the other way around, but I didn't think it would play well with Yerzhan. "Projects don't have to be dismissed. There are other ways to resist. Delays. Labor disputes. Poor construction. Materials shortages. Rebuilds."

The numbers on the display ticked toward eighty. "You've been thinking about this for a while, haven't you?"

"I wont lie to you. It's on my mind. A lot. Because the fact of the matter is I care. I care about Mars, Yer. I care about you and Smithy and Kelsey, about Wicker and Mustapha, about everybody we work with. I want things to get better, but they won't unless *we* make it better. Progress doesn't happen as a matter of course. It only occurs when passionate, dedicated individuals commit to making it happen."

The display flashed eighty-one, and the doors opened. Yer and I stepped into a stiff breeze, clipping ourselves onto the safety systems attached to the bare girders. I glanced across the expanse of Isidis, the sun's glare turning the Mylamene-covered streets into rivers of molten plastic. My eyes trailed to the edge of the temporary flooring, and even now, after two and a half months, I felt a flicker of fear at the thought of the safeties failing.

"I said you had a way with words, Jordan," said Yer through the intercom. "Didn't realize how right I was."

"That doesn't tell me a lot about what you're thinking."

Yer clapped me on the shoulder. "It means I feel the same way you do. I don't think I'm quite as idealistic, but still. Now what do you say we get some welding done?"

I hefted my bag. "Point me in the right direction."

Yer did just that. As I settled down, perched on the edge of a metal skeleton with the world open before me, I got a message via Net.

It was from Winsor. *Time to move, kid. Got a new assignment for you.*

I vaguely wondered if the man had impeccable timing or was still spying on me, but I actually had a good idea of which of the two it was. Either way, I didn't respond right away. I'd move, sure. I always did, continuing to spread the word. But my work here wasn't done. I needed more time.

36

JULY 1, 2179

I SAT IN A RIDESHARE, parked at the side of the road while the occasional heavy truck rumbled by. The building across the street from me was a mixed-use commercial complex with a fifty percent occupancy rate, which wasn't surprising given the structure's proximity to New Chennai's industrial sector. From tax records, it appeared the owner had tried to sell the building to a plastics manufacturer seven years ago, but the deal had fallen through after a survey of the property revealed issues with the underlying soils. Still, the building puttered along, with the businesses within mostly going under every few years, the landlord lowering rents in response, and the entrepreneurs being replaced by new ones with fresh hopes and fewer debts.

Among the newer businesses was a place by the name of Micron Consulting. I'd been alerted to their existence by the tech experts at Counterterrorism. When I'd sent them the bank information provided by Divya Anagal, they'd immediately gone to work unearthing the address associated with Vikram Nandi's account. They'd found it nestled among the bank's servers, but it pointed back to his apartment in Ms. Anagal's complex. However, when accessing his statements, they'd found recurring payments to the commercial building's landlord, made on the behalf of Micron Consulting. Conveniently enough, the payments had begun immediately following his exit from his previous residence. It wasn't proof that he was staying there, but he wouldn't be the first to reside in a shuttered business in the hopes of attracting less attention. I'd spent several months living in a boarded up beauty salon during my apprenticeship under Winsor Salt, after all.

When I'd first received the information from Counterterrorism, I'd discreetly scoped the commercial building out, scanning for RF signals from hidden cameras using my tablet and setting up a few microcams of my own at key locations. Luckily, there was another business on the same floor as Nandi's consulting firm, so even if he'd been watching—which my scans suggested he wasn't—he wouldn't have been able to distinguish me from any other discerning patron of Country Jack Padhi's homemade earthenware jars, one of which now sat on the nightstand of my hotel room. Upon returning to said room last night, I'd watched the security footage from the microcams I'd set up. Sure enough, at about nine P.M. that evening, a man had exited the elevators, walked past Padhi's jar shop, and entered the firm.

I couldn't be a hundred percent sure it was Vikram Nandi who waltzed in, but his face matched the picture in Nandi's employee profile from the New Chennai Medical Center. I counted it as a strike.

The question at that point had been how to proceed. If I'd been in a USC controlled territory, the answer would've been simple. I'd put in the call and USC Counterterrorism teams would swarm the business, take Nandi into custody, and begin the process of interrogating him. But I wasn't in USC territory, and as I'd already discovered, the Mukt government had a frosty relationship with my employer. They wouldn't be willing to do our dirty work for us. If we presented our evidence to them, it was possible they'd take Nandi into custody, but that would first require sharing *all* of our information with them. That meant explaining to them why I'd cracked several of their government and private servers, set up illegal surveillance in multiple edifices, and terrorized and illegally questioned a security guard after breaking into his home. Even if we managed to present Nandi as a threat without disclosing my actions, there was no guarantee the Mukt would decide to take action against the man, not without evidence that he'd committed murder. Given the loose thread connecting him to the diplomats and our inability to identify their cause of death, we didn't have it. Not yet.

So I'd gone to the top and called the Inspector General for guidance on how to proceed. From my meeting with the man, I'd gathered the impression he was disciplined and logical. Once again, he didn't disappoint. After filling him in on the details, he told me what I already believed—that the case work I'd done was top notch but that we didn't have conclusive evidence Nandi had poisoned the three ambassadors. Once we had that evidence, we could take action. USC Counterterrorism wasn't above a clandestine extraction, nor were they above continuing to use me in ways that skirted local laws, but we needed evidence before taking any drastic measures.

Which brought me back to to the commercial complex. I'd had my eyes glued to the microcam feeds for the past three days, taking note of Nandi's entrances and exits from his place of business. Luckily for me, he kept a regular schedule. He went in and out a fair amount in the evenings between the hours of eight and eleven, but he regularly left his business at ten in the morning and didn't return until after seven.

My clock read ten to one. I checked the items in my jacket, silenced my tablet, and opened the door on the rideshare.

Nobody bothered me as I entered the building's fast airlock and headed up the elevators to the fourth floor. The microcams I'd installed in the halls gave me the benefit of surveillance, precluding any need to look over my shoulder for watchful eyes. I needn't have bothered even checking those. Barely a soul perused the wares in Jack Padhi's store, and no one cast a glance at me as I wandered past it to the face of Micron Consulting. I'd done my homework, so the door opened at my touch as the tablet in my pocket sent the digital equivalent of Nandi's thumbprint into the console at the door's side.

I'd clipped my mask to my belt after going through the airlock, but I'd kept my jacket and gloves on. I pushed the door closed behind me with print-free fingers as the motion activated lights flickered on around me.

The place wasn't anything special to look at. The main floor was largely empty, with only a few dusty shelves clustered at the center. I spotted a bed in one corner as well as a desk, a small dining table bookended by a pair of chairs, a couple stand lamps, and a sofa chair situated in front of a holoprojector. A number of plates had been stacked on the table, many of them with dried sauces crusted onto the ceramic, but the place didn't smell as foul as most bachelors pads. It barely held any scent at all other than a faint tickle of artificial lemon cleaner. I strained my ears for sounds of motion, but I failed to detect any. Nonetheless, I kept my muscles coiled, ready to spring at a moment's notice.

I walked past the shelves, noting the floors had been mopped clean despite the general disorder. I treaded softly, checking to make sure my boots weren't leaving prints as I headed toward the living nook. No tablets rested atop the bed or the dining table, so I turned to the holo. I activated it and brought up the menu, looking at the most recently accessed steams. The bulk were politics and news related, though several looked like extremist stuff, their thumbnails full of bold print, outlandish claims, and graphic images. There were a couple scripted streaming services among the fringe content. From looking through them, it appeared Nandi enjoyed the odd baking show alongside his political propaganda.

I flicked the holo off and turned my attention to the closed doors at the side of the room. A restroom sign hung over one. The other had no identification. Neither had a keypad next to them, but when I tested the unmarked door, I found it locked. A glance at the handle revealed the mechanical system that kept it shut.

It had been a while since I'd picked a lock, but I remembered how to do it. I could still hear Winsor's voice when he'd forced me to learn. *A good intelligence agent needs to be able to handle any situation on the fly.* For all his faults, Winsor had been a good mentor.

I had a torsion wrench and a couple picks in a pouch in my interior coat pocket, but the lock looked about as simple as they came. It wouldn't require much finesse to pry open, so I opted for the lowest-skill item in my tool kit: a bump key. I slipped it from my pocket, inserted it into the lock, and gave it a hard whack with the base of my palm. I turned the key as the blow landed, the force of it sending the interior pins flying into their sockets. The lock clicked open without a fight.

I slipped inside, and I knew from the first glimmer of stainless steel and glass that I'd found what I'd been looking for. Jars and vials filled the racks of a converted supply closet, all of them covered with labels listing chemical compositions and concentrations. Materials safety data sheets had been tucked alongside universal pictograms for flammability, corrosivity, and toxicity. Pressurized tanks of gas stood in the corner next to a long desk, one covered with medical and scientific instruments, some of which I was familiar with—an optical microscope, a centrifuge, and an autoclave—and others with which I wasn't, including a polished boxy system that looked like it might be pressurized. Maybe some sort of spectrometer?

Syringes caught my eye as I stepped to the desk, but it was something else I reached for. A tablet, sitting next to the optical microscope. I flicked it on and pulled off my glove to let me access the touch screen. Unsurprisingly, the device was filled with scientific data, not to mention thousands of medical papers. I opened the text browser and read the names of the most recently accessed titles. *Respiratory uptake rates of fine particulate matter and their effect on brainstem astroblastomas via vascular transmission. Nuclear abnormalities in vascular smooth muscle cells (VSMCs) due to NOTCH7 mutations. The effects of inorganic microsolids on blood-brain barrier transmission rates.* I could barely understand the titles. Given what I knew of Nandi's background, I was surprised he could either.

I sorted the articles by frequency of access and again scanned the titles. None of them mentioned synflurane, but the most accessed title did contain the word graphite. I opened it. I got as far as the lead author's name before my eyes widened.

She was involved? It couldn't be.

I began scanning the abstract, trying to process the information as quickly as I could, but the language was too advanced for me. I couldn't understand it. The words swam in my eyes, turning into a jumble—literally.

The tablet slipped from my hand, clanging against the table. I stumbled, barely catching myself against the desk. That's when I smelled it. A faint, sweet scent in the air, reminiscent of candied almonds.

I turned my head, the room now starting to spin, and forced my eyes onto the pressurized tanks of gas in the corner. *The synflurane.* I hadn't forgotten about it—but I'd forgotten to check the closet for microcams and sensors as I had in the hallway outside. Pairing the mechanical lock on the door with a more advanced detection system had been a nice touch on Nandi's part.

I wasn't so dumb as to think I could outrun the gas's effects, but I had to act fast. I pulled my Net and initiated emergency protocols, but an error flashed as the script I'd written failed to connect to a wireless network. Something was blocking my Net's online access, something that must've activated at the same time as the system pumping synflurane into the closet. I couldn't get a message to Counterterrorism.

I could've panicked. It was the logical thing to do. But twenty-five years of living under an assumed identity with death a single slip-up away had hardened me. It was those years of experience that allowed me to spend my last few seconds of consciousness in action instead of wallowing in fear. As darkness crept in, I reached into my jacket pocket and pulled out my shock pen. The jars of chemicals on the shelves in front of me had turned into a haze, so I relied on memory to tell me which one to grab.

I fumbled at the jug's lid, feeling the ridges of the cap but seeing only darkness. My fingers felt like sausages as I brought the shock pen forward. It clattered as it hit glass, but I couldn't tell if I'd hit pay dirt or merely the side. I hoped for the best as I tried to replace the cap, but an iron will could only do so much against an aerosolized anesthetic.

I fell into the darkness, but I didn't feel the slap of the floor underneath me. I just kept falling.

37

AUGUST 18, 2160

I STOOD in the shadow of a hulking cargo hauler, the cold winds of the Terra Cimmeria buffeting me as I waited for the exterior airlock to open. In my years on Mars, I'd ridden all manner of transports, but the hauler in front of me dwarfed them all. I couldn't have touched the tops of the tires even with a well-timed jump, and the roof of the hauler was higher than the tires by a factor of three. If dumped into the middle of one of the major metropolises, the thing could've destroyed whole city blocks with ease, mostly by ripping through the protective Mylamene layer overhead, but I wouldn't bet against the thing in a demolition derby, either.

The door puffed open in front of me, or rather above me. A ladder hung from the wheel well, so I hooked my feet onto the rungs, grabbed the handholds, and hoisted myself into the airlock. The exterior door snapped shut behind me, trapping me in a space the size of a small closet. I couldn't even move my arms. I waited as the pumps cycled, ignoring the mumblings of claustrophobia as I prayed the interior door wouldn't get jammed.

After a minute, the lock snapped open, revealing a shaft with another ladder as narrow and restrictive as the airlock. I shuffled in sideways and kept my arms close to my body as I pulled myself up the rungs. It was slow going, but even in the massive transport, I didn't have far to go. I reached the hatch at the top, pulled myself through, and barely managed to avoid flopping to the floor gracelessly like a fish.

A burly guy with a beard big enough to swallow me stood in front of the hatch. He stuck a hand out as I drew myself up. "I take it you're Jordan?"

I unlatched my helmet and took it off. "That's right. You must be Helmuth."

"In the flesh." We shook hands. "I guess I'm hard to miss. Even people who don't know what to expect often tell me I look like a Helmuth. Must be the beard."

In addition to the all-consuming facial hair, the man also had arms the size of tree trunks. His handshake suggested they contained more muscle than fat, though it was impossible to tell thanks to the thick flannel shirt he wore. His wasn't a body type I saw on Mars often.

"Guess so," I said. "Hey, thanks for the ride. I really appreciate it."

Helmuth flicked his hand dismissively. "Don't mention it. I take passengers whenever I have the room. It's the neighborly thing to do. The normal transports don't travel near often enough out here, I tell you. Besides, I enjoy the company. Babysitting these metal beasts is a great life for hermits, but for those of us who like to chat and laugh, it's not the most fulfilling of occupations."

I glanced around the cabin, which wasn't much more spacious than the airlock and access hatch. It stretched the entire width of the vehicle, but it was *narrow,* with a captain's chair set in front of a huge bank of controls below a comically small observation window. A bench built into the back wall was flanked by flaps that could be folded into an approximation of a table, and a pair of bunks were tucked inside the wall beside them. There must've been a bathroom somewhere, but I couldn't see it off the bat.

"Nice and cozy in here," I said.

Helmuth snorted. "Yeah, these babies are even fatter than me, but they don't allocate a lot of space to *living* cargo. You get used to it. Ready to go?"

"I hope so. If I forgot anything, I'm not going back for it now."

"That's the spirit. Have a seat while I get this beast moving. Its max speed isn't anything to get excited about, and time is money."

I stripped off my Suit while Helmuth manned the controls. The hauler crawled into motion, so slowly that if not for the hum of the motors I wouldn't have sensed we'd moved. I suspected there was more to setting the hauler on its path than hitting the accelerator, though, because Helmuth spent a good ten minutes checking displays, flicking through readouts, and making minor adjustments on his panel. Eventually, he grew content with the results of his tinkering and joined me on the bench.

"All good?" I said.

"Oh, yeah. This girl could take a direct strike from a tactical orbital laser and come out unscathed. She's finicky is all. Takes her time warming up to me even though I've known her for years. She's like my ex-wife in that regard. Hah!"

I wasn't sure if I should laugh. "That doesn't sound like a great quality."

"If you're talking about my ex-wife, I agree. Explains the *ex* part." Helmuth slapped the table. "So. Tell me something good. What pulls you away from the Kepler mines? Because I have a pretty good idea what brought you out in the first place." The big man hooked his thumb in the direction of the cargo bay holding hundreds of tons of nitratine.

"Same as everyone else, I guess," I said. "Opportunity."

"Yeah, but the opportunities are at the mines," said Helmuth. "The people who are lucky enough to get those jobs usually don't squander them. Don't tell me they're laying people off again. Wouldn't make sense, what with the loads I keep hauling week after week."

"No layoffs," I said. "Production's up. Actually, I think they're hiring. But I'm not the sort who stays in one spot too long. I get antsy."

"Same here. That's why I'm a driver. Course I usually do the same routes over and over, but I switch it up every now and then. How long were you at the mines?"

"Hard to remember. Two and a half months I think."

Helmuth whistled. "Not long. And before that?"

I smiled. "Before that I was working at the shipyard outside Hooke in the Argyre Planitia, but I've done everything under the sun. I've worked in construction. Transportation. Agriculture. You name it, I've probably dabbled in it."

"Sounds to me like you hate every job you've ever tried."

"On the contrary. I'm addicted to work. I wouldn't keep trying new ones if I knew I hated them all. Besides. I can't afford to stop."

I meant it figuratively, but Helmuth took me literally. "I hear that. But it sounds like the economy's taking a turn for the better. You just said the consortium is hiring. The folks I've talked to say things are picking up in the cities, too—at least in some ways."

"*Some ways?*"

Helmuth lifted an eyebrow. "You keep up with the news?"

"When I can't avoid it."

Helmuth shrugged. "Stability breeds prosperity. From everything I can tell, the globe's seeing more of the former than it's had in some time. Spaceports and shipping lanes are open and largely safe. No sabotages to the vactrain line in months. Fewer demonstrations. None of which means people are better off, mind you, but their bank accounts are. It's stability nonetheless."

"What do you mean by that?"

Helmuth waved a hand. "Never mind. I shouldn't be talking

politics. It's bad for business, and it puts us in an awkward spot if we're to be together for the next week and we end up disagreeing on something. Suffice it to say I wish people could all just get along."

"People can. There are always enough good ones to crowd out the bad. I'm not sure you can say the same about institutions."

Helmuth snorted. "Something tells me you're too smart for your own good. You ever going to tell me what's pulling you out of Kepler?"

"Like I said. Opportunity. A chance to see more of the world. Talk to more of my fellow men and women. Learn a thing or two. Maybe make a difference somewhere along the line."

Helmuth smiled. "I think we're going to get along just fine, Jordan."

HELMUTH and I shared stories for the next few days, but Helmuth broke his promise. He did get political. That didn't surprise me. What did was that as he poked and probed and asked questions, it became increasingly obvious *he* was trying to recruit *me* to the resistance.

It put me in an odd position, one I'd never encountered before. I couldn't give myself up for what I was. I couldn't know precisely what motivated Helmuth, who he was connected to, whether or not he was an active partisan or merely a sympathizer, and he was always smart enough to imply, never to state things outright. But it made it easy to listen, easy to nod my head and smile and agree with the issues he brought up for discussion. The more I listened, the more I realized Helmuth hadn't always been on the side of Mars. He was an Earth transplant, too. He'd grown up under blue skies with warm breezes tickling his face, but economics had forced him out. Though he'd started as an outsider, he'd grown to find acceptance among the dust and ice. He'd listened to the stories of those he shuttled in his hauler, and it changed him.

Just as it had me.

It gave me pride to know I wasn't the only one. That there were others, either working within the system or rooting on the sidelines. And it gave me an incentive to keep going.

Heaven knows I needed it, because I'd lied, too. I did keep tabs on the news, and it was decidedly bleak, at least for the resistance. USC forces controlled vast swaths of the wastes. Even in the cities, rebel cells had been pushed further underground. Public sentiment for the cause was dwindling, which Marina used as motivation to keep me in my current role. According to her, contacts she'd made and forces she'd garnered as a result of my outreach efforts had been crucial to keeping the resistance afloat.

I doubted the honesty of her communications at times, but I was nonetheless surprised when five days into my overland trip in Helmuth's hauler I received an encrypted message from Marina. Two sentences long, straight and to the point, as was her style: *Recent chatter suggests a shift in enemy strategy. Return home as soon as possible for a change in assignment.*

I lay there in bed that night, mulling the words. I wanted to talk to Marina to learn about what had changed, but there were reasons for the short message. Encrypted calls and video chats were harder to hide from USC satellites, and Marina wouldn't risk sharing anything over a channel that wasn't a hundred percent secure. Regardless of her motivations, one thing was clear. My two and a half years spent abroad were finally over.

Almost, anyway. Marina had said to return as soon as possible, but there was one stop I needed to make before I returned.

38

JULY 1, 2179

IN MY EXPERIENCE, waking up from a drug-induced loss of consciousness is quite different than waking up from a jab to the chin or a cudgel to the base of the head. With the latter, your senses trickle in slowly but surely. Your brain senses smells and sounds: the scent of bacon frying in a pan, the clap of shoes against a hard floor. These senses filter in as your brain regains the ability to think, and because the process occurs slowly, you have the ability to consider your options before you act—sometimes before you open your eyes. I'd been in situations where an enemy had been in a position of power over me, thinking I was unconscious when in fact I was listening to every word he spoke and gathering data for a sudden counterattack.

Anyone who's ever had their wisdom teeth extracted knows waking up from anesthesia is nothing like that. The process of regaining consciousness is sudden and disorienting. Time shifts without any knowledge of it on your behalf. One moment you're settling into a chair, talking to a doctor, and the next thing you know you're in a rideshare, waving to a nurse as they close the door. Not only do you not remember what happened during the operation, but you've forgotten a good potion of what happened to you before you received the anesthesia, too.

So it was that I blinked and found myself tied to a chair in a vaguely familiar room, the scent in my nostrils that of lemon cleaner instead of mint tooth polish and the voice in my ears not a gentle nurse's but that of angry pundits arguing on a newsfeed. I swiveled my head to the side, taking note of an unfamiliar dark-skinned man in a sofa chair in front of a holo, spooning a tube chicken and rice dish into his mouth. He kept eating for a few seconds, the speakers blaring, before he sensed my gaze. His head turned and our eyes met. He smiled, showing a mouthful of bright teeth.

"Nandi," I said, suddenly recognizing him from his New Chennai Medical Center employee profile. He wore a short beard that he hadn't in the records, and his dark brown eyes had a dangerous quality to them that no photograph could convey. I pulled my Net messenger at the sight of him, but an alert blinked red. I didn't have any service. Something was blocking me. Had the same been true before I'd been dosed? I couldn't remember.

Vikram nodded and stood, taking his bowl to the round table beside him. "That's right," he said in a patronizing tone. "I imagine everything is coming back now."

Not everything. I remembered walking into his apartment. Looking around. The visual of the room I'd captured when I first entered coalesced with the one I saw now. I glanced toward the far wall, the one with the door. I remembered walking toward it. Testing the handle. Taking a key from my pocket. Then what?

Nandi watched me as I processed my surroundings, following my eyes. He nodded in a self-assure manner. "It's no rush. Take your time. Everyone reacts to the anesthetic differently. Some people babble nonstop for an hour before regaining consciousness. You? Not so much. You spoke for a while about being followed.

Something about a leopard? I'm not really sure. It didn't make a lot of sense, and your voice was slurred."

I had to assume the man was lying to me, but I didn't focus on it. I was too busy trying to remember what had happened. I'd opened the door. Found the miniature lab with the chemicals and the analysis equipment. But what had I done in there? *The tablet!* That was it. I'd found it and started reading. And then...?

"You're pensive, and still very quiet." Nandi pulled a chair from his table and set it before me. He sat in a fluid motion, his relaxed manner obvious. "Are you always this way, or only when you've been tied to a chair?"

I hadn't tested the restraints. It wouldn't be wise to do so with him staring at me, but I knew I was well secured thanks to the numbness in my fingertips. Hopefully the blood flow hadn't been restricted long enough to cause serious damage. "I needed a moment to get my bearings."

"Ah. You've found your tongue. That's good, for both of us but especially for you."

"Is that a threat, Mr. Nandi?"

"More of a statement of fact. I realize you're still recovering your senses, but I have to imagine you've taken note of your current predicament."

I had, but I wasn't about to let the fact that I was immobilized dictate the terms of our engagement. I'd played the game before, usually from the other side. That didn't mean I couldn't handle myself from the weaker position. I had to do my best to extend the conversation and to keep Nandi off guard long enough to formulate a plan.

I nodded toward the closet door. "That was clever. Pairing a mechanical lock with... what? A laser tripwire? Or just a camera?"

"You liked that? It was nothing special. A simple motion sensor. Enough to alert me to your presence."

The bit about the motion sensor seemed important. I couldn't remember why, though. *Damn the synflurane.*

Nandi waggled a finger at me. "You see, I was expecting you. Well, not necessarily you, but rather someone of your ilk, Mr...?"

I didn't give him my name. Either he already knew it and was playing dumb, or he truly had no idea who I was, in which case he'd already underestimated me.

Nandi sighed. "I see. Well, I'll learn your name soon enough. For the time being, I'll call you Gora."

Traditionally, Gora was a term the Hindi used to refer to anyone with a lighter skin color, but the Mukt used it to refer to anyone who was ignorant of their culture. "Why do you presume I'm an outsider?"

"Well for one thing, around here it's considered a grave offense to break into a man's place of business and search through his possessions in the hope of incriminating him. But really, it's just a standard, low-level insult for your kind."

I snorted. "I'd think my actions are worthy of more than a *low-level* insult."

Nandi smiled as he crossed his legs. "You surprise me, Gora. Your ability to stay calm under pressure is impressive. I would've expected you to be more tense given the circumstances."

If he expected that, then he really *didn't* know who I was. "Why?"

Nandi blinked. "Perhaps I should give you more time. Clearly the synflurane hasn't fully worn off if you're asking me that."

"You misunderstand me, Nandi. Let's dispense with the banter. You may not know who I am, specifically, but by now you know who I work for. My tablet may be encrypted, but someone with your level of technical knowhow is capable of checking what *sort* of encryption its running." I nodded to my tablet, which lay on the dining table alongside my jacket, gloves, respirator, and the remaining contents of my pockets: my lock-picking set, a multitool, extra microcams, a scanning attachment for my tablet, a prepaid credit card, my pistol, and the electrodes for my shock pen, but not the pen itself. Had Nandi appropriated it? "If you checked my encryption software, you'll know I'm working with USC, which I'm sure you guessed the instant you got the alert that your closet had been breached. You'd known someone like me was coming after you the instant you attacked our diplomats. If you're not an idiot—and I've followed you enough to know you're anything but— then you'll know USC agents don't work alone. That's why I'm not concerned about my well-being."

Nandi raised an eyebrow. "You're expecting a team of your fellow agents to break down my door, take me into custody, and save you?"

"I didn't come here on a whim, Nandi. My superiors know where I am at all times." Or at least, they did when I wanted them to.

"You said we should dispense with the banter, Gora. I assumed that meant we wouldn't deceive each other anymore. You know as well as I that you were unable to deliver your distress call before losing consciousness."

I actually didn't remember that. It was good to know I'd had enough of my wits about me to try. It meant I might've tried something else to protect against my inevitable capture, as well. "Lack of communication can be as telling as the act itself. I was supposed to spend at most a half hour here before leaving."

"But you did. Don't you remember?" Nandi smiled again as he pulled his own tablet from his pocket. He turned it on, tapped it a couple times, and turned the screen so I could see.

On a maps app, a blue dot moved along a street I didn't recognize, but it was definitely in New Chennai. Nandi tapped it. "That's you."

I looked up from the tablet. "A transponder?"

"Moved via drone. Eventually, I'll have the drone service

deliver it to your hotel, but for the time being, it's sufficient to have it moving about the city. I've paused it at a cafe for three-quarters of an hour in case anyone is paying attention."

It was a clever move. The sort of thing I'd do. "That won't be enough to throw my friends off my trail. I communicate regularly. They get suspicious when I don't."

"I believe you. Luckily for me, you were working here alone, were you not? Which means once your friends at—Counterterrorism, probably?—notice that you're not acting like yourself, it'll be a few hours until anyone arrives. I give myself twenty-four hours, give or take, before I'm at risk, and we'll be long gone by then."

"We?"

"I wouldn't leave you behind, would I? You're too valuable. Don't get me wrong. You've thrown a wrench in my plans. I doubt I'll be able to move all my equipment before your USC associates arrive, but the data is the most important part, and I take that with me everywhere. As I can you."

"You're stronger than you look, then."

Nandi smiled again. "Thankfully, I won't have to carry you. That would attract too much attention. But I have a cocktail of drugs I plan on injecting you with that will make you much more suggestible. I doubt you'll give me any issues once I administer them, and they'll provide the added benefit of making you more than willing to tell me everything you know. We'll start with the basics, such as your name and which hotel you're staying at and move from there. Don't worry. I won't keep you drugged indefinitely. That would interfere with the study."

I didn't like the direction the conversation was headed. "What sort of study would that be? Do you plan to torture and psychoanalyze me as you go?"

Nandi shook his head. "Despite whatever you might think of me, I'm not that brutish. I don't torture people. My study will be medical in nature. I just wish I didn't have to wait a week for the effects to present."

I narrowed an eye. "A week?"

"That's right. That's about how long it took with your ambassadors, isn't it?"

A chill ran through me. I glanced at my arm, which was tightly secured to the chair with the rest of me. My jacket lay on the table with the rest of my belongings, so I was down to my shirtsleeves. The cloth was rumpled, perhaps from the process of being secured to the chair, but neither of the buttons at my cuff were fastened instead of the usual two.

I stared at the cloth, imagining the speck of dried blood I'd find at the vein over my elbow pit when I pulled the sleeve back, and tried not to panic.

A week, Nandi had said. That was roughly how long it had taken for the first of the diplomats to perish. I had time. The frightening part was no one, not me, not Trinh Pham, not anyone at USC knew what had caused the ambassadors' hearts to stop beating. But Nandi did. Something told me he wasn't the only one.

It took an exertion of self will, but I kept my voice measured. "What are you playing at, Vikram? You're not a doctor. Not a bioengineer. You're a computer scientist with a few years of nursing experience. Developing bioweapons isn't up your alley."

"Who says I *develop* them?"

"If you don't, then you're not as smart as I thought. You're tinkering with a force you don't understand. If you play with fire, you're going to get burned."

"Soldiers don't need to know how guns work to point them in the right direction and pull the trigger. Besides, I know more that you think. That's why I'm going to take thorough notes as I watch you. Any data points I collect will ultimately aid my brotherhood. But enough chit chat. It's time to move, and your head's cleared enough that it should be safe to give you the next injection."

Nandi stood and took a step toward the converted closet door. My mind raced as I tried to think of something—anything—that would postpone the inevitable. "What do you use in your cocktail, Vikram? Midazolam? Propofol? Amobarbital? You realize if you mix those in the wrong quantities, you could kill me. As you said, I'm too valuable to waste."

Nandi stopped and turned. He approached me deliberately, leaned over, and pressed a hand against my shoulder. "You weigh, what? Ninety-five kilos, give or take? I'll measure it right, though it might take me a moment given the mess you made of my lab. You knocked two full shelves over when you hit the ground, you know. But in case you're thinking of taking advantage of any time spent outside my presence—" His hand squeezed. "—be aware that I'm watching you. Constantly. So don't try anything. Because as much as it would go against my nature, when pushed, I *can* be brutish."

Nandi smiled, his teeth abnormally sharp in my mind's eye. His footfalls echoed off the floor as he crossed to the closet door, threw it open, and disappeared inside, but I only noticed him in my periphery. My mind was already hard at work, cycling through ideas. If he had cameras on me, it would be useless to try and free myself from my bonds. I gave my wrists a slight twist, feeling the zip tie bite against them. If I could generate leverage, I could break them, but doing so from the confines of the chair was impossible, and if I so much as tipped the thing over, Vikram would be on me in a moment. That said, it was up to me to formulate an escape. My Net still showed no external wireless signal, so I couldn't even contact local police, much less anyone at Counterterrorism.

Think, Drake, think. If I could convince Nandi not to inject me, it would give me more time, but he wasn't weak-willed enough for me to talk him out of his plans. Perhaps I could pretend to lose consciousness before I actually did, taking him unawares when he released me from my restraints, but despite his background in computer science, Nandi also had experience in nursing. He'd measure his dose correctly, he'd know when I was truly gone, and he'd be sure to test me before setting me free and coercing me into following him to his next safe house.

I heard a clunk from the lab, and I thought about what Nandi had said. I'd taken out two shelves of chemicals when I'd lost consciousness and fallen to the floor. Had that been on purpose? I didn't put it past myself to take drastic action before losing my grip on reality, but stumbling into a shelf didn't sound like a deliberate act. If only I could remember what I'd done after picking up Vikram's tablet!

Maybe eventually it would come to me, but it hadn't yet, and I was running out of time. I glanced at the table again, wondering if I could hop my chair over and get a grasp on my pistol before Nandi returned. As my eyes passed over my pistol, they paused on a patch of empty space next to a coil of electrodes.

My shock pen. It wasn't there. Nandi hadn't hidden my pistol. Why would he have taken the pen?

I pulled up the pen app and focused on it. I might not have access to online Net features or be able to get a message out, but the shock pen didn't require either. It was on a short-distance, personal area network protocol normally used for headphones.

I prayed that I'd known what I was doing and initiated a maximum shock delivery for the pen.

From inside the closet I heard a pop and a crackle. A moment later a cloud of black and orange erupted from where a wall had existed a fraction of a second earlier. A wave picked me up and threw me against the far wall, bringing with it an explosive cacophony. My head whipped and something at my back cracked. Whether it was my spine or the chair wasn't immediately obvious.

I groaned as I rolled onto my knees, my butt held in the air by the chair strapped to me. Heat radiated against my cheek. I turned my head to find the wall gone and the lab within consumed by angry flames, belching thick black smoke that roiled across the ceiling. The smoke swirled, and I felt something cool against my face, fighting back against the heat of the flames. The building's sprinkler system. If an alarm had gone off, I couldn't hear it over the roar of the fire and the ringing in my own ears.

I lowered my eyes as the sprinkler spat at me and saw what I'd missed on first glance. Nandi lay prone on the floor, unmoving, covered with insulation and debris, his clothing smoldering. His burns weren't as bad as might be expected, but I had no doubt he was dead. Shock waves were unforgiving to the human body. Christ, what sort of chemical had I paired with the shock pen? I suppose it didn't matter. Once one exploded, the rest hadn't waited to add their fuel to the fire.

I didn't have time to think about it. The chemical fire blazed merrily, unfazed by the sprinkler's efforts, and the room was filling with smoke. I set a Net timer, figuring it would take firefighters no more than six minutes to arrive. I'd already wasted one.

I flexed my back, hoping not to feel searing pain down my spine. Instead I felt only a moderate bite. The chair gave, however, bending at the base. I stumbled to my feet, clawing at the wall for support, but I didn't use it as a crutch. I launched myself as high in the air as I could, twisted in midair, and braced myself. The chair crunched underneath me as I hit the ground, sending a wave of pain through an already battered body.

I ignored it. I rose again, and again launched myself. This time, the chair surrendered upon impact. I shook myself free of the pieces, twisting my body like a pretzel, wiggling my arms low behind my back. Legs up. Feet through the hole. Then I was on my feet. Arms overhead and onto my knees as quickly and with as much force as I could. The ties at my wrists snapped. I lunged for my multitool, which had been blasted against the wall with my other belongings. A slice from the knife blade freed my legs.

Thousands of pinpricks stung my fingers as blood returned to the flesh, and my lungs screamed as chemical smoke poured into my nostrils. As I found my respirator and strapped it to my face, I for the first time said a blessing for the ease of the system over full Suits.

I checked my clock as I threw on my jacket and crammed as many of my belongings as I could find into my pockets. Three minutes gone. At least another unaccounted for.

I tucked away my pistol last, but I didn't turn for the door. I held an arm against my face to shield me from the increasing heat of the fire, scanning the floor for one last thing.

I found it tucked underneath one of the overturned shelving units in the middle of the office space. Nandi's tablet, its screen smashed to slivers.

I threw it in my pocket, and only then did I run.

39

AUGUST 26, 2160

THE THUMBPRINT READER beside the salon door beeped when I pressed my flesh against it, and the door unlocked. I pushed it open, breathing in the musty scent. Black paint still covered the exterior glass, keeping the interior in shadow. I stepped inside, my footsteps muted by the thin layer of dust that coated the floor. I scanned my eyes across the desks and chairs and mirrors, then crossed to what I'd turned into my office. The bed I'd procured was still there, as was the squat rack. The vending machine I'd fixed stood in the corner, silent and dark. Someone had unplugged it. Maybe I'd done it before I'd left. I must've. I know I'd turned off the air conditioning system.

Though I'd never asked him, part of me assumed Winsor would've sold the place after I left. Then again, he'd been adamant he hadn't bought it for me but as an emergency escape in the event he needed it. I guess he'd told the truth about that, and that he remained as paranoid as ever.

I didn't expect anything less.

I crossed to the cabinets with the bottles of shampoo and conditioner, which remained stocked with the most popular brands of a half decade prior. The cabinet next to it with the bleach and nail polish remover appeared undisturbed as well.

I leaned forward and peered closely at the cabinet's twin handles. A thin auburn hair lay over them, a hair I'd recovered from my tuxedo the night of my encounter with Francesca. It was barely visible unless you knew to look for it.

I'd turned the air conditioning off because of it.

I SAT on one of the benches in Melody Park, enjoying the sun's lazy descent through the tips of the trees. It wasn't the same view as the one I'd watched during my dawn runs through Olympus's waking neighborhoods, but it was close enough, brightening the sky with the same hints of breathable blue.

I took a deep breath and let it out slowly. I'd enjoyed the fleeting months spent at the salon, studying, maintaining some semblance of a schedule, knowing I'd fall asleep in the same bed I woke up in, but when I thought back to who'd undergone those tests with Winsor, who'd quarreled with the old man, who'd resisted him at every turn, I could barely recognize the individual. Then again, the Ambrose who'd undertaken Marina's quest to find Winsor wasn't the same one who'd been captured three years before, and the one who'd stood in the Bernhard Center in Kalamazoo watching Los Angeles getting nuked on replay was a different soul still.

I was too young to have lived so many lives. I wondered how many more I would get.

A tired voice sighed as it took the spot on the bench beside me. I didn't turn to look at its owner. I'd made him as soon as he cleared the trees.

"Well, you look older," said Winsor.

"Not sure if that's an insult," I said. "It's fair either way. I feel like I've aged four lifetimes."

I peered at the man out of the corner of my eyes. He looked about the same, which was to say ragged and cold and with maybe ten percent less hair than he'd had before. He didn't look directly at me either.

The rumble of street noise carried through the trees toward us, muted by the pine needles. I didn't rush the conversation. Neither did Winsor.

"I wasn't expecting you back," he said eventually.

"You had no reason to."

"Was there a problem? Did the stamping plant in Elysium refuse to take you in? You could've sent a message."

"I didn't go to Elysium. I've been recalled."

"Oh." More silence. "I'm not sure if that's a good or a bad thing."

I missed the breeze. I would've given anything for the sound of wind tickling the leaves. "Me neither."

"So what brings you back to Olympus?"

"It's easy to sever ties with someone remotely. It's better to thank them in person."

"That sounds final."

"Pretty sure it is. Marina asked me to come back, and it's easy to see why. I think my efforts made a difference, but not enough of one. Support is fizzling despite everything I've done. USC's grip keeps tightening. It's time for a new approach. I'll find out which soon enough."

Winsor snorted. "I thought by now you would've realized your path is up to you. I honestly thought you would've stopped taking directions from me long ago."

I looked at Winsor. "If I didn't have a sense of my own agency, I wouldn't be here. I followed your suggestions because they were good ones. I'm here because I made the choice to be."

"You done?"

"No. I've always been in charge of my choices. I chose to stay with Marina after I was captured. I came to that decision on my own after discovering the truth of the nuclear attack on my homeland, also on my own. I chose to seek you out because I put my trust in Marina. She thought finding you was the best use of my time and abilities, and I decided she was right. I stuck around because I knew that your methods aside, the lessons you were teaching me were ones I needed to learn. I kept at it because I knew that despite the fact I'd rather be at my friends' sides, I was needed elsewhere. I sacrificed. I chose to. That's on me. But you? You didn't have to take part. I didn't give you much of a choice, to be fair, but you helped me. You didn't treat it like a joke. So thanks for putting me on the right path."

The old man snorted, which I think was as thorough an expression of gratitude as he was capable of.

We sat there for a while. Just when I'd come to the conclusion there wasn't anything else to say between us, Winsor surprised me. "Why'd you ask me to meet you here?"

"It's public. Crowded, but not too crowded. Lots of exits. I paid attention."

"That's not what I meant. This place means something to you."

I wanted to ask if he'd been spying on me, but I knew the answer. He knew I'd come through here every morning on my runs. I didn't need to volunteer anything else. "It reminds me of home. Of the journey I've taken. Watching the sun through the trees... It's cathartic, in a way."

"*Cathartic?*"

I sighed. "If I squint, while the sun's setting, the trees remind me of the rocket boosters sitting on pads in Titusville. Even when I don't, they remind me of Earth. Of home. Of the journey I took to get here, and the people I lost along the way."

"Like Ranbir?"

I'd become a lot better at hiding my emotions, but I wasn't totally prepared for him to bring up that name. I guess I shouldn't have been surprised he'd done his research. He'd had plenty of time. "Yes. Like Ranbir, and Cal. Their deaths still haunt me. Near deaths, too. I still try to keep tabs on those who remain. Maarten, especially. I regret a lot of my time spent with him. I can't help but feel if I'd been a better friend, a better mentor, that he would've turned out different. Now he's a major in charge of an entire company, helping set policy, making decisions that impact the behavior of those underneath him. I failed myself by not seeing who he was earlier in life. But Phoebe is by far the worst. I'll never forgive myself for what happened to her. I've always felt that if things between us hadn't soured, she'd still be with us, but that's nothing more than wishful thinking."

"It's never too late to repair a relationship, kid. Trust me. I speak from experience."

I turned to face the old man, for the first time confused. "It's too late when they're dead."

Winsor's eyes softened. "Sorry. I thought you were still talking about Phoebe."

"I *am* talking about Phoebe."

Winsor's brow furrowed. "Then why the wistful sorrow? She's not dead."

I blinked, the words not quite registering. *"What?"*

40

JULY 1, 2179

AS I FLED the burning commercial building, I didn't bother retrieving the transponder that was mimicking my Net signal. Fact of the matter was Nandi's use of one had saved me the bother of setting one up myself.

After a three minute stop at my hotel for a change of clothes, some bandages, and to grab my bags, I was off again in a rideshare to the closest rail station. With night well underway, it wasn't a challenge to grab a seat on the next train. Within an hour of being tossed ten meters through the air by a violent explosion and with my ears still afflicted by tinnitus, I watched New Chennai fade behind me through a clear plastic window.

I tried to clear my head as the kilometers disappeared underneath my seat, but the knowledge that I'd been injected with a deadly, experimental drug lingered at the dark recesses of my mind. I had at least a week, I told myself, probably more to reverse the effects of whatever Vikram Nandi had dosed me with. The problem was that I had no idea what it was.

But *she* might. The woman whose name had been listed as a lead author on so many of Nandi's favorite journal articles.

I would've read more of the papers on Nandi's tablet to

educate myself on the subject of blood-brain interactions and how long it took for foreign particles to leach into cerebral tissues, but the tablet I'd recovered from the fire was trashed—which wasn't to say the memory had been wiped. I'd pulled files from fire ravaged devices multiple times as a cop, but I lacked the equipment to do so at the moment. Maybe once I reached Utopia, but I'd be hard pressed to find time once I arrived there. Given the fact that Nandi's transponder had provided me with temporary invisibility, now was the perfect time to make another visit in Utopia that I'd been putting off—assuming I lived long enough to make it.

I reached the Niesten station at just after midnight, then made a quick transfer onto a train headed east. Since I knew I wouldn't fall asleep in a million years in my current state, I spent the hours flying across the black Martian wastes delving into the Utopian public security camera database, which wasn't as easy to crack as I'd hoped. Thankfully, I made some headway as the train pulled into the Utopia Main station and set a script to analyze some footage in search of a familiar face.

With the local time reading four-thirty, I snagged another rideshare and gave it an address from memory. The vehicle hummed and sped off, navigating the empty streets with ease. My clock read two minutes past five as I stepped out of the cab onto a quiet street lined with ornate townhomes, the sidewalks flush with trees and heavily manicured bushes. The homes themselves might not've been enormous, but the fact that they were single family units at all made them exorbitantly expensive. Their proximity to the city center was another factor.

With my bag in hand, I approached the nearest house, climbed the steps to the door, and pressed on the intercom.

A light on the console lit up, but nothing else happened. I tried again, with similar results. It wasn't until the fifth try that the screen lit up. I saw a man, his face lined with sleep and illuminated by the light on his tablet. Pillows were in the frame, as well as a dark headrest. He groaned. "What the hell do you want?"

I didn't know the man—or more accurately, we'd never met. I knew who he was though. The benefits of thorough research. "Put Phoebe on, Lars. This is important."

He blinked. "Who are you?"

"Put Phoebe on, Lars."

He grunted, rolled over, and shook the woman beside him. She blinked slowly, a sense of awareness slowly returning to her almond-shaped eyes. Lars spoke. "Guy at the door says he wants to see you."

She grabbed the tablet and blinked again, her hazel eyes finally focusing on the tablet. They widened. "Ambrose?"

"Phoebe. Sorry to wake you. We need to talk."

41

AUGUST 26, 2160

I BLINKED AGAIN, still unable to comprehend what Winsor had said. "Come again?"

"Phoebe," he said. "Phoebe Zhao, right? Your fling in the corps? She's alive."

A creeping darkness lingered at the edge of my vision. "What the hell do you mean she's alive?"

Winsor squinted at me. "Uh... that she's not dead? I don't know how else you could interpret that."

"That's impossible. She was shot in the head. I saw it happen."

"And clearly she survived, unless USC's records are part of a giant conspiracy I don't know about. *Is* there a giant conspiracy?"

"You're freaking me out, man. Make some sense."

Winsor sighed. "I delved into your past after you first showed up. To make sure you were who you said you were. You can't blame me. I needed to make sure you could be trusted. Obviously, that involved understanding your time in the military, up to and including your capture. As part of that, I did some research on the people you knew at the time. Your friend Phoebe didn't die. She's in Utopia, working at USC's Community Hospital. I figured you would've kept tabs on your old squad mates after you left them behind."

"I did. I mean, not at first, but eventually I got around to it. The ones who were still in the squad. The ones who *weren't dead*." But it was true. I'd never specifically looked into Phoebe's death. Maybe because it was too raw, too emotional, but also because I'd been certain of her death. Why relive something that was only going to cause me further grief? Besides, her name had never shown up in any of the status reports my script collected for me about the actions of Maarten, Janeece, or any of the other remaining members of Zeta squad.

Winsor looked ashamed. "Kid, I'm sorry you had to learn this from me. I wasn't trying to turn this moment into *this*. In my defense, I thought you knew. Why would you have assumed she died in that attack?"

"Because I saw it with…" The words died on my tongue. Yes, I'd watched her get shot. But that wasn't why I'd assumed she'd died. It's because *Marina* told me she had.

It took all the will I had to retain my composure. I gave Winsor a curt nod. "Thanks for your help." Then I turned and raced toward the nearest street.

THE RIDESHARE WOVE through traffic at a snail's pace. I wished I had Winsor's access to the system AI that he'd once used to test me and almost kill me at the same time. It would get me to the vactrain station faster, even if it might bring the authorities down on my head.

The encrypted call connected a half-dozen blocks from the park. Marina's voice sounded in my head, a trace of concern woven among her words. "Ambrose. Where are you? I'd expected you to arrive—"

"How could you not tell me Phoebe is alive?"

"*Phoebe?* Who's Phoebe?"

I felt the anger boiling over inside me. The Net transmission probably couldn't do it justice. "The girl I asked you about when we first met. My girlfriend while I was in the corps. She was with me when you took me. When you initiated the Net attack against my squad in the tunnels near Cassini."

"I'm not following. What does this have to do with—"

"*You told me she was dead, Marina.* When you first came into my quarters and confronted me, I asked you, and you said... You said..." I hesitated, trying to remember Marina's exact words. I remembered the instance quite clearly. I'd been sitting in a small room, my quarters after being captured. I'd just woken, and Marina came in, revealing herself as my antagonist for the first time. She'd asked me questions, mostly about why I'd fought back against Maarten, which I realized in retrospect she'd done to gauge my sentiment toward their movement. Before she'd left, I'd asked her about Phoebe, but I couldn't remember my exact words. Perhaps I hadn't asked about Phoebe directly. I think I'd asked about my friends in general. How had Marina responded? I could've sworn she'd told me Phoebe had died, but maybe she'd merely alluded to it. How had she put it? Something about Mars not being kind to those who took bullets in vacuum.

"Look, Ambrose, I'm trying to remember the incident you're referring to, but that was years ago. You asked me about your friend. Phoebe, you said. Right. I told you she was dead. I must've thought she was. You're saying she isn't?"

I didn't let my uncertainty over our conversation douse my anger. "*You're damned right she isn't!* How the hell did you not know that?"

"Calm down, Ambrose. You're talking about a raid that happened almost six years ago. If you'll recall, you and I were trading attacks on each other's comms. You sniffed me out and convinced your leadership to launch an attack on us. I was monitoring you the whole time, but that doesn't mean any of us were ready to have several squads of marines descend on our base within twenty-four hours. We had to scramble to get crews and equipment out while we sabotaged most of the surrounding infrastructure. The Net attack we used to incapacitate you was planned in haste. We didn't expect the melee that erupted when you and your old squad butted heads over our potential prisoners. We didn't expect bullets to fly, and we certainly didn't expect any self-inflicted casualties on your side. You have to remember, *you* were our target. You were the one who had the skills I sought and had the frame of mind to listen to what I had to say. So you'll forgive me if I didn't pay close attention to who died and who didn't as I fled with the rest of the resistance from your former employer's muzzle."

The rideshare turned a corner, and I checked my map to see how far it was to the vactrain station. The online schedule listed a westbound departure in twenty minutes. "It doesn't change the fact that you lied to me, Marina. I asked you about Phoebe for a reason. I could've gone the rest of my life without seeing Maarten and it wouldn't have bothered me. Watkins. Janeece. Zeta squad. Lambda squad. I could've taken them or left them. But Phoebe? She *meant* something to me."

And I didn't say it, but the fact of the matter was I may never have joined Marina and the rebels if I'd known Phoebe was alive. That one severed relationship might've changed the course of my life, and it was all a lie.

"I didn't deceive you, Ambrose," said Marina. "Not knowingly. If I misrepresented the truth, it was out of ignorance, not malice. To be honest, I stopped paying attention to your old squad mates after we brought you aboard. I couldn't tell you what any of them are up to beyond what little of their activities makes it into my daily briefings. I figured if anything, you'd have been the one to keep up to date on their lives."

"I have. At least I have for the members of Zeta squad, even if they've since been promoted out of the squad. But I didn't keep track of members who'd been dismissed. I didn't even know there'd been any. Do you know why? Because I thought the only one who wasn't accounted for was *dead*."

Marina's voice remained measured despite my ferocity. "Ambrose, where are you? We need to talk. The message I sent you the other day was explicit. There are rumblings in our intercepted comms that suggest something major is ongoing."

Five more blocks until the vactrain station. "It's going to have to wait."

Marina paused. "My asking you to come back wasn't a request."

"And I didn't ask permission."

"Ambrose... what are you planning?"

"It should be obvious by now, don't you think?"

Marina finally lost her calm. *"Are you crazy?* If she's still on Mars, you can't go to her. Everyone thinks you're a prisoner of war. Any contact with people you knew before we captured you threatens not only you but our entire operation."

"I haven't forgotten the rules, Marina. I'm still playing by them. But I've spent two and a half years out from under your wing and I haven't been recognized yet."

"You haven't tried to contact anyone you knew, either."

The vactrain station grew in my window. "Sorry, Marina. This is something I have to do."

Marina started to say something, but I ended the call. As the cab came to a stop, I hopped out and booked it toward the trains.

42

JULY 2, 2179

I SAT in a padded chair in a white room at the Utopia-Turing University Research Hospital. A synthblood infuser hummed quietly beside me, the display showing the machine's tanks were full and maintained at a pristine 98.6 degrees. Normally, the machines provided synthblood to those who'd lost at least 750 milliliters of the real stuff in a traumatic accident, but like the old hemodialysis machines, the thing could just as easily filter blood out of the body and replace it with the synthetic, lab-grown kind. It was mostly for ridding the body of blood borne pathogens, but it could just as easily be used to remove poisons—or whatever I'd been injected with.

Phoebe Zhao had already done the hard work of locating the cephalic vein in my upper arm and attaching the input line. I felt the prick of the second needle and looked down to see her carefully insert the draw line into the basilic artery at my elbow pit.

I glanced out the window at the sky, which had started to turn from black to a dark purple. My clock read five past six.

Phoebe taped the second line into place and moved to the infuser. She tapped at the display a few times before affixing me with a cool glance. "You're going to feel a sensation of blood flow when I turn this on. You might even get a little light headed. Both are normal. Are you ready?"

"I've been through worse. Let's do it."

"Here goes nothing, then."

Phoebe activated the machine. The two sites where the catheters had been attached suddenly felt cool, and curiously enough, I did feel like I was bleeding. It was an odd sensation.

"For future reference, the phrase *here goes nothing* doesn't inspire a lot of confidence that a procedure is going to work."

Phoebe sat in the chair against the wall. She swiped a hand through her hair, putting a few of the loose black strands back into place. Back when we'd first met a quarter century ago in the marines, she'd worn her hair in a pony-tail, but after taking a bullet to the brain and having a portion of her skull reconstructed, she'd switched to parting it on the side. Twenty-five years later, she'd cropped her hair shorter, but she still parted it the same way.

"What do you want me to say, Ambrose?" she said. "I don't know if this will work. I'm guessing based on what you've told me. The *very little* you've told me."

"I'm not trying to be intentionally obtuse, Phoebe. I don't know much about what I was injected with. All I know is it's the same substance that was administered to three USC ambassadors who all died within a week and a half of exposure. It doesn't appear to be biological in nature. The USC base where the ambassadors worked was put into lockdown in the wake of their deaths, and no one else died or suffered adverse symptoms in the two weeks that followed. Multiple toxicology screens weren't able to identify it, as well. The only hint I have to the nature of the chemical I was injected with comes from the autopsies performed on the dead. The coroner at my former precinct was certain all three died of cardiac arrest. She wasn't sure what might've caused it, but she found graphite deposits in the major veins that feed the brain stem and cerebellum. She said she'd never seen anything like it, but I have to assume that's what caused the heart failures."

"I don't see any method by which graphitic deposits in the basilar arteries could lead to cardiac arrest, unless they led to full on blockages, which you've said wasn't that case. Which suggests..."

Phoebe sat there in thought. At the end of her stint in the corps, she'd gone on to get her medical degree and become a top notch researcher, one who specialized in using advanced sub-cranial mesh architectures to help people who'd suffered traumatic brain injuries, like her, to successfully reintegrate their Nets. Her medical expertise was one of the reasons I'd tracked her down following my interaction with Vikram Nandi. The fact that Nandi had been researching her papers was another, but there was a third reason even beyond those two obvious ones. A reason *very* few people knew about.

"Which suggests what?" I said.

"That the graphite deposits didn't cause the cardiac arrest. At least not directly."

I glanced at the infuser. It could administer liters of synthblood in less than a minute, but replacing real blood with the synthetic version took quite a bit longer. The two had to be separated as the draw line removed a mixture from the body. "I've got time for an explanation."

"How's your understanding of how the Net interacts with the human brain?"

"From a software perspective, very good. If you're talking about how the Net mesh interacts with the cerebrum on a biological level, then I don't understand it anywhere near as well as you do. I have a fundamental knowledge of the science, though. The brain functions via electrical impulses, same as the Net."

Phoebe nodded. "It can only access the portions of the brain it's in contact with, namely the cerebral cortex and the cerebellum. It's a function of how the mesh unfolds as it's injected into the subarachnoid space between the brain and skull."

"Which is why the Net can't regulate hormone levels, or at least not without more intrusive elective surgeries. Because hormone levels are controlled by the hypothalamus in the center of the brain. Though I know you've been working on methods to make Net mesh unfolding more tailorable and less dangerous for people with abnormal brain geometries."

"That's right. Don't tell me you've been reading my research papers."

"Only the old ones. And a new one that I didn't get far into before I was knocked unconscious. I actually remember the bit about the hypothalamus from one of our conversations decades ago."

Phoebe lifted an eyebrow. "We talked about that stuff back then?"

We had. The only reason I remembered was because I'd been trying to get into Phoebe's pants at the time, and the wink she'd given me when talking about birth control hormones had cemented itself in my teenage mind.

Remembering those times brought a faint smile to my lips, but it was more wistfulness than a longing to return to the days of yore. Phoebe and I had been so naive back then. Life had been easier, if not necessarily better. "Yeah. In retrospect it should've been obvious you'd go into medicine at the end of your service. But what does any of this have to do with the injection I got?"

"You said the graphite was deposited throughout the basilar and cerebral arteries, right? Ambrose, graphite is *conductive.*"

I paused, the gears upstairs grinding. "Are you suggesting the graphite was a conduit for electrical signals to pass into the innermost parts of the brain?"

"The medulla, at the base of the brain stem, controls heart

function. If you can administer an electrical impulse to the correct portion, you can stop someone's heart from beating. I know because I've done the opposite. I've worked with patients who had irregular heart function as a result of trauma, and we were able to restore normal function precisely by connecting the medulla to the Net mesh—not via deposited graphite, but via a microwire. Still threaded through the cranial arteries, though."

Suddenly I understood why Nandi had been researching Phoebe's work. "You're saying the ambassadors to New Chennai could've been killed on command? Via remote signal through their Nets?"

"If the graphite had created a conductive link between the mesh surrounding the cerebellum and the medulla oblongata, yes. You'd have to have access to someone's Net functions to do so, but that's more up your alley than mine."

"*Christ.* That's what I was injected with?"

"I'm guessing, but you can be sure I'm going to take a close look at the blood I'm sucking out of you. For what it's worth, graphite doesn't behave that way on its own."

"How would someone program it to selectively deposit the way it did?"

Phoebe shrugged. "Not sure. Could be a biological precursor. MEMS. I have no idea without looking at the deposits. I assume your coroner didn't take the graphite under an electron microscope?"

I shook my head. "Not to my knowledge." I swallowed a lump. "Let's assume you're right, Phoebe. What does that mean for my prognosis?"

"It means you probably have nothing to worry about. As you said, the people who died from this were exposed days before they perished. It's no surprise why. Theoretically, a graphite solution in your bloodstream could deposit along the basilar and cerebral arterial walls immediately, but it couldn't establish contact to the brain that quickly. You're familiar with the blood-brain barrier?"

I recalled the articles I'd glanced at on the way over. "More than I was a day ago."

"Drugs, or suspensions of any microparticulate solution, have to cross a barrier of sorts to get into the brain. It's an unfortunate fact of life for the medical community, but it's an evolutionary necessity. It's probably also the reason you're still alive. That and the fact that the person who administered the injection died in a violent explosion."

"Because someone has to send the kill signal."

"I would presume," said Phoebe. "But that leads to a more important question. Ambrose, what the hell have you gotten yourself into? Were you investigating this on behalf of USC, or is this work related to *something else?*" Her voice dropped at that last part, perhaps unintentionally.

I glanced at the door. I hadn't heard much in the realm of crowd noise since arriving, just the steady hum and occasional beep of the synthblood infuser. It was still early for activity at a research hospital, though foot traffic would pick up soon. "Are we in a secure location?"

"As far as anyone knows, this room is empty. I didn't sign you in."

"You know I mean more than that. What about you?"

"To the best of my knowledge, no one within USC knows about me. Except for you. Technically, you work for them now."

If Phoebe said we weren't being watched, I believed her. She knew what she was doing. "And here you made it seem like *I* was the one keeping tabs on *you.*"

"I know you moved to Counterterrorism. That's about it. In my defense, that stunt of yours with the rogue detectives made the news, even here in Utopia."

I nodded. "The reasons behind my move to Counterterrorism are twofold. I wanted to continue stopping violent killers in their tracks, and I needed access to USC's inner network to come up with a solution to Martian independence that doesn't involve open warfare. But my investigation of Vikram Nandi was entirely driven by USC."

Phoebe's face scrunched. *"Nandi?"*

"Yeah. He's the guy who dosed me and killed the diplomats. He had a number of your research papers on his tablet, but I was hoping it was because of your work. Don't tell me you knew the man."

"I didn't. But I am familiar with *a* Nandi. Karam. He was a graduate student of mine, a joint tutorship between myself and Professor Elliot Schweinfurt in Bioengineering. Karam was brilliant. Probably the smartest student I ever met."

I blinked. "Finally. Things are starting to make sense."

"It's not like that, Ambrose. Karam wasn't a terrorist. He wouldn't be involved in this sort of thing. Besides, Nandi is a very common last name."

"Coincidences might happen in life, Phoebe, but they're as rare as ice on Venus in my line of work." I pulled up my Net file on Vikram, the one Elysium Counterterrorism agents had put together for me as soon as I'd identified the man through his employment history. I hadn't bothered to look at his family history, but I did now. "Yup. Vikram Nandi. Born to Ramaeshwara and Priya Nandi. Has two siblings. Samara and Karam. He's involved, Phoebe. I *knew* he wasn't working alone. He didn't have the knowledge base to pull something like this off."

Phoebe didn't say anything.

It gave me pause. "Phoebe... why are you so sure he wasn't a terrorist? Did you recruit him?"

She met my eyes. "This was over a decade ago, Ambrose."

"What happened?"

She didn't flinch. "I didn't treat him any differently than anyone else I thought could be an asset. We talked. About Mars. About our cultures, about the communities we came from. About the challenges we'd faced and about our hopes for the future. I felt him out. I got the impression he didn't share my desire to make a change, at least not the way I wanted him to, so I didn't pursue him. That's it. If he suspected I was involved with the resistance, it would've been a wild guess on his behalf, not anything based on evidence."

Ever since we'd parted ways twenty years ago, Phoebe and I had shared similar goals. We both wanted to free Mars from USC's oppressive yoke, but we had different ideas about how it should be done. Phoebe's strategy was one of mitigation. Of slowly pushing USC actions and policies toward a future where Mars was more independent and valued. Mine was a more drastic approach. I maintained Mars needed a clean break from USC, one that could only be achieved through revolution. That meant bloodshed, however, something Phoebe couldn't condone. I'd always known it would be inevitable. The key was making it meaningful. Trading it for a change that was permanent.

"Where can I find him, Phoebe?"

She shook her head. "If I knew, I'd tell you. I haven't heard from him in close to a decade. After he graduated from the program, he returned to New Chennai. I thought he would do great things, but as the months and years rolled by, I never heard a word from him. I assumed he'd taken a different path in life. I'd never imagined something like this."

I sighed. "That's bad for me, but good for you. Still, this isn't a positive development. You were the mentor of a man who's now suspected of developing a bioweapon used in the murder of three people, and the attempted murder of at least one more. For all I know, there have been others. I can try to keep the information from USC for a while, but sooner or later they'll find out."

"Let them. I mentored Karam in medicine, not terrorism. I have nothing to hide."

I cocked my head.

"As far as Karam is concerned, that's accurate. USC won't know a thing. I've been hiding as long as you have, Ambrose, and I've taken fewer risks along the way. If they investigate me, they'll find nothing but my record as a physician and researcher."

The infuser beeped. I turned to look at the display. "Is this thing done?"

Phoebe stood and checked the readout. "Your blood is ninety-eight percent synthetic. We could get the last one and a half percent if you're willing to give it another twenty minutes."

"I'll take my chances." I waved at the catheters. "Take these out. I need to go."

Phoebe grabbed an alcohol pad and began to draw the needle from my upper arm. "So soon? You just arrived."

"As far as USC is concerned, I'm still in New Chennai. I'd rather they never learn I was here. Besides, I have other work to do before I leave."

The needle came out. Phoebe wiped me off, then began on the second. "Still planning your revolution?"

"You said you followed the news about my last case in the Elysium police department. The city was balanced on a razor's edge at the possibility of the Snow Leopard's return, Phoebe. That energy hasn't gone anywhere. It's building. If someone doesn't channel that energy into a useful outlet, it'll explode, same as it did the last time the red planet rose up. That didn't work out so well for Mars the last time. I'd like to avoid that if possible."

She removed the second needle and wiped away the trickle of blood that followed. "I know you're clever, Ambrose. I know you're careful, and thoughtful, and that you consider the impact of your actions. I know you've been working at this for two decades, but you have to understand it's not going to work the way you want it to. You can't free Mars without people dying. Are you prepared to accept that? To be responsible for that fact?"

I rose and grabbed my jacket. "Phoebe, people are going to die whether I act or not. The question is whether anything is accomplished through their sacrifice."

"Are you going to be one of the ones who makes that sacrifice?"

The coat enveloped me. "I hope not."

I turned for the door, but her voice stopped me.

"Ambrose? It was good seeing you."

I met her eyes, and images of happier times flashed before me. "Likewise. Take care, Phoebe."

"You, too."

The sun crested the horizon in the window behind Phoebe. I turned and didn't look back.

THE DOOR GROANED on tired hinges as I pushed it shut behind me, moving slowly due to its massive size. It was more of a cargo hatch than anything intended for human use—the thing even had a locking wheel on it instead of a mechanical or electronic latch—but it was the only unlocked entrance to the building I'd been able to find. As the last few centimeters of space between it and the wall disappeared, I turned and stared into the darkness, giving my eyes a moment to adjust.

I stood in a cavernous warehouse—an old textiles factory based on city records and the remaining equipment that dotted the floor. As my pupils dilated in response to the dim light filtering through windows up high, I spotted dozens of industrial looms, each of them attached to feeding mechanisms that could hold bolts of cloth large enough to cover full soccer pitches. The bolts were all gone, however, and the looms were covered with a fine layer of rust.

I didn't know where within the factory I needed to go, but I figured the floor wasn't it. I headed to the far side, toward some walled off space that might've belonged to the factory foreman or support staff. My footfalls made more sound than I would've liked, but I wasn't too concerned. I kept my gait loose, and I didn't reach for the pistol tucked away in my jacket.

I opened the door to what I presumed were offices to find an even more oppressive darkness within. I stepped inside, noting the dark outlines of a conference table and office chairs beyond. There was something else, too. A vertical line in the wall before me, illuminated by a pale glow.

I skirted the table to the illuminated line, feeling my way around the corner. In the distance, I saw the source of the light. Another pale glow, this time coming from a horizontal line. Light creeping under a door.

I followed it, pausing outside as I located the glimmer of the door knob. I took hold of it, twisted, and stepped in.

Bright light blinded me, and I lifted an arm to shield me from the glare. As I did so, I heard a metallic click.

"Don't move a muscle. Not one."

The voice was a third of an octave lower than I remembered it, but it was also different. More confident. More seasoned. "Hello, Fabia."

"Drake...?"

The light dimmed, and I brought my arm down. A young woman with frizzy golden hair stood to the side of the light, a pistol gripped tight in her hand and pointed steadfastly at my chest. She was taller than I remembered, with fuller lips, higher cheeks, and a sterner face, but she was still the same girl who I'd last seen lugging a backpack around, complaining to Jorge about her geometry assignments.

"Been a while, girl. How've you been?"

"Christ, Drake..." Fabia took two steps and fell into me, wrapping me in a giant hug. She squeezed me tight, the pistol in her hand digging into my back.

I ignored it, hugging her in return. "It's good to see you, too."

"Yeah. It's been too long." Fabia pulled back, her hands moving to my shoulders. She frowned as she took a better look at me. "Damn. You look like shit."

"In my defense, I've been knocked out, tied up, blown up, and had all of my blood replaced in the last twenty-four hours. I also haven't slept in a day and a half."

"Jesus. I simply meant you looked old."

"Oh. *Thanks?"*

Fabia smiled. "You're welcome, you old windbag."

"I'm forty-three, not a hundred and forty-three. Give me a break."

"Still ancient as far as I'm concerned."

The conversation had brought a smile to my lips, too, but it didn't last. "Look. Fabia. I'm sorry about your dad. If I'd have known what he intended..."

She released me and took a step back, the look on her face one of self-admonition. Like me, she preferred to keep her emotions in check rather than let them run free, even if all they led to was a harmless hug and a joke or two.

She shook her head as she holstered her pistol. "Don't apologize. You didn't know. The whole point of our organization is to keep other people from knowing. That way when someone gets captured, it doesn't jeopardize everyone else. My dad knew taking on those Snow Leopard wannabes would put him in danger. It's a risk he entered into willingly. Besides, it's not as if the shootout that killed him was planned."

"No, it wasn't."

The two of us stood there in silence, the ease with which we'd joked suddenly lost.

Fabia leaned against a table at the room's side. "You going to tell me how you found me?"

"Nothing out of the ordinary. I hacked the street cams. Pretty easy once I knew I was supposed to be looking for you."

"And how *did* you know to look for me? Did my dad tell you we were working together?"

"No," I said, "though in retrospect it made total sense. I tracked you from the jacket you left in that elevator shaft after you fire-bombed Shao Wen's apartment. Nice work, by the way. You didn't leave many clues."

"You tracked me from a *jacket?* How... Never mind. I don't want to know."

"Let's just say it eventually made me curious if anyone attended your father's funeral."

Fabia took the mention of the event in stride. "I figured you would've been looking for me in Elysium, not here."

I took a seat in one of the room's unoccupied chairs next to a makeshift cot. "I was at first, but then Sophia noticed someone broke into the Utopian water extraction facility. It didn't take a great leap of faith to assume it might've been someone who wanted to continue to investigate USC's ice thefts."

"Back it up. *Sophia?*"

"My girlfriend. Are you going to pretend you didn't know I was dating someone?"

"Honestly, my dad and I intentionally steered clear of you and everyone else on the EPD throughout that crime spree."

"And you didn't bother to look up what I'd been up to after my name got plastered across the news in the event's aftermath?"

Fabia shrugged. "I mean... I might've. But it's not like I've met her. Is she one of us?"

"Someone who enjoys hanging out in dark abandoned factories? Could be a fetish of hers. I'm not sure."

"A member of the resistance, numb nuts."

I smiled. "Sort of. She's new to the game."

Fabia flicked a hand at the door. "Did you bring her?"

"I wish. I haven't seen her in a month."

"Probably for the best, unless she's ready to be tied up, knocked out, and blown up, too. And please don't make any more fetish jokes."

"I'll demur. Though I wouldn't have minded having her at my back. She needs training, but she's tough. Might've been able to get me out of the jam I was in *without* the use of explosive chemicals."

Fabia waved her hand at me. "Well. Go on. I assume that's why you're here. You need help blowing up more things or tracking down the folks who did it."

"No, that's a separate business entirely. I need to talk to you about the resistance."

Fabia laughed out loud, her mirth filling the small office. "Don't ever change, Drake." She sat down in the only other chair in the room, opposite me. "Alright. I'm listening."

"How well connected are you to the remaining cells?"

"Probably as well as anyone who's left. My dad was in contact with all of them, or at least all the ones left from when you guys disbanded. I'm sure more have cropped up. I haven't been in contact with all of them myself, not directly and not recently, but I could if need be. Why?"

"What's the sentiment among the resistance, Fabia? Does everyone know about the ice theft in Elysium? How are they reacting to it?"

She shrugged. "I can't answer that. I'm not on a group chat with the other cells, but as far as our people? It's the same as everyone else on Mars feels, Drake. People are tired of being ground under USC's heel. They're angry. They're frustrated. But they're scared, too. They'd be stupid not to be."

"Is anyone talking about taking up arms? Seriously considering it, I mean."

"Some always are, but not the public. They might if the ice stuff can be proven and it gets out, though."

"Fabia, we can't let that happen."

"What? Let people fight for their rights or tell them the truth about USC? If USC is stealing from the public, we can't keep it from them. Literally. We have no chance, regardless of whether you or I might think that's the right course of action."

"That may be true, but we can influence the decisions of those around us. The actions they choose to take in response. We need to temper those."

Fabia looked at me with downturned lips. "You can't hold back a tide, Drake. More importantly, why are you so desperate to do so in the first place?"

"Because if we act now, we'll fail, Fabia. Same as your father did, same as your mother did, same as I did when I was with them. But if we wait a little longer—sixteen months—we'll have a chance."

Fabia lifted an eyebrow. "That's an oddly specific amount of time."

"I have a plan, Fabia. A way we can rid ourselves of USC. Permanently."

"I'm not sure that's possible."

"It is. Or at least it might be."

Fabia leaned back in her chair. "Okay. Let's hear it."

I took a deep breath, and then I told her.

FABIA PACED across the floor of her small room, flipping a credit card between her fingers.

"Well?" She hadn't said a word in over two minutes. To be fair, I'd been talking most of that time, but still.

She stopped and met my gaze in full, her brow creased with concern. "You want my honest opinion?"

"Yes."

"It's the craziest god-damned plan I've ever heard, Drake. I don't even know if it's physically possible."

"I downloaded some software. Made some preliminary calculations. I think it is, though we'd need to consult with subject matter experts to be sure. Astrophysicists. Orbital dynamicists. Space flight engineers."

"You downloaded some software. Right. Yeah. We'll need lots of consultations."

"Do we have any folks that fit the bill in the resistance?"

"Maybe? I couldn't say. If not, I'm sure we can buy their services."

"No way," I said. "No one on the outside finds out about this. If USC gets a whiff of it, we're done, and we miss our chance. It has to be people we trust. People *you* trust. This is why I need your help. I've been divorced from the others for too long."

"That's a tall order."

"I know. And the same has to apply to anyone who knows about this. The hackers and the software guys. Anyone you recruit to organize the response once we set the wheels in motion. This has to be the most clandestine operation the resistance has ever attempted."

"Oh, *the most* clandestine? Is that it?"

"No, it's not. Because while we're both doing this, you have to pacify the more warlike elements among our ranks. We can't risk open warfare with USC until we pull this off. It'll be chaos, otherwise."

Fabia collapsed into her chair. She wiped her hands across her face and sighed. "Christ. I don't know..."

"I know this is overwhelming. Not just the task in front of us, but the implications of what I'm proposing, too. I don't take either lightly. I'm not proposing we rush into this without taking every precaution possible, but we don't have a ton of time to waste either. Trust me. I've thought about this for twenty years. This is the only solution that has ever crossed my mind that might actually work."

Fabia hung her head. "Maybe. I just..."

"What is it?"

Fabia took a moment. "Two months ago I knew what I was doing, Ambrose. I had direction. And as soon as *he* was gone... It's not that I doubt myself, but I don't feel like I'm ready. Not for *this*."

"Can I give you a piece of advice?"

"Couldn't hurt."

"Nobody ever feels like they're ready. In truth, they never are. Not for this sort of work, because there's always something on the horizon that'll take you by surprise. The key is knowing that the unknown is coming and having confidence in your ability to deal with it when it does."

Fabia stared at the floor, unconvinced.

I reached out and gripped her shoulder. "I believe in you, Fabia. Jorge believed in you. Most importantly, your mother believed in you. I've met a lot of tough, intelligent women in my life, but she might've been the best of them all. You may have gotten your father's looks, but you got her spirit, without a doubt."

Fabia snorted. "Is that an insult wrapped in a compliment?"

"Not at all. Jorge was a good-looking guy. Though I always told him he would've looked better without his beard." I checked my clock. "It's getting late. I've got to go."

Fabia nodded without asking why. "I'll be in contact. I'll need a couple weeks at least to gather the intelligence we need and to find the right people."

"I think we have a month, tops. Maybe two. Then we'll have to get the ball rolling."

"Understood."

I turned toward the hall, but I paused at the door. "Maybe when this is all over, you can hop back over to Elysium. Meet Sophia. I think she'd like you."

Fabia smiled. "I'd like that. But even when it's over, I'm not sure it'll really be over."

"Maybe not. It never is. Take care, kid."

And I stepped back into the darkness.

43

AUGUST 27, 2160

IN MY TRAVELS of Mars under Winsor's guiding hand, I'd never more than passed through Utopia. There was a reason for that. The metropolis was where I'd spent the most amount of time in USC's grasp, my days in the mining colony of Cassini notwithstanding. Logically, there remained the most people in Utopia who could recognize me should we cross paths on a city street or in a cafe. The odds weren't great, of course. Utopia's population exceeded sixteen million, and during my time in the corps, I'd interacted with perhaps a hundred individuals who might remember me six years later. I doubted if even a third of them remained in the city, but espionage efforts throughout history had been derailed by similar chance encounters of minuscule probability. Avoiding the city entirely had been the safe choice.

As my vactrain whipped through the flat expanse of the Elysium Planitia in the early light of dawn, I wondered if anyone who'd met me would even recognize me now. I hadn't changed much physically. My hair was longer but still on the short side. I'd lost some of my bulk thanks to the combination of Martian gravity and work demands that limited my opportunities for exercise. I didn't shave as often as I used to, preferring to buzz my stubble short instead of taking it to the skin. It was underneath the layers of flesh and bone that the transformation had occurred. It wasn't that I'd learned to run in low gravity or that I'd picked up Martian colloquialisms and added them to my repertoire. It wasn't that I'd committed the geography of the planet to memory or that I'd familiarized myself enough with the major cities to know which parts to go to for sightseeing, shopping, cheap housing, or to get knifed in the back. It wasn't even that I'd grown accustomed to the taste of the local maché or that I knew the difference between government agencies owned by USC and those who merely partnered with them. It was a combination of all that. More than anything, it wasn't about how much I'd learned or how I'd adapted to the environment. It was about how I saw the world.

I remembered when I'd first arrived on Mars, touching down at the Utopia spaceport outside the city. I wasn't a slack-jawed yokel. Spending weeks hurtling through vacuum had dulled the novelty of spaceflight, and the harsh realities of war and death had already hardened me before I ever set foot on the regolith. But I'd nonetheless viewed the world with a different eye, one born of inexperience and ignorance and fear. That first day as I'd sat on the backs of the open transports, riding toward USC's base in the center of the city, every person I'd seen had been a foreigner, a partisan, an enemy. Every building a nest of hostility, every monument a reminder of the tens of millions of kilometers between me and my home. Even in my time spent huddling in resistance tunnels, executing digital attacks against USC servers, my sense of isolation had never been extinguished, and though my anger and fear had been redirected, they hadn't disappeared. It wasn't until Winsor sent me delving into the planet's heart that I'd torn the shroud from my eyes. That I'd seen Mars and its people in a new light. That I'd found a purpose and a sense of place.

Mars is home. Mars is love. Mars is death. I finally understood it. I hoped the death wasn't imminent, however.

I TOOK a rideshare from the vactrain station into downtown, directing my cab to take a nonstandard route to my destination, one that passed within sight of USC's Utopia West base. I didn't tempt fate by stopping the car at the station's gates and snapping a video or two. I merely looked upon the installation from the window of my car, eying the Marauders and transports parked in hangars beyond the barriers at the entrance, soldiers in crisp navy uniforms passing in groups from one building to the next. I could see the top of the mess hall, the barracks I'd shared with Maarten, the addition to the hangars where we'd planned raids against Red cells in the Utopian suburbs. In a flash it was gone, blocked by the walls of apartment complexes as the car plowed relentlessly along the city streets, all of it pushed behind me, memories included.

On a whim, I directed the cab to stop a few blocks shy of my destination, choosing instead to walk the final distance along the crowded sidewalks. I popped into a cafe along the way and ordered a coffee to go, hoping the brew might rejuvenate me after my night spent on the vactrain. I took my time, stopping outside shops to browse the latest fashion trends before crossing into a tree-lined area by the name of Burns Park. It showed green in my minimap but turned out to be little more than a couple basketball courts ringed by a running path. When I stepped past the trees at the edge, the street noise intensified and I saw what I'd come to find: USC Community Hospital.

During my time in the city, it had run without affiliation, and USC doctors had operated out of a makeshift medical ward inside Utopia West. When I'd been hit in the leg by shrapnel during my first patrol duty assignment, it was in the medical ward where doctors had replaced the severed arteries in my legs with synthetic ones. The ward still existed, but following a string of resistance attacks, many of the military's cases had been outsourced to

Community Hospital, which had since been absorbed under USC supervision as part of a wartime mandate. It was there I'd find Phoebe.

I'd done my research on her during the vactrain ride. Winsor was right. She hadn't died after being shot during the firefight that saw me captured at the hands of Marina and the rest of the Snow Leopards, but it had been close. The bullet had indeed hit her in the head as I'd remembered, which was a bad enough injury to sustain even without factoring in Mars's atmosphere. Luckily, Zeta squad's medic, Nakamoto, had been near enough to Phoebe when she went down to apply an emergency hardening gel to her helmet to stop the loss of oxygen from her Suit.

That's when her luck ceased. Around that moment, Marina's Net attack hit us, allowing the resistance to capture me and flee with the last of their members. It was during that fifteen minute stretch that things got bad for Phoebe real quick. The bullet had impacted her on an angle, striking her underneath the cheek, traveling into the brain along the left side of her skull, and back out again. On the one hand, the fact that the bullet hadn't lodged itself in her cerebrum was a good thing, because the hole left in the back of her skull relieved some of the cranial pressure caused by swelling of her brain in response to the trauma. On the other hand, blood from the wound seeped into her throat as she lay on the ground waiting for medical care, meaning she almost drowned in her own blood while her body struggled to overcome the dip in oxygen available to her as a result of her helmet's pressure failure.

As soon as the Net attack faded, Company C's medics evaluated Phoebe as they rushed her out of the tunnels, but at that point she was nearly dead. Only via administration of a supercooled hyperoxygenated air mixture into her Suit were the medics able to slow her heart and brain function enough to get her to a secure facility before she lost hold of the thread of life she clung to.

Even after consulting her medical files, I wasn't sure how she'd done it. My theory was that she was simply too stubborn to die. Either way, her recovery hadn't been easy. Soul-crushing would've been a better way to put it. She stayed in a medically-induced coma in Cassini for two months until she was stable enough to be moved, at which point she was transported to Utopia for further surgeries. At that point, she'd been honorably discharged, because even the USC brass were smart enough to realize she'd never fight again. It explained why I'd never come across her in my spying on the members of Zeta squad months afterwards.

In Utopia, Phoebe continued to receive a steady stream of treatments, from reconstructive surgeries to physical therapy to cognitive rehabilitation. She wasn't released from the hospital for close to seven months, and it took another half year after that for her rehabilitation specialists to declare she'd regained normal cognitive and motor function.

In a cruel twist of fate, however, being released from her doctor's care after being honorably discharged didn't mean her contract with USC had been voided. It simply meant USC didn't expect her to see action in the field. Apparently, her new superior officers at Utopia West tried to push her into administrative work, but Phoebe had nothing of it. She'd instead forced her way back into the hospital and found a spot on the physical therapy team, helping other enlistees who'd suffered wounds similar to hers get back on their feet. She'd done that for a year before being accepted to study medicine, which she'd done for four years while continuing to meet her obligations to USC. She'd only recently graduated and begun her residency, of which she had several more years before she'd be treated with any level of respect by her peers.

I stood there at the street corner, my eyes on the hospital, knowing Phoebe stood somewhere within the building's thick walls. What would it be like to see her again? Would she faint? Welcome me with open arms? Stare at me with complete and total confusion? Or would she scream for help, calling her superiors to report my sudden and unexpected return?

There was only one way to find out.

I brought up my Net interface and made another secure call. It connected shortly. Marina spoke. "Ambrose. Thank god. I've been trying to get a hold of you for almost a day."

"I know. I chose not to respond."

"Well, I'm glad you've finally come to your senses. We need to meet. If you're willing to come back into the fold—"

"Cut the crap, Marina. If you want to meet, you know where I am." I ended the communication abruptly.

I waited there, watching cars and pedestrians go by. A couple minutes passed before I felt someone approach from behind.

Marina crossed the running path and came to a stop beside me, looking uncomfortable. "How did you know I was here?"

"I made you during the ride from the vactrain station. Not you, specifically. At that point all I knew is I was being followed. Rideshare traffic wouldn't have routed a cab behind me along the path I took. I physically spotted you while I grabbed coffee. I stopped a few times after that to make sure you were alone."

Marina didn't look at me. "Salt taught you well."

"Should've used the street cams to follow me instead."

"I would've if I'd had time to crack their system. You didn't give me much to work with."

"If I'd had the time, I would've cracked them myself and known you were spying on me."

Marina sniffed. "Or so you think. I remember beating you at that game before."

The jab drew a smile from my lips, despite the circumstances. "How'd you get here?"

"Tunnels followed by overland transport," she said. "Luckily I was close enough to intercept you. I couldn't track you via Net trace, not since we disabled your beacon after capturing you, but I knew you were coming in via train. As long as I was able to arrive at the station before you, I knew I could follow you."

"I made it too easy. I never should've called you. I got emotional."

Marina remained quiet for a moment. "It's okay to get emotional, Ambrose. I didn't realize what she meant to you. Maybe a few years ago I couldn't have related but... circumstances change. But you have to know what you're doing right now, what you're planning? It's beyond foolish. You're smarter than this."

"I didn't lose my mind overnight, Marina. I've been hiding in plain sight for years, and I've only gotten better over time. Besides, I keep an eye on USC chatter same as you do. Anyone who ever knew me assumes I'm dead or still in your custody."

"Well, revealing yourself to your former lover is a surefire way to ensure at least *one* person knows you're not. And clearly you haven't been keeping a good enough eye on USC's communications, otherwise you'd have paid more attention to the command I gave you. Something is going on, Ambrose. I don't know what exactly, but there's a meeting of USC military officials happening here in Utopia soon. Perhaps as soon as tomorrow."

I lifted an eyebrow. "So that's why you were close by."

"Yes."

"And you don't know what the meeting is about?"

Marina shook her head.

I sighed. "I understand your concern, Marina, but I have to see her. I have to talk to her. I know it's a risk and I know it goes against the rules, but for Christ's sake, not everything in life can revolve around the cause. Isn't that part of what we're fighting for? The right to live freely, to choose for ourselves, the right to the fruits of our labors and to spend time with the people we cherish? You of all people should understand that."

Marina locked gaze with me, her eyes softer than they normally were. "Yes. I do."

"Then you understand why I need to see Phoebe. I promise I won't risk you or myself or the cause itself. I'll do it right."

"Of course you will," said Marina. "I wouldn't expect anything less from you. But that doesn't mean mistakes can't happen. That's why I'm going to help you do it."

44

JULY 2, 2179

I COLLAPSED in the vactrain seat, blinked, and found myself in Elysium, the train filled with passengers grabbing their bags and heading for the exits. I had to check my clock to convince myself time had in fact passed, because as far as I was concerned I might as well have entered a wormhole. A glance at the darkened skies and the Elysium skyline gave proof to the reality of the situation.

I stumbled off the train, feeling slightly more human if still far from refreshed. I wanted nothing more than to catch a ride to Sophia's, kiss her a few times, and fall into a coma, but instead I directed my rideshare to the Counterterrorism offices. It was after hours, but given the events of the last thirty hours, I figured someone who'd be interested in talking to me would be on the scene.

The guards at the entrance didn't blink at my appearance, but they didn't know any more about the inner workings of the organization than did the taco vendor who ran the food stand outside. It wasn't until I rode the elevators up and headed in the direction of Director Schmidt's office that I got the reaction I was expecting.

I found the director hunched over his desk, a half-dozen holos superimposed before him. The door was open, but I paused at the frame and knocked regardless. "Director Schmidt?"

He looked up, sporting bags under his eyes that hadn't been there the last time I'd seen him. His eyes widened. "Agent Drake? *Christ almighty.*"

He shot out of his chair and grasped me by the hand, shaking vigorously. "You're a sight for sore eyes, let me tell you. We thought you were still in New Chennai. What the hell happened?"

"Ran into some trouble. Vikram Nandi got the drop on me. I had to improvise."

"That's what you call burning down his building?"

"You heard?"

"Agent, we may not have as many eyes and ears in New Chennai as we'd like, but we get their newsfeeds. That building's incineration was one of last night's top stories, especially given that a body was recovered from the fire. We couldn't figure out what the hell started it. As far as we knew from Net-tracking data, you'd left Nandi's hours earlier. That said, we didn't figure it was an accident."

"Nandi dosed me and reproduced my Net signal using a transponder while I was under. Sent it around town via drone. And the fire certainly wasn't an accident. It was my only way out."

"I don't doubt it, Agent. Why the hell didn't you get in contact, though?"

"Sir, I had reason to believe local authorities were in hot pursuit of me after I left Nandi's. I figured the transponder was a blessing in disguise, given that they might be tracking me without my knowledge. I left it on to throw them off my scent and got the hell out of dodge as quickly as I could. To be fair, I could've initiated contact upon arrival in Isidis, but I figured the vactrain would get me here soon enough. Now I can deliver my report in person."

"Speaking of which, have a seat. I need to record this for our records, not to mention the Inspector General will want to hear it in the morning." He waved at the chair in front of his desk as he returned to his own seat.

I sat, thankful to be off my feet.

A small microcam built into the Director's desk flared to life. "We're all set, Agent. Start at the beginning."

I told him everything, as detailed and as accurate as I was capable of. Up through my escape from the fire the only changes I made to my story were in the omission of Nandi's injection of me with the graphite-based solution and in the omission of Phoebe's name from the list of papers upon Vikram's tablet. I'd turn the latter over soon enough, and they'd recover the data. If they wanted to apply significance to the inclusion of her research among the rest, that would be up to them, but I wasn't about to let them know I'd had her replace my blood with the synthetic version.

Upon my exit from Nandi's, my story started to veer from the truth. I kept myself in New Chennai for longer than I really had, though I described most of my time spent there as hiding from local authorities. I related my exodus via overland rail and vactrain, including my stop in Utopia, though I described it as a ploy to lose agents who I suspected might still be in pursuit of me. I had to craft my story carefully because in the event that the department asked for memory-based Net records of my flight, I'd need to provide them. By weaving the story I had, I could provide them with snippets that proved what I'd claimed, cobbled together from the actions I'd taken in the time spent between visits to Phoebe and Fabia. All I'd need to do to legitimize them would be hack the timestamps.

Schmidt took it all in silence, letting me finish before deactivating the camera. He rapped his fingers against the desk, rubbing his tongue across his teeth as he did so.

"You killed Vikram," he said after a pause. "We confirmed from local sources it was his body that was recovered from the fire. In your opinion, where does that leave the state of the investigation?"

As with the rest of my testimony, I had to be careful. I couldn't reveal what I'd learned from Phoebe—but I *could* suggest the truth of it and find evidence to support my case in the future. "Sir, in my opinion, Vikram wasn't working alone. He didn't have the requisite medical experience or background to suggest he'd be capable of engineering *any* bioweapon, much less one as curious as the one he used. Have you looked at the graphite deposits unearthed during the autopsies?"

"Some," said Schmidt. "We're still trying to nail down the chemical precursor that was used to deliver them. We have a few theories about how it might've been used to kill our men and women, but nothing definitive yet."

"The point is, to my knowledge, it's not something anyone has previously used as a weapon. Nandi's background suggests he didn't make it himself. He also mentioned a 'brotherhood' in his conversation with me. I don't think it was a name, simply a designation. Regardless, it further suggests Nandi was a part of something larger than himself. Unfortunately, given the public nature of the way I freed myself from the man's custody, whoever was working with him almost certainly is now aware that we're after them."

Schmidt nodded. "I agree with you on both counts, Agent, but don't beat yourself up over it. Without your efforts, we wouldn't know about Nandi at all. As is, we have one dangerous radical disposed of, and we should have a bead on his associates soon enough. Trust me. It's always a process, and the rabbit hole always goes deeper than you expect. There'll be plenty of time to figure out where to go tomorrow. You've earned some rest. You look even more tired than I feel."

I didn't need any more encouragement. I stood, giving Schmidt a nod. "That I am, sir. I hope you won't be far behind me."

"I'll send a message to the Inspector General and be on the next elevator. Call your rideshare now or I might swipe it."

I chuckled. "Yes, sir."

"And Agent Drake? Good work."

I tipped my head in acknowledgment, but I didn't let that slow me from pulling my rideshare app.

I WOKE at the sound of the front door. I cracked my eyes in time to see Sophia waltz into the living room with a bag in hand.

"Hey," I said weakly.

She froze, my words reaching her a fraction of a second before the realization of my presence did. Her face quickly cycled through the normal progression: fright at the unexpected, tension as a result of self-preservation, immediately followed by relief.

The bag hit the floor, and Sophia launched herself at me. Her arms wrapped around my neck, and her tender lips pressed against mine. They paused there for a while, drinking me in, her body weight sinking into me. I wouldn't have minded if lips and body both stayed all night.

Eventually, Sophia pulled back, the cool apartment air sweeping between our bodies. Her hands moved to cup my face. Her dark eyes were soft but her nose downturned. "You know, it strikes me that I should be upset with you for not calling."

"I guess I should count my lucky stars that I'm so irresistibly kissable, then."

Sophia's nose tilted up, but a hint of a smile tickled her lips. "Among other things. Did you just get in? You look exhausted."

"What gave it away? That I fell asleep on your couch in my shoes and coat?"

"It was a hint. You also look like you got into a fight with an auto-grooming machine. And *lost.*"

"It's been a long few days."

Sophia lifted an eyebrow.

I sighed. "I promise I'll tell you everything. The important thing is I got the guy who killed the USC diplomats. He won't be a problem anymore."

The second eyebrow joined the first. "You killed him?"

"He forced my hand."

"Well, that *is* good news. And it explains your grooming issues."

I'd dated tough women before Sophia, but I don't think any of them would've reacted quite the same way to the revelation that I'd recently killed a man. "I have other news that's potentially better. I found Fabia."

That seemed to shock Sophia more than the news of Vikram's death. "You did? Where?"

"In Utopia. You were right. She was the one to break into the water extraction facility. I was able to track her from there using security cams, though she didn't make it easy. She's like a ground-hog. Goes underground at the first chance, every time."

"That's wonderful. And?"

"And your work was instrumental to helping me find her. Really. Without the starting point of the water extraction facility, I never would've tracked her."

Sophia smiled for real this time. "Oh, sweetheart. I wasn't looking for validation, though I appreciate you giving credit where it's due. I meant, what then? For all the talk of finding this Fabia woman, you never told me why you were so desperate to locate her. Did you talk? Are we joining forces? Did you hatch a plan to remove USC from power?"

"Yes, to all three, in various degrees. Though we didn't hatch a plan together. I proposed one. She was rather taken aback by it."

Sophia blinked. "You already had a plan?"

"Yes."

Sophia moved off me and settled onto the couch, leaving a half foot of space between us. "You didn't tell me you had a plan."

I breathed deeply. I'd been afraid of this. "Sophia, it's not because I don't trust you that I hadn't mentioned it. The plan's been coming together in my mind for some time now, but it only recently coalesced. I didn't know how to express it to anyone without it sounding utterly crazy. Even more importantly, I didn't want to tell it to you for fear of you thinking less of me."

"Is that it? Darling, I won't think less of you for having half-baked ideas."

"That's not what I mean." I stood and started to pace, simply to put more space between us. "I mean, if you knew what my plan was, you might question my core. The fundamental essence inside me."

"Ambrose, what are you talking about? We had this discussion already. I know you're no saint. You're a flesh and blood man who's made good decisions and bad. I'm not sure you've taken any of them lightly. What I like about you is you're thoughtful and passionate and driven, and you always consider the ramifications of even the smallest actions. You always look at the bigger picture. If this crazy plan of yours is the best you've come up with, I trust it has serious merits. Short of you planning a genocide, I can't imagine it'll affect how I view you."

I took a moment, trying to think of how to respond. "When you were in school, you learned about Earth's global warming in history class, right?"

Sophia blinked, clearly confused. "Yes."

"I remember reading about a politician of the time. I can't remember his name. He made the argument that if the oceans rose a centimeter every year, year after year, eventually inundating New York and Singapore and Bangkok, it wouldn't constitute a tragedy because there would be time to engineer solutions to the changes. It would only be a tragedy if the oceans rose ten meters overnight. Then some eight years after the man's statements, the west antarctic ice sheet broke off and fell into the ocean, and the oceans did rise by about two and a half meters in a matter of hours."

"I've read about that. What of it?"

I met Sophia's eyes. "My plan is more west antarctic ice shelf and less gradual global warming. It's going to cause a lot of immediate pain to a lot of folks. People will die. It's not a possibility. It's a certainty. There will be misery and despair. But it's also the only way I've come up with to give us a fighting chance against USC, and every other option creates death, misery, and despair, too. It's possible my plan creates the least."

Sophia nodded. "I believe you."

"Knowing that, do you still want to hear it?"

Sophia didn't respond right away. She thought it over. One more thing I liked about her. "I do."

And so I told her, and Sophia became the third person to discover how I planned to overthrow the tyrants of Mars.

45

AUGUST 29, 2160

MY CLOCK READ quarter till eleven as I trudged up the clean-swept concrete steps in the Community Hospital's stairwell, heading toward the tenth and final floor. A badge with my picture swung from the front pocket of my white coat, listing me as Dr. Henry Marsden. As I approached the door, the lock automatically clicked opened in response to the chip in my badge. Given that I'd gained access to the hospital's security, I could've unlocked the door remotely via Net, but having a functional badge that pointed to a thorough bio I'd uploaded into the system was more efficient and less conspicuous.

I pushed my way into the corridor beyond, the door closing behind me with a soft click. Shadows lay across the hospital corridor, with only soft lights from strips near the floorboards providing a cool glow. A similar glow was visible through the windows, radiating from the streetlights of the city below.

I walked purposefully, the scent of industrial cleaner thick in my nostrils. There was a time not so long ago where I might've fussed with my coat, checked my badge, avoided eye contact with passing staff, or paused to check my minimap as I went, all tells that might've given someone who didn't recognize me pause, but years of living a lie in public had replaced the blood in my veins with ice. I wasn't worried about being recognized. I'd gone through the hospital's employee and patient database with a fine-toothed comb. One nurse who'd attended to me during my injuries worked in the trauma ward on the third floor, not to mention a doctor who might've seen my face in USC's facilities once upon a time. Both worked day shifts, and my surveillance efforts showed both were at home, probably sound asleep in their beds. The only other individual in the building who'd ever set eyes on me was my target.

Phoebe.

The blood within me felt less icy just thinking about her. I hoped I knew what I was doing.

I turned down a side corridor, past the central elevators, and through a pair of secure doors into the ICU. The two nurses at the station didn't even look at me as I passed, their eyes glued to displays flashing streams of patient biometrics. I nodded my head in their direction nonetheless before heading down the hallway to my left. I followed it to the second to last door on the right.

There I paused. I took a deep breath, looked into the camera in the corner of the hall by the windows, nodded once, and pushed my way in.

The room into which I passed was lighted in the same manner as the hallway, with thin strips providing a soft glow near the floor. Hospital records indicated the room was occupied by a coma patient who'd been unconscious since suffering a brain hemorrhage falling down a flight of stairs, but it was the woman at the foot of the bed that interested me. She stood there in a white doctor's coat, comparing metrics from a bed-mounted display to the vitals on her tablet. Her dark hair was cut shorter than I remembered it, falling across her cheeks in a simple bob. The nighttime lighting placed half her face in shadow, but the features I could see were unmistakable. The straight, low-profile nose. The large, almond-shaped eyes.

I couldn't tear my eyes from her.

Phoebe's fingers flicked at her tablet a few times before she looked up. "Just checked Mrs. Chen's EEG and CBFs, and..." Her brow furrowed. "Oh. I'm sorry. I thought Dr. Durrani was the attending tonight."

I thought I'd prepared myself to face her, but in that moment, I couldn't summon a single word to my lips. All I could do was stare at her and remember. Remember the way she'd shared awkward, inappropriate tips on our first vactrain ride. Remember the sight of her emerging from the training pool on Luna, dripping wet and graceful as a mermaid. Remember her soft touch and the special smile she'd only shared with me after intimate moments. Remember the sadness etched into her face as she'd told me she couldn't see me anymore in the wake of my demotion. All I could do was remember and tremble.

The furrows in her brow deepened. "I'm sorry, you are..."

It was then I realized the baseboard lights didn't extend to the door. I stood in shadow. I took two steps forward. "Phoebe..."

Her eyes widened, and her jaw fell. She took a step back, then another before stumbling. I lurched forward, but she caught herself and collapsed into a sofa chair. "My God... *Ambrose?*"

"It's me, Phoebe."

The confusion froze her face. "But... I... don't understand. I thought you were in Red custody. Or worse. I thought you were..."

"Dead? I know the feeling. I've thought you were for the last six years. Until a few days ago."

I wasn't sure what I was expecting from Phoebe, but she didn't cry. She didn't embrace me. She merely sat there in shock, unable to process what she was seeing.

"What are you doing here?" she asked. "Were you rescued? Did you escape? Why are you dressed as a doctor? Are you in medical school? Why does your badge say Marsden?"

"Slow down. I came because I wanted to see you, Phoebe. I promise I'll explain anything you want to know about me, but first

—" I pulled a small electronic device from my pocket, barely larger than a pill, and held it between my fingers. "I'm going to need you to grant me access to your Net."

"What?" Phoebe blinked. "What are you talking about? What is that?"

"It's a Net transponder. It can simulate signals from a Net that's been deactivated or disconnected from the public network."

"Why would I need to do that? Ambrose, what's going on?"

"I'll be happy to explain everything, but I need you to trust me first."

Phoebe seared me with her look, her shock and confusion slicing at my emotional core. *"Trust you?* Ambrose, I haven't seen you in years, haven't heard from you, haven't heard anything *about* you. Now you show up during my work hours dressed like a doctor, refusing to answer simple questions. And you're asking me for my *trust?* What am I supposed to say? None of this makes any sense."

I wanted to reach out, to touch her, to comfort her, but I couldn't. That wasn't who I was anymore. Not to her, at least.

I took a seat on the other sofa chair. "I understand how strange this is, Phoebe. It wasn't my intention to come here and cause you any grief, I promise. I just wanted to see you. It's been so long."

Phoebe looked at me, a wistfulness in her eyes, but she didn't say a thing.

"You want to know why you should trust me. I know it may seem irrelevant, but please, answer me a simple question. Why are you doing what you do?"

Phoebe blinked, her confusion over my presence morphing into confusion of a more manageable sort. "What do you mean?"

"After discovering you were alive, I tried to familiarize myself with your past. That's how I found out you were here, working at USC Community. Why did you go into medicine after your injury?"

Phoebe took a moment to respond. "Ambrose, I should've died.

When last I saw you... I don't remember anything until about five months after that incident. Medicine saved my life. It was an approved course of action following my discharge from the corps. I owed it to the field."

"Not to the field. Only to the people around you."

"Excuse me?"

I sighed. "We didn't leave each other's lives on the best of terms, but that doesn't mean I've forgotten you, Phoebe. Who you really were. You joined the corps for the same reasons I did. Because you wanted to make a difference. Because you wanted to protect the ones you loved. Because you wanted to stand up for what was right and for people who didn't have the ability to do it for themselves. You thought that path was laid out before you, easily accessible by a rocket booster to Mars. It was only after months spent on freezing ground that you realized it wasn't. But you didn't give up. The corps may not have offered you a path to your goals, but you found one anyway. A way to help people. A way to protect them. A way to make a difference. I admire that, because I've tried to follow the same path myself.

"I won't tell you I haven't changed in the years we've spent apart. I'm not the same kid you met on that train to Titusville, but in my heart, in the ways that matter, I'm exactly the same. I think you are, too. That's why I'm asking you to trust me for a moment."

Phoebe kept my gaze, her lips slightly parted. She glanced at the coma patient, then back at me. In the background, a medical device beeped gently, intermittently. I'd only now noticed it.

"I don't love you anymore, Ambrose. You have to know that."

"I know. To be honest, I'm not sure either of us knew what love was when we met."

Phoebe nodded. She gestured at the transponder. "How does that work?"

"Just connect to it via Net. Grant me access. I'll take care of the rest."

Phoebe did as I asked. "You know, I tried to contact you once. After the raid. Is this how you've remained off grid the whole time?"

"One of many ways." I activated the transponder through my Net interface. "That's it. As far as anyone else knows, you're still right here in Room 1052, but your Net won't record anything I tell you until we reactivate its connection."

This time Phoebe glanced at the door. "Why wouldn't you want that recorded?"

"I mentioned how we're the same, Phoebe. You're been bettering yourself, studying medicine, trying to heal those affected by the war. I realized the war wasn't helping anyone, as well, but I've taken a different path to pay penance for it."

"Are you saying... you deserted?"

"No, Phoebe. I was captured. I was a prisoner—at first."

It didn't come all at once, but the anger grew as Phoebe processed what I'd told her. "I understand your resentment at USC. I didn't sign up for the journey I got either, but the Reds *bombed our home,* Ambrose. They're murderers. Terrorists. You can't possibly tell me you *joined* them?"

I always knew we'd get to this point in the conversation. It was the inevitable landing spot. And so I told her—everything. About how I'd come to the conclusion that USC had initiated the nuclear strike on Los Angeles, killing millions in an effort to boost their own war effort against Martian rebels. About how the Snow Leopard who'd claimed responsibility was nothing more than a digital simulation, and that USC had released the video to lay the bombing at the feet of the Reds. I explained how I'd been captured, how I'd been recruited, what I'd done in the years I'd been missing, and how I'd worked, rather fruitlessly, to bring a stop to USC's subjugation of Mars.

Phoebe sat through it all stone-faced, her initial shock having morphed into something far more serious. When I finished, she sat there in silence.

"Well," I said eventually. "Say something."

Phoebe shook her head. "I understand you wanting to see me, Ambrose. If I'm being honest, there's always been a part of me that wanted to see you again, too. But you could've spied on me from afar, or if you had to say hello, you could've lied. Told me you'd been freed, that you were on your way home to get away from it all. I would've believed you. It would've been better... Better than this."

I noticed she didn't dispute any of the things I'd told her. Didn't fight me on any of my claims. "I trust you, Phoebe. I've always trusted you, and I thought you deserved the truth. That's why I told you."

"What if I would've been happier not knowing?"

"You never struck me as the blissfully ignorant type." I stood and grabbed the transponder. "I've stayed too long. You should get back to work, and I should go."

"Yes." She rose on unsteady legs. "But... what happens now?"

"Ideally? I fade away. No one ever knows I was here except you, and you never mention I was here, although I can't stop you if you wish it otherwise."

"That can't be it. There has to be more."

"I didn't lie to you, Phoebe. I came to see you and to be honest with you. I thought I'd missed my chance six years ago. But I'll never bat away the outstretched hand of a friend."

"The answer hasn't changed in the years we've spent apart, Ambrose. I can't be that for you anymore."

"Would you be interested in being an ally, instead?"

Phoebe shook her head. "I don't know if I can be that, either. Even knowing what you've told me, I don't know if I feel the same way you do. I need time."

"That's okay." I wanted to reach out and touch her, but I didn't. "Take care, Phoebe. It was good seeing you."

I turned toward the door.

Her voice stopped me in my tracks. "Ambrose, wait. Will I ever see you again?"

"Only if you want to. Now that I know you're here, it won't be hard for you to get in touch."

I FELT strange as I walked down the hall, past the nurse's station toward the ICU's exit. On the one hand, my reunion with Phoebe could've gone far worse. She hadn't screamed, hadn't threatened to turn me in, or slapped me, but at the same time, it hadn't gone as well as I could've hoped. I hadn't expected us to fall into each other's arms, to share a cry or a passionate kiss. I knew our relationship had long since scattered on the wind. And I'd gotten closure. I could finally move on, finally commit my full focus to the path in front of me, but I'd nonetheless hoped Phoebe would've been more open to the sentiments expressed in my speech.

I pushed through the security doors and headed for the stairs. Behind me, the doors took longer to click shut than they should've, and I heard light footsteps. I didn't look back. I'd expected them.

The elevators dinged in front of me. A door opened, spitting out a trio, two men and a woman in crisp blue USC uniforms. I'd already begun nodding a casual greeting as I moved to pass them when the woman in the front spoke.

"Private Drake?"

We locked eyes. It couldn't be, but it was. Major Watkins, now Lieutenant Colonel Watkins, stood before me, staring at me in shock.

46

JULY 29, 2179

IT ONLY TOOK me a few days to cobble together a credible argument for how Karam Nandi was involved in the development of the bioweapon that killed the ambassadors at Terby Station. Luckily, none of my superior officers at Counterterrorism contradicted my hypothesis. The more research we did on Vikram, the more obvious it became to the entire team that he wasn't responsible for the development of the graphite-based poison, and it wasn't a leap to shift the suspicion for said development to his brother Karam. In fact, the more I researched the man, the more I convinced myself he was responsible, beyond even the level of certainty I'd felt after discussing the matter with Phoebe.

By all accounts, the man was a genius. He'd enrolled in secondary school two years early and would've gone to college three years before his peers if not for the fact that he'd spent a year honing his musical dexterity in the presence of legendary piano virtuoso Yanny Bajpeyi. Of course he graduated as his school's valedictorian, and he went on to graduate from Jalapal Academy of Higher Education with highest honors despite majoring in both biomedical engineering and chemistry, captaining the college's debate team, and authoring a hundred and fifty page undergrad-

uate thesis on the effects of socioeconomic disparities on the liveli-
hoods of Mukt youth in different regions of the Hellas basin. All
that occurred *before* he studied medicine and completed his residency under Phoebe at Utopia-Turing University.

Unfortunately, while I was able to track Karam's educational
record quite well, I found the man himself to be much more
elusive. After leaving Phoebe's side a decade ago, whether due to
Phoebe's influence or not, he became a ghost. Even with the
combined power of every USC database at my fingertips, I couldn't
locate him. I searched bank records, credit cards, communications
backlogs, employment records, tax records, local utility and
internet providers, even ticket sales for vactrains and spaceports,
but I couldn't find anything related to Karam Nandi more recent
than May of 2170—at least, not for the *correct* Karam Nandi. It
was a common enough name after all.

I was left with the inescapable conclusion that Karam had been
going under one or more assumed names for the past decade, and I
didn't have any idea what they might be. That alone wasn't a problem. The fact that our traditional methods of unearthing enemy
agent aliases weren't working was.

As far as I was concerned, the key to uprooting Karam lay in
his connection to his brother, Vikram. The two had been in
communication, of that I was sure, but in killing Vikram, I'd
severed the one indisputable remaining link that I could use to find
the other, not to mention likely driven Karam even further
underground.

I didn't despair at first. I tracked every delivery Vikram had
sent and received going back as far as the databases would let me,
but it appeared the equipment in his laboratory had all been
purchased legally from reputable third parties. The chemicals likewise, except for the ones he'd stolen from the New Chennai
Medical Center, and none of his personal deliveries were ever
made to Karam. Whatever exchanges the two of them must've

made had to have occurred via dead drops or other untraceable means. Similarly, call and message records obtained from Net providers didn't indicate that Vikram had contacted Karam within the last decade, even after weaseling out the actual recipients of Vikram's encrypted messages, most of which appeared to be encrypted as a force of habit. Worse still, if Vikram had been in contact with any members of his 'brotherhood' besides Karam, it wasn't apparent from the records. Either their terrorist organization only consisted of the two of them, or their members were far better concealed than they had any right to be. Given the complexities involved in keeping large groups hidden from sight, I assumed it was the former. The bright side of that was that our adversary was a single man, working alone, with only his wits and skills keeping him hidden. The bad part was that said man seemed to have an abundance of both.

With traditional digital tracking methods failing us, we moved to other, more conventional means. We set up surveillance of Vikram's burned building, of his parents' home, and of any family and friends from the brothers' previous lives. Through three weeks, none of it had yielded results. As Karam's profile coalesced, I figured it never would.

I didn't give up though. It wasn't in my nature. A man as dangerous and brilliant as Karam Nandi could do immense damage, not just to USC but to humanity as a whole. He needed to be found, but I also couldn't ignore my work with Fabia. Deadlines were approaching that couldn't be missed. Deadlines I couldn't ignore.

As usual, it was up to me to figure out how to balance the two.

I KNOCKED on Director Schmidt's door. "Director? You got a minute?"

He looked up from his holos. "Agent Drake. Sure." He wiped a few. "What's up?"

"Did you get that report I sent you earlier this morning?"

Schmidt's brow furrowed. "Report. Uh... I'm sure I did, but I haven't gotten to it yet. Too many other things going on. Remind me?"

I stepped into the Director's office and stood behind one of the chairs, grasping the seat back. "It was about Vikram Nandi's internet search history. We'd analyzed everything that was data mined from his new place, but I finally got around to looking through the results of his searches at his previous apartment. The one he'd been at during his Medical Center days."

"Anything interesting?"

That was shorthand for tell me so I don't have to read the report. "Maybe. Many of the searches were for mundane, everyday stuff. Who's selling the brand of hand lotion I like? When's the new Canderous Ford interactie coming out? What's tomorrow's weather? The usual. And there were all the expected medical, chemical, and biological searches related to the bioweapon he used. I also found a few searches related to our diplomats' travels to New Chennai, indicating he'd been targeting them for a while, as well as a bunch of random, one-off queries. But three months before he left his apartment, so maybe nine months ago, he made a series of queries that seemed out of the ordinary. He was researching a number of disparate locations in and around Olympus. The Gold-water Bank Stadium, the Olympus Aquarium, and the observatory on top of Mount Olympus, among others."

"You think he was planning a vacation?"

"My first thought was that he might be picking a target."

Schmidt rubbed his chin. "I suppose he might've dabbled in explosives as well as bioweapons. Or he might've had a new trans-mission method in mind, even that far back. From what you describe, it sounds like he might've been trying to hide his true object of interest with a bunch of random bullshit. Did you find any odd searches after that initial string that would suggest what that might be?"

I shook my head. "Thought of that, too, but no. Nothing."

Schmidt snorted. "Maybe he *was* planning a vacation. Do we have knowledge of his whereabouts at the time?"

"Not really. It was shortly after he'd left his job at NCMC. It's possible he actually went to Olympus."

"You want to go check it out?"

"I'd like to, yes. If he showed his face at any of those locations... it might be a lead."

"Given how cold the trail on his brother has gotten, I'd say any lead would be worth celebrating. How soon can you leave?"

"I've only been on this job a few months, but I've been training for it my whole life. I have a bag packed at my desk. I'll hail a rideshare."

THE VACTRAIN RIDE TO Olympus only took an afternoon. The overland transport to the Olympus Mons Observatory took substantially longer than that. Despite the fact that I'd lived in Olympus for months during my stint with Winsor Salt and that I'd been on Mars for over twenty-five years, I'd never once scaled the largest volcano in the solar system, nor had I even paid it much attention. Never once had I taken a day trip from Olympus to gaze upon its majesty, but that was the sort of thing Earther tourists tried to do. Native Martians knew better.

Olympus Mons is simply too big to enjoy. Despite its prodigious height—almost three times that of Mount Everest—Olympus Mons doesn't look like much because it's too large to take in all at once. If plucked from its home and set down on Earth, the entire thing wouldn't even fit in the state of Arizona. Because it's so big and because the slope is so gentle, the curvature of the planet limits how much of it you can see at any given time. From the base, all you can see is a slowly ascending mound that eventually curves off the edge of the planet, and only by looking away from the mountain can you notice a difference in the height of the horizon. Supposedly, the same is true at the top of the volcano, though I'd heard the view of the sheer cliffs that fall into the caldera is pretty impressive.

So instead of staring at the volcano's shallow slopes from the window of my transport, transfixed by its imperceptible majesty, I double checked my files on Vikram Nandi and wondered if my intel on the Observatory was accurate.

A little more than a day after departing, my transport reached the peak of the mountain, though I wouldn't have known it if not for the presence of the small community at the top. It wasn't much. Perhaps three dozen structures: apartments, an infirmary, and a modest motel among them. A field of solar panels stretched to the north of the settlement, a more economical solution than operating and staffing a full fusion reactor, and to the east, a kilometer removed from the rest of the buildings, was the Olympus Mons Observatory. It, too, underwhelmed, though the gleaming silver dome certainly *looked* like the sort of structure science fiction writers of old expected Mars to be dotted with one day.

I knew better than to be fooled by appearances. The observatory housed a scope with an effective aperture of over eighteen meters, far larger than anything on Mauna Kea or the Canary Islands on Earth, making it the most powerful terrestrial optical telescope ever built. The astronomers in charge of it still had to deal with occasional dust storms and high altitude orographic clouds, but when the atmosphere played nice, the images it produced of the Jovian moons were downright spectacular.

The transport dropped me off near the base of the dome. The operator had told me there was an underground tunnel with moving walkways connecting the observatory with the rest of the settlement, which would be helpful for when I'd have to retire to the hotel, but for the time being, I still had to deal with airlocks. I changed and cycled and braved the winds and cycled and changed again, and when I'd packed my Suit into my bag and visited the lavatory, I went in search of a woman by the name of Hanna Kieliszkowski.

I didn't have to look far. By the time I got out of the staging area into the domed roof beyond, I spotted a series of offices curving off in a hallway to my right. A woman in a trim grey skirt suit with wavy brown hair that fell to her shoulders spotted me through the windows in the first office. She waved and hopped from her seat.

"Hi, there," she said as she bustled into the hall. "You must be Mr. Drake. Er... Agent Drake? Which do you prefer?"

I shook the hand she offered. It was floppy, but professional. "Either is fine. You must be Miss Kieliszkowski."

"Please. Call me Hanna. I've been expecting you. Obviously. It's not every day that we get a visit from someone in Counterterrorism."

"To be fair, it's not every day I visit an observatory. This is my first time here, actually."

Hanna' face lit up. "Is it? It's a remarkable piece of engineering. A real testament to the astronomers, technicians, and contractors who put it together. Would you like a tour?"

"Eventually, yes. Should we speak in your office first?"

"Oh. Of course. Please. After you."

I followed the young woman's outstretched hand, noting the name plate on her door with the titles "Staff Services" and "Community Events" underneath it. I took a seat as Hanna closed the door.

"So, Mr. Drake," she said as she headed to her chair. "What can I help you with? The initial communication I received from you was rather vague, if I'm being honest."

"That was by design. In my field of work, it's in the interest of everyone involved to be judicious with information. The very opposite of scientific research, I know. Suffice it to say I'm on the hunt for someone who may or may not have come through here posing as a tourist nine months ago. You organize tours for the observatory, correct?"

"Among other things, yes. I also give the tours, and I work with the company who organizes the tour groups in Olympus. Can I ask the name of the individual you're looking for?"

I pulled my tablet from my pocket, set it on Hanna's desk, and activated the holo feature. An image flared to life at eye level. "Vikram Nandi. Mid thirties. He may have taken measures to hide his features while he was here, but I doubt it."

Hanna's brow furrowed. "Hmm. He doesn't look familiar, but if you give me a moment to pull up our visitor lists..."

"That won't he helpful. He wouldn't have travelled under his real name. Though I will need access to those lists later, as well as some other records you may have on file."

"Certainly, Mr. Drake. But I have to ask... This man. Mr. Nandi. You said he might've been posing as a tourist. If he didn't come to look at the telescope, why would he have come?"

I adjusted myself in the seat. "That's classified information."

"I see." Hanna fell silent, and she looked a little confused.

"Tell me, Hanna. What sort of work goes on here at the observatory?"

The young woman perked again. "Oh. All sorts, Mr. Drake. Loads of scientific research for one. You may have heard about the discovery of the trans-Neptunian object seven one seven five nine eight Cresphontes? That was discovered by our astronomers. But there are hundreds more projects and proposals underway at any given time. To do them justice would take all day, and even then I'm sure I'd miss half of them. But scientific studies are only allotted half the time on the telescope and supporting equipment.

We also perform a lot of routine work for USC and Martian municipalities. We track satellites, rocket trajectories, and we're closely involved with USC's space division working on traffic management."

"When you say satellites, do you mean natural or man made?"

"Both. Ultimately, the tracking is done to ensure the safety of space travel for anyone arriving or departing from Mars. Timing launch and landing windows to make sure no one hits space debris may not be as large of a challenge here as it is on Earth, but it's a vital and complicated task."

"I have no doubt." I reached over and grabbed my tablet, wiping the holo as I put it into my pocket. "Alright, Miss Kieliszkowski. I'll take that tour now, if you're still willing. Afterwards I'm going to need your help with those files."

The young woman shot out of her seat. A smile stretched her lips. "It would be my pleasure, Mr. Drake. Please, come with me."

47

AUGUST 29, 2160

WHEREAS PHOEBE HAD GROWN and changed, Watkins looked the same as ever. The same chin length sandy-blonde hair. The same cold, blue-eyed stare. The same tension in her jaw, and the same aura of callous severity. She was staring right at me, and she'd spoken my name.

I froze, unsure what to do. I couldn't run. That would only heighten her suspicions. I couldn't claim she'd made a mistake—she'd already recognized me, and I hadn't bothered to mask my appearance. Would the lies Phoebe had suggested I use on her work on Watkins? Doubtful. She'd want to know every detail of my release, and there remained a good chance she was still looking for me, still trying to track down my whereabout after losing me in the tunnels so many years back.

Panic gripped me. Blood pounded in my ears. The moisture seemed to have left my tongue, leaving my mouth thick and mealy. Watkins took a step toward me, her face ghostly pale. "Drake? Is that you?"

It was then I realized I *did* know what I had to do, but I didn't want to do it. Winsor had walked me through this scenario, but we'd never practiced it. It wasn't the sort of thing you *could* practice.

My lips parted, but before I could say a word, a firm hand pushed me to the side. Marina swept into the space I'd occupied, a glint of steel in her hand. Watkins' eyes barely had time to widen before the suppressed pistol in Marina's hand spat out a *pat pat.* Watkins grunted as red sprouted from her chest.

Time slowed as Marina pivoted. Two more shots escaped her pistol's muzzle. *Pat pat.* One of Watkins' escorts grimaced and stumbled, flecks of blood spraying into the air. Watkins still hadn't hit the ground. Marina swung her arm back to the other side, but the second of Marina's escorts wasn't waiting to die. His arm flashed to his side. A pistol filled his grip. Not a suppressed pistol like Marina's, but a standard USC issue Browning Hi-Power V3.

I lurched toward the man, but I was too late. He fired at the same time Marina did, the crack of his pistol like a firecracker going off in my ear. Bullets hit him in the chest as my forearm swept into his hand. The gun flew, clattering off the wall. I grabbed the man by the upper arm, twisted, and spun. I hacked a heavy blow into the side of his neck, right at the carotid artery. The man collapsed in a heap, losing consciousness as the blood pressure in his brain dropped abruptly from my strike, although the bullets in his chest couldn't have helped either.

Marina stumbled forward, clutching her chest with her free hand. She wheezed as she flicked her pistol at the prone bodies on the floor. More taps, three sets of two. *Pat pat, pat pat, pat pat,* as she sent bullets flying into the skulls of Watkins and her compatriots, scrambling their brains so nothing could be posthumously extracted via Net. As she swiveled toward the man who'd pulled his gun, I saw the red spreading from underneath her hand.

I flew into action without hesitation. I grabbed Marina by the arm and burst into a run, turning the corner past the elevators before heading toward the stairwell. Behind me, I could already hear distant sounds of commotion, but I didn't look back. Marina groaned and stumbled as we ran. I slipped an arm around her torso to help take her weight, but I didn't slow. Luckily no one exited their rooms in the fifteen seconds it took us to reach the stairs. I slammed my hip against the release and pushed through, dragging Marina with me down the steps as I pulled up my hospital security Net interface. As soon as I heard the click of the latch, I activated all the locks on the top floor, but I left the elevators operational as a distraction. If anything, authorities would be using them to head up, and I'd rather they take them than the stairs.

I checked the surveillance cameras as I helped Marina down the steps—the live feeds, not the falsified loops I'd spliced into the system that showed no trace of me wandering the halls or of Marina wandering them in my wake, keeping an eye on me. Two nurses had arrived on the scene. One was applying chest compressions to Watkins, screaming at the other who was calling for help.

Thanks to the false feeds, I wasn't concerned about anyone recognizing us as Watkins' murderers, but police would be on the scene in minutes. Everyone in the hospital would be a suspect, most of all the woman who was bleeding from a gunshot wound to the chest.

I glanced at Marina as we raced down the stairs. Her face was pale, more from shock than from loss of blood at this point. Her breath rasped as it crawled from her throat, and the stain on the front of her shirt was spreading.

"Want me to take a look?"

"Later," she sputtered.

We sprinted toward the first floor as quickly as we could. I kept an eye on the security cameras, making sure no one was heading toward us, though I'd locked all the entrances to our stairwell. As we approached the ground floor landing, I pulled Marina to the side. She resisted, grunting in pain. "We need to get out of here. *Now!*"

"I agree, which is why we can't afford to be stopped by a nurse who happens to see your chest. Which pocket has the foam injector?"

Marina sucked air through her teeth. "Left."

I reached into Marina's pocket and extracted the applicator. I pinched off the nozzle tip. "This is going to sting."

She nodded. I pulled Marina's bloodied hand from her chest and slid the nozzle into the blood-filled cavity left behind by the gunshot. I depressed the button and the applicator hissed, injecting a rapidly expanding biodegradable foam into the wound. Marina hissed and arched her back into the wall as the antiseptics in the foam reached nearby nerve endings.

I stripped off my doctor's jacket and forced Marina into it, ignoring her groans of pain as I pushed her arms through the coat sleeves. "Hand in your pocket. It's a dead giveaway. Lean forward a little. Can't let the coat touch your wound. The foam'll bleed through soon enough. Can you walk without grimacing?"

Marina nodded weakly.

"I'll be right by you. Slow and steady. Can't show any emotion."

I opened the door and held it for her as we walked through. Hallway activity wasn't as frantic as I'd feared, though camera footage from near the elevators showed a beehive of activity. A doctor and nurse pair raced past us, not even looking our way as we headed away from the front of the hospital.

Marina and I had put together contingency plans for different scenarios. In the event everything went perfectly and Phoebe didn't threaten to expose me, we would've walked out of the building one after the other and dusted our hands of the situation, wiping the security systems as we left. Even though I'd been confident Phoebe wouldn't react with hostility to my presence, we'd put a contingency in place for if she did. Marina had suggested, only somewhat jokingly, that eliminating her would be the only way to ensure her perpetual silence, but I'd made it exceedingly clear I'd never put her in harm's way, much less cause her harm directly. Instead I'd agreed to inject her with a fast-acting benzodiazepine that would muddle her memories, all while I tinkered with her Net via the transponder to eliminate any evidence of my presence.

Both of those situations encompassed our business as normal scenarios, but unfortunately we'd landed in one of the shit-hits-the-fan scenarios instead. We'd anticipated a situation where I was stopped, questioned, or otherwise unmasked. We'd even considered a situation where one of us was stabbed, shot, or otherwise injured. We knew where to go and what to do.

Marina's pace slowed as we reached the loading bay, so I placed a hand on her back and gave her a subtle nudge. The street cameras showed a barrage of police cars pouring into the circle at the front of the hospital. Officers jumped from their vehicles and raced toward the entrance as we reached the garage in back. Paramedics rolled a gurney from the ambulance parked at the far side, but several other vehicles sat unattended in the half-dozen adjacent spots. Checking over my shoulder to make sure no one was watching, I hopped into one of the empty ambulances, pulled Marina up behind me, and closed the door.

I'd only cracked the hospital security and not the city-wide street camera system, so escaping via foot from the hospital presented a problem, hence the need for alternate transportation. I hadn't hacked the traffic AI that controlled the hospital's ambulances, but that didn't mean I wasn't prepared. The near death experience I'd suffered years ago at the hands of Winsor's out of control rideshare had added an important item to my study list, and I'd refreshed my training in the past couple days. As Marina fell into the gurney, I locked the exterior doors, found the access panel at the front of the truck, pulled it off, and located the onboard computer. I slid a thumb drive into the wired port, and within seconds, I'd gained access to the vehicle controls.

Marina groaned as she pulled bandages and anesthetics from drawers at the ambulance's side. She ripped her coat open, pressing a thick wad of sterilized gauze against her blood-soaked shirt. With her teeth, she tore open the wrapping on a hypodermic needle, pulled it from the plastic, jabbed it into her shoulder, and depressed the syringe. She stifled a cry as the narcotic flooded her muscle tissue. An intravenous injection would've done her more good, but she'd need my help for that.

I was eager to give it, but we weren't out of the woods yet. I transferred a destination to the onboard computer and enabled the emergency mode. The truck lurched and pulled out of its spot, its siren blaring as it sped from the garage and out the hospital's back entrance, hurtling into the darkened Utopian streets.

48

AUGUST 23, 2179

THE ENGINES BELLOWED out a deep rumble, and a moment later, the forceful tug of acceleration pushed me firmly into my seat. My stomach lurched, more at the thought of flying again than due to the increased gs.

It was hard to believe, but the last time I'd ridden a rocket had been in my service to the marine corps. In all the time since the highest I'd risen had been the penthouse of one of Elysium's skyscrapers—or the summit of Olympus Mons, if one was being technical about it. Perhaps if air travel existed on Mars, the act of launching myself through the skies wouldn't seem so foreign, but I hadn't been on a commercial airliner since leaving Earth, either.

I glanced out the porthole at the rapidly receding red earth below and told myself it would be fine. Rockets were perfectly safe. Safer than rideshares. Infinitely safer than any profession I'd ever had. But repeating the logical mantra didn't help, because my fear wasn't grounded in logic. Nor was it grounded in acrophobia.

It was grounded in memory.

I shared the tiny cabin aboard my Mark VII Juno Class with three other flyers: a wealthy old geezer fulfilling the second leg of his bucket list back to Earth and a pair of young USC enlistees, a tall kid with east Asian features and a crisp haircut and an equally tall dark-skinned girl with an even shorter, crisper hairdo. If I craned my head to the side I could've looked at either of them, but I refused to do so, fearing I might not see them at all. That I might see someone else instead.

I still remembered the look on Ranbir's face after the shrapnel from the surface to air missile hit us. His mouth twisted in agony from the tiny bits of metal that had torn a hellish, bloody path through his intestines, lungs, and chest. Him laying there, unable to move thanks to the straps keeping him securely tied to his cot. I remembered the red mist that floated out of his chest cavity, hanging in the air before my eyes. The essence of his life slowly fading.

There had been nothing I could do for him. Nothing anyone could do but wait and watch him die.

I kept my eyes on the ground below, hoping the endless sea of rust would dull my memories, because looking to the heavens wouldn't be any better.

I doubted I'd be able to spot it if I tried, but we were headed to USC's Phobos base. The same base where USC doctors had spirited Ranbir's still warm corpse away without letting me say a final goodbye. Misery waited for me there, too.

At least this time, I was fairly sure no one would fire upon my ship. The blood would remain in my memories. For now.

I CAUGHT a brief glimpse of the moon as we eased sideways into the waiting arms of a rocket clamp, but I barely recognized it. When last I'd visited Phobos, the USC base had been a distinct entity. A cluster of connected bunkers, warehouses, and hangers surrounded by pads for rocket landings and takeoffs, with nothing more than lightly packed dust and rubble beyond that. In the twenty-five years since I'd stopped there, the base had consumed the moon. Literally. Though I knew from previous research that pristine portions of Phobos remained, none of them were within eyeshot. Buildings, cranes, and concrete covered every square meter of the moon's surface. Fusion reactors, ship yards, rail hubs. They were all there, and I knew that portions of the base extended for a hundred meters beneath the surface. It got me to wondering. Phobos only had a diameter of twenty kilometers, though it didn't have enough of a gravitational pull to force itself into a sphere. Given enough time, could humans hollow it out? Turn the entire moon into a floating colony?

When I'd been born, the idea would've been laughable, but in fifty years, USC had transformed Phobos from a hunk of floating dust and rock to a thriving port through which every freighter and passenger ship from Earth stopped. It was the establishment of the orbiting community that had allowed trade and travel to flourish, and it was the relentless nature of humanity that had transformed it in a mere half century. We never stopped. We never gave up. We could do anything we put our minds to, no matter how ambitious— or at least that was the story I told myself. Now that I'd arrived, my own larger-than-life plan seemed more impossible than ever.

I disembarked the ship and headed into the interconnected web of buildings, showing my credentials to USC flunkies as I worked my way up the food chain. After taking a magrail to an administrative building on the outskirts of the USC complex only to be rerouted back to the shipyards where I started, I eventually made it to the office of a man by the name of Mike Shedd, the Associate Director of Freight Operations for USC Phobos. According to the Inspector General, he and his direct superior were the only ones who'd received the report regarding Karam Nandi, but having wasted almost two hours getting as far as I had, I figured the *associate* director was as good as I was going to get.

Of course, I might've been optimistic in that estimation. The man wasn't in his office, so with the help of an ornery administrative assistant, I went on the hunt yet again. Luckily, as cantankerous as the assistant might be, she did know the associate director's schedule. Together, we tracked him to one of the base's unpressurized warehouses where I found him inspecting a pile of spare Mark VIII fuel canisters that had come loose the previous day after a tether malfunction.

I pulled myself along one of the guide wires set up along the warehouse floor, avoiding pushing off with my feet to keep from flying away. The gravity on Phobos was practically undetectable, though you'd eventually settle to the ground if you stood perfectly still.

I reached out to the man via the comm channel in my Suit as I closed on him. "Director Shedd? Coming in behind you."

The man turned, a tablet in hand. His glare-retardant mask didn't give me a good look at his face, but he tilted his head in the direction of the assistant who'd followed me to the warehouse floor. The man stayed that way for a moment. When I glanced back, I found my helper had started to retreat. They must've used a private line.

A harsh voice crackled to life on my channel. "So. You're the Counterterrorism guy."

"Agent Ambrose Drake. Nice to meet you, Director." My security cable jerked against the guide wire as I pulled myself the last meter in. Apparently I needed to work on my touch.

"Cut the crap, Agent. Why the hell are you here?"

So that was how it was going to be, was it? "I'm sorry, Director. I was under the impression you'd received a copy of my report from the Inspector General."

"Sure I did. And I read it. It's a bunch of garbage."

I was practiced at keeping my cool, but this guy wasn't making it easy. "Director, the *garbage* you're referring to represents one of the top security threats in all of Counterterrorism and perhaps the first international terrorist threat since the Snow Leopard. Suspect One in our report, Karam Nandi, is a highly intelligent bioweapons expert. He understands computer systems better than individuals who've spent decades in cybersecurity, and he's not working alone. The fact that we uncovered evidence he and his brother hacked third-party servers at the Olympus Mons Observatory and used their direct connection to Phobos to modify shipping manifests should concern you."

"I'm going to tell you the same thing I told your Inspector General, Agent. No one has ever smuggled their way onto a USC vessel, and no one ever will. We have a series of checks in place to make sure everything on board a ship is accounted for."

"What's your justification for saying it's never happened? That you didn't catch anyone in the act?"

"Weight is tracked aboard every USC vessel. Fuel weight. Cargo weight. Water weight. Compressed air weight. Food stuffs are tracked, as are oxygenation levels. Last time I checked, people eat, drink, breathe, and crap whether or not they're in a cabin or stuffed in a box in a cargo bay."

"Freight mass can be swapped for food and supplies. Urine can be recycled using kits purchased online at Congo. The additional strain of a single individual on a ship's oxygenator wouldn't even register. It would be the same as if a few people exercised for a few extra hours a day. I don't doubt you have safeguards in place to prevent people from sneaking aboard vessels, but it could be done."

The comm channel was silent, and Shedd didn't budge. "You know what your report didn't address, Agent? Why the hell this suspect of yours would bother going to all this hassle to get to Earth."

"Mr. Nandi has taken every precaution possible over the past ten years to erase himself from public life. He's practically a ghost. He'd never expose himself by taking commercial travel. But if you're asking why he'd bother traveling to Earth in the first place, the answer should be obvious. USC's major bases of operations are on either Earth or Luna. The headquarters are there. Not to mention Earth's population is a hundred times that of Mars. More importantly, it's a single interconnected biome. If he has his eyes set on unleashing a biological disaster, something that could wipe out populations, Earth is the place to do it."

Shedd shook his head. "I still think you're off your rocker—a position I made clear to your superior."

"Thankfully, he has more faith in me than you do. I'm going to need a copy of every shipping manifest of every vessel on a Phobos to Earth trajectory for the last seven months. Let's make it nine to be on the safe side."

"You can get that from my assistant."

"I haven't yet."

Shedd scoffed. "Is that why you came all the way up here? To harass me in person to make me hand over the records faster?"

It wasn't the *only* reason. "I spent over fifteen years as a detective. Files are useful, but they paint a limited picture of the truth. I prefer to investigate things personally."

Shedd turned back to his tablet. "The manifests you want are for ships that aren't here anymore. The files may not paint the entire picture, but they're the only one you're going to get."

"I'll be the judge of that." I wanted to stomp off, but I had to settle for launching myself back along the guideline.

I LAY in my reclining chair in my room on Phobos, strapped in to keep from bouncing around every time I crossed my legs. My stomach remained in a perpetual state of unease, same as it had been when I first launched. I'd never particularly cared for microgravity, but I think I'd tolerated it better when I was young.

A grumble from my belly told me part of the problem was

hunger, but I ignored the complaint. I was close, and I wasn't about to stop now.

I inputted commands furiously into my Net terminal, watching them appear faster than I could've typed them on a keyboard. I flipped back and forth between the scripts I was running in the background, watching them probe the encrypted Phobos servers to test the delay. For two days, I'd banged my head into a wall trying to hack through the security system—until one of my attempts had timed out with an unexpected error code, giving me the idea for a denial of service attack. If I could successfully overload the servers, even for a microsecond, it might give the worm I'd written a chance to get in.

So far, I hadn't had any success, but I was also trying not to leave any tracks, something I couldn't have done from down in Elysium. I needed local terminal access to remove suspicion, not to mention that latency issues would've made the attempt physically impossible from ground level. Still, I had to be careful. I'd confined my DoS attacks to fractions of seconds themselves, hoping not to alert humans. Internal computer logs I could take care of later, should I get in. For now, I'd coopted a few more easily hacked Phobos servers to help me. In a moment, I'd have the combined computer might of three flight operations buildings, Phobos's power grid management system, and the moon's transportation servers blast the encrypted orbital tracking server with ten microseconds of digital vomit.

I checked my work and initiated the blast.

There wasn't anything to watch, and it happened too quickly for me to process anyway. I simply checked my login access to the orbital tracking server afterwards and found that I was in.

I was in.

I breathed a sigh of relief, but I didn't pop open a squeeze pouch of champagne. My work had only just begun.

49

AUGUST 30, 2160

I RACED through a tunnel deep beneath Utopia, Marina breathing raggedly in my arms. A light from the tablet in my pocket sent shadows racing through the darkness, dancing across rough-hewn rocks walls. I'd strapped a wrist monitor to Marina in the ambulance and linked it to my medical scanner. I brought her vitals up via Net and gulped at what I saw. Her blood oxygenation was down, and her blood pressure continued to drop.

I picked up the pace.

I'd wanted to address her wound in the ambulance, but there hadn't been enough time. As we'd raced through the streets, zipping past cars pulled to the side of the road, I'd treated her as best I'd could. I'd administered an intravenous analgesic for her pain, as well as a mild anxiolytic to reduce her anxiety. I'd applied more antiseptic to the wound's exterior, bandaged it, and put it into a compression sleeve, but that was all I'd had time for. News of the triple murder surged onto the police band before we'd even left the hospital, and the chatter only intensified as the minutes ticked on. Journalists wouldn't be far behind the police, and I figured we had less than ten minutes before someone figured out one of the ambulances was missing and not on call.

It took us eight to arrive at our drop. I'd pulled the ambulance into an alley we'd scouted, one that happened not to have street cam coverage. When our ride came to a stop, I'd pulled Marina from the back and helped her into the back entrance of the nearest building, an abandoned synth meat lab that we had under surveillance. The ambulance pulled away, following my instructions to drive around the city until it either ran out of juice or was pulled over by authorities, while I descended to the lab's basement and through an access point into the city's network of underground tunnels.

Marina hadn't made it more than a hundred meters before collapsing. She tried to fight me off, more with words than fists, but I'd ignored her protests. I picked her up and kept running, thankful that I'd kept up my exercise regimen and that Marina weighed the equivalent of what a child would on Earth.

Something appeared out of the darkness ahead, a stretch of rusted metal rungs hanging from a shaft before a wall of solid rock. I checked my minimap to make sure we'd reached the end of the line, but even if I'd somehow taken a wrong turn, there was only one way to go. Marina grunted and muttered curses as I shifted her over my shoulder, wrapped my fingers around the rungs, and started pulling.

Luckily, I hadn't lost myself in the tunnels. At the top of the shaft, I found a few items we'd left the day before: a pair of Suits, complete with Bacteria Buddies and helmets, a change of clothing, several liters of water, and a backpack loaded with firearms, prepaid credit slips, meal bars, and first aid supplies.

I didn't need anything from the backpack—I'd already scavenged what I could from the ambulance, and the overland transport Marina had parked in the Martian wastes would have more than we'd need—but the Suits were a different story.

I checked the time. Half past midnight, close to the time when the clock would roll back to double zeroes after accounting for the extra thirty seven minutes each day had to offer. That didn't leave a lot of time to get through the airlocks above, skip to Marina's transport, and drive to the nearest underground resistance tunnel before dawn.

Weather on the surface was calm. I couldn't count on a dust storm to bail me out, which meant I might get stuck in the open during the day, exposed to the prying eyes of USC satellites. There should be countless other transports roaming the edges of the city, though. No one would have any reason to suspect ours.

As I glanced at Marina, wheezing in pain, her eyes only vaguely taking stock of our surroundings, I had to hope it would be enough.

I grabbed the Suits and started pulling the smaller of the pair over Marina's legs.

AIR SWIRLED around me in a rush, the sound filling my ears as I waited for the pumps to finish cycling. As the burst of sound died, I cranked on the door handle and pushed into the cabin of the transport. I'd initiated the route as soon as I'd closed the exterior airlock door, and I felt the transport rumbling underneath me as it headed for the nearest tunnel access point.

I still held Marina in my arms. I lay her on one of the cots built into the side of the vehicle and pulled off her helmet. Her eyes fluttered, but I wasn't sure if she saw me. "Marina? Marina, can you hear me?"

She muttered something, but it was too soft for me to make sense of it. Her eyes looked dilated, and the vitals streaming to me through her wrist scanner were only getting worse.

I tore the medical kit from one of the transport's storage cabinets and threw it open, searching desperately for the items I'd need. I drew gloves onto my fingers, and a pair of trauma shears filled my hand. I unzipped the front of Marina's Suit and cut through the compression sleeve and bandages I'd applied. They came away saturated with blood, the clothes underneath dark red and stuck to her skin. I cut those off and peeled them away, too.

The gunshot wound stared at me from her breast, a ragged hole yawning from living flesh. I squeezed my eyes shut and took a deep breath. I wasn't a doctor, though I'd pretended to be one in the past. I'd studied medicine as a result of my espionage work, and I'd learned basic first aid, first in the corps then as part of my field work for the resistance. First aid was a far cry from surgery, but Marina was fading. I couldn't sit on the sidelines.

I swallowed back bile as I pulled the diagnostic lamp over my forehead. I pulled more anesthetics from the medical kit, then I selected a pair of forceps. After taking another deep breath, I pulled the foam plug from Marina's chest with one set of forceps and clamped the wound open with the other. I leaned in, adjusting my headlamp as I probed the wound.

Marina groaned weakly, signaling the need for more painkillers. I didn't administer them right away. I wouldn't need to, because I couldn't operate on her.

I wasn't an expert, but I knew the difference between muscle and lung tissue. The bullet was lodged in the latter.

50

AUGUST 29, 2180

EVENTUALLY, I stopped trying to find Karam, though Counterterrorism gave up long before I did. It's not so much that his trail went cold. More that there was never a trail to follow in the first place.

No one could label me a quitter, though. I followed every lead, every clue, and every moth-eaten shred of evidence from his brother Vikram's digital legacy. I revisited the building which I'd burned down in making my escape, and I hacked into the New Chennai Police Department to steal their file on his death as well. I kept up surveillance on Karam's family, on his childhood friends, and on acquaintances of Vikram's, but none of them produced a damn thing. I even went back to Karam's apprenticeship under Phoebe and attempted to pick him up using old surveillance footage, but after the man graduated, he disappeared into thin air. One day he'd been living life as a medical resident, and the next he'd slipped from the system. I hadn't even been able to locate the moment when he disappeared. I figured he'd retroactively doctored the footage of his departure, but there was no way to tell. The logs that recorded those sort of things had been rewritten thousands of times by the time I got to them.

For a while, my superiors at Counterterrorism held out hope that the brothers were part of a broader network, but the lack of any whisper of their plans through intelligence gathering channels suggested otherwise. Vikram and Karam were vectors that pointed only at each other, and I'd eliminated one. At times it worried me, knowing I'd killed the brother of a brilliant man hell bent on creating a weapon that could murder people in their sleep, but I wasn't normal. I was too rational, and I knew Karam wouldn't risk his operation for something as petty as revenge. Why kill one man when the action could jeopardize the murder of millions? But losing Karam's scent like a speck of dust in the Martian wind grated at me. I hated loose ends.

At least I had other projects to keep me busy. Despite my talks with Fabia, Mars refused to cooperate. Though the case with the false Snow Leopard had momentarily quenched Elysium's taste for upheaval, the same wasn't true of other Martian cities. Rhetoric on newsfeeds intensified. Civil discourse deteriorated, and angry civilians began committing politically-motivated violence at elevated rates. Attacks against public figures crossed our desks at Counterterrorism every week. Riots weren't uncommon, either, though they weren't all political in nature. Many were economically motivated. Inflation rates kept rising, especially in regards to food, but water and energy had also been affected. The latter two were particularly hard for people to swallow given USC had only paid lip service to talks of restructuring their service deals with the major municipalities.

Then in June, the dam broke when the Utopia Tribune published an explosive expose accusing USC of knowingly and maliciously exposing a hundred trillion liters of Martian ice to atmospheric conditions, resulting in their loss from proven reserves. Despite not having worked at the EPD for over a year, I'd still received a call from Captain Reyes minutes after the report went live, in part to ask if I'd had any knowledge that it was coming and in part to assure me she hadn't been a party to the reporting. Ultimately, after months of research and investigation, the EPD hadn't felt comfortable with the case they'd put together and had neglected to bring charges against USC's Water Services Division, but the threshold for proving guilt under the rule of law and establishing a connection in a news publication were far different.

Regardless of who leaked the story to whom, the end result was the same: chaos. A week's worth, give or take. Citizens flooded the streets around the Elysium and Utopia water extraction facilities, picketing and burning things and preventing anyone from getting in or out. Police couldn't get through the masses of people, and to be honest, many of the cops assigned to the task weren't thrilled with the idea of protecting USC from consequence. In Elysium, a group of budding revolutionaries initiated an attack on the adjoining water treatment plant, causing the place to be evacuated for a day, and a series of bombings at underground pumping stations caused water to be lost to portions of the city for days.

USC didn't sit on its collective ass in the immediate aftermath. They deployed troops to keep the peace at key holdings around the city, but they also responded to the accusations in the smartest way possible: by immediately condemning the loss of ice, blaming a combination of mechanical failures and gross incompetence on the behalf of its employees, throwing numerous people under the bus, and vowing to perform a thorough public investigation of the accusations. I doubted such an investigation would ever take place, certainly not an unbiased one, but the commitment to finding *the truth* was enough to temper the flames of rebellion, at least temporarily. Most people have a fundamental faith in due process, after all, just as they have jobs they can't leave behind to protest for days on end. Open conflict was once again postponed, while people continued to toil in frustration, for less pay than they needed, with the world slowly crumbling around them.

Meanwhile, the revolution I'd planned with Fabia continued

along its trajectory, slowly but steadily, and I kept chugging away at my job, thankful as much for the opportunities it provided as for the paycheck. At least I had Sophia to fall back on if times got tough. Something told me her family's mob money would weather any political storm.

Then on one morning in late August, after kissing Sophia at the door of our apartment—formerly hers—and catching a rideshare into work, I received a call from someone I hadn't expected to hear from again. Phoebe Zhao.

I picked up right away. "Phoebe. Hey."

Her voice had that same straightforward quality to it as the last time we'd spoken, the same as it had twenty years ago. "Morning, Ambrose. Have a minute?"

I eyed the traffic jam in front of my car. My map showed an estimated fifteen minutes until I arrived at Counterterrorism. "Sure. What's up?"

"I'm at a neuroscience conference in Chandrayaan. A large one. There's over twenty-five hundred doctors and industry professionals here. I gave a talk yesterday as an invited speaker on the state of advances in Net-assisted neural regrowth in victims of traumatic brain injury. You know that's been a recent focus of mine?"

"You're talking about regrowth of dead brain cells? I try to keep tabs on what you publish, but I don't read the articles."

"I don't expect you to. And yes, you have the general gist of it. It's an interesting topic, but the entire field is expanding so quickly it's hard to stay atop it. Fundamentally, it's about using the Net as a medical tool instead of as a method of connectivity and about coming up with new ways to expand the limits of the Net from a medical standpoint. Some of the talks I attended were eye-opening. We're talking about implants that penetrate deeper into regions of the brain than ever before. New, less intrusive methods of Net insertion. People are proposing ways to have the Net coalesce from a nanoparticulate solution in the bloodstream instead of being injected as a flexible mesh into the brain's subarachnoid space. In theory, it could provide a better brain meld than the traditional one-piece mesh."

I'd sat up straighter at the mention of injectable nanoparticulate solutions. "Okay."

"That's not all. Yesterday, I attended a talk about those nanoparticulate solutions. A spirited question and answer session followed it that addressed methods of delivery. Ingestion and inhalation were discussed as possible options, given both are used as drug delivery mechanisms."

"As fascinating as this is, Phoebe, I can't understand your motivation for sharing it with me."

Phoebe took a deep breath. "Last night, after the talks had wrapped for the day, I received a call from Professor Daksh Prabhu at Chandrayaan Polytechnic. I've met him before. We're not friends, but we are colleagues. He'd been unable to attend the conference due to other obligations, but he was watching the livestream, including talks about the nanoparticulates. He wanted to ask my opinion of some of the topics of discussion. Absorption speeds. Deposition rates. How the brain would react to different stimuli. Very pointed questions. It was a stimulating talk, but... something about it felt off to me."

"Off how?"

"I couldn't say exactly. The research seemed different from what I was used to seeing him publish, and the questions were very advanced. Very technical. Above the level of what anyone at the conference had proposed. I got the feeling he was intentionally beating around the bush. That he knew ten times what he was telling me. Not to mention... Well, this might seem strange, but I got the impression the man's cadence was different. The speed at which he spoke and replied was quicker than I thought it should be. I can't explain it. It bothered me all night, so this morning, I called Dr. Prabhu back.

"He never called me, Ambrose. He swore he hadn't. But it was him. His voice. I'd spoken to him, from his number. He called me."

My mind swirled, trying to make sense of it. "How did his cadence seem? This morning, I mean."

"Normal. Unhurried."

I wiped a hand through my hair. "There are ways of falsifying voice signatures. Same as there are ways of misrepresenting call identifications."

"I know, Ambrose. I don't have any evidence to support it, but... I think it was *him*."

She didn't have to say who she meant. Karam Nandi. "Is there anything else I should know?"

"Yes. The questions he asked me. They were related to *inhaled* nanoparticle absorption rates. The effects of long term exposures. Do you catch my drift?"

Inhaled nanoparticles that affected Net function. "Yes, I think I understand. How long are you going to be at the conference?"

"Through the end of the week. Why?"

I tapped my fingers on the armrest. "I'll be in touch, Phoebe. I appreciate you calling."

"Of course. Take care, Ambrose."

"You, too."

The call cut off, and I checked my minimap. Traffic had worsened, and I still had about ten minutes until arrival at work. I stared out the window, thinking about what Phoebe had told me. About inhaled nanoparticles. About the level of discourse she'd engaged in over the phone. How it had even left *her* in the dust.

Dust. On Mars, it had always been a threat, but never a weapon.

I knew what I had to do. The question was who else should know.

I KNOCKED on Director Schmidt's office door. He looked up. "Agent Drake. Come in."

I did. "Don't you ever leave your office? You're aware of the health benefits of exercise, aren't you, Director?"

He wiped his holos. "Don't nag me. I get enough of that from my wife. Besides, you're one to talk. You haven't had an assignment outside the city in almost two months."

"Outside the city, sure. But I get up and visit the coffee machine every now and then."

Schmidt gave me a nod. "What's on your mind?"

"I need to take a few days off for a family matter. Is that going to be a problem?"

"We don't have any pressing cases at the moment. We'll cover for you." He lifted an eyebrow. "Having issues with your girlfriend?"

"Nothing like that. Things are going quite well with Sophia, actually."

That elicited a smile. "I probably shouldn't pry, but this family matter... it wouldn't include any sort of long term commitment, would it?"

"I would've planned that further in advance, sir, but I'm definitely not against the idea. Just hard to find time to give it serious thought with the world in the state it's in."

Schmidt leaned forward in his chair. "Let me give you a piece of advice, Ambrose. There's always something else going on in your life, whether it's moving or work or literal bombs going off down the street. The world's crazy, all the time, for all of us, but having someone there to help you through it cuts down on the insanity. Makes it more palatable."

Over the past year I'd found that the Director liked to take the occasional preachy tangent. There was a fatherly instinct that came out of him unprompted, even though I was close to the same age as him. "I agree with that wholeheartedly, sir."

He waved a hand. "I'm not trying to push you. I've only met Sophia once, but it seemed to me that family issues aside..." He shrugged in a knowing sort of way, as if so say, what are you waiting for? "Anyway. When do you expect to be back?"

"Monday at the latest, I would think."

"Alright. Take care then, Agent."

"Thanks, sir. I'll do my best."

51

AUGUST 30, 2160

THE VOICE STARTLED me out of my reverie. "Ambrose..."

I turned in my chair and found Marina's eyes were open. I hopped out of my seat and took a spot next to her on the cot. "Marina. How are you? Can I get you anything?"

Her eyes passed over me, but they seemed to be focused on the wall at my back. She spoke softly, and her voice warbled. "Where are we?"

"In the transport you left parked outside the city," I said. "About forty kilometers outside the edge of the pressure barrier."

"What time...?" She trailed off.

"Twenty after six. Close to dawn."

A twinge went through her face. "We'll be caught... in the open. Have to stop."

"We're not stopping until I get you into more capable hands than mine. You hear me? You're going to be okay. I promise."

"It's... not about me. About the cause."

"The cause can suck it for once. I'm not going to let you become a martyr. Not to mention nobody knows we're here. As far as USC is concerned, this is an automated gas hauler on a hop to the carbon aggregators south of town. I'll sneak you out the bottom and into the tunnels when we slow over the hatches."

"It's... still risky."

"It's better than switching the active camo on and dumping our waste heat into the salt block in the floor. Sneaking around works at night. Better to hide in plain sight during the day."

"You're... too cocky."

On the contrary. I was petrified of failure, but of the immediate sort. Of losing Marina. The cause would go on without either of us, but there were people who cared for and depended upon us—her more than me.

"I've evaluated the situation. I'm taking the best course of action."

Marina cracked a smile and tried to laugh, but a chest spasm cut off her chortle before it started. I'd injected her wound with foam, bandaged it, and put it back under compression, but at my skill level, I'd do more harm than good attempting anything more.

"You're killing me, Ambrose. Literally."

I smiled though I didn't feel any mirth. "Technically, you're the one who forced yourself into my affairs, regardless of whether I wanted your help or not. Metaphorically speaking, you're killing yourself."

"Ah. There's the attitude... that I've missed."

"You're misremembering. I used to be a saint. It's the years away that have taught me to be so self-assured."

"You wish. You've always... been a bit... of an ass. I would've cut you loose... ages ago... if you weren't so damn good at what you do. You're probably the best... I've ever worked with."

Marina closed her eyes, and I feared she might've faded out of consciousness despite the medication I'd given to keep her alert. I was checking her vitals to make sure she wasn't in immediate danger when I heard her speak again.

"Who was it?"

"What do you mean?"

"In the... hospital. The woman. Two men... I killed."

I hesitated. "The woman was Lieutenant Colonel Marjory Watkins. She was my superior officer during my stint in the corps, though at the time she'd only been a major. I don't know who the men were. Friends. Colleagues. Escorts, maybe."

Marina swallowed, the pain obvious on her face. "What would you have done... if I hadn't been there?"

"You mean if you hadn't killed them?"

"Yes."

I'd replayed the incident a hundred times in my mind while Marina faded in and out of consciousness, so I knew the answer. I'd known as the incident unfolded. "I would've killed her, but not fast enough for it to have mattered. Her presence shocked me. I hesitated. By the time I would've reacted, her entourage would've had their guns out. So perhaps it's more accurate to say I would've tried to kill her. I probably would've failed."

"You... see the problem?"

I didn't get angry. "For all my training, that's the sort of thing you can't emulate. I have experience with it now. I'll do better next time." If there *was* a next time. I'd rather there wasn't.

"And... your friend? Phoebe?"

"What about her?"

Marina's eyes still hadn't opened. "We had... contingencies. But... not to cover... death of someone else."

"Phoebe won't give me up. I'm confident in the conversation we had. In who she is as a person."

"She was... confident... in you, too. Before you went missing. Before... you murdered your superior."

The thought chilled me. Phoebe hadn't known Marina was tailing me. She had no idea I wasn't acting alone. When the news of the murder reached her ears, she could only have assumed one thing, especially after she discovered Watkins' identity. Phoebe now knew I was a murderer, or at the very least suspected it. I'd challenged every assumption she'd held about me in our long overdue reunion, but the truths I'd told her were at odds with the incident that occurred mere hallways from where we'd met.

The simple fact was, I didn't know how she'd take it. What was going through her mind. How she'd react or who she'd tell. All I knew was that as of *this* moment, my name and face hadn't been shot through the air to every mobile connected device in Utopia.

I considered my words carefully. "You know I respect the cause, Marina. I wouldn't do anything to put it directly in harms way. I know the rules are in place for a reason. But sometimes, they have to be bent. There are people we have to trust. The right ones, at least. That was the crux of my mission outside HQ. It was up to me to decide who to share information with. Besides, if there aren't people we can share our experiences with... what's the point of it all?"

I waited for a fiery rebuke, telling me I was a reckless buffoon and that we'd discuss it at length later, but none came. "Marina?"

I jumped, pulling her vitals as I leapt, but a flicker of motion preceded the shallow rise of her breast. I sighed and collapsed into my chair, my extremities tingling from adrenaline.

I checked my clock. Two hours until we reached the tunnels.

AS I SAT THERE, trying to will the minutes past, I replayed the night's events in my head. My conversation with Phoebe, her every reaction, bodily and spoken. The way she'd looked at me, concern in her eyes but emotionally separated from me by a chasm of time and experience. Most importantly, I couldn't stop reliving my encounter with Watkins. Despite their impossible speed, I could trace the paths the bullets took as they flew through the air. I remembered perfectly the way Watkins jerked as the shots hit her.

The spray of her blood. The metallic scent of it in the air and on my tongue. The way she crumpled and hit the ground, the shock on her face abruptly replaced with agony.

Her death would haunt me for a long time, I was sure of it, but I couldn't let myself fall down that hole. Not now, with Marina's life in my hands. I had to stay awake. Clear. Focused.

So I wondered for the umpteenth time what she'd been doing in that elevator at that precise moment in time.

I didn't believe in coincidences. I had a greater probability of spontaneously disassociating into a soup of free radicals than of running into Watkins by sheer chance, which meant she'd been there for a reason. That reason had to have been Phoebe. I'd done the research. Checked the hospital's files. No one who worked there or was being treated there had any direct connection to my time at USC other than Phoebe. She was the only connection to Watkins, and it made sense she might visit her. Surely Watkins would've remembered the raid in which I was taken and in which Phoebe almost died. It was a black mark on her otherwise sterling record.

But what brought Watkins to Utopia in the first place? My scripts kept track of her and the remaining members of what had once been Zeta squad. The last time I'd checked, she'd been deployed in the Terra Sabaea with the rest of her battalion, so I delved online to investigate the issue further. I'd hacked my way into USC servers so many times that I could do it in my sleep, so gaining access to troop movement records wasn't an issue. They indicated the battalion was still there, two hundred kilometers north of the vactrain line. Try as I might, I couldn't find any record of Watkins being recalled—which indicated Watkins had been extracted in secret. But why? Marina had mentioned a meeting of high level USC officials taking place in the city. Had it included Watkins? I didn't know if she was high-ranking enough to qualify, but if the meeting was secret, that would explain why she would've dropped in on Phoebe unannounced.

Whispers pulled me from the maze of my own thoughts, and I turned toward Marina. Her lips were moving without making so much as a whisper. I leaned in close, but I could only catch a few scattered words. You. Why. Please. Can't. Love.

Love. That one stuck in my mind as I gripped her shoulder, giving her a shake as I spoke her name, hoping to wake her.

My touch didn't register, and she continued to whisper. I pulled up her vitals and my heart sank at what I saw. Her brain activity was elevated, but her heart and lung function had fallen precipitously. I double-checked the location of the transport and performed some mental math regarding the speed of the underground pod awaiting us in the tunnel. I didn't like the results I came up with.

Love you. Two more words that I pulled from the sub-audible conversation. I froze as I realized she wasn't talking to me, or even to herself. She was making a call.

Jorge reached out as soon as her lips stopped moving. I should've rung him when we'd first taken off in the ambulance, but in my panicked state, I hadn't considered the possibility. I'd been on my own so long that the idea of calling for help seemed foreign.

I didn't pull any punches in our conversation. I gave him the facts. How Marina had been shot. What treatment I'd administered. The location of our transport, our speed, and our bearing. Marina's physical condition. Everything that was relevant to the situation.

Jorge took it as well as could be expected. He didn't say much, and his voice remained impassive throughout the exchange. He simply asked me to keep him appraised of any changes and wished me god speed.

Anger I could've dealt with. Unbridled rage, cursing, threats even.

But Jorge's response, one of pain and fear hidden behind a thin veneer of professionalism was worse. It dug into me like a hot knife, searing the soft core underneath. I wanted to say I was sorry, that it was my fault and that he could take out his aggression on me, but it would've been a lie. I'd acted independently in seeking out Phoebe. I hadn't told Marina of my plans. I hadn't asked for her help. She'd volunteered it freely, and I'd made the smart choice to accept it. Working together had provided the best chance of mission success, both for me and for the cause.

That's why Jorge didn't attack me. Because he knew as well as Marina did that every action we took in support of the resistance put us in danger. Every action exposed us, and we accepted those risks. We found them worthwhile.

It didn't mean the consequences didn't hurt.

I hung my head in my hands as I logged off, wanting to cry, but no tears would come. Maybe it was because the years I'd spent in solitary service had dulled me to the pain of others. Maybe it was because I'd conditioned myself to prepare for trauma or because I'd forced myself into a state of vigilance, pushing my emotions into a box until such a point where the people who depended upon me weren't in peril and I could deal with them in peace.

Maybe it was a mixture of all three. Certainly, I'd prepared for the worst. Not only had Marina and I established escape protocols in the event of our injury, but we'd set up surveillance bots to keep track of local news, police movements, and USC actions in the event we'd been forced to flee. Those indicated that authorities remained in the dark with regards to our identities and location. Our efforts to control hospital security had succeeded, and Phoebe's trust for the moment had held.

But the worst betrayals are the ones you don't expect. As the Net alert popped into my vision, I knew at once that the worst had indeed come.

52

AUGUST 30, 2180

I REACHED out and tapped my tablet to stop the recording. "For what it's worth, I agree with you. That wasn't the same Dr. Prabhu as before."

I sat in Phoebe's hotel room. She stood to the side of the round table within, resting against the wall with her arms crossed tightly over her stomach. "Counterterrorism won't know you accessed the telecoms database to get those audio files?"

"As far as USC and TelSat are concerned, these calls never happened. I already wiped them from the server. The only copies are the ones left on my tablet."

"And the call signal?"

"I triangulated it before I deleted the data from the server. The metadata was set to show the call as coming from Dr. Prabhu while he was at Chandrayaan Polytechnic, but the call actually pinged off satellites flying over New Bangalore. Have some faith, Phoebe."

She chewed on her lip, refusing to meet my eye. "What now, Ambrose?"

"Now I finish what Karam and his brother started over a year ago."

Phoebe snorted. "You say that so nonchalantly. As if his life means nothing to you."

"It doesn't. I've spent hundreds of hours thinking about him, studying him, analyzing every fragment of his past, but I don't know him, not the way you do. So you're right. He doesn't matter to me. What matters are the lives he could extinguish if he unleashes an airborne bioweapon that can cause people's hearts to stop with a wireless signal."

Phoebe shook her head. "He wasn't like this when he worked with me."

"I wasn't this way when I met you, either."

She looked at me with sad eyes. "No. You weren't. Can you even find him?"

"The satellites gave me a precise location, but he might've moved. Even if he has, I have other tools at my disposal. I've been tracking elemental graphite sales for over a year. That and the satellite data gives me a starting point. I think it'll be enough."

Phoebe looked out her window at the convention center below. She was quiet for a while, and I thought I might've angered her instead of merely disappointed her. "I'm scared, Ambrose."

I stood and grabbed my tablet. "You shouldn't be. I'll get him. Karam won't be able to unleash his plague on us."

She turned back to me. "That's not what I meant. I'm afraid for Mars. Every day it gets worse. Every day we're one step closer to open conflict. People aren't afraid to talk about it in public anymore. Not in Utopia and not in Chandrayaan. War is coming."

"Perhaps it is, but I'll do my damnedest to make sure it doesn't take the same trajectory as before."

Phoebe's nostrils flared. "And how do you plan to do that? You're very clever. You always have been, but you're one man. *You can't change this.*"

"That's the thing about trajectories, Phoebe. It doesn't take much effort to change them. The right push at the right time. That's it."

"Metaphors don't win wars, Ambrose."

I took a step toward the door. "I was sorry to hear about you and Lars."

Phoebe nodded, refusing to meet my eyes. "It wasn't meant to be."

"I guess not. Take care of yourself, Phoebe. I mean it. War or not, the next few months are going to be rough. Try to stay safe."

"And you try not to kill us all."

"I'll do my best."

I headed out of her room, letting the door click shut behind me. As I walked toward the elevator, I made a call.

It didn't take long for Fabia to pick up. "What's up, old man?"

"I'm going to need your help."

I STOOD in the chill night air, feeling the cold bite my hands and stiffen my fingers. At least I'd been smart enough to dress in layers.

A horn blared in the distance, the sound shrill and eerie. My thick cap and hood muffled the noise, but it was the bitterly cold, CO_2-laden air that made it sound the way it did. Though I'd long since acclimated to the breathing masks used in the Hellas Basin, I didn't think I'd ever get used to the sound the breeze made whistling through the buildings, a deathly moan that spoke of the relentless power of dust and time.

A chill ran through me, but I shook it off, staying focused on the storefront across the street from me. A car passed by. Along the sidewalk, a couple walked briskly in the opposite direction. Neither of the pair looked into the alley in which I stood. Even if they had, they wouldn't have spotted me. The streetlights cast nothing but shadows into the spot I'd claimed.

Another car passed by, then another. I checked my clock. Seven past ten. The last customer who'd entered the pharmacy had left at ten till, so unless there was someone who'd been in there for hours, hiding behind a shelf of cold, flu, and sinus medication, it was down to the clerk. I'd caught glimpses of him walking back and forth, presumably checking to make sure everything was in order for the morning shift. It was what he'd done the last two nights.

The pharmacy's lights dimmed, and at exactly ten after, the clerk exited the fast airlock at the front of the building, his coat wrapped tightly around him. He shuffled off down the street in the direction of the subway station. I set my alarm for five minutes. He'd be gone in two, but better to be safe than sorry.

As the clock ticked down, I ran through everything in my mind. I glanced at the building blueprints one last time, taking note of the path I'd take through the pharmacy and into the much older, much less up to code subleased section beneath it. I took stock of where I'd placed each tool in my possession, from my pistol to my emergency transmitter, which would function along the trail of breadcrumbs I'd already begun to spread. And I recalled in full detail the conversation I'd had with Fabia. I could still picture the uncertain look she'd given me as I'd laid it all down. *Are you sure you want to play it this way?* Of course. I'd studied Karam for over a year. I knew him as intimately as anyone, and I knew what he'd expect. I knew how he'd react. I had to play my hand appropriately.

When the timer hit zero, I left my pocket of darkness. I hustled out of the alley, checked for cars before crossing the street, and proceeded to the pharmacy's entrance. Thanks to the computer work I'd already done, a quick scan of my tablet at the security console unlocked the airlock door. A bare fifteen seconds later, I was inside. The lights tried to brighten to full luminescence, but the signal from my tablet preempted them, keeping them at night levels. Similarly, the security cameras in the corners had been momentarily disabled. Should anyone check the feed at a later date, all they'd find was looped footage from a night three months ago with the time-stamp adjusted.

I slapped a mini transmitter on the side of a cosmetics shelf as I moved to the back of the store. There, I used my tablet to access another locked door. I affixed another transmitter to the door frame as I moved into darkness. I activated the light on my breathing mask as the door clicked behind me, illuminating a storage room filled with products for the shelves in front. One more door opened under my tablet's digital coaxing, and I found myself at the head of a set of metal stairs leading underground. I moved down them slowly, trying to keep my footfalls from producing a sound. I peered at the sides of the staircase, at the old, roughly cemented walls covered with a polymer clear coat and at the bare electrical wiring overhead. I knew from the blueprints I'd uncovered that the underground portions of the pharmacy hadn't been touched in a half century, at least not by a licensed contractor, but clearly someone had made improvements.

As I took in my surroundings, I brought up my Net and initiated a kill order for one of the sets of security cameras in the pharmacy behind me. As I'd found out during my initial scans, pharmacy management weren't the only ones with eyes on the building. Karam was, too. I'd left his microcams on at first, but now I switched them to a similar looped feed as I'd used on the official cameras. If all went according to plan, he'd be too busy preparing for my arrival to anticipate the switch.

My feet hit the hard-packed dirt at the bottom, and I turned the corner into a long hallway. I stuck another mini transmitter to the wall as I walked, taking each step carefully and methodically. My muscles ached from tension, ready to explode at a moment's notice, but I didn't pull my pistol. I knew where it was, and in a hallway as narrow as this one, I preferred having my hands free.

I checked my Net cams and transmitters, then checked the

clock. My mask flashlight cut a swath across the hallway. At about the center point of the pharmacy above, based on the blueprints, the hall sprouted a series of offshoots. Several led to old storage rooms. One of them had service elevator access. Not the one I planned on accessing, though.

I turned to the door at my right, which gleamed sliver in the light of my mask-mounted flashlight. It, along with the electrical wiring, had also been updated in the last half century.

There wasn't a security console next to the door. I hadn't been sure if there'd be one. Tentatively, I reached out and grasped the handle. I applied a smidge of torque, and it responded without a fight. Slowly and as quietly as possible, I turned it the rest of the way and pushed. As the door opened, I heard a scuff behind me.

I couldn't have turned if I wanted to. A distinct *pat* split the air, followed quickly by two more, but thanks to the blinding pain that erupted from my rib cage following the first, I didn't focus so much on the second two. I crumped to the floor inside the edge of the door, groaning as I turned onto my side. I tried to reach into my coat for my pistol, but I was too slow. The figure behind me approached and leveled their pistol at my heart. Another round cracked free of the silenced barrel, slamming me in the torso and pulling the breath from my lungs.

The pain spread like fire across my chest. My head slammed against the floor from the force of the round, sending the light from my mask careening across the hallway behind me. It illuminated Karam for only an instant. His crease-lined forehead. His trim beard, speckled with grey. His cold, unfeeling eyes.

He didn't say a thing. Didn't gloat. Didn't rage. Didn't present a manifesto. He simply unloaded two more rounds into my chest.

Spots flashed in my eyes as the pain overtook me, so I missed most of what happened next, but thanks to the suppressor on Karam's pistol, my ears still worked. I heard a dull thwack, a grunt, and a couple soft blows.

I blinked a few times, and when I was once again able to focus, it was a different soul who knelt in the door's open frame, one with frizzy golden hair and a less icy stare.

Fabia pulled Karam's wrists together and quickly zip-tied them, then did the same to the man's feet. She ripped a piece of tape from a roll and slapped it over his mouth, then checked his pulse. He was still alive. Even from my position on the floor, I could hear his quiet breathing.

Only then did Fabia join me. "Christ, Drake. I counted a half-dozen shots. Did he hit you with all six?"

I groaned in response as I ripped my mask from my face.

"Seriously, are you okay?"

I managed to nod, though my verbal response was barely a whisper. Even that made my chest erupt in flames. "Three to the back, three to the chest. He followed protocols. Didn't waste any shots."

"Your Suit stopped them all?"

I felt at my jacket. I found one of the bullet holes in the fabric, but when I probed it, my fingers came away dry. "Looks like. It's military strength after all. I think I broke a few ribs, though."

"You know, when you told me you were going to dress in layers, this wasn't what I'd expected. How did you know you'd get shot?"

"I didn't, but this isn't my first rodeo. I prepared for anything. And I didn't know how far behind me you'd be. You could've been faster if we're being honest."

"Yeah, I was eight seconds slow. Kind of hard to avoid given that I had to give you enough of a head start so that when you switched the cameras over, Karam wouldn't see me following you."

"Stop being rational and help me up, would you?"

Fabia extended a hand. I gripped it and used it to pull myself up—which was a hell of a lot harder than I expected. The pain in my chest nearly buckled my legs.

Fabia eyed my grimace and the fact that I used the wall for support. "You sure you're okay?"

"I will be. The important thing is we got Karam."

"I can't have you crapping out on me, Drake. We have a lot to do still."

"Get him in a chair. I'll be fine. Give me a minute."

Fabia activated the lights, illuminating the interior of Karam's underground laboratory. She grabbed Karam by the arms and moved him inside. I stood to the side, breathing shallowly and gathering my strength.

As bad as the pain was, it wasn't the fire that consumed my chest that forced me to pause. It was the moment itself. More than a year after I'd started looking, after hundreds of hours spent searching databases, tapping communications, and overturning every rock larger than a shoebox, I'd finally found him. I'd finally captured Karam Nandi.

And no one would ever know.

53

AUGUST 30, 2160

I STARED at the Net message for several minutes, digesting its contents. It came from a bot I'd set up myself, so I knew the information was accurate—and I knew that I didn't have long to act.

Nonetheless, I kept my composure. I triple-checked the information and made sure my systems hadn't been breached. I hacked into the USC servers that had been on the receiving end of the missive and checked to make sure they'd been adequately doctored. Then I prepared myself for what I had to do, which was by far the hardest part.

I couldn't risk losing the connection in the subterranean tunnels, so when I was a half hour away from the access hatch and with Marina in as stable a condition as I could get, I made the call.

Winsor picked up in short order. "Kid. This is unexpected."

His voice was casual. Unhurried. I responded in kind. "I'm sure my arrival a few days ago was more unexpected. Consider this a follow-up."

"Yeah. Speaking of which, you have to know I didn't intend to spring that info on you. I assumed you knew about the fate of your former squad mates. All of them."

"Yes. I believe that you did."

"So you don't hold my sharing that knowledge against me?"

"Not that, no."

I think I detected a genuine measure of relief in the man's voice. It was odd, given the circumstances. "Good. When you ran off after I told you, I thought I might've spurred you into a rash decision."

"You did, but just because the decision was rash doesn't mean the actions I took were. I'm not that reckless."

"Not anymore, anyway. So did you meet her? Your old fling, I mean."

"I did, and while the details of our conversation matter to me, I doubt they do to you. It's not what I called to talk about, in any case."

"What's on your mind then, kid?"

"I think you know."

Winsor was silent for a while. For a moment I thought he might hang up on me, but that wasn't his style. "Yeah... Well, I guess I'm not surprised you've been keeping tabs on me. I always thought you would. I know I always gave you a hard time, but after those first few weeks of you bumbling about, I came to realize you actually knew what you were doing for the most part."

"Thanks. I'm surprised you didn't check your computer systems for bugs, though."

"Who says I didn't? I replaced all the hardware in my apartment after you left, just to be on the safe side. Did you tap me remotely?"

I'd actually planted the bug in his building's wireless routing infrastructure, assuming he'd check all the systems in his own possession. Part of me wanted to tell him, but we were still at a point in our conversation where a slip-up could cost me everything. "I was paying attention. That's all you need to know."

Winsor snickered. "Rule number two. Don't offer anything you don't have to. Good to see you're playing by the rules, kid. But honestly, I'm surprised you're not more upset."

"I'm not more upset precisely because I *am* playing by the rules," I said. "Rule number one. The most important. Never trust anyone. I trusted you when I first met you, and you chewed me out well enough that I never forgot the lesson."

Winsor sighed. "Can I speak to you frankly for a moment, kid?"

"I'd welcome it."

"For what it's worth, I'm sorry. I actually kind of like you. You're like me except you learned the important lessons at a younger age. And I still believe in a free Mars, it's just that as I've gotten older, I've realized my sacrifice, your sacrifice, any of ours doesn't mean a whole hell of a lot in the grand scheme of things. For all I tried when I was younger, my efforts never made a lick of difference, and they sure as shit won't make one now. So when I got that call from USC and they gave me the choice of staring at the inside of a concrete box for the rest of my life or giving them everything I knew... well, it wasn't a hard choice to make. But know that if I'd had a choice, I wouldn't have given *you* up."

I couldn't tell him, but it was only because he *had* given me up that I'd learned anything was wrong in the first place. My surveillance bot wasn't the most sophisticated piece of AI. It processed ingoing and outgoing communications to or from Winsor looking for specific written or audible cues, specifically any mention of me, Marina, Jorge, my other compatriots, or the resistance in general, as well as monitoring the sources and destinations for said data. But USC had been clever. Upon locating Winsor—a feat which I had no idea how they'd achieved—they'd reached out to him via a source I didn't know was associated with them, and they hadn't mentioned any of the cues the bot had been searching for. Winsor hadn't either in his initial response. It was only in the last returned message where he'd given up my name, Marina's, and Jorge's in return for his freedom.

Except that message never arrived as composed. My AI wasn't the best, but it did more than collate date. It could also modify messages on the fly. Written messages were child's play, but my AI did the same for visual and auditory messages as well, thanks to some creative coding and the visual effects program we'd used in the resistance to fake the Snow Leopard videos. Ultimately, Winsor had sent a written message to USC with our names and information, but even if he'd spoken to someone via Net, they never would've heard him say my name. Wendy Comstock would've been the head of Martian counterintelligence, and my identity would've been that of Smitty Gerhart.

I wouldn't feel so defeated if that were all Winsor had sent along, but USC hadn't merely asked for names. They'd asked for places. Data. Everything. And Winsor had passed along as much as he could. He didn't know everything. Not even close. In that respect, I'd played by the rebellion's rules. But he knew enough. He'd sent information correctly hinting at the locations of three-quarters of resistance strongholds, as well as a few more that were long obsolete. His cooperation must've precipitated the meeting among military heads. They knew they'd turned their target and would soon have all the information they needed. Troop mobilization wouldn't be far behind.

I gathered my strength. "If nothing else, I appreciate you being honest with me, Winsor. Given this is probably the last time we'll ever speak, you mind if I be equally frank with you?"

"Go ahead, kid. Hit me with whatever you've got."

Clearly he anticipated an insult, but I surprised him. "I hate the rules. I think they're bullshit. Especially rule number one. Don't trust anyone. It's an awful rule. I understand its basis in self-preservation, but it's a horrible motto to live by. There are people we should be able to trust. People we care about. People with whom life is worth sharing. Without people to trust and confide in, the freedom we're fighting for isn't worth a damn."

"Well... you may be right," said Winsor after a moment. "But you've chosen a path. It's not up to you which rules to follow and which ones to ignore. Especially when ignoring the wrong rule can get you killed."

I snorted. "Yeah. Even though I may despise them, I have followed them. *All* of them. Including the third one."

Winsor misinterpreted my meaning. "Look, kid. I'm not expecting you to give up. I know you'll do what you can to protect the movement. I'm sure you'll find a way to slink into the shadows, to keep the fight going a little longer. I'd be disappointed if you didn't."

I'd double-checked Winsor's position via GPS before I called him. He hadn't moved throughout our conversation, but now I brought up the feed from his building's security cameras, which I'd hacked soon after I'd come under his wing.

I swallowed hard, my tongue thick in my throat. "Can you do me one last favor, Winsor?"

"I can't make any guarantees."

"Tell Rowdy I'm sorry."

"For what? He's the one who actually liked you."

"I know."

I sent the signal. It whisked away at the speed of light, bouncing off an orbiting satellite before beaming down, through the router in Winsor's building and into the receiver I'd hidden in the bowels of his dilapidated couch. The call turned to static as the triacetone triperoxide I'd synthesized from the leftover nail polish and bleach in the salon ignited. The feed from the security cam in the hallway outside his apartment shook, but the apartment door stood fast. I'd activated the bolts to keep it in place for when emergency services tried to force their way in, but it was a redundancy I wouldn't need. Winsor's GPS signal had already winked out of existence.

I didn't shed a single tear. Instead, I checked how far away we were from the tunnel access hatch.

54

SEPTEMBER 3, 2180

KARAM'S EYES FLICKERED, then snapped open. They focused on me, sitting in a chair before him. His look was one of surprise. "You're alive."

I'd been staring at Nandi for almost an hour, so I'd had time to get over the shock of coming face to face with a rival who until tonight had been purely theoretical. I pulled my jacket back, revealing the thick interwoven bands of the pressure suit underneath. The painkillers I'd taken were helping, but I nonetheless moved slowly. "I came prepared."

Karam's gaze flicked to Fabia, who leaned against one of the man's lab tables, then down to the bonds that kept him tightly fastened to his chair. He blinked a few times, and I suspect he was trying—and failing—to access his Net. "Yes. It seems you did."

"Do you know who I am, Mr. Nandi?"

Karam cocked his head to the side. "Don't patronize me, Mr. Drake. Do you really think I'd be unfamiliar with my brother's murderer?"

"I didn't murder your brother. He intended to kill me. I acted in self-defense."

"Is that the sort of man you are, Mr. Drake? The sort who hides behind semantics?"

I didn't flinch. "I killed him. It wasn't premeditated, and it wasn't unlawful given his intentions, but I won't hide behind words. I intended to take him into custody. I'm not upset that he died instead. He murdered three civilians and would've murdered more if I hadn't stopped him."

"You consider three agents of your parent corporation to be civilians? Three people whose job it is to present your employer's fist as an open hand?"

I didn't take the bait. "Tell me about the drug, Karam."

He lifted an eyebrow. "We tested it on your ambassadors over a year ago and you're still uncertain about it?"

"It works by deposition of a conductive pathway from the Net to the innermost portions of the brain via the cardiovascular system. We isolated the precursor you used when your brother injected our people with it. We don't understand it as well as you do, but I doubt anyone does. I wasn't asking about that iteration of the drug, though. I want to know about the aerosol version."

Karam's eyes narrowed, and it took him a second longer to respond than it should've. "You tapped Dr. Zhao's comms. That's how you found me."

It amused me that despite everything else, Karam's concern was with how I'd tracked him. Then again, if I were in his shoes, I'd wonder the same thing. "No. She called me."

"She called you?"

"So you *can* be taken off guard. She and I have known each other for decades. I'm not surprised she never mentioned me. I think she's tried hard to forget me."

Karam didn't say anything, but I could see the rage building within him. In his mind, he'd been caught thanks to a coincidence. It was a simplistic way of thinking of it, but he probably couldn't conceive of anyone being good enough to track him on their own, just as he hadn't conceived of me coming after him with help at my back.

"Tell me about the airborne version of your graphite nanoparticles, Karam. How far along are you in the development?"

Karam smiled a sinister smile. "You don't know? If so, you're exceedingly confident for a man who's aware of that deployment system and happens to be standing in *my* lab."

"I already told you. I came prepared." I turned on my tablet and showed him one of the apps. "I took control of the building's HVAC systems before I came down. Your brother got the drop on me once with a similar ruse. I wasn't going to let it happen again."

Karam sagged, his last trick anticipated and intercepted.

"Do you have the drug ready?"

"It's not a drug. It's a graphitic nanoparticle bonded to an organic molecule that—"

"I don't care what you call it, Nandi. Is it functional? Have you tested it?"

The man shook his head, but without any vigor. "Not the aerosol, no. You know that if you talked to Dr. Zhao."

"You overestimate my ability to understand the science involved. How close are you to developing it, Karam? Weeks? Months? Years?"

Angry color returned to the man's cheeks. "Why does it matter to you? Do you plan to finish my work? Does USC intend to use my efforts to enrich their already bloated coffers or as yet another method to force their will upon those who disagree with them?"

"I don't know what USC intends, but I don't plan on giving them the option to do any of those things."

For the first time, Karam looked at me with confusion. He glanced at Fabia again, who still hadn't moved or spoken. "Who are you?"

"Who I appear to be, for the most part. A Counterterrorism agent who doesn't condone mass murder as a negotiating tactic.

Not as a first option, anyway." I leaned back in my chair. "Tell me, Karam. Why did you do it? Why dedicate the last decade of your life to developing a chemical that could kill others with a Net signal? What were you hoping to achieve?"

Karam's confusion left him, but rage didn't replace it. His eyes were filled with sadness, instead. "It must be nice to live in a bubble of one's own naivete. To be able to look around you and see a world in which a future exists for you and your children. For all your time spent among us, Mr. Drake, you must not have looked around you very hard otherwise you would've seen the lengths USC has gone to to oust us from our homes. Their stated goal is and always has been the terraformation of Mars. We live in the Hellas Basin, but we are men, not fish. In a couple short months, when their captured comet arrives in orbit and they begin breaking pieces off, what will we do then? Where will we go when USC fills the skies with imported ice and the seas swallow us whole? *Where?*"

My face remained a mask, but the man's words cut me deep. Everything he accused USC of, I was guilty of as well. I didn't consider myself a monster, but my plan for Mars's freedom didn't solve the Mukt's problems, either. It would simply force them into an impossible choice. Perhaps if Karam knew what I'd planned, he would've risked his safety to attack me in Elysium, and Vikram's attempt on my life would've been justified. But I had to believe that a free Mars, even one plagued by hardship as it struggled to gain its independence, would ultimately serve all Martians better than one governed from afar. USC imposed misery out of greed. The misery I'd impart would at least serve a purpose.

"You tried to create a weapon to wipe out mankind, Nandi, not stop USC. There's a difference."

"Weapons are tools. How they're used is up to the ones who hold them."

"Your brother said a similar thing, but you're both wrong.

Weapons, by definition, can only be used for harm, which is why I intend to destroy your research, Karam. It's too dangerous. The world isn't ready for it."

Karam's eyebrow lifted. "Once again, you tell me what *you* intend. What of the company you work for? Do you not care what they think?"

"In some matters, yes. Not in this one."

Karam was silent for a while. "If *you* are in charge, what do *you* intend of me?"

"There are a couple options. I could turn you over to USC."

Nandi's eyes hardened. "I would rather die."

I stood. "I thought you might say that. Do you mean it?"

Nandi didn't flinch. "You killed the only family I cared for. My dream is dead, too. Why shouldn't I be?"

I shook my head. I'd always known it would come to this. I couldn't leave the man free, but his willingness to take part only made the deed infinitesimally easier. "You have all your research here at the lab, or is some hidden elsewhere?"

"You really plan to destroy it? To keep it out of USC's hands?"

"Yes."

Nandi stared at me. Weighing my words. "All my equipment and supplies are here. I have an additional copy of my research on a third-party encrypted server. I have it linked from my computer." He nodded toward a workstation at the wall.

I slipped my pistol from my jacket. "Any last requests?"

"You don't waste time, do you?" The man averted his eyes. "I would ask that I die by my own research, but even the accelerated version of the serum I've developed would take days. I can't imagine you would grant me that luxury. Do it from behind, please."

"I can only hope one day I face death with as much resolve as you, Karam."

I hobbled to the back of the chair, pistol in hand.

Fabia joined me. "Drake. I can do this if you need me to."

I shook my head. "There's enough blood on my hands already. I knew this day would come. I'm ready."

Fabia nodded, and I didn't delay the inevitable. I leveled my pistol and pulled the trigger.

OUR RIDESHARE SLOWED as it turned a corner. Somewhere in the distance, I heard a horn blare, and I imagined the sound of sirens converging on the pharmacy. I pitied the work of the firefighters. The blaze we set would turn everything within the building to fine ash. We couldn't leave any trace of Nandi's lab or of our presence, but it wasn't thoughts of capture or even of Karam's killing that plagued me. It was thoughts of my plans for Mars's freedom. Nandi's speech had opened old wounds, and I still didn't know if I was doing the right thing. Not that I could change the course of events now. As I'd said to Phoebe, I'd already changed the trajectory.

I felt a jab at my shoulder and heard Fabia's voice. "We're here."

I looked up from the car's floor mats, blinking away my reverie. The rideshare had stopped outside the apartment building with the room Fabia and I had rented for the night. It was a modest place no one would look at twice.

Fabia nodded at me, her eyes shadowed by her breather mask. "You sure you're okay?"

"It's been an emotional night. Let's get some sleep."

We slipped out of the rideshare and transitioned into the apartment complex. The previous two days, the lobby at the base of the building had been empty, but tonight a cluster of individuals stood among the seats, riveted to a holo. Not one of them looked our way as we entered. None of them said a word among themselves, and I knew something was gravely wrong.

I glanced toward the holo, my mask still on, and took stock of what I saw. A small white speck glowed among a backdrop of stars. In the foreground, a man in a crisp suit gestured toward the space scene and spoke in a disjointed fashion. The ticker at the bottom of the screen read "Swift-Tuttle Crisis: Comet on Collision Course for Phobos."

Fabia's shoulders sagged. "*Shit.* They found out."

I didn't panic. "We always knew they would. It was only a matter of time. Come on. Let's get our things. We have decisions to make."

55

AUGUST 31, 2160

I EYED the medical team amassed on the platform as my pod slid to a halt on the rail line. I'd never bothered pressurizing the pod, instead leaving it be after crawling through the hidden access hatch and into the tunnels with Marina in my arms. She lay there in her Suit, motionless as the pod doors snapped open and the nurses poured inside. With a practiced ease, they shifted Marina onto a gurney and sped down the platform, turning into the airlock nearest the medical bay. People hustled back and forth, moving supplies and gesturing to each other while additional pods lined up for loading, while others stood there in a daze, casting their gaze everywhere but seeing nothing.

I moved through it all at a measured pace, my heart empty. I reached the airlock well after the nurses had, so I waited as it cycled and spit them out before taking my turn. The air poured over me, hissing its displeasure, and then I was out the other side into the underground base. With my helmet removed, the chaos was more audible. Shouts and orders filled my ears, accompanied by the patter of feet and the clatter of motion as I made my way into the makeshift hospital.

A crowd of professionals surrounded Marina, some with

metallic paddles in hand and others with intravenous needles, all of them doing what they could. Attaching electrodes, intubating, taking measurements. I'd always trusted doctors to act rationally, but I had to assume they were acting more for my benefit than Marina's. They'd had access to her vitals. They must've seen her heartbeat flatline twenty minutes ago, same as I had. Same as Jorge had.

He stood there, a couple meters from the foot of the bed into which Marina had been transferred, his face frozen in fear. One of his hands hovered in the air, reaching toward the bed, but his feet didn't move. Neither did the rest of him.

I didn't want to be there. Didn't want anything to do with the situation, but my wishing for an alternate reality wouldn't make it magically appear.

I took a few steps toward him. The beeping of medical devices and the orders from the doctors drowned out my voice, forcing me to repeat myself. "Jorge. *Jorge.*"

He turned toward me the second time, tears streaming down his cheeks before disappearing into his beard. He looked at me in shock, agony and loneliness written in his every crease. He lunged at me, and I stiffened in anticipation of the blow.

He swallowed me in a hug instead. He sobbed uncontrollably on my shoulder, clinging to me for dear life. I squeezed him back, letting his tears slide off the fabric of my Suit. His weight dragged on me, as if his legs wouldn't support him, and I had to struggle to keep him upright. I held him for a minute as the world moved around us, soaking in his pain, sharing in his loss.

It wasn't until the tears slowed that I found my voice. "I'm so sorry. God, I tried. I did everything I could."

He shook his head and tried to speak, but words wouldn't come out. He turned and set eyes on Marina's still form. Again he froze. I didn't know what was best for him, but I figured distance couldn't hurt, so with an arm around his back, I nudged him away from the doctors and into the hall.

When the door closed behind us I tried again. "It's my fault, Jorge. I should've pushed her away. Been more forceful in rejecting her when she offered to help. I should've acted faster when we ran into my old superior. If I hadn't hesitated... I could've beaten them. Stopped everyone before a single shot was fired."

Jorge gripped me by the arm with more strength than I thought he had left. "No. Don't blame yourself for this, Ambrose."

"But I could've—"

"*No.*" His grip tightened, and he looked me square in the face with his watery eyes. "I talked to Marina before she left. She knew what she was getting into. She went after you to protect you. She succeeded. She won."

I couldn't contradict him. He was right, after all. She'd saved me. Helped me escape. Protected me from capture, and in doing so, had protected the entire resistance. Rule number three. But victories were fleeting in our profession, and even in victory there was consequence. The ultimate one.

"Still. I'm sorry, Jorge. Anything you need..."

Jorge wiped the tears from his cheeks and took a deep breath, trying to compose himself. "Someday, maybe. Not now. How are things looking on the surface?"

While I'd travelled via pod, he'd charged me with keeping track of troop movements, and by god, there were a lot of them. They'd started moving before I'd finished my conversation with Winsor, and while informant channels had lit up like Christmas trees within minutes of his death, USC hadn't paused to mourn him. Knowing how they operated, they'd probably sent news of his murder to officers and followed it with instructions to transition operations into overdrive.

"It's not looking good. There's a major strike force headed here as we speak. I estimate they'll be here within ten hours. Additional forces are moving on our positions in the Lunae Planum, Daedalia Planum, Terra Sirenum, Terra Cimmeria, and Noachis Terra. All of them are expected to make first contact in anywhere from four to twelve hours. While I can't base it in evidence, I suspect the attacks won't go as well for us as they did when I was first captured. USC has learned from every strike they've made against us. They'll be ready this time. All of which leads me to believe we need to get out of here as fast as possible—a conclusion you've come to independently." I glanced past Jorge as another member of the resistance raced down the hallway, panic in her eyes.

Jorge followed my gaze. "We should've eliminated Winsor the moment you left his presence. If there's one thing I regret, it's how we dealt with him. I agreed with Marina when she sent you to find him, but... I guess we couldn't have known."

"It's not who we are, Jorge. His death is due to his own choices. But we don't operate that way. If we did, we wouldn't be any better than the enemy." I thought about the nuclear weapon that had murdered millions. *Well, we'd be a little better. But not much.*

Jorge wobbled, and he leaned against a wall to steady himself. His voice still warbled when he spoke, and despite his efforts, his tears hadn't fully dried. "We've always known this was a possibility. That a leak would give us away. We didn't think we'd be exposed on so many fronts simultaneously, but we're still prepared. We have explosives. We're rigging them now. We'll destroy every record and spray down every surface with genetic dissolvers, but I can't help but think about how much we're going to lose. Resources. Data. Facilities. It's overwhelming. The worst part is the people, though. There are too many of us and too few bases to which we can flee. Some of us are going to be captured, Ambrose. There's no way around it."

"We'll make it work, Jorge. I've been living in the field for years. Not everyone here has my experience, I get that, but we don't need to be centrally located. Those we can't pack into the bases that are still secure can be distributed through the major population centers. We'll survive. We'll keep fighting."

"Of course we will. But we're not going to redistribute anyone. We're implementing shadow protocols."

I blinked. *"You're disbanding the counterintelligence?"*

"Given the circumstances, it's the only logical choice. Leave emotion aside for a moment, Ambrose. Look honestly at what we're facing. The full might of USC's Martian forces are bearing down on us, and we have nothing to counter them with. Not to mention the centralized strategy we've adopted for the past five years isn't working. It's why Marina sent you out in the first place. To increase recruitment. To build your skills for when we'd need to make a change. This is it."

"Yes, but—"

"Daddy!"

The little girl's voice cut across the background hum. She ran down the hall, pigtails bouncing, her little legs carrying her as fast as they could. Jorge whirled at the sound of her, scooping her in his arms as she approached.

"Daddy, I'm scared! Where's mommy? Is she back?"

Jorge's voice cracked, and fresh tears welled in his eyes. "It's alright, pumpkin. Mommy isn't here now, but everything's going to be okay. I'm here for you."

Jorge asked her something about where someone was, maybe her caretaker, but I barely heard him. Something inside me broke. She was only an infant when I'd last seen her, swaddled in her crib. Because of me, my actions, my choices, she'd never get to know the woman who loved her most. She'd never remember her.

Because of me.

God, I hated the rules.

I felt hot tears on my cheeks as Jorge turned back to me, his equally wet as he shushed his daughter. "Ambrose. It's time. The shadow protocols are all we have left. We can keep fighting. Keep trying. But for Fabia's sake and the sake of every child like her, we have to pack it in. We owe it to her. To everyone."

I nodded, words sticking in my throat. I stepped forward and pulled Jorge into a hug. Fabia pulled back, squirming as I gave her father a hug, but I didn't let her discomfort stop me.

"I owe you so much, Jorge," I said between tears. "I'm going to miss you."

He pounded me on the back with his free arm. "Likewise. You know what you need to do."

I took a deep breath. "I do."

56

SEPTEMBER 4, 2180

IT WAS amateur astronomers who figured it out, specifically those from the M/Red Planet Gazers on the social media news aggregator site Marsin. They'd been watching Swift-Tuttle's orbit since its last gravitational slingshot around Earth in 2177. They got a kick out of pointing their telescopes at anything closer than the Jovian moons, and collectively they'd pulled together a sizable pot for the first person who could post a picture of the comet's tail on its final approach. Most of the members of the group treated is as recreational fun, but a man who went by the online handle of Hardcore_TailChaser was determined to snap the first picture. He was the one who tracked the comet for two months straight and calculated its final trajectory. I could only imagine his surprise when he realized the comet's tail would appear about eighteen hours earlier than it should've.

He would've shared his findings earlier except for the fact that he was sure he was wrong. He didn't have the best equipment. He knew even the slightest misalignment would produce incorrect conclusions, which is why he continued to check and recheck his data for about two weeks longer than he really had to. Eventually, he convinced himself that what his telescope was telling him was the truth. Swift-Tuttle wasn't on track to be captured in Mars's orbit. It was coming in a smidge too fast, and more worryingly—it was on track to collide with Phobos.

The other members of M/Red Planet Gazers laughed at him when he first posted his findings. Some of them made crude jokes about him having more success if he chased real tail instead of the astral variety, but a few of them checked his results against anomalies in their own data. When three more of the message board's more senior contributors posted explanations of why they thought Hardcore_TailChaser might be right, all hell broke loose. The post gained ten thousand upvotes in a matter of hours, and thanks to an infusion of apocalypse-hungry nutcases from the M/Doom Clock sub group, the post was quickly elevated to the front page of all Marsin. Local news groups picked it up from there, and it wasn't long before the story had made it to the national feeds.

As of 1:00 AM local time in New Bangalore, as Fabia and I boarded a train headed toward the Niesten station at the northern tip of the Hellas Basin, the newsfeeds had yet to find any experts that had any idea of what the hell was going on. A few had managed to interview astronomers from various colleges around Mars, all of whom looked bleary eyed and uncertain, but all of them refused to validate the amateur astronomers' data until they had a chance to check on the comet's path with their own equipment. The newsfeeds, being starved for content and with limited astronomers to contact, had to expand their pool of interview subjects to just about anyone with first-hand knowledge of the story, including senior members of of the M/Red Planet Gazers group. However, it was an interview with one of the M/Doom Clock users that actually hit closest to home.

I watched the thing unfold live via Net. NGNN's Felicity Jones patiently nodded as a long-haired guy with a two-year beard identified only as Jim "Panhandle" Duncan outlined his theory, that rogue USC agents had taken control of the remaining ion cannons and thrusters still attached to Swift-Tuttle and burned them in secret, using the last of the fuel reserves which had otherwise been saved for course corrections to nudge the comet into an orbit that would cause it to plunge into Phobos on its way down to Mars, where the debris from both would end life as we knew it, praise Ba'al.

The fact that he guessed I was a rogue USC agent was a nice touch, but he'd gotten a lot of the end part of his theory wrong. Swift-Tuttle *was* on a collision course with Phobos, true, but it wouldn't fall into Mars. If the calculations the astrodynamicists, Fabia, and I had worked with were right, Swift-Tuttle would slam into Phobos, breaking it apart into a few thousand pieces, roughly ninety-five percent of which would be ejected into the asteroid belt. The bigger question was what would happen to Swift-Tuttle. We had detailed knowledge of Phobos's composition thanks to the extensive construction USC had undertaken there, but Swift-Tuttle was a much bigger question mark. Based on the models, after colliding with Phobos the comet should bounce off into an eccentric orbit around the sun where it would slowly outgas over the centuries before plunging into Jupiter in the late 2800s. However, if the comet ruptured catastrophically upon impact, anywhere from five to twenty-five percent of the mass could rain down on Mars. Thanks to Phobos's orbit and the timing of the impact, the mass should fall along the Martian equator, thus avoiding the major cities, though it would demolish the transglobal vactrain line. Nonetheless, it was a potentially *massive* amount of mass to introduce at one time. In the worst case scenario, it could introduce enough ice to flood the Hellas Basin with water—*liquid* water thanks to the sheer amount of heat the burn up of the comet would bring with it. For a time, Mars could grow to be warmer than Earth.

But we didn't know. Therein lay the fear.

Of course, none of the newsfeeds knew that. They could only

speculate, and along with their speculation, all of them raised the same question: How could this happen?

Not by accident, that was for sure. I hadn't been able to do it all myself, much as I'd initially wanted. The first step had been to hack the Olympus Mons Observatory's primary telescope, from which astronomers who worked with USC tracked Swift-Tuttle, but we couldn't simply doctor the tracking data generated by the system. Many of the metrics were generated automatically, but the capture of Swift-Tuttle was one of the most important projects in the history of USC. Real people, most of them career astronomers, monitored the comet's progress on a daily basis. If data generated by their tracking didn't match what they saw, they'd immediately know something was wrong.

So we'd had to match what they saw to the data. With the help of software experts who'd worked on the faked Snow Leopard videos during the last rebellion, we'd generated visual overlays of Swift-Tuttle that we'd added to the imagery generated by the telescope. When anyone pointed Olympus Mons's pride and joy toward Swift-Tuttle, all they saw was the comet exactly where it should've been, and the tracking data confirmed it.

Hacking the observatory was only enough to keep our activities from being detected, however, which was why I'd lied about Karam's plans to Counterterrorism to get them to send me to Phobos in person. There, I'd eventually hacked into the servers that controlled the ion thrusters and control systems still present on Swift-Tuttle. Since no one could physically check fuel levels of the propulsion systems on the comet, I was able to fudge the numbers in those databases while I burned the reserves to push Swift-Tuttle into its new trajectory, but my work hadn't been done. I'd still had to hack the reconnaissance satellites orbiting Phobos for initiatives we'd launch in the immediate preamble to the comet's arrival.

While the newsfeed commentators wondered how Swift-Tuttle's trajectory had been so badly bungled and debated about whether or not the world was about to come to an end, I concerned myself with what would happen next. I'd always expected USC would realize Swift-Tuttle's trajectory was off weeks before the impact. Certainly, once the comet's tail appeared, it would be impossible to hide. Even if the people in charge of monitoring it didn't pick up on the changes in velocity and orientation, Fabia and I had agreed we'd need to leak the truth at least a month before impact. In our estimation, it would take that long to evacuate the Hellas Basin in something resembling a peaceful and organized manner.

We were prepared for USC to learn the truth. The question was how they'd respond. We'd intentionally kept their options limited. In performing our celestial nudge, we'd used the full reserves of all thruster systems left strapped to the comet in the wake of the initial maneuver performed in 2126, leaving nothing for USC to work with when they eventually regained control. USC wouldn't be able to redirect it with what was there. That left two options. One was the nuclear option—literally. They might launch a superheavy nuclear weapon into the comet, blasting it to pieces, but Fabia and I knew they wouldn't take that route. Nuking the comet wouldn't change its trajectory. Instead, it would break it into tens of thousands of smaller projectiles which in turn would sweep a larger cone through space than did the comet itself. At least half of the pieces would bombard Mars at high speed without being captured in orbit. The result would be catastrophic. Every man and woman on Mars would be killed, and as cold and callous as USC was, they'd never risk that. To USC, Mars was an asset.

That left one serious option on the table: an all out blitz to get new teams to land on Swift-Tuttle, where they could conceivably push the comet out of its current trajectory and back into space. USC would lose the most valuable piece of space debris in the history of mankind, but depending on how much of a push they gave it and in what direction, it might not be lost forever. They could use Mars as another gravitational slingshot and with a few more nudges over time, they might be able to bring Swift-Tuttle back to Mars in another fifty to a hundred and fifty years.

Doing so wouldn't be easy. The closer Swift-Tuttle got to Mars, the more energy would be required to change its trajectory enough to avoid catastrophe. The only reason I'd been able to nudge the comet enough was because I'd made my push a year ago. It was questionable if USC could generate enough thrust to move Swift-Tuttle into a favorable orbit at all, but based on simulations our astrodynamicist had run and given we had little more than six weeks until impact—forty-five days, to be exact—it *might* be possible. USC would have to fill nearly every ship they had with fuel and launch them toward Swift-Tuttle, fill the existing thruster tanks, and blast like crazy, all within the next week, otherwise the window would close.

Fabia and I both knew they would try. In fact, we'd bet on it.

Now that the cat had finally been let out of the bag, Fabia and I chatted logistics on an encrypted comm channel as our train hummed toward Niesten. We'd have to mobilize sooner than expected, but everyone involved had trained. They knew to be ready at the drop of a hat. We were using people we trusted. We'd get the job done. The evacuation of the Mukt settlements was what worried me most. It would take a diplomatic effort grander than we were capable of to make them leave in a civil, timely fashion. It wouldn't be easy, but once the Mukt realized the inescapable truth of Swift-Tuttle's approach, they'd make it happen. The USC settlements would accommodate their influx, whether USC wanted them or not. They'd have to. People weren't monsters, even if the company they worked for might be.

At roughly three-thirty in the morning, with all plans laid as best as I could and with an hour left until arrival in Niesten, I made a final call to Sophia.

She answered after a few rings, her voice slow to respond. "Hey."

"Hey, Sophia. How long have you been asleep?"

"Uh... Five hours, give or take? Why? What's going on?"

"You should check the news. Everyone's talking about Swift-Tuttle."

Her voice solidified. "It's time?"

"It's time. Do you have your bug-out bag ready?"

"I've had it by my bed for the last six months, right next to yours. Want me to grab both of them?"

"Yes. Meet me in Utopia. You know where."

"You got it. But Ambrose?"

"Yes?"

"Is it going to work?"

I took a deep breath. "Only time will tell. I think so."

"Okay. I'll see you soon. I love you."

"I love you, too."

I ended the call and settled back into my seat. With luck, I'd be able to catch an hour of sleep. God only knew I'd need it.

57

SEPTEMBER 1, 2160

THE LIGHT BLINDED me as the door burst inward on its hinges. I squinted as a trio of uniformed marines burst into the door, rifles in hand. The one in front kept her Badass trained on me as she took note of the room's lone bed, desk, and the toilet in the corner. Her eyes flicked to my white jumpsuit, and she called out over her shoulder. "Krastenov. Looks like we have a prisoner." She gestured at me with the rifle. "You got a name?"

I stood, blinking, staring at them in disbelief. "You're USC. Does that... Does that mean...?"

"That the Reds are all gone? Yeah. I'm guessing they didn't tell you."

I glanced from one marine to the next, my mouth hanging open. "I haven't spoken to anyone in over a day. My handler stopped coming. I heard noises and activity, but no one would talk to me. Then a few hours ago I heard the explosions. God, I thought I was going to die. The power went out for a while before coming back, but I was certain I'd lose air pressure."

"Yeah," said the woman in front of me. "The Reds must've learned we were coming. Blasted a good two-thirds of this place. The air circulation systems survived, but if you'd been another twenty meters to the east, you would've been past the last pressure door. Guess you got lucky."

I snarled. "I don't even remember how long I've been here. Five years? Six? Don't talk to me about getting *lucky*."

"Six years? Damn." The woman's eyebrows rose. "What did you say your name was?"

"I didn't. Ambrose. Ambrose Drake."

"Hey Wu. Pleasanton. You guys keep canvasing the rooms. I'm going to move this guy higher up the chain."

The other two marines nodded their acknowledgment, and the woman waved for me to follow her. I walked behind her slowly, staring at everything in awe even though the hallways didn't look any different than they had twelve hours ago. Marines swarmed everywhere. In the conference rooms, in the grow farm, in the quarters, but of familiar resistance faces, I saw not one.

The elevators blinked angrily, so we skirted them and took the stairs up two flights. The woman led me into a thicker mass of armed combatants, nodding at the one posted at the door to the mess hall. "Spellman. Shiravadakar still here?"

"Yeah, he's with the Major. You found someone?"

She nodded as the man stepped aside. The dining tables had been pushed against the walls to make way for marines. My escort led me right into the thick of them.

"Excuse me. Lieutenant Shiravadakar? Major Stanić? Something you might want to see here."

"Major *Stanić?*" I said.

I didn't have to hide my surprise as the crowd parted. There, standing amid the soldiers was none other than my former roommate and training partner, Maarten Stanić, his shoulders as broad and burly as ever but with additional stripes of command adorning them. He did a double take as he looked at me, his eyes widening.

"Holy shit. *Ambrose!*"

He pushed past the Lieutenant beside him and swallowed me

in a hug. I stiffened, disarmed by his response. The last time I'd seen him, we'd been firing at each other across darkened vacuum in a panic.

He gave me a good squeeze before pulling back. "Christ, it's good to see you. You look like shit, man. What the hell happened to all your muscle?"

Years of trading running for weight training in Martian gravity had melted it away, but I took the opening. "The box they kept me in wasn't a great gym. Did someone call you *Major?*"

Maarten snorted, and he actually smiled. In his case, I guess time did heal all wounds. "A lot's changed since we lost you, Ambrose. Jesus, I still can't believe it's you. We all thought you were dead. I mean, Watkins always held out hope, but..." His jaw tightened.

"Major Watkins?"

"Lieutenant Colonel now. Until recently." He took a step back. His demeanor had changed the instant he'd thought of our former commander, the spark of friendship dying and pulling him back to the present. "As I said, a lot's changed since you were captured. We'll catch you up. Shiravadakar. Get him to the medics. Someone should take a look at him."

"Yes, sir," said the tall, chocolate-skinned man next to him. "Drake, was it? Could you come with me?"

"Sure," I said. "But... I have questions. *A lot* of questions."

"I'm sure you do," said Maarten. "For now, Ambrose, all you need to know is that you're finally going home."

I LAY in a hospital bed in a USC base near Pollack Crater. Medics in Maarten's company had looked me over following our conversation, but after the day long overland trip to the base proper, the professionals with degrees had wanted a more thorough crack at me. I'd told them time and time again as they poked and prodded me that I was fine, that nutrition had been adequate in the Red's care and that other than suffering in isolation for the better part of six years, I otherwise hadn't been abused, certainly not physically. Doctors being doctors, they refused to believe a word I told them, or maybe they needed to perform the tests to satisfy protocols. Either way, I was forced to wait in bed, cooling my heels until someone decided I was good to go.

Perhaps the holdup wasn't medical. I figured sooner or later, someone would come to talk to me about my experiences in custody. Not a psychotherapist, though I wouldn't be surprised if one of them showed up, too. Rather a representative from USC intelligence—probably several. They'd ask me questions. Lots of them. Questions for days, and I'd answer them all. I'd trained for years for the shadow protocols, more thoroughly than for anything else. Intricate details of fraudulent handlers filled my brain, along with memories of my time under lock and key, but should the questioners ask about my Net records, they'd be sorely disappointed. The Reds had disabled my Net for the *entire* time they'd imprisoned me, which explained why USC had never been able to track me. Only after reuniting with Maarten's company had I been able to reinitialize it.

As I sat there, anticipating the questions for the umpteenth time, I received a message. I was bored enough that I would've opened and read anything, but the identity of the sender spurred me into action quicker than anticipated.

Ambrose. This is Phoebe. I heard you'd been found and rescued. What a relief! I know it's been years, but I wanted to message you to let you know I'm alive and well. How are you doing? Please reach out, if you have a chance.

I stared at the words, trying to decipher what hidden meaning might lay behind them. The fact that I sat in USC custody, confined to a hospital bed but otherwise free, meant she'd kept our encounter private despite Watkins' death. Was she messaging me to keep up appearances? Was she warning me? Or was there something else I was missing? I took my time composing a response, knowing everything I sent would be monitored.

Phoebe. I'm a little overwhelmed. I thought you'd been killed in the encounter before my capture. You can't believe how relieved I am to hear you're okay. And yes, I'm fine. Adapting to my new environment. You might not believe it, but it was none other than Maarten who freed me. I can't believe he's a major now, but there are a lot of things that seem strange to me. I didn't get much of a chance to talk to him, but he told me about Watkins. I can't believe it happened around the corner from you. How are you handling it?

The minutes stretched as I waited for her response, knowing the follow up would tell me everything I needed to know. Eventually it came.

It's been difficult dealing with her loss. Authorities are still looking for the individual who killed her, but I can't help but feel responsible for her death. I've been told she was coming to visit me. She'd done so once, years ago. If not for me, she'd never have walked into that violent situation. Still, I know I shouldn't blame myself. I didn't pull the trigger that killed her. Her blood is on the hands of another.

I knew she'd left the ending open intentionally. I wrote back quickly this time.

I can commiserate. I remember situations we experienced while we were deployed where people died as a result of our actions, both directly and indirectly. After all these years, the blood of the few I've killed has never washed away. I've learned to live with the indirect deaths, though. They hurt, it's true, but you have to tell yourself it wasn't your fault. That even though you could've acted differently to avoid disaster, the choices you made at the time and those of the people around you weren't wrong. Your situation with Watkins seems like one of the latter.

Her reply didn't take as long in coming this time.

It would seem to be. Thanks for talking me through it, Ambrose.

I breathed a sigh of relief, but I wasn't quite done.

I'd love to catch up at some point, Phoebe. There are so many things I feel ignorant of after my time in custody. I doubt it'll be soon, however, as I can't predict what the future holds for me now that I'm back with USC. If I reach out at a later date, will that be alright?

Another quick reply.

As long as you remain true to yourself, I'll always be your ally, Ambrose. If you need my assistance, don't hesitate to ask.

I closed the messaging app, and for the first time since being reunited with Maarten, I felt a glimmer of hope. The path before me was shadowed, rugged, and unbelievably treacherous—but at least I'd have a friend to help me navigate it.

58

OCTOBER 19, 2180

WITHIN MINUTES of the news of Swift-Tuttle going public, I severed my access to USC's satellites and other Phobos-controlled remote systems, initiating an exit protocol that would remove the last vestigial traces of my presence and cripple their servers for a period of hours to days, depending on how good their IT professionals were. Nonetheless, we continued to monitor their communications via other secret channels—not that we really needed to. The doomsday scenario of Swift-Tuttle impacting Phobos was the only story that mattered to anyone, on Earth as well as Mars. USC couldn't keep their intentions secret. Every news organization, every city state, and every major government on Earth pressured USC relentlessly for a plan to avert catastrophe. Within twenty-four hours of the news of Swift-Tuttle's trajectory becoming public, USC's CEO Wibke Gunkel appeared for a press conference that ended up being the second most watched live event in human history, behind only the 2174 World Cup final between China and Brazil.

In the conference, Gunkel characterized the comet's modified orbital path as a vicious attack on behalf of Martian separatist forces, which was absolutely true. She also laid out an emergency

plan to shift the comet's trajectory by launching an armada from
Phobos to refuel the thrusters on Swift-Tuttle, pretty much exactly
as Fabia and I had predicted. Space travel between Earth and Mars
would be halted immediately to divert resources to the project, and
all Mars-based spaceports would focus solely on providing supplies
and manpower to the redirection efforts.

Thanks to calculations from our astrodynamicist, Fabia and I
knew to a precision of about a hundred kilograms how much fuel it
would take for USC to push Swift-Tuttle out of a path of destruc-
tion. At the rate of transfer available to them with the rockets and
tankers already on Mars and around Phobos, we estimated it would
take five to six days of shuttling methane and liquid oxygen from
the refineries on Mars to Phobos to make the attempt.

We gave them three days before we struck. At 2:47 AM on the
morning of September 8th, resistance forces detonated explosives
on refineries and fuel reserve tanks at all major USC spaceports:
Utopia, Elysium, Isidis, and Olympus, as well as a couple other
minor ports at Hale and Schiaparelli. USC had increased security
at all spaceports in the wake of the news of Swift-Tuttle, perhaps
anticipating the way we'd try to thwart them. What they hadn't
anticipated was that we'd set explosive charges in place two and a
half months prior.

I watched via remote feed as the explosives detonated in
unison. They weren't particularly impressive displays. The liquid
methane and oxygen used in USC rockets were kept in separate
tanks, and neither could burn on their own in the carbon dioxide-
rich Martian atmosphere. At each spaceport, I saw a couple bright
flashes, then heard a roar as the supercooled liquids boiled into the
skies above. Perhaps more important than the sabotage of the tanks
was that of the refinery equipment. USC didn't make public the
severity of the damage, but comms channels showed USC engineers estimated it would take weeks to get the facilities up and
running again. Weeks that they didn't have.

USC's second public address came a couple days after the attacks at the spaceports and was decidedly more somber than the first. Wibke Gunkel, looking defeated, announced what Fabia and I already knew: that there was nothing else they could do. They'd considered launching a fleet from Luna, but given the orbital positions of Earth and Mars, it would take nineteen days for the ships to reach Phobos and a few more to arrive at Swift-Tuttle. Even with unlimited fuel, that didn't leave enough time for them to modify Swift-Tuttle's trajectory to a satisfactory new one, which was a moot point because the incoming ships from Luna couldn't make the trip in nineteen days without burning their fuel reserves and needing to be refilled. There was no plan B. Swift-Tuttle would impact Phobos.

I wish I could say I was overjoyed after watching the conference, but I wasn't. For all the orbital simulations we'd run, I still didn't know how things would play out. I didn't know how Swift-Tuttle and Phobos would fracture upon impact, how much of either would enter the atmosphere, at what trajectories or at what speeds. I didn't know if I'd saved Mars or doomed it.

Some people didn't think the former was a possibility. I talked to Phoebe once and only once in the weeks preceding the impact. She couldn't believe what I'd done and more importantly couldn't comprehend why. I tried to explain it to her. The Luna to Phobos pipeline was USC's lifeblood. The existence of the two moon bases outside their respective planets' gravity wells was what allowed USC to send massive ships laden with soldiers and equipment in a matter of weeks. In reality, traveling from Earth to Mars was challenging. It was only traveling from Earth to Luna to Phobos to Mars that was easy.

Phoebe didn't want to hear it. She didn't want to hear that USC's entire fleet would have to be redesigned to allow it to land directly on Mars from Luna, that the rate at which USC could deliver soldiers and cargo to Mars would be cut to a fraction of what it had been. To her, what mattered was that I might've sentenced a few hundred million people to death.

Maybe she was right.

At least Mars would be prepared. In the aftermath of USC's second press conference, all planetary efforts turned toward preparing for impact. USC evacuated Phobos, securing what gear they could in Mars-based settlements. The Mukt organized as well as could be hoped. Trains and transports ran twenty-four and a half hours a day, shuttling people from New Chennai and Chandrayaan and New Bangalore into the USC controlled cities, the latter of which worked tirelessly to put up temporary housing, expand food production, install life support systems, and keep the peace. Emergency protocols were established for when debris inevitably destroyed portions of the Mylamene barriers over the cities. Factories worked overtime to produce goods that were in short supply while scientists ran models continuously, trying to predict the full range of effects that the introduction of water ice and ammonia from Swift-Tuttle might create.

For Fabia, Sophia, and I, there was work to do behind the scenes. We prepared documents to release to the people, ones that laid out in no uncertain terms the level of USC's involvement in the water theft scandal and how they'd planned to use the water from Swift-Tuttle to enrich their shareholders at the expense of Martians. We also prepared a video proving the resistance had nothing to do with the nuking of Los Angeles in 2154 and that explained our theories for why USC had perpetrated the act themselves. We didn't release either, however. For the time being, the planet's priorities were in the right place. Only after as many people had been saved and as many resources protected, only after Swift-Tuttle's rubble rained down and people awakened to a new sky above them would we release what we knew. Perhaps everyone would be prepared for the revolution then.

But not yet.

I STOOD in the cold dark of midnight, my Suit tight against my skin. Behind me, a hatch to an underground resistance outpost in the obscure reaches of the Arabia Terra stood open, but I'd cast my eyes to the sky instead.

Swift-Tuttle's tail shone bright among the stars, like a contrail from the world's most powerful jet. To my eye, it moved slowly, but it did so faster than the bright speck before it. Phobos. I checked my clock. Less than a minute to go.

My heart raced, and I felt cold sweat at my brow. I reconsidered every decision I'd made for the past year and a half, the doubts racing through my mind. Phoebe's harsh words, Fabia's suspicions, even Karam's death. The latter had nothing to do with my actions with the resistance, but there was guilt and sorrow associated with him, and that's what arose. I'd never felt more uncertain, never more afraid, never more full of self-doubt.

The impact itself wasn't as spectacular as I'd expected. From my vantage point ten thousand kilometers away, the contact looked like a monochromatic firework, with bright sparks flying in all directions. No sound paired with it, just a flash of light and a sparkle of debris.

For a few moments afterwards, there was nothing. The burst in the heavens dimmed, obscured by the comet's tail, but soon enough new spots appeared. Points of light in the far distance, leaving trails behind them in the sky. Hundreds. Thousands perhaps. The midnight sky turned purple, then blue, then a rage-filled reddish orange that spoke of brimstone and hellfire.

As the heavens burned, I heard the rumble, and the ground started to shake.

Sophia spoke in my ear via the helmet's private channel. "Please, Ambrose. Come underground. It's not safe."

I didn't argue. I turned and headed down the hatch, my Suit aglow with heavenly fire, and I wondered what I'd done.

THE HATCH CREAKED as I pushed it back up. A fierce wind buffeted me as I pulled myself onto the Martian regolith. Dawn had come, or so my clock assured me. Clouds stretched as far as I could see, glowing burnt orange rather than the traditional butterscotch.

The wind that hit me felt stronger than I was used to, but it lacked its usual bite. I checked the thermometer on my Suit and was surprised to see the temperature was only a few degrees below freezing. In the distance, an opaque cloud obscured my view. A wall of dust stretched from one end of the southern horizon to the other. A storm was coming. A massive one.

The wind buffeted me again, and a flicker of something bright whistled past me. Not rust red dust but something grey, like tarnished silverware. I held out a hand. The wind swirled, and a few of the particles collected on my palm, lead gray from the Phobos dust but unmistakable from my Michigan youth: snowflakes.

I tilted my head up, watching the snowflakes slide across my helmet's faceplate. Mars had survived. How many of its children had survived alongside it? How many would survive what was to come?

The lead gray snow seemed prophetic, the frozen specks the color of bullets. Lead and snow. There would be much of both to come.

ABOUT THE AUTHOR

Hi. I'm Alex P. Berg, author of *Lead and Snow*. Well, this is it. Drake has made his choice, and Mars will feel the impact for the rest of its history. But the fight for Mars isn't over. USC won't back down, but neither will Ambrose. Find out if Drake is able to free Mars once and for all in the thrilling conclusion to the Tyrants of Mars trilogy, *Iron and Rain*.

Can't wait for the next Tyrants of Mars novel? Why not try my Daggers & Steele series? It features paranormal homicide detectives Jake Daggers and Shay Steele solving crimes in the fictional metropolis of New Welwic, a city filled with mystery, strange creatures, and more than its fair share of magic. The complete ten book series is available now, so what are you waiting for! Read it today! You can even buy the complete series in a single low-priced omnibus volume.

Word of mouth is **critical** to my success. If you enjoyed this novel, please consider leaving a positive review on Amazon. Even if it's only a line or two, it would be a *huge* help. Thanks!

Want to connect? Visit me at www.alexpberg.com or contact me on social media.

For a complete list of my books, please visit: www.alexpberg.com/books/.